An Accidental Spy

JOLYN JONES

PORTIA PUBLISHING

Copyright © Jolyn Jones 2014

Jolyn Jones has asserted her right under the Copyright Designs and Patents Act 1988 to be indentified as the author of this work

All rights reserved. No part of this publication may be reproduced, distributed or transmitted in any form or by any means, including photocopying, recording, or other electronic or mechanical methods, without the express permission of the author.

Visit the author's website at www.jolynjones.com

Publisher's Note: This is a work of fiction. Names, characters, places, and incidents are a product of the author's imagination. Locales and public names are sometimes used for atmospheric purposes. Any resemblance to actual people, living or dead, or to businesses, companies, events, institutions, or locales is completely coincidental.

Book Layout ©2014 BookDesignTemplates.com
Cover design by Author Design Studio

A CIP catalogue record is available from the British Library

An Accidental Spy/ Jolyn Jones - 1st paperback edition
Published simultaneously in the UK and USA
Portia Publishing
ISBN 978-1-897680-01-8

To Allan

I was a pilot flying an airplane and it just happened that where I was flying made what I was doing spying.

–FRANCIS GARY POWERS

Acknowledgements

During the gestation of this novel many people and organisations have assisted in the research and historical background to this story. There are of course many historical books and accounts of the Spanish Civil war and I have listed some for those who may be interested in further reading. Paul Preston's books are a major source of authoritative information and have been particularly useful.

The University of Barcelona's library was the main source of original material about the war including contemporary newspaper accounts especially in La Vanguardia. The Thomas Cook Library kindly allowed me access to their archives to obtain information about package tours to Spain before the Second World War.

The account of the fiesta is based upon participation in actual fiestas in Ibiza and Menorca a long time ago.

I am indebted to the work of Abel Paz for the account of the fighting in Barcelona. The spy training is based on information supplied by Harry Verlander about the later training of the Jedburghs, a secret operations group, who were trained for sabotage and dropped into France in the months leading up to D-Day. The information for the poisoned garden episode is based on the wonderful Poison Garden at Alnwick Castle where visitors are encouraged to learn but not touch.

The original inspiration for the novel came from participating in a walking holiday in Andalucía run by the inestimable Hugh and Jane Arbuthnott of www.arbuthnottholidays.com.

Among the many individuals who have helped me, special mention must be made of Concepcion Muńoz, Moira Allan, Suzy Greaves and Stephanie Hale.

My husband has been constantly supportive. Lastly my Birman cats have kept a paw on things every step of the way, including direct editorial action in deleting sections not to their liking.

1

If Verity had intended to take up a career as a spy, she would not have started by going on a tour round Europe with her maiden aunt. Verity already had a different career mapped out for her by her father. As a lawyer with no sons to follow him into the profession, his only daughter was going to have to fill the void. Someone had to be able to take over the family firm when he retired. So that was it – by 1934 Verity had nearly completed her training and a lawyer she would be. Becoming a spy was purely accidental.

Captain Luis Moreno was a handsome young man who, at twenty-five, knew that he had great power over women. With his looks, his uniform, a commanding manner, and charm that he could turn on like a light, he was irresistible to women. This morning he was not at his best - it was after all only six in the morning when the door of his room was kicked open as he lay sprawled on his bed, still fast asleep. Moreno turned over, an oath dying on his lips as he saw that his visitor was not an orderly with his hot water but the Colonel from the barracks in Mallorca. Jumping to his feet, he stood to attention but felt disadvantaged by having to stand there naked, his feet cold on the rough surface of the stone floor.

"You've ordered an arrest?" said the Colonel, who already knew this fact perfectly well. "A saboteur? No, let me see, a foreigner, so a spy. What are the facts?" he barked, not giving Moreno any chance to explain.

"Come to the office directly when you are properly dressed. By then," he added, "your patrols that I saw sweeping the town, will have brought the spy in."

The Colonel swept out leaving Moreno to wash, shave, dress and present himself in double quick time as the Colonel, a noted disciplinarian, did not put up with fools lightly.

What had brought the Colonel here so early this morning on an unscheduled visit, wondered Moreno? Appearing in the office - his own office as it happened - the Captain snapped his heels together smartly and saluted the Colonel, now that he was in uniform. The Colonel's gaze appeared to be focused on his own highly polished boots that were resting lightly on the Captain's desk in front of him.

"Our troops are scouring the island for an English woman. Why?" the Colonel asked.

"Sir, I attempted to interrogate her last night and she assaulted me and got away."

"Assaulted you?"

"Yes Sir," said Moreno, reluctant to furnish the details.

"And this was in the course of an interrogation?" said the Colonel crisply.

"Yes, Sir. I was seeking information from her when she assaulted me."

"Assaulted you?"

"She pushed me in a fountain, Sir."

"So, you met this woman last night and questioned her. Where were your escorts?"

"I was on my own Sir. I left my men at the café where I had found her," said Moreno, anxious to supply actual facts wherever possible.

"So," said the Colonel again, "you find and arrest a suspected spy in a café, you leave your men at the café and take the suspect along the street to a fountain out of sight of the café."

"Yes Sir," Moreno confirmed unhappily.

"Was she pretty, this suspect of yours?" asked the Colonel. Moreno did not reply.

"And then you stand by the fountain. Or perhaps you were sitting down, yes, that is more likely. You do not want to be overheard, so love talk perhaps, rather than questions of spying, of sabotage?"

Moreno knew better than to answer rhetorical questions. He looked steadfastly at a dusty patch on the wall above the Colonel's head and said nothing.

"You attempt to take liberties with her, she sees her chance and pushes you in the fountain. Am I right?" he suddenly fired at the Captain.

"Sir, I..." But the Colonel now turned his attention from his polished boots to Moreno, and his look was withering.

"So, the gallant Captain turns out the garrison to arrest a girl who bested him in what he thought he was best at, making love. Am I right? I'd better warn you that I have already spoken to the men who were with you last night. I was intrigued to find out the details of this sudden alert without the embellishments you would have felt compelled to add."

"Sir, you've decided that my conduct was dishonourable without asking for my own explanation first. I demand to offer my explanations to General Franco himself, he appointed me here."

"In that case you'd better report to him in Palma at once. You'll find the patrol boat at the quay. I suppose that by the time you see the General you will have had time to think up a plausible story. You'll get away with it as usual."

Moreno was turning red with anger as he saluted and left the room. He saw his most reliable sergeant crossing the square to intercept him.

"No sign of the girl, Sir. We found the hotel where the girl was staying. A Miss Verity Fleming, travelling with an older lady they think is her aunt. They've both gone, during the night apparently. It looks as though they left in a hurry leaving all their belongings behind. I thought you might want this" he said, handing over Verity's sketchbook. "The men made enquiries all round the town, but she's simply disappeared."

"Very suspicious," said Moreno. "They've probably fled the island. This proves my theory that the girl is a spy who was looking at the military defences of Ibiza. I was right all along."

The sergeant looked at him in astonishment. He had seen the Captain's amorous pursuit of the girl but the ways of officers were often hard to fathom. Now he'd turned the girl into a spy, had he? Oh well, if that was the way he wanted it.

Captain Moreno arrived at headquarters in Palma in time to be invited to join the General and his staff for breakfast in the mess. It was not that General Franco was a sociable man, just that being rather short he hated anyone to have the advantage of height by standing. Franco remembered that Moreno had been a model student at the army academy at Zaragoza whilst he was its director and was always interested to see how his protégées were faring.

The General was a thin man with a small moustache and staring cold eyes. It was as well for an officer to have rehearsed any report that needed to be delivered to Franco since otherwise his gaze could reduce a man to stumbling incoherence. Moreno had thought through precisely what to say to the General. After breakfast in the mess, Moreno made his personal, and much embellished, report to General Franco.

"So I think Sir that this girl must have sought me out to try and obtain information about the military defences of the islands." said Moreno in his most earnest manner.

"You said that she is British?"

"Yes Sir."

"The British Government proclaim a non interventionist policy but can never resist meddling in other countries' business," said Franco, mulling over what Moreno had reported. "Do you think this woman might have had communist backing?"

"That was my first thought Sir," responded Moreno untruthfully. Fortunately for him all his military training had enabled him to impassively tell a senior officer whatever the officer wanted to hear without regard to the truth. Then he produced his final irrefutable evidence for the General.

"My men found this sketchbook in her room" he said placing it on the table in front of Franco. The general leafed through sketch after sketch of Ibiza views including the garrison sitting on atop of the city and its military defences.

"Mmm," Franco wondered for a moment and then made a swift decision.

Following this interview Verity Fleming was formally listed as a spy, wanted for questioning. Moreno, far from being disgraced by the incident, had been commended by the General for his perspicacity in spotting and pursuing a spy of English origin, but who was undoubtedly spying for the Communists, whom Franco thought were the cause of all Spain's troubles. Moreno had carefully removed from the sketchbook everything that did not fit the espionage theory before handing it over. He had found Helen's simple sketch of Verity herself and had placed it in his pocketbook for safekeeping; the rest of the sketches he had discarded.

As a reward, the General decided that Moreno should serve as an aide on his own staff for the time being. Trustworthy men such as Moreno, trained in the General's own academy, were worth their weight in gold to him.

Whilst Moreno was pleased with the overall outcome of the affair, he swore to himself that however long it took, one day he would get even with that bitch, Verity, for soaking him in the fountain.

Verity thought she was very fortunate to have the opportunity to tour Europe with her mother's sister,

Aunt Constance, who loved to travel and was the complete antithesis of her own dead, distantly remembered and constantly inebriated mother. Constance, a good-looking woman of mature years, had almost too much energy and was no-one's idea of a maiden aunt. She thought it would be good for Verity to widen her outlook from that of her narrow-minded father and learn to speak out a bit more. It was often very hard to understand exactly what Verity was feeling or thinking. She included Verity in her travel plans for the summer of 1934, just after Verity's twentieth birthday. Verity's father had thought that his sister in law would be a suitable companion and chaperone for someone of Verity's tender age. In the latter he was mistaken, for Constance, a passionate and vivacious woman in her early forties still attracted men wherever she went and had nothing of the spinster aunt in her nature.

It was when Constance and Verity had reached Ibiza, one of the Balearic Islands of Spain, that Verity had met Helen, who was travelling with her short, stout and very Welsh parents. They were all staying in the town of Ibiza and Verity and Helen had taken to one another immediately and started to go about together unchaperoned in the heat of the day.

It was Helen who had found out about the fiesta to be held that evening, the Festival of San Juan. She had been told that there would be bonfires and horsemen, but she was not too sure of the detail other than that it involved masked men dressed in black and mounted on black horses.

"Do come," she pleaded. "My parents have promised to come too so we won't get into any scrapes."

Verity knew that her Aunt was dining with an old acquaintance, Don César, this evening. She was expected to join them to preserve her Aunt's good name as Don César was a married man. Certainly, Constance had attracted numerous admirers wherever they went but scandal, no!

"We'll meet up at the Plaza after dinner," directed Helen. "They say that the fiesta doesn't get going until midnight."

Constance and Verity were staying at the Grand Hotel which stood on the corner of the Paseo Vara de Rey and lived up to its grandiose name so long as the traveller was prepared to ignore the peeling paint on the walls and the fact that the furniture had seen better days some decades ago. Colonial in looks, its shady interior provided large cool rooms and was a favourite lodging for foreign visitors who only had a few minutes walk to reach it when they disembarked from the ships that called twice weekly.

What was appropriate dress for a fiesta, wondered Verity? Something cheerful, she decided. Goodness knows what time the fiesta would end if it did not start until midnight. Verity was not particularly dress or fashion conscious. She kept her unruly dark hair as short as possible, whether or not bobbed hair was in fashion, as hats usually bounced off her hair, taking the restraining hatpins with them.

She knocked on her Aunt's door. Constance had been writing letters but readily turned to a discussion of the fiesta and described the fun and excitement of Spanish fiestas, the noise, the music, the jostling crowds dressed in their best, street bonfires and a general public disregard for safety.

"They always go just that bit too far, so don't get carried away just because everyone else does," she warned Verity.

"Will you come too?"

"No, I'm looking forward to a tête-à-tête with Don César," she said frankly, "so you go with Helen and her parents and have fun. It'll probably be the only fiesta you'll see on this trip."

At dinner that evening, Constance was effervescent. Conversation always flowed when she was around and she had a knack of making her companions feel happy and pleased with themselves. Don César looked across the table at Constance and her niece. He had known and loved Constance for many years and now he studied the younger woman to seek out signs of the aunt in the niece. Verity had striking violet eyes looking out of an oval face with a creamy complexion, framed by a mop of dark hair. He would not describe her as beautiful now, but in a few years she would be a woman of great beauty. He thought that many women were pretty when young but quickly lost that attraction. A woman who matured into beauty had something worth far more because it could last a lifetime; Verity was not only going to be like Constance, but might even eclipse her. He sighed and wished himself young again.

"Tonight there'll be dancing, music and bonfires in the squares," he said, "but the centre of events is up in the old town in the two largest Plazas. As midnight strikes, twelve horsemen on black stallions ride through the great gate into the plaza. Menorca has much the same festival, but this one is better. The best of the island's young horsemen are chosen. They dress in black and their leader wears a scarlet band around his hat and a scarlet sash around his waist. The crowd taunts and tries to unseat them, whilst each horseman aims to sweep up and carry off a young lady who takes his fancy. The horsemen chase all over town."

"And then what?" asked Constance.

"Then the people dampen down the fires and go home to their beds."

He turned to Verity. "You'll see extraordinary feats of horsemanship tonight, a wonderful sight and very exciting, but keep well clear of the horses hooves, someone always gets trampled. I'd hoped my nephew would take you to the fiesta but he was otherwise engaged. Just make sure that you don't get accidently scooped up by a horseman!"

Roberto had protested to him that this was a special night and he wasn't going to give up something he was looking forward to in order to accompany an English lady lawyer to the fiesta, that was asking too much. Don César hadn't insisted, a surly companion would not have been much fun for Verity.

"Could you escort Verity up to the square, so that she can join Helen and her parents?" asked Aunt Constance. "Then join me for a brandy."

Verity noticed the intensity of the look that they exchanged and for a moment wondered whether there was something between them. Don César smiled and stood up offering Verity his arm.

Verity took the proffered arm as a guard against stumbling on the uneven cobblestones. They walked along the narrow dark streets leading to the great gateway that pierced the thick town walls, the noise of the crowds already spilling over into the lower town. Don César is a very good looking man thought Verity - old of course, but very charming and gallant and with a certain something that was not apparent in men of his age in England. He still had the lithe and supple figure of a much younger man. He placed his other hand over hers as it rested on his arm and Verity felt a tingle run through her. Ridiculous, she thought, this man is almost as old as my father and he's clearly very keen on Constance. However, she did not remove her hand.

The scent of flowers was strong on the warm night air, cascades of bougainvillaea, hibiscus, and honeysuckle everywhere. The noise was growing as they walked up the steep ramp towards the high stone arch of the gateway, snatches of music, and a rabble of voices as excited families pushed past them and surged through the colonnade into the plaza.

"How do we find your friends?" asked Don César.

"They'll meet me over by the water pump at eleven thirty."

He looked at his watch and saw that it was eleven twenty five.

"I'll be all right," Verity said, "you go on back to Constance. She'll be waiting for you."

"Abandon you in this crowd? Never! You must be handed over safely," he said laughing.

"I'm not a parcel," she said, angry that he should treat her like a child. At that moment a crowd of young men surged by, knocking against her, and she would have fallen but for his arm as he reached out and drew her firmly to him, shielding her from the excesses of the crowd. She was facing into the square, looking at the throng of people jostling for position and feeling protected and remote from the crowd. Then it was as though lips lightly touched the nape of her neck. A wave of emotion ran through her, just as the crowd surged forward taking her with them, and there were

Helen and her parents waving at her, their faces wreathed in smiles.

She turned to look for Don César to introduce him, but he was gone. Verity felt she must have imagined the light kiss - in this crowd everyone was being jostled. Helen was chattering excitedly, telling her what was to happen during the fiesta.

Verity looked about her, eyeing the beautiful costumes of the girls, such fine embroidery on their shawls, white ornate blouses and black skirts. Each girl had her head covered in a white scarf, some of them of white lace and others in fine cambric; Verity knew that white signified unmarried status. All the girls had rows of bright gold necklaces over their ornate shawls and some carried coquettish fans. Many had rings on each finger, she gathered that the number of rings worn by a girl had a special significance, but didn't know what it was.

Helen was explaining to her that the girls were anxious to attract a horseman but also to tease and escape him for as long as possible; it would be a particular honour for the girl who attracted the attentions and pursuit of the leader of the horsemen, probably the equivalent of a good eligible "catch" at home. The rituals of courtship tonight demanded that the Spanish girls captivate, but play hard to get.

The young men in the crowd had also dressed in their best. Anxious not to be outdone by the horsemen, they wore traditional red headgear that was somewhere between a beret and a hat, elaborate red waistcoats, embroidered white shirts and white trousers. Clearly, they were seeking conquests of their own.

The bonfires crackled, flames leaping up high in the square, singeing the leaves of the trees. A good thing the normal washing lines had been taken in, thought Verity, because by day washing danced high in the air strung on co-operative lines across the street from balcony to balcony. The flames lit up flowers in the window boxes and turned the geraniums strange orange and purple colours in the unnatural light. Waiters from inns around the square piled more wood on the bonfires; it looked as though they were taking the opportunity to get rid of broken chairs and other rubbish. The music began to swell as voices in the far part of the square began singing, the sound swelling until the whole square seemed to be joining in. Verity felt the excitement growing as she stood arm in arm with Helen.

Helen whispered, "I've told my parents that we've been invited to join the family of someone who works at our Pension for the evening to view the fiesta so they'll be going in a minute. As soon as they've gone we'll be off."

When Maria from the Pension appeared beside them, her parents kissed Helen and departed, a pathway opening up through the crowd before them, down which they progressed in stately fashion. As they

disappeared from sight, Helen grabbed Verity's arm and pulled her away.
"Quick, we'll go with Maria and then we're going to dress up and join in."

2

Maria led the girls into an ill-lit side street, darted down a passage and entered a dark arched doorway where she lifted the latch. Two elderly women in black sat on either side of a fireplace, the room lit by an oil lamp which spluttered and gave out an erratic light. Maria introduced the women as her grandmother and aunt. Helen's plan was for them to disguise themselves as locals and join in, with Maria to show them what to do. It sounded much more fun than sitting and watching and after all why did they need chaperoning? It was an outdated local custom as far as the girls were concerned and if Maria's family approved of her joining in, why shouldn't they? As a lawyer, Verity normally stuck to the rules imposed on her, but after all, she thought, what harm could come of it?

The women chattered volubly as they expertly dressed Helen and Verity in embroidered black shawls round their shoulders and white lace shawls to cover their heads; the shawls looked very special, perhaps antique. Maria explained in her halting English that they had belonged to her family for several generations, worn on special occasions. The old ladies hung rows of gold chains round the girls' necks and finally offered a selection of large rings, encouraging them to find a ring for every finger.

"But doesn't your family mind lending them to us?" Verity questioned.

"They regard it as an honour that you English ladies should wear them," Maria said above the continuing chatter of the old ladies as they deftly thrust gnarled fingers into Helen's long hair, twisting it this way and that and pinning it down with beautiful combs. The enveloping embroidered shawls almost hid their English dresses. Finally, they were thrust in front of the distorted glass of an old mirror.

Verity looked with surprise at the images reflected back at them. Whilst nothing could make Helen look Spanish, with her long fair hair pinned up and covered by a white shawl, she looked sophisticated and elegant. Verity's own reflection astonished her even more; with her dark hair, a truly imperious Spanish lady stared back at her. True, her hair was short rather than piled up on top in the local manner, but with ornamental combs and a lace shawl, her reflection looked very Spanish. Verity felt taller and more commanding, even though to her eye the white skin of her face and rosy cheeks rather detracted from the image. She felt like a different person, ready for any adventure.

Maria, already dressed magnificently in her own finery, was hastening them out of the door. Hurriedly calling their thanks to the old ladies, they were hustled out into the dark passage and back to the plaza where the great gateway of the Portal Nou loomed above them, reflected in the light of the fires.

"Stay close to me," Maria admonished them. "Be ready to run; we run in and out of the passages. Stay close and keep within the town walls."

The noise in the square had quietened, apart that is from a gaggle of youths drinking heavily and lurching about near the largest bonfire, impervious to the expectant atmosphere that had affected everyone else. The girls waited as the hands of the clock closed on midnight, the crackle of the bonfire loud in their ears. Then they caught the sound of galloping hooves and into the crowded square swept a phalanx of horsemen, with black clothes, black masks, black hats and black horses.

As the horsemen rode in, there were cheers from the men in the crowd and answering shouts from the riders. The horsemen rode straight into the crowd, women screamed snatching small children from the paths of dangerous hooves. Verity thought it was like a medieval play being enacted before her. She watched the horsemen parading round, bowing, and raising their hats to the ladies as the families withdrew to the safe outer edges of the square, leaving the senoritas and the young men surrounding and taunting the horsemen. The withdrawal of the family groups had been sudden and Verity felt vulnerable, like a pebble left isolated and exposed on the beach by the ebbing tide. The horsemen paraded round the group, following their leader who was resplendent in a red sash, sizing up the assembled beauty of Ciudad de Ibiza. The bolder of the young men in the crowd made sudden rushes at the riders and tried to unseat them. However, they were big horses ridden by good horsemen who brushed off the young men easily.

Verity felt the rising excitement as the twelve horsemen withdrew at their leader's signal to circle the fountain.

"Follow me," shouted Maria as a horn sounded and the circling horsemen wheeled and rode straight at the crowd of girls who scattered and fled. Verity and Helen ran after Maria down a passageway, round a corner and up an alley. The sounds of hooves were everywhere, magnified by the high walls of the houses. Maria paused for a moment in the shelter of an archway, listening.

"They ride in twos and threes so it is safe now; when they ride singly, it is dangerous. Now we must tease them." Saying this, she pulled a red scarf out of her pocket and waved it out of the archway. It was answered by a cry from down the street and a clatter of hooves. Maria laughed and ran off down the alley with the girls following hard on her heels. They could hear the horsemen entering the alleyway and then Maria ran nimbly up some narrow stone steps ahead of them which Verity guessed led on to the city walls. Verity was last, hampered by the fact that Helen – who was in front of her - did not seem to be as fleet of foot as Verity hoped. She could hear a horse's breath behind her as it neared the foot of the steps.

As Verity turned the first corner of the stone steps, she looked back and saw to her astonishment that one of the horsemen was urging his horse up the steps. She stood for a moment transfixed by the unexpected sight, surely straight out of a movie. A shout from Maria above recalled her and she shot up the last flight of steps to join the others on the path along the walls. Looking back, she saw that the horseman had found the last corner too narrow for his horse to manoeuvre. He took off his hat with a flourish and waved it, the crimson scarf tied around it glinting in the lamplight. Then, with a remarkably elegant display of horsemanship, he backed his horse down the steps.

The girls ran light-footed along the wall, looking down at the elaborate ritual being enacted in the dimly lit streets below. Female figures dashing in and out of archways pursued by cheering, whooping riders. Now and then, they saw a pursuer corner his prey.

They were now on a section of the wall lit by braziers. Silhouetted by the light, their progress could be seen from below. A shout and a clatter of hooves and then a horseman, resplendent in scarlet sash, appeared in front of them on the wall. It was the same horseman who had backed his horse down the steps behind Verity when the way became too narrow. Maria disappeared down the nearest flight of steps with alacrity. "He's the Leader," she called over her shoulder as she skipped lightly down the dark stairs.

Verity could hear the clatter of hooves starting to descend as she reached the bottom of the flight. Ahead of her, she saw Maria and Helen disappearing down a passageway. More steps, and up they went, another passageway with low archways that seemed no deterrent to their persecutor whose horse seemed remarkably surefooted on this uneven ground. The passageways were exceedingly steep as they wound their way up the hill. Maria dived through the open door of a house to the cries of the family assembled inside. Joining her, Verity thought for a moment that they had found sanctuary but the family were already pushing them towards the back of the house and out through a rear door. A commotion behind them announced the arrival of a horseman who was clearly trying to ride into the house but being vigorously and noisily repelled by a householder with a broom.

Verity's breath was coming in gasps, as was Helen's ahead of her. She paused to get her breath, but immediately the sound of the pursuing hooves forced her on again. Surely, she thought, they had completed a circuit of the old town by now; there could hardly be any of the narrow streets they had not explored already.

"Must stop," Verity called to Maria as a stitch in her side became overwhelming.

"In here," called Maria pounding on an inn door. The door opened wide revealing a crowd of people within. Horse's hooves sounded on the stones of the street behind Verity and a hand reached out from behind but she twisted away and almost fell through the doorway into a covered stone courtyard of an inn with a staircase ahead of her.

She saw Maria and Helen on the staircase and tried to reach them, as people shouted and screamed as the horseman rode through the arched doorway and, ducking under the lintel, forced his horse into the courtyard to the foot of the staircase and on to the first step, brushing off all attempts to stop him. The cries from the crowd seemed to be divided equally between those who were encouraging the horseman and those who feared that the staircase would give way under the weight. Foremost amongst the latter was the landlord, a thin man in a dirty apron, who loudly wailed his misfortune.

As Verity turned to face the rider, his horse's feet planted firmly on the uneven staircase waiting for his master's command, the crowd fell silent. The scarlet-sashed horseman was smiling now, his teeth gleaming in contrast beneath the black mask through which icy blue eyes gazed hypnotically at Verity. She felt some gesture was called for and, blushing, curtsied deeply to him. He extended his arm and held out a hand to claim her.

Then a voice cried out from the gallery above her.

"¡Déjala, es inglesa! The lady's a visitor, a guest in our country, do not touch her!"

The horseman responded angrily in a stream of Spanish, gesticulating with his whip. Verity felt the tension rising and knew she needed to do something more to divert his anger. Taking a red rose from her hair she threw it to the horseman and he deftly caught it. His smile had a hint of menace as he bent towards her. Only Verity heard his whispered words.

"They saved you this time but I will find you. Next time you will not escape..."

With that he backed his horse out, scattering onlookers as he went, accompanied by the good-natured cheers of those who had gathered in the courtyard.

A hand gently touched Verity's arm.

"Come," said the young man who had called from the gallery, leading her up the stairs to where Helen and Maria were waiting in a large room above.

"You've made a conquest there," said Helen.

"He could be a dangerous enemy," said the young man. "That was Luis Moreno, an army officer garrisoned here. He has much power and is greatly feared for his ruthlessness."

"But surely," said Helen "that power only extends to his soldiers?"

"You're wrong," said the young man who introduced himself as Juan. Verity felt foolish that this young man could speak English when she knew so little Spanish.

A young man with a red embroidered waistcoat admonished Maria: "What were you thinking of, dressing up these English ladies in this foolish way?"

Verity felt rather as though she was a child who had been caught out wearing fancy dress to a party that turned out to be for adults only. Maria let rip in Spanish but her critic continued undeterred.

"You should know better! Many of the horsemen tonight were cavalrymen, not the local boys. The army is training here and if we defy them we put ourselves and our families in peril."

Another young man joined in.

"They took my uncle's farm from him when he refused to let them use his fields for training. They turned him and my aunt out and didn't even let them take their belongings. They let them leave in a horse and cart but that was all."

Verity shivered and pulled her borrowed shawl more tightly around her.

A serving woman was pouring hot wine into glasses and handing them round. It tasted divine to Verity after the exertions of the last hour or so, even though she did not normally drink alcohol - a reaction to the distant memories of her mother who always smelled of gin and heavy perfume. Maybe there was a time and place for alcohol in moderation, she thought.

The young man continued, "Not a peseta have they received. If the country is on a war footing, no compensation is payable."

"And who said the country is on a war footing?"

"It stands to reason," said the young man. But his argument was shouted down by his friends, who'd heard it all before. The four young men continued a heated discussion which flowed around and over the girls. Maria obviously found the discussion of little interest but continued to gaze at the young man with the red waistcoat .

"He's my second cousin, Felipe," she explained to the girls. "He's at the University in Barcelona and is very clever."

Felipe, his face lit by the passion of his argument, was waving his hands around to enhance his point.

"We will make our republic just like France," said one. The others jeered.

"You will make us like the French?"

"Well, we don't want the King back; the monarchy's always been corrupt and useless!"

"The government is even more corrupt and useless," said a handsome young man in an embroidered blue waistcoat.

"You should know, Roberto," said Juan "Your uncle, Don César de los Ríos, is one of them."

Verity perked up. She had never guessed that Don César was a member of the Spanish Government, Constance had never mentioned it, surely she must know? Before she could say anything, Roberto answered.

"He's not corrupt, he tries to stamp out corruption: he feels for the people and carries their message to the Cortes."

"And what good does that do? What we need is action, not words."

Juan turned to the girls.

"Since we were little, we've had many different governments; they seemed to change every few minutes. None of them could resolve the war in Morocco or the unrest in Barcelona. As for the army, they do exactly what they like and take no notice of the government. Union membership has surged, especially in Andalusia and Barcelona, as lots of people think that they could improve things by violence through the Unions."

Felipe took up the story.

"At one point, we had army dictatorship under Miguel Primo de Rivera but he kept our King in place."

Juan exploded, "De Rivera thought he was receiving 'Divine Guidance' – but no-one else did. He squashed the existing political parties as he didn't like them and actually thought that another better governing class would materialise who would govern by goodwill. Can you imagine?"

Roberto joined in, "The rich went on evading taxes, the poor got poorer and life became more difficult than ever."

Juan continued, "The dictator resigned and the King went into exile. Since then we've had the lot: Anarchists, Socialists and Trotskyites, all vying for power on one side, and on the other side, rich landowners supported by the Church. You can guess who's been winning."

"And don't forget the Fascists," said Felipe. "The Cortes introduced land reform but it's never really been implemented and the Fascists have been increasing."

Helen said musingly "So you're saying that each new government spends its time undoing the measures that the previous government introduced but doesn't make any real progress in getting to the root of the inequality, before it too is overthrown?"

Verity looked at Helen in surprise; nothing in their light-hearted conversations to date had prepared her for a serious side to Helen.

Everyone started to talk at once, pleased to be able to explain their many and diverse points of view to any newcomers prepared to listen to them. The volume of noise went up and up. Verity's attention was focused on Felipe, whilst Juan held Helen's attention with ardently right wing views. The girls did their best to follow the argument back and forth, but it was next to impossible. At home her contemporaries rarely discussed politics, and never with the passion of these young men who cared very deeply about the direction which their country might take. Eventually the excitement of the evening, the exertion, and the lateness of the hour overcame her and she found herself beginning to nod off.

"We must take the ladies home," said Juan, rising.

Juan and Felipe escorted them out into the warm night air. They walked slowly through the quiet streets. When they reached the plaza, it was almost empty, save for a knot of watchmen standing by the embers of a dying fire.

"Are things really as bad as your friends suggest?" Verity asked Felipe who was walking by her.

"They don't exaggerate," he said sombrely. "There are many factions in Spain at the moment; if they cannot unite, then Spain will split apart."

"And if they do unite?" queried Verity.

"Then the King will never return. The army is powerful and waiting its time; it may put down any insurrection, but then take over the country itself."

"Not in support of the Government?"

"No, they'll support their own ends. That's where the Government makes their biggest mistake, thinking that they command the army."

They had turned into the street where Maria's home was. The girls removed their shawls, combs, jewellery and mantillas and handed them to her with their thanks. Maria kissed them lightly on both cheeks and went in.

The girls walked on, the excitement of the evening draining away with the removal of their finery. Verity saw that the sky was beginning to lighten over the harbour, revealing a line of dark clouds on the horizon. A waft of sewer smells assaulted her nose and she was not surprised to see a dead rat in their path, which Juan casually booted aside. Verity realised that dawn could not be too far away and wondered what the new day would bring.

3

"Tell me all about it," said Constance at lunch the next day, "and don't miss out any detail."
Verity's story came out in a rush as she began to describe all the events of the evening, anxious to recount every detail in a way that she would never have done with her father. He would have been horrified by the whole thing, not interested like Aunt Constance.
"What was this horseman of yours like?" asked Constance.
"Well, probably tall; it's difficult to judge the height of a man on a horse, everyone is tall on horseback."
Constance smiled encouragement.
"He had a good strong face - what I could see of it below the mask," Verity continued, from which her aunt, knowing Verity's dislike of beards and moustaches, deduced that he was clean-shaven.
"I saw he'd got black hair when his hat was dislodged as he rode through the doorway and piercing deep blue

eyes, just like the vicar's wife's, the sort that go straight through you and know immediately that you haven't said your prayers every day like you ought to have."

"Hmm," said Constance, "I'll make enquiries."

"Really, Aunt, it's not as though I'll ever see him again."

"I hope you're right if your new friends say he's a tough army officer."

"Well, yes."

"They seem to have summed up the situation here in Spain pretty well, perhaps we should move on." She mused on the situation while Verity tried to decide if she should tell her about the remark one of the boys had made about Don César and the fact that she had met his nephew, Roberto. Then her aunt's words grabbed her attention.

"I don't think we'll go back through Spain as I originally intended, perhaps we should take the boat to Marseilles. Anyway, we can discuss that later, now tell me about this girl Maria. Perhaps we ought to make a present to her family as a thank-you for the loan of the shawl. These mantillas are very precious family heirlooms; it was kind of them to lend them to you."

The rest of the lunch was taken up with planning the purchase of a suitable present for Maria's family.

Verity met up with Helen later in the Plaza and found her in an unusually sombre mood.

"Do you really think there will be a war in Spain?" Helen asked. "Juan and the others seemed absolutely convinced of it last night."

"I don't know," said Verity. "Let's go somewhere we can talk – and perhaps do some sketching as well."

"We'll walk over the headland until we find somewhere with a view," Helen suggested.

Verity was inclined to be somewhat serious for her age - it went with her lawyer's training and the lack of brothers and sisters. She was not used to discussing what she thought with anyone, her father's views were absolute as far as his household was concerned. It was different with her contemporaries, but even then she always let others express their views first before hesitantly expressing her own. Often the conversation moved on before she had the chance to say anything. She had been attracted to Helen because she was fun loving, and Verity had had little fun in her life. It now became apparent to her that Helen had a serious side too.

The girls finally found the perfect spot and sat down facing the sea with all its translucent colours where the light picked out the changes in the depth of the water. They got out their sketch pads and then sat in silence looking at the gorgeous view for a few minutes, and then Helen blurted out: "Have I told you that I've persuaded my parents to let me train as a nurse?"

"No," said Verity in amazement.

"It's something I've always wanted to do. Now I've worn their opposition down at last," Helen grinned. "I start at St Thomas's Hospital in London in September - they've accepted me for a three year training course; I've started reading the textbooks already. I may not be brainy like you," she said looking at Verity, "but if war comes, I'll be ready."

"What do you mean? You're surely not planning to come back here?"

"Why not? They'll need nurses," said Helen, her eyes shining.

Verity was appalled at the thought. "Well, surely there will be plenty of Spanish nurses to cope, and anyway," she continued unconvincingly, "it won't be our war."

"Don't you understand? You heard Juan last night. It will be a struggle for justice, for the people, for right."

Verity had not expected to hear a passionate speech from Helen. It seemed to her an overreaction to a lively late night discussion.

"You're a lawyer," said Helen, "don't you spend your time fighting for justice for the people?"

"In a way, but it doesn't often seem like that. My father does very little criminal work. Even when he does, it's defending petty thieves."

"But if they're innocent you get them off?" demanded Helen.

"Yes, but..."

Helen interrupted, "So you fight for justice!"

"In a way, but usually we're simply acting for a client who is suing a neighbour about a boundary dispute."

"There," said Helen triumphantly, "what are most wars but boundary disputes?!"

"But if there is a war in Spain it won't be about a boundary dispute."

"The principle's the same. As a lawyer you're bound to fight for what's right."

"Yes, but in the Courts, not in the field!"

"It's the same difference," concluded Helen stubbornly.

They were quiet for a while, deep in thought as they sketched. Verity was concentrating on the land and seascape before her, whilst Helen, unbeknown to Verity, was quietly doing a pencil drawing of her friend.

Verity had never looked at her own reasons for being a lawyer; it had always been taken for granted that it was what she would do. Her father had wanted a son to take over his solicitor's practice in due course and, not having one, had decided that Verity would do so instead. Was fighting for justice what she wanted to do, she wondered? She really had no idea, she had never even thought about it until now.

Helen said suddenly, "Juan has promised to escort us to a café after dinner tonight. You will come, won't you?"

Verity realised that, without her, Helen could not go either.

"This is for you," Helen said thrusting the sketch at her. "Ten thirty tonight."
Verity looked at the little drawing of herself, distracted from their discussion as Helen had intended.
"But I don't know whether I'll be free," began Verity, but Helen was already off up the path leaving her with no choice.

Over dinner, she discussed the problems that beset Spain with Aunt Constance and Don César, who was again in attendance on her aunt. Whilst Don César, as she might have expected, thought the opinions of the young men inflammatory, his own thoughts also led him to believe that war was inevitable. Verity wondered what kind of position Don César held in the Government but her aunt's conversation, brilliant and optimistic as usual, stopped her from asking. Besides, Don César's worries were clear enough.
"There are too many divisions between the people," he was saying. "At one end the clergy and the rich and privileged, with the Army always ready to defend them; at the other, peasants with no land, no livelihood and no prospects. In the middle, there are those who make their money in industry and commerce. Many of the poor people are taking the communist standpoint, collectivism and the community working for all, with no man favoured above another. But there's no way it can work in practice. A belief is growing among the peasants that the land belongs to everyone, there've

already been isolated cases of the peasants seizing the land."

"Presumably the land owners paid a fair price for the land in the first place?" asked Verity, a lawyer to her core.

"No! It was often the spoils of battle. Give a sword or an axe to a Spanish nobleman and he will fight until he reaches the sea, and sometimes even that didn't stop him. Just think of Cortes destroying the Aztecs," said Don César his eyes shining with fervour. "Sometimes, powerful people simply fenced the land off centuries ago and built a house on it, just as they did in your country. The monasteries and the King owned much of the land and they granted rights to people to live on it and make a living from it. A great deal of the land is still owned by the monasteries and cultivated by others, but the rents are too high for the poor quality of the land. There's a lot of resentment against the monasteries, and in some parts of Spain that bitterness extends to all of the clergy as well."

Verity compared it in her mind to home. Was there equality in England? No, there were wide inequalities, but it seemed to her that even events like the Jarrow March had not generated the antagonism and hatred that she was beginning to become aware of here in Spain.

After dinner, Verity waited in the lobby until Helen arrived. They were shortly joined by Juan who escorted the girls to a café where many families were still finishing their evening meal. Above the hubbub, Verity heard the sound of a guitar that grew in volume as they passed through an archway and into the back room that was filled with younger people, noise and music. Fresh glasses and wine were placed in front of them as people moved up to make room at the long table. Verity noticed immediately that Roberto was there and just how handsome and animated his face was as he talked to his friends.

Juan explained, "These are the friends I grew up and went to school with. Some of them are now at University in Barcelona, like me. Jaime's training to be a doctor, Antonio and Jose over there are at the Law faculty with me, and Felipe, sitting next to you, is training to be an architect."

Felipe said enthusiastically, "Barcelona is a wonderful place to train as an architect. Do you know it?"

Verity had been there on her way to the Balearic Islands and explained that she had spent a couple of days in the city with her aunt visiting its sights. That was enough to set Felipe off, he was clearly very proud of the city that he had adopted as his own and especially of the famous architects who had contributed to it.

One of the others rounded on him, mocking.

"He's talking of Barcelona as though it was merely a collection of buildings, when it is the heart of Catalonia."

Verity had barely even heard of Catalonia; Felipe explained that the area of Spain called Catalonia had been granted autonomy in return for its support of the Government.

Verity did not want another solemn lecture on the complexities of Spanish politics and let her attention wander to the saturnine guitarist who was playing mournful music to which no-one appeared to be listening. But on the other hand, mused Verity, his music set the tone for the sombre discussions around the table. Whenever he finished playing there was a noisy display of approval. He would take a short break and then begin another tune that, to Verity's untutored ear, sounded very much like the one before. His music seemed overwhelmingly sad.

After a while, Verity began to receive the impression that, far from being ignored, the guitarist was actually orchestrating the discussion around him whilst exhibiting total absorption in his own music. He looked up and saw Verity watching him, but made no acknowledgement, he simply stared at her and then went back to his playing. Eventually he moved on to a piece that was not of the mournful flamenco type of music, but was insistent and rhythmic and had Verity tapping her foot.

A lithe young man sitting near her rose and began to move in time with the music, then started to drum his heels insistently on the tiled floor. It made a rhythmic staccato sound that was impossible to ignore. The talkers turned and watched the dancer and encouraged him with cheers and cries of "Ole!"

Verity saw that guitarist and dancer formed a partnership, as first one took the lead in the rhythm, then the other. Everyone was marking the tempo with fierce hollow handclaps. The pace built up, the music had caught everyone's attention and conversation had ceased. All eyes were on the duo that they urged on to an impossible crescendo of blurred fingers and stamping feet. The music stopped at its climax; there was a moment's silence, then a roar of approval. The guitarist rose and made a slight bow.

During this entertainment, Verity suddenly noticed that she and Helen were the only women left in the room. When they had arrived there had been women and children in the café eating. She interrupted Felipe to ask why this was.

"Spanish women don't have the freedom you English have. They're not expected to take part in café society; it is for the men to debate, argue, and make decisions. It is for women to look after the home and the needs of her family, whether she is married or not. Women are welcome to eat out with their families, but they then return home to put the children to bed and await the return of their men folk."

Somehow, when Felipe described the role of a Spanish woman like this, it sounded archaic, but it was really not much different from how things were at home, where she and Helen would probably have been condemned as 'loose' girls for sitting with young men talking late into the night. Some things were much the same wherever you were. But would they have had the same atmosphere of music and vibrant discussion in a public house at home? Verity somehow doubted it, even though she had never actually been in a public house.

The talk round the table had turned to fascism.

Felipe explained, "On the mainland it is tougher, student life is not easy now. We have our studies for our professions but behind everything is politics. We are safe here with our friends, even when we do not agree with them, but we cannot walk safely in Barcelona. Any man may be your enemy without even knowing your name, because he suspects that you support this party or that party. You don't walk alone in dark streets in Barcelona."

Verity felt a shiver run down her spine. "Is it really that bad?"

"Yes," said Felipe, "haven't you heard of our death..." Felipe jerked as Juan stopped him by kicking him hard on the shins under the table. With an effort, Juan endeavoured to turn the conversation away and asked how long the girls were staying. Helen started to reply but faltered as the room fell quiet. Looking up from the table, they were mesmerised by the sight that confronted them. Three soldiers stood in the archway, two with their rifles raised and pointing directly into the room.

4

The room had fallen silent and Verity felt the chill that went through it. One of the soldiers was an officer and as he stepped forward and surveyed the room, Verity recognised the piercing blue eyes that last night had been the only features visible behind the black mask. The eyes swept over the others around the table and then focused on her. Felipe's arm imperceptibly vanished from the back of her chair.

The officer stepped forward, bowed and announced himself, "Captain Luis Moreno." She half expected him to say "at your service" but he did not. Instead he extended his hand, "Come."

She was not sure whether this was an invitation or an order, but a glance at her suddenly mute friends convinced her that there was no question of not doing what this arrogant man ordered. She rose and followed him out into the square. His men stayed behind in the café doorway and none of Verity's new friends dared move to accompany her.

The captain had her arm in a firm grip and led her along to an ill-lit square with a fountain gushing in the centre. He stopped by the low stone wall of the fountain and turned to face her so abruptly that she cannoned into him, as he had no doubt intended.

"Why did you run from me last night?" he demanded. "You were my prize; I sought you out after seeing you in the square. According to the rules of the fiesta I won you and you had no business refusing to come with me," he said, keeping his grip on her arm.

"I'm sorry; it was very silly of me to take part when I didn't know the rules. I didn't mean to make you angry," she said looking up into those piercing, uncomfortable eyes.

"You make me look a fool before all the others. Every young woman in Cuidad de Ibiza wishes for me to make love to her, all but you, who entices me only to reject me!"

What incredible male vanity! How was she to get out of this? There was no-one about in this dark and neglected square to come to her rescue even if anyone would dare to interfere with an army officer. She looked up at him and his mouth came down on hers. It pinned her as effectively as his hand had previously, angry and hard at first, and then his tongue probed her mouth in a way that was new to her, his arms holding her firmly to him.

She could feel his strength as he angrily kissed her. For Verity, kisses had always been gentle exchanges, not at all like this brutal assault on her mouth, but there seemed nothing she could do but submit, however much she hated to do so. Surely someone would come by and for propriety's sake he would stop.

She realised that whilst one arm was pinning her firmly against him, his free hand was exploring her body. Verity tried to struggle against his intimate and unwanted caresses but he held her in such a powerful grip that her struggles seemed more like the beating of a butterfly's wings. She reasoned with herself, he can't harm me, not here in a street where people might see. She thought she'd better not antagonise him further and stopped struggling. His mouth, which had been bruising her lips, became softer, his hands gentler. She found against all the odds that he was arousing pleasurable sensations in her as he sank to a sitting position on the low wall around the fountain, drawing her on to his knee.

Verity had never sat on a man's knee in her life until now. He was kissing her neck passionately and murmuring, but whether they were endearments or threats she could not tell. Against her will, waves of pleasure ran through her as one of his hands found its way inside her dress and caressed her breasts. She tried unsuccessfully to push his hand away and as she did so she became aware that his other hand was caressing the bare skin of her thigh above her stocking. They were in a public place, what if anyone should see them? Her reputation would be ruined forever, even though there seemed to be no-one around at the moment. She felt mortified and knew she must stop him but was becoming overwhelmed by the sensations overtaking her own body; no-one had ever touched her this way before. Surely, she thought, this man must have more than two hands - they seemed to be all over her. Then to her horror, she realised that she was reacting to his touch and moving with his caresses. How could she be responding to this lecherous, demanding man who only last night had seemed a gallant and chivalrous knight on his black horse? She was ashamed of herself. This had gone too far already, she must get away.

She gave up trying to remove his hands and instead rested her hands lightly on his chest. He relaxed as she did so and Verity shoved him as hard as she could and threw herself sideways. He overbalanced and toppled slowly into the fountain without as much as a cry. Verity fell on the ground but was up again immediately and only looked back long enough to see him sodden and struggling to get up as the fountain gushed relentlessly over him.

She could not help herself - she laughed out loud at the sight of him. Then she was running down the street as fast as she could.

Captain Luis Moreno was an expert in making love. He did not mind whether his conquests were young girls or experienced married women, he enjoyed them all. Apart from the pleasure, it was useful for finding out what was going on; all the family secrets came out on the pillow and these secrets he could and did make use of.

No one was ever going to be chasing after him with their bastard babies, he knew too much. He had not been born into the officer class, he had come up through the ranks on account of his excellent military skills, which, combined with ruthlessness, was what he reckoned took a soldier to the top. Garrisoned in Ibiza town for four months, he had used the time to good effect, learning the geography of the island and meeting all the local officials in his day-to-day work. He made sure to find out where their true sympathies lay, through their daughters, their sisters, and, sometimes, their wives. He knew the truth about all the prominent citizens of the island.

Moreno had dreamt up the idea of replacing the local leader of the horsemen in the fiesta as he relished the idea of the chase and the capture; he was getting bored with the lack of military action on this island. He had taken two trusted men with him just before midnight, waylaid the horsemen on their way to the square, and

removed their leader who had been left trussed up, with Moreno occupying his gilded saddle for the foray.
The other horsemen had been forced to take their lead from him and it had given the fiesta a new dimension of excitement. He had spotted the foreign girl as soon as he entered the square, her borrowed plumes marking her as a participant in the night's action. He had also marked one or two other targets amongst the girls, as he saw no reason to limit his actions to merely one. After all, the local girls were just as attractive. He had carried out other skirmishes on horseback, but this time it was purely for pleasure that he had hunted down the foreign girl.
At first he thought the girl would be an easy target, since, as a stranger to Ibiza, she could not know the streets, alleyways and passages as he did. He soon realised that at least one of the others with her must be a local girl since they used routes that his target could never otherwise have known. He had had to use his military skill to track her and cut off her path, which had eventually led to her taking refuge in that wretched inn from which he had been unable to wrest her.
He was pleased with her gesture of handing over the flower from her hair. It had style and promise and made her even more desirable. It was in cheerful mood that he had ridden away from the inn, rounded a corner, and found a local girl whom he had easily scooped up on the saddle in front of him and carried

triumphantly (and on her part compliantly) back to the barracks with him. At first he had been pleased by her attentions to him as the victorious horseman, but quickly tired of her. It was the other girl, the English one, he wanted.

The next evening he had set out to find the English girl and, when he had found her, to separate her from her friends. He had expected her to capitulate quickly – no woman ever refused him. Shyness, perhaps, had prevailed on the previous evening and he was prepared for once to make allowances - after all, he had never seduced a foreign girl before, perhaps they had different customs. He had intended to take her off to a room nearby which he often borrowed for the purposes of seduction. He cursed the fact that he had not taken her there straight from the café. She could not have run away so easily from him there.

Whilst she had struggled at first, she soon responded to his touch, just like all the others. He was sure that he had aroused passion in her and that she wanted him as much as he wanted her, so it was with complete astonishment that he had been overbalanced. Before he had realised what was happening, he had fallen backwards into the fountain where the water gushed relentlessly over him, soaking his uniform through. Then she had stood there and laughed. Laughed!

Astonishment and then anger took hold of him. How dare she? Did she not know who he was? His honour was at stake, she was not going to get away with this. He would bring a charge against her for assault, he would have her brought in and taken to the cells. A little softening up by the guards would soon put her in the right frame of mind. He was not going to be cheated of what he wanted by a mere girl.

He liked a challenge and he thought, surprising himself, he was a little tired of "yes" women. It could be the diversion he had been looking for, to while away the time in this place.

Just before dawn was the best time for an arrest to instil the right degree of terror. Make sure to take them unawares through sleep. It would work just as well in this case, even if the purpose was more personal. He walked back to the barracks humming a little tune, not entirely displeased with his evening. He was still humming as he gave the orders for Verity's arrest, and then went off to bed.

Verity had run for all she was worth through the streets of Ibiza to find shelter from him. After a while, she realised he was not pursuing her and headed at once for the hotel and her aunt, forgetting her friends at the café. Perhaps Constance could obtain Don César's help. She was sure he could protect her from the repercussions of having pushed this proud officer into the fountain, even if he had richly deserved it.

Reaching the hotel, Verity went up the stairs and knocked quietly at her aunt's bedroom door.

Constance soon let her in. Verity found that some kind of shock had set in and she was shaking as her aunt enfolded her in her arms and led her to sit on the bed. Verity stopped shaking out of sheer surprise when she saw Don César sitting up in her aunt's bed. She had suspected something, but was still amazed. How discreet they had been. Astonished as she was, a thought came to her mind; she had forgotten to tell her aunt that she had met Roberto, Don César's nephew.

Brushing this distraction aside, she told them her story quickly and with economy. She did not need to repeat anything.

"You're right to be afraid," said Don César, "he's a dangerous man who might well issue a warrant for your arrest on assault or some trumped up charge, or he might take other equally effective action against you. I doubt that even I could protect you from the army."

"Never mind," he continued. "Give me 30 minutes to arrange a plan to take you both off the island. Pack a case with essentials; the rest of your luggage can be sent on later. There is not a moment to be lost as arrests are generally carried out before dawn. They're not uncommon," he added seeing the look of surprise on the faces of both women.

They moved into action immediately, gathering belongings to pile into a small holdall as Don César left the room. He was soon back with a solution; he had sent his nephew to look for a trustworthy fisherman who could take both women in his fishing boat over to neighbouring Mallorca, where they could catch the steamer to Marseilles. Roberto would be waiting for them at the harbour. Less than half an hour after Verity's arrival back at the hotel, they crept quietly downstairs and out through a side door. Don César carried their bag whilst Verity and her aunt moved quickly over the cobbled stones towards the harbour where the smell of fish vied for dominance with the ever-present smell of sewage. They slowed as they reached the harbour and picked their way cautiously over ropes, cables and fishing tackle until a figure detached itself from the shadow of the harbour wall and materialised into the form of Roberto.

"The boat is waiting for you," Roberto said, addressing Verity. "They will take you and your aunt to Mallorca. I'm sorry I cannot go with you, I must remain with my uncle."

Verity had time to wonder what kind of activity could demand Roberto's presence near Don César.

"Who's on board?" queried Verity.

"The skipper and two crew members - local men who have been with him for years. They will fish after they have dropped you off. That way it's not suspicious."

Don César was saying goodbye to Constance as Roberto helped Verity on board. He handed their bag to the waiting men, only dimly seen in the darkness, who stowed it on board. Roberto introduced the skipper, who showed Verity into the cramped crew quarters where she could sit without being in the way of the work of the boat. Verity turned to Roberto.

"Go now," she said. "I can't thank you and your uncle enough for all you have done for me." Stooping down he kissed her on each cheek, then vanished quickly.

On the quayside, Constance was talking quickly with Don César as to the possible implications for their own relationship.

"Nothing will come between us," he assured her, kissing her gently.

"It is easy to say," she said, "but you have to stay here for your work and I worry so much about your safety."

The engines of the boat began to throb. Don César helped Constance on board and squeezed her hand in farewell. The crew released the ropes and hauled them onboard; the boat chugged slowly out of the harbour with only the stars to witness their departure.

It was a strange end to their long, lazy holiday. Verity found it difficult to comprehend how it had suddenly taken so deadly a turn and had clearly put so many people in jeopardy. She and Constance talked in a desultory fashion but Verity, having had no sleep, finally succumbed. Constance cradled Verity's head on her shoulder and then helped her into a more comfortable position on a bunk where for the time being she slept soundly as the water rhythmically hit the side of the boat.

5

When Verity awoke - stiff and feeling sick - the dawn light was filtering through the cabin portholes. She had never been a good sea traveller and now she felt the rolling motion of the boat was going to make her sick. She emerged on the deck just in time to vomit over the stern. She immediately felt a bit better; the fresh air helped but there was an overall stench of fish and machine oil that continued to make her queasy. Aunt Constance was sitting on an upturned box apparently mending a fishing net and wearing, improbably, a stained fisherman's jersey and hat. She hailed Verity who picked her way through the tangle of ropes, drums and fishing gear to join her.

"A boat carrying the flag of the Spanish Army passed within hailing distance so the skipper suggested that I would avoid attracting attention if I borrowed some clothing and looked busy," she explained. "He told them that we were going to the fishing grounds off Mallorca and they went on their way. If you work on the other side of this net, we could soon have it repaired," she added.

Verity did as she was bidden, thinking how full of surprises her aunt was. She had seemed during their tour round Europe to be the quintessential Englishwoman, keen on their seeing every tourist sight, missing nothing in their quest for knowledge, making sure that Verity saw and appreciated all the wonders of the rich past of France, Italy and Spain. Constance had always gone to bed early so as to be fresh for the morning sightseeing and was appreciative of every little service that anyone had rendered to them. She was solicitous of her niece's welfare, but not unduly restrictive of her freedom.

Now in one night Verity had found her aunt in bed with a very handsome Spaniard, had seen her rise to the challenge of a sudden flight from danger and now here she was sitting dressed as a Spanish fisherman mending a net. Verity decided that she really didn't know her aunt very well and that it was about time she did.

It was cold on deck with the sea breeze and Verity was relieved when one of the men smilingly passed her a jersey. Verity felt ashamed that she had spent so long travelling through Spain without learning much more of the language than how to say "please" and "thank you." She would have to start to learn Spanish, as she would certainly need it when she returned to Spain. Returned? Her aunt took up the theme as though Verity had spoken aloud.

"You must definitely learn Spanish; I've missed so much by not getting a better grasp of the language. I can understand much of what people say but always find it so difficult to make myself understood. You're young; start now and I'm sure you will grasp a new language quickly."

"I will," said Verity. "But how can such a little thing, like pushing that man away, have had such repercussions. I didn't intend to push him into the fountain, it just happened."

"It's not just big things that have repercussions. You might appear to ignore someone one morning because you were daydreaming and didn't actually see them. They might feel affronted and you make an enemy for life. Or a man asks you out and you accept and your life goes in one direction; but if you refuse, it goes in another. Most people think it is the big decisions in life that matter, but it isn't. It's the little ones that affect the course of our lives. Walk up a street at a particular time and you may well meet someone who will change your life, or something happens in that street that will do so. Decide to stay at home that day and your life simply goes on as before."

"You're not saying I shouldn't have pushed him away, are you?"

"Of course not! You did the only thing you could, you didn't have any alternative." Constance left it at that.

Verity changed tack. "Are you going to marry Don César?" she asked abruptly.

"No, he has a wife from whom he has been separated for years. He's a Catholic so will never divorce - he cannot marry me," she said simply. "We make the most of our time together but we try to make sure that there will never be any scandal associated with his name. After all, he has an important post in one of the Ministries in Madrid. He'll go back there shortly and resume his duties."

"Do you mind my asking about him?"

"No. It's wonderful to be able to talk about it – it's not a luxury that I can indulge often," she said with a smile that gave Verity an insight into the lonely years of loving someone from whom she must always be separated. Verity felt very guilty that she had been the cause of cutting short their time together. "And you," continued her aunt, "have you left your heart in Spain?" Constance had noted that Verity had clearly already met the handsome Roberto who had seen them off.

"In some ways, yes, but not with anyone in particular, but with Spain itself."

"Ah! That's far more dangerous than being in love with an individual. You can grow out of love with a person as life changes you, but with a country, there is always more to entrance you each time you visit. It's not as fickle as a lover."

A glimpse of Roberto's smile and his farewell kiss came to Verity's mind but she forced herself to concentrate on mending the net. When they had finished they sat companionably side by side, one on a box, the other on a coil of rope, ducking as spray sometimes arched over them and talking occasionally until the island of Mallorca came into sight.

It is always a jolt to return home after a holiday, but when it has been a particularly eventful one, it is even harder to settle down again. Verity was finding it very difficult to adjust.

However, returning to her father's office in Ruislip had some compensation as she had now been given an office of her own, although the room, newly fitted with a desk and chair, still smelled musty from the boxes of deeds stacked high along one wall.

As an articled clerk who had successfully completed her examinations, she was well on the way to qualifying as a solicitor. There would be no more exams and she would be admitted to the Roll of Solicitors in a short time. It would be quite a landmark as there were still only a handful of women who had qualified as solicitors.

Now, her father had promoted her to her own office, able to see clients on her own and held out by him as competent to do the clients' work; it meant a lot to her. Obviously, he would continue to vet the clients she would see, but it was definitely promotion and she felt pleased and encouraged. However, the daily routine did all seem very dull after her continental tour and the adventures that ended it.

Her father was a stickler for getting things right in the office. He was the same at home and it had not made for a happy childhood for Verity. There had never been any hugs and kisses as she grew up. She was expected to behave like a small adult, always serious and responsible. She knew that deep down he loved her but was quite incapable of showing it. A nod or a 'well done' was the only sign of his approval. Incurring his displeasure meant that he spent even more time at his London Club than usual. She hoped that she would not grow too much in his image.

Verity had told her father about much of her travels and filled him in on the political situation developing in Spain, but he had been dismissive, reiterating the British Government's viewpoint. Verity and Constance had agreed not to talk to anyone about their sudden departure from the Balearic Islands. The circumstances seemed too bizarre when viewed from outside Spain. Had she really been in danger? Verity did not know, but certainly had felt the real fear of those around her. She had not yet heard from Helen but expected to receive a letter from her when she and her parents returned home to Swansea in a week or so.

Verity decided that she must start reading the foreign news with more attention in future, her natural insularity gone for good. She had never been one for reading the news about countries she knew nothing about, but Aunt Constance had succeeded in her aim of broadening both Verity's education and her mind.

Verity relished the independence of having her own office and thought it the best home- coming present her father could have given her. She knew that the secretaries and the office boy must have worked very hard to clear all but one wall of deed boxes and move them elsewhere. They must have been covered in dust for days, moving at least two decades of office debris. Unfortunately none of this prevented her from feeling locked in by the four walls of the office to which she was now confined.

The staff were all pleased to see her obvious pleasure in the new arrangements. Verity thanked them for their hard work on her first day back in the office when she found the two secretaries in the narrow little scullery that passed for the office kitchen, where they were making tea for themselves and the clients.

The secretaries started to talk about the latest office panic, blaming Bernard, the new office boy, for a lost document. Verity knew it was much more likely that one of the girls had misfiled it but knew better than to voice her thoughts. One of the unwritten rules of the office was that things were always blamed on the office boy of the moment, regardless of whether he might have had anything to do with the mishap. The boy was out and about for most of the day so generally never even knew that he was being blamed, and probably wouldn't have cared anyway. However, it did keep the peace between the secretaries and their bosses if there was always a convenient scapegoat.

Bernard was a cheeky boy of 16 with a slightly red face, sandy hair and an ear-to-ear grin that took some shifting. He turned up at the office on his bicycle each morning at eight to help open the post before the secretaries arrived at 8.45. The secretaries, Patricia and Joan, were several years older than Verity. Both accordingly adopted a sophisticated air when dealing with her, regardless of the fact that she was the daughter of the boss and likely to be a partner in the firm herself as soon as she qualified.

Their offices were on Ruislip High Street and Verity's new office was at the back where she could look out on to the garden, behind which crescents of new houses were rising. The new residents tended to be recently married couples, the men taking the Metropolitan line train into London or Uxbridge to their work. It took just under an hour to get into Central London, the early stages of the journey passing through meadows with cattle and sheep, then gradually becoming suburban as the density of houses increased from Harrow onwards.

Verity's own home was about twenty minutes' walk from the office, on the edge of Mad Bess Wood. Some days she cycled, but since it was uphill all the way home, she mostly liked to walk, tending to linger at the duck pond to watch the delight of the children feeding the ducks. They were very well fed ducks; with the new housing populated mostly by young married couples, there were many toddlers whose mothers brought them regularly to feed the birds, while the adults sat on the benches and chatted to one another.

Verity and her father lived in a large Victorian house on Breakspear Road, backing on to the meadows below Mad Bess Wood and a stone's throw from Park Wood. The two woods were indistinguishable from one another in variety of trees, but Park Wood covered a larger area and therefore was easier to get lost in, if you did not know every inch of it as Verity did. It bordered the Ruislip Lido and at weekends in summer trippers from London would throng the place and stray into the woods.

Mad Bess Wood was Verity's own favourite place. The dells where the bluebells and primroses grew had been her childhood playground, the secluded woodland pond a secret place to sit and work out her problems. Few knew of the pond for it was well hidden, no path led directly to it. Here, Verity sat on a large flat stone that had been warmed by the sun, her back against the solid trunk of an oak, the sun's setting rays reflected red in the water.

The sun vanished behind the trees in a glow of red and, looking up, Verity saw a figure flitting through the trees towards her. Not the phantom Mad Bess but an altogether more solid figure. Verity recognised Richard's outline. Richard, now 24, was tall, slim and newly qualified as an accountant. He lived a couple of doors from Verity with his parents. Richard and Verity had been childhood friends in so far as a boy will ever be friends with a girl several years his junior. As there were few other children in the vicinity, he had allowed her to play with him. He still knew where to look for Verity when he needed to talk. They had an easy familiarity and he often took Verity to dances and other social activities. Verity supposed that eventually they would become a couple and marry, that seemed to be the general expectation of their families; it was just that actual romance was lacking but maybe things would change now she was nearly twenty-one. She was looking forward to telling Richard all about her holiday as she did not really have any other friends.

Richard cut her off as soon as she started to tell him about her travels. "You've been away so long, first with those wretched solicitors' examinations; why you needed to take those I don't know. Couldn't you just have looked after your father's house for him, he needs someone to do that," he said peevishly. "And then this dilettante idea of doing the Grand Tour with an elderly relative. It's really time you settled down."

The gross unfairness of his words left her speechless, which gave him just the opportunity he needed to tell her about the dances and outings which he had planned that they should go to this summer, and in particular about next Saturday's tennis club dance where Richard was a leading light. Verity played a social game of tennis now and then, but was not really interested in it, nor indeed very good at it.

"Couldn't you find someone else to go with you?" she said, shocking Richard to the core.

"Find someone else?" he spluttered. "You'll come with me and that's that. Stop being so high and mighty and do what I want for once. You've been away for months and it's about time you thought of something other than your own pleasure."

"Pleasure? Doing exams is not pleasure, you surely know that."

"Well, it was selfish of you to be away so long."

They walked back home not speaking. Outside her house he said, not looking at her, "Seven o'clock Saturday," and stalked off leaving her seething.

6

In the office next morning, Bernard sidled into Verity's room.

"Hello," said Verity, "shouldn't you be out doing your deliveries?"

"Don't you start, Miss! There's enough of them giving me orders. Your father, he wants me to take something urgent in one direction but Joan says I must do a delivery in the opposite direction first. They must think I'm bleeding Malcolm Campbell on me bike. Anyhow, I saw this bit about Spain in The Times when I was cutting out yesterday's Law Reports and thought you'd want to see it. Just been there haven't you, Miss?" Thrusting a cutting at her, he was off to do his Malcolm Campbell imitation. She heard his cheerful whistling as he set off, pursued by wailing noises from Joan who saw that he'd set off in the opposite direction from that of her urgent delivery.

Verity examined the cutting - it was a rather dull report about the Spanish Minister for War who was visiting the Balearic Islands with a General Franco whom the report described as a hero of Spain's Moroccan campaigns and commander of the Balearic Island's military defences. It brought it all back to her, the fear of being pursued by Captain Moreno and his soldiers, their escape and her sickness in that tossing boat and the stench of fish. She blotted it out by turning her attention to the task in hand, drafting a summons.

Finally, on Friday night there was a letter waiting for her at home from Helen.

June 1934

Dear Verity,

Whatever happened to you? I do hope you are safely home. I have been so anxious – you walked out of the café with that army officer and never came back and none of us knew what to think. We left the café as soon as the soldiers went. Juan and Felipe escorted me back to the inn as soon as the soldiers left, but there was absolutely no sign of you.

Then in the early hours of the morning there was banging at the front door and soldiers came in looking for you. We all had to go downstairs in our night clothes whilst they searched the place. Fortunately for me, they didn't seem to know that I'd been with you the night before. Maria was very frightened and said that they were looking for you and they said that you had assaulted an army officer. I assume it was that Captain Moreno; good for you that you clearly gave him what for! I was afraid that otherwise he might have assaulted you, which would have been so much worse. The soldiers insisted upon asking us about you but their English wasn't very good so they didn't get very far. However, Mum and Pop were quite upset about being questioned and said if they had been with us nothing would have happened and have been blaming themselves. They haven't let me out of their sight since, which has been very frustrating for me, but I can hardly blame them.

Anyway, they decided we ought to leave the island as fast as we could and, as the ferry was due in, they managed to secure us places on board that day and we left within a few hours. Everyone was worried that there might be repercussions. I managed to exchange addresses with Juan and he said that Felipe had asked for your address so I gave him it too, maybe a little romance might come your way? I'd certainly like to have a little romance with Juan! What a good thing you and I had already exchanged addresses or I would have had no way of finding out what happened to you and that would have been unendurable. You must write as soon as possible to tell me how you and your

aunt did your vanishing trick, very clever I must say as no-one at all seemed to have any idea where you had gone or how you had left the island.
Now do write to me the instant you get this letter and tell me all. I'll be coming to London soon and then we must meet up.
Much love
Helen

If only it had been Roberto who had asked for her address, thought Verity. She could barely remember what Felipe looked like but she well remembered Roberto's handsome looks. She thought about Helen's parents and how alarmed and indignant they must have been about the soldiers visit to their lodgings and flustered as they hurried their arrangements to leave the island. They were pleasant, friendly, trusting people and Verity was sorry that they had suffered on her account. Who else had suffered as a result of her actions she wondered? She longed for Helen's arrival in London so that they could meet and talk, but in the meantime rushed for pen and paper to reply.

Verity's first driving licence had been waiting for her when she got home from her holiday; it was simply a matter of paying the appropriate fee to the authority. Richard had taken her out in his car to show her the rudiments of driving as her father didn't have a car. Richard had an MG sports car, though it was often erratic. It was a magnificent beast with a sleek body and large headlamps high on the front of the car. Richard thought that driving round in an MG enhanced his image with young ladies, and he was right.

By Saturday morning she had decided to ignore Richard's stupid remarks and arranged to go out with him in his sports car for driving practice. She was relieved to find that she hadn't forgotten anything after the long interlude since her last lesson. Richard was quite complimentary for once and thought she had grasped all the basics; now it would simply be lots of practice. Verity walked into the house afterwards thinking about what dress to wear for the dance that night. She must make sure that it was ironed in good time and would ask Violet to do it since she was far better at ironing fancy things. Violet was their maid, who, along with their cook, Doris, and a part-time gardener, made up their household. Her mother had never contributed to the running of the house in any way while she was alive, Doris and Violet had always managed things between them. Now they were adjusting to increasing input from Verity.

Since the death of Verity's mother, the house had been a quiet place with none of the gay parties that her mother had thrown regularly.

Entering the hallway she saw two letters waiting for her on the hall table. Picking them up, she saw that one had Spanish stamps on it. Felipe's name and an address in Barcelona were written on the back, in writing that was distinctly different from the English style. The other envelope was typewritten. Pocketing it she ran up to her room and sat down to open Felipe's letter. She took out the closely written sheets of flimsy paper and then felt a pang of disappointment: it was all in Spanish. She scanned each sheet carefully but could only make out the odd word. Why had she imagined that just because Felipe could speak some English he could also write it? She would have to get a Spanish dictionary and do her best with that.

In the evening, Richard picked her up promptly at seven. She was wearing the freshly ironed green dress, green shoes and a pretty green comb in her hair. "A touch of Spain," she said to herself as she looked in the mirror to secure the comb.

They drove to the Tennis Club at Eastcote and Richard took her arm possessively as they entered the Club. Verity wondered whether it was to ward off the hordes of female admirers whom Richard attracted, both for his fine playing and personable looks. On the other hand, there seemed to have been a change in their relationship since her return from holiday. Was Spain some kind of passage to womanhood for her, she wondered? Had Richard picked up on this, or was it simply some kind of jealousy on his part, wanting from her some kind of acknowledgement that they had a special relationship? She did not think she could cope with this at the moment.

The events of her holiday had been momentous and yes, she had changed. She not only had a new political understanding but also an awakened sexual awareness. Her quick arousal at the touch of Captain Moreno had surprised and shocked her. How was it, she thought, that she could react to the touch of a man whom she had instinctively disliked and feared? Then there was Roberto; she had only seen him twice but she couldn't forget him. And that night at the harbour he had kissed her, even if it was just on her cheeks.

She had liked Felipe and it would be good to get to know him better, but how she longed to be able to read and understand his letter, containing as it must news of all those new and interesting people she had met. She became aware that Richard was talking to her loudly.

"I said, would you mind if I left you for a short while? There are a few people I must see. I'll leave you with Peter and Betty," he said bringing her to a halt in front of his friends.

"Oh no, of course," she said as he disappeared into the crowd. Peter was his best friend, tall with blond hair that was just slightly too long. He took her by the hand and pulled her into the window bay that he and Betty had commandeered.

"You looked deep in thought," Peter said, and then, scrutinising her, "My word, you do look well - your holiday must have agreed with you. Where was it, France or Italy or Spain?"

"All three," she said switching to the social necessities of the moment and launched into an animated discussion with them. Betty did not work and in consequence she spent much of her time in sporting activities, tennis in the summer and riding in the winter. At twenty, Betty's ambition was to get married and have babies.

Verity considered briefly whether she wanted to do the same. The answer was easy, no she did not! On the other hand, did she actually want a career in the law? Was a career incompatible with a husband? Working women were expected to relinquish their jobs and change to the role of homemaker on marriage. Whether this applied when you were the daughter of the boss was something that she had never considered, she had assumed that she would become a solicitor and a partner in the firm and that would be her life. She had never thought any further. Now, with the exhilaration of travel and adventure, could she still settle down to the quiet life of a suburban solicitor?

Peter, having supplied them with drinks, took Betty off to dance while Verity sat thinking about her future and idly watching the swirling couples from the depths of the bay, sipping at her lukewarm drink. She noticed Richard was twirling a girl round the floor and thought with relief that perhaps she had been imagining his possessiveness earlier. Whilst graceful on the tennis court, he was awkward on the dance floor. Verity noticed with amusement that the girl, whose name Verity thought was Milly, or perhaps Molly, was trying to snuggle up to Richard but clearly finding his hold so awkward that she was tripping over his feet. She reminded Verity of a limpet and Verity thought that Richard, whether he liked it or not, was probably stuck with her for the evening.

The dance ended and Betty returned whilst Peter headed off to the bar again.

"Don't you mind Richard dancing with that dreadful little Molly?" asked Betty.

"Why should I? We only came together this evening because we live in the same road."

"Oh, I wasn't sure. Richard seemed so restless whilst you were away that I thought perhaps there might be something between you," Betty probed.

"I'm handy as a partner for outings, that's all," said Verity watching Richard across the floor, still trying to detach the limpet. Peter returned with fresh drinks in glasses that seemed as wet on the outside as on the inside.

The band struck up again and Peter offered Verity his hand and escorted her on to the dance floor.

"You're looking very pretty tonight," he said into her ear, "and I really like that comb in your hair - it looks, well, exotic. Richard is a lucky man, even though at the moment he doesn't seem to realise it," he said indicating where Richard had apparently given in and taken the limpet back on the floor.

"Lucky?" she asked, following his gaze.

"Oh, not with her. Her father's the new manager of the Bank in Ruislip High Street; Richard promised her father that he'd introduce her to people at the club tonight, all in the line of business you understand. But it seems as though she doesn't want to meet anyone else at the moment. Poor Richard!"

Peter, like Betty, seemed to believe there was something between Richard and Verity. She was going to reply but the music was becoming too loud for conversation. Verity relaxed and enjoyed herself. Betty, she could see, was dancing again, so at the end of this dance Peter retained her for the next dance. When the dance ended, Peter led her outside to the terrace. Richard was there and turned to her, greeting her effusively and taking her arm whilst dropping the limpet's with distaste. Peter stepped in and took the limpet back into the clubhouse, the girl going with him reluctantly.

"There is only so much I will do in the line of business," Richard said. "I thought I was never going to be rid of her. Why didn't you come and rescue me?" he asked plaintively.

"I didn't realise you wanted to be rescued, you looked as though you were getting on fine," she retorted.

Later, back in the clubhouse, the room became noisier and noisier, the voices around her loud and the band overwhelming. Almost as overwhelming was her desire to get out of there and go home where she could think properly. Richard claimed her with alacrity for the last dance - Verity suspected this was to avoid the hovering limpet. He drew her in closely and led her firmly round the dance floor, weaving his way through the throng to a corner of the floor where they had some space to themselves. He did not take advantage of the space but continued to hold her closely. She realised, with surprise, that he was aroused. Surely not by her - how could he be aroused by a girl he had known since she was a baby? She tried to loosen his grip but without success and they danced on to slow smoochy music for what seemed to Verity an interminable length of time. As the last notes of the music sounded, Richard swung her out through the French doors and on to the terrace.

As his face closed on hers, she heard a girl's voice say, "Oh, there you are Richard, I've been looking for you everywhere," and he broke away and turned to face Molly. Verity was left feeling awkward and embarrassed by being caught in an embrace that she did not want, by a girl who was obviously jealous and must have been watching them closely for the whole of the last dance. Verity went to fetch her wrap from the cloakroom and emerging found that Richard was waiting for her, still with the limpet in tow.

"Molly needs a lift and as she lives in Ruislip, we can drop her off," he said with forced brightness.

By the time the three of them were safely installed in his car, Molly had persuaded Richard that it would be far preferable to drop Verity off first as she would be so uncomfortable in the back of the car. Why Richard agreed, Verity wasn't sure, but she was glad to be dropped off without further complications. She thought that Richard must be attracted to Molly in some degree or he would never have agreed to take her home.

It was only when she undressed for bed that she remembered the other letter that had arrived that morning and took it from her dressing table and opened it. The letter was from the Overseas Trade section of the Foreign Ministry, asking Verity to make an appointment to see a Mr Jones when she was next in London. He said it was something to do with the Spanish trip. Verity was mystified as to the reason for the letter - what could Mr Jones possible want to see her about? She would telephone Constance in the morning and see what she advised. She could always make an appointment to see Mr Jones when up in London at the High Court next week. It somehow seemed a good idea not to mention it to her father.

Verity, lying in bed thinking about the strange letter, heard the distinctive sound of Richard's car drawing up outside his parents' house. Where had he been all that time, she wondered? Then she put the thought out of her mind: he was entitled to his privacy as much as she was to hers and there were more important things in her life now than what Richard might be doing. Whilst considering all the changes that were occurring in her life and how she might respond, she turned over and fell asleep.

7

Constance suggested making an appointment to see Mr Jones at the earliest opportunity, to find out what he wanted. Verity had to go up to London to the Law Courts once or twice a month to issue writs and summonses for the firm. She loved going to London, so the arrangement suited everyone and she was able to make an appointment to see Mr Jones on the following Thursday. The address she was given for the meeting was not Whitehall, as she had expected, but Baker Street. As a bonus she was able to arrange to meet up with Helen afterwards for lunch.

The Baker Street office of Mr Jones was only marked by a small brass plate on the door bearing the name 'Jones & Brown Trading'. She went up to the first floor as directed and was soon shown into a spacious office with no filing cabinets, no files spread around, no books, no pictures, no clutter at all, save for a single piece of paper in the middle of the desk. It was totally anonymous, as was the man behind the desk.

Mr Jones, having asked her to sit down, said nothing further but simply sat looking at her. She found it quite unnerving but thought to herself that he knew why he had summoned her, she didn't, and she was darned if she was going to break the silence. She thought they must have sat staring at one another for at least five minutes. She was mentally making a shopping list when he finally smiled a thin smile and said, "Now tell me about your trip to Europe," as though they were in the middle of a conversation instead of just starting one.

"Why?" responded Verity.

Meeting up with Helen later at a Lyons Corner House she told her about the strange interview.

"After a bit of flannel about promoting tourism and trade with Spain, which seemed pretty phoney to me, Mr Jones at last came out with the fact that he knew that a warrant had been issued for my arrest by the Spanish Authorities and that he needed to know what it was all about. I had the impression he had already checked up on my credentials and was satisfied that I hadn't done anything criminal. So I told him the whole story as I didn't think that I had done anything to be ashamed of, and certainly not anything that might embarrass the British Government!"

"What did he have to say to that?"

"He was quiet for a bit and then he came straight out and told me that my name had appeared on a list of foreign agents, spies he meant, that the Spanish Government wanted for questioning! Can you believe it? Since the British Government knew I wasn't spying for them they wanted to interview me to find out what it was all about and make sure I wasn't spying for anyone else."

"And did he believe you?"

"I think so; he smiled rather at the thought of Captain Moreno getting drenched in the fountain and said it must have cooled his ardour. He gave me his card and said that if I planned to visit Spain in the future, to contact him first."

"A spy? They've got you posted as a spy? You've got to be joking. It's just too bizarre!" Musing, Helen added, "Right now it's hard to believe that we took part in that mad chase and that you had to flee like that. It doesn't make any sense."

"It doesn't, does it? Sometimes I think that I dreamt it all and that I'll wake up and find that none of it took place. I still have nightmares about the chase around the streets and it always ends up with me being cornered, and a hand reaching out to grasp me, and then the sheer fright wakes me up."

"But it was fun at the time, wasn't it," said Helen, seeking reassurance.

"Of course! When we were just larking about teasing some young men on horseback. Then it turned into something altogether more serious, an adults' game, and I wasn't prepared for it," said Verity honestly. "I keep asking myself whether there was something else I should have done. I behaved like a bit of a flirt and then when it came to it, chickened out!"

"I'm sure it was just as well you did - Juan told me later that evening about Captain Moreno's reputation - he's known for his womanising. Just as well you got away from him or who knows what might have happened. Juan says that the fiesta was never like that before. When a young woman was captured by a horseman she would scream for her honour, but it was all just a bit of fun. She'd be quite safe and knew that nothing more than a kiss would be demanded. They'd both enjoy it and then she'd be returned honourably to the Square and all the other girls would be jealous. Otherwise no one at all would have joined in."

Verity shuddered whilst Helen went on, "It was just that horrible man who barged in and changed the rules to suit himself. We didn't know that and nor did anyone else. It seems the authorities are proposing either banning the fiesta in future or, at any rate, banning the horsemen. Apparently, Ibiza adopted the idea of the horsemen from the Menorcan Fiesta. There's a backlash now and people are saying they ought to return to their own traditions."

"Was it my fault?" said Verity humbly.

"Don't be silly. Even if you hadn't been there at all, the Captain would have captured some poor girl and had his way with her. We were lucky to get out of it so well." Then Helen reflected that maybe Verity had not got out of it too well: the night escape from the island and finding herself listed as a spy would be fairly shattering for anyone. Whilst Verity was outwardly calm, she was in turmoil inwardly. Helen turned the conversation to other things.

Verity was relieved to find that she and Helen were just as good friends here at home as they had been in Ibiza. It was good to have a girl friend she could confide in. Helen's enthusiasm for her new career in nursing was very refreshing and Verity was soon drawn into the details of Helen's new life in London.

Later, Constance was reassuring when Verity called at her flat to tell her about the interview with Mr Jones. Whilst outwardly supportive, Constance was privately worried by this development as it was impossible to conjecture what the consequences might be for Verity. She fervently hoped that there would be no consequences for Don César, but then there was no reason why his part in their escape should come to light.

That afternoon Mr Jones had spent a considerable amount of time thinking about Verity. He was quite satisfied that she would be an asset to his team, as had already been suggested to him, but he had to see her for himself to make sure. He liked the way she had not attempted to say anything at all during the initial long silence with which he had intended to intimidate her. She had simply gazed back at him calmly until in the end it was he who broke the silence - unusual to find that in a girl. She had given a good account of herself and with training she would come along nicely. He would probably wait until she had qualified as a solicitor before he made any move - after all in law she was still a minor. He would bide his time and keep an eye on her in the meantime.

Verity for her part had guessed that the inscrutable Mr Jones must be a representative of the intelligence services and that she had clearly been interviewed for some kind of job. She had no doubt that she would hear from him again in due course and in the meantime it added to her dilemma about her future.
She was making progress with translating Felipe's letter, having already started local tuition in Spanish. Felipe described the political situation in Barcelona and how the ordinary people were seething about various injustices, and said that lots of small incidents of violence were taking place. Many of the numerous political parties and workers' unions were at loggerheads both with one another and the employers and were reputed to be hiring their own private gunmen to defend themselves.

Felipe said that if you went out at night by yourself, you might be cornered by one of the factions and beaten up. The trouble was that if several of the students went out at night together, they risked being taken for a rival gang and beaten up anyway, so there was no safety in numbers. He and his friends were adopting the strategy of meeting at one of the students' lodgings, and then all of them staying there until dawn, when they would filter home through the byways of the city.

Verity sat looking out of her office window at the quiet ordered suburban estates of Ruislip and to the fields beyond and found it hard to imagine what it was like to be afraid to go home at night and have to wait for the safety of dawn. How was she to reply, and if she wrote in English, would Felipe be able to understand her letter? She decided that this would have to be his problem - after all he had started the correspondence. She went to the cubby-hole kitchen to make herself some tea and found Bernard perched on a stool, engrossed in reading yesterday's discarded Times.

"Hello Miss! You're looking a bit serious. Shall I bring your tea in when the kettle's boiled?"

"You are good to me, Bernard."

"Well, someone has to look after you – them two never do," he said gesturing in the direction of the secretaries' office. "By the way, did that Mr Richard leave a message on your desk for you?"

"What do you mean?" she replied puzzled.

"The gentleman came in and said he wanted you and walked along to your office before I could tell him you weren't there. I went along with a cup of char for him a few minutes later and he was reading a letter on your desk."

"What letter?"

"Think it was in a strange hand and there were some notes of yours with it. Saw it when he put it down all hurried like when I walked in. Then he said he wouldn't wait after all and rushed off. I thought he might have left you a message."

Typical Richard sticking his nose in her business, thought Verity. She wondered what he had made of the letter. One thing was sure, he wouldn't approve.

Bernard in the meantime was sticking a none too clean finger on his atlas to show her where Barcelona was. Verity looked at it with interest; her years at a girls' school had given her a conventional education which, when she thought about it, was of little actual use in the modern world.

She felt ashamed that with all her educational advantages over Bernard that he actually seemed to know more than she did simply with the aid of his children's atlas. They pored over the atlas together, chatting away until a door banged, indicating the return of the staff from lunch.

"I'll bring that tea in, Miss," Bernard said and, feeling that she had been dismissed, Verity went back to her room.

When he came in with the tea a few minutes later, having used the china reserved for clients, he hovered over her desk.

"Miss," he finally said, "I always go out on me bike on Sunday afternoons, generally over to Denham or one of them little villages, and I wondered," looking her directly in the eye, "whether you'd like to come for a ride this coming Sunday?"

Verity looked at him: young, earnest, impressionable and apparently really wanting her company. She was far too old to go for bike rides with a boy of Bernard's age. However, she wasn't actually doing anything this Sunday and it would be a shame to disappoint him.

"That would be very nice, Bernard. Shall I bring a picnic tea?"

"Wonderful, Miss," he said, grinning all over his freckled face. "2.15 by the pond?"

She was glad he had suggested meeting by the pond, he was bound to be too embarrassed to come up to the house, and she, for her part, would rather her father didn't know. She somehow thought he would disapprove of even so innocent an outing with the office boy.

After her Saturday driving lesson Richard said, "Found a great little pub, thought I might take you there for lunch tomorrow."

"Sorry, Richard. I'm going out and won't have time for lunch with you." She was certainly not going to keep her Sundays free on the off chance that he might want her company.

Richard looked put out. "Where are you going? Is it with one of your new Spanish friends?" he said with disdain.

"Oh, I'm just going out for a ride." She definitely wasn't going to mention young Bernard.

"You mean on your bike? Who are you going with and why can't you change it to another time?" The questioning made Verity exasperated.

"Nobody you know, and having promised, I intend to keep my promise." Seeing Richard's glower, she added, "And you must understand that I'm not going to keep my weekends free just in case you drop by."

"I see," said Richard, drawing up outside her house with a screech of brakes and, leaning over, opening the door for her. He drove off not returning her wave.

Well, if he wants to behave stupidly that's up to him, she thought, and went in to consult the cook about what they could have for the picnic.

Sunday was bright and sunny. Her father had gone to lunch with friends, so Verity had something to eat in the kitchen before tying the wicker picnic basket on to the carrier of her bike.

She reached the pond a little before two fifteen but Bernard was there already, looking a little anxious until he caught sight of her. She remembered then that he didn't possess a watch. Together they set off down the road and were soon bowling along the country lanes, Bernard a little in front but frequently looking over his shoulder to make sure that she was keeping up with him. The air was clear and good and there was little traffic on the roads. Reaching Denham village, Bernard very nearly cycled straight into the back of Richard's car, parked outside a pub. He had again been looking over his shoulder and only her warning shout made him turn and swerve in time.

Bernard turned down a lane at the end of the village where a stream ran alongside the lane. They went over a little bridge and then he stopped and got off his bike. Verity did likewise and followed him a little way along the bank until he stopped under the shade of a large oak. She undid the basket from her bike and Bernard propped both bikes up against the far side of the tree.

"Would you like some lemonade?" she said, getting out the bottle of homemade drink. It was very sharp but thirst quenching after their ride. Bernard put the bottle in the stream to keep cool, securing it to a bush on the bank with a piece of string.

They sat on the bank talking, mostly about Spain and Verity's still vivid impressions of it and all the people she had met. She also told him about Helen, now safely launched on her nursing career at St Thomas's Hospital. Her friends and acquaintances all came alive for him as he prompted her with questions.

"You ain't in love with any of them are you, Miss?" She laughed at the fact that he was prepared to ask her outright what others dared not. Indeed, she had not even asked herself the question.

"No, I don't think so, Bernard. I knew them all for such a short time but they were exhilarating to be with." They were certainly a contrast with conventional sneaky Richard, she thought, and went on, "They made Spain come alive for me, not just as a place to have a holiday but as a country. They covered so many different points of view between them and each of them believed passionately that he had the answer to Spain's problems. I'm not sure I understand it all even now."

"They couldn't all be right, could they, Miss? Who sounded the most right?"

"How could I tell? Each of them was equally convincing."

"I've been reading in the papers about what's happening," and he told her about what he had read, which was mostly the point of view of the new Unions in Spain with whom he clearly felt an affinity.

Bernard definitely had a good brain, thought Verity - untutored, but learning fast. Maybe she could help him with books and discussion. He was telling her about the Pathe News which he had seen at the cinema on Friday night and which had featured briefly the growing unrest amongst the agricultural workers in Spain. She had not been to the cinema for several weeks and had missed the Pathe News reports. She resolved to go to the cinema this coming week.

As they sat listening to the gentle sound of the stream washing over smooth stones and watching tiny fish dart about in the clear waters, they heard a car turn into the lane. I just know it's going to be Richard, thought Verity. It was. The car was slowing and Verity could see him clearly now, the limpet clinging beside him and both of them laughing delightedly. Then the note of the engine changed and the car roared off, leaving the smell of burnt oil lingering on the air and the tranquillity by the stream gone.

"Let's go," said Verity, "it'll take us a while to get back as we've got that long uphill ride." They repacked the hamper and got back on their bikes, the peaceful companionship of the afternoon over.

8

That same afternoon, Felipe lay panting in the dirt of a Barcelona ditch, pressed hard up against a stone wall to make himself as inconspicuous as possible. He and some friends had gathered for lunch at a bar in the Barri Gotic, the oldest part of the city, a noisy convivial occasion in the bar's gloomy depths. As they left together and emerged into the street, they were momentarily blinded by the strong sunlight. Before they were fully aware of what was happening, they found themselves surrounded by a jostling, menacing, blue-shirted gang, chanting and pushing them around, shouting, "Arriba Espana! Espana Una! Espana Libre! Espana Grande!" waving makeshift clubs of chair legs, table legs and iron bars. The noise made it worse and it was impossible for Felipe to think, as he and the others ducked and weaved to avoid the flailing clubs.

Felipe heard the sharp crack of a bone breaking, and then realised that the sound was caused by a cudgel which had caught his arm. The blow spun him round with its force, just in time to duck sideways to avoid another blow aimed at his head. His arm hung at an odd angle and the pain was appalling, coming in waves advancing up his arm. He saw that his friends were scattering before the onslaught and he ran too, without thought as to where he was going, tucking his arm into his jacket for support as he ran, feet pounding after him.

The narrow medieval alleys of the Gothic quarter around the cathedral formed a web of linking passageways which, taken at speed, could just as easily land the pursued in the arms of his pursuers, as allow him to lose them. The city seemed to be deserted for the siesta: there were no pedestrians, no crowds to hide in, and the dusty heat of the overhead sun illuminated the city streets and alleys far too well to provide sanctuary. Once Felipe almost ran straight back into the arms of the three men who were chasing him. He had immediately dived into a side passage and zigzagged sufficiently to be fairly sure of having thrown them off. After all, they could just as easily beat up any other passer-by instead of him; he did not think it personal. For good measure, he scaled a wall, dropped into a ditch on the far side, and lay there panting. Freed from the diversion of escape, the pain was overcoming him and making him feel sick. He realised that he would need to seek medical aid, but for the moment he would lie where he was until he could be sure the gangs of blue-shirted thugs had scattered and gone.

The afternoon wore on with the sound of sporadic outbreaks of fighting. Some of it was sufficiently near at hand to ensure that Felipe continued to lie prone in the ditch, hoping to avoid attention. It sounded as though large bands of men were prowling the streets causing destruction and beating up anyone in their path.

The blue-shirted men were bound to be members of the pro-Nazi militia, the Falange, which many students on the Right were joining. The Falange, founded the previous year by Jose Antonio Primo de Rivera, had merged with a pro-Nazi party. Felipe had heard of it as a small but reputedly violent group committed to a utopian form of forceful nationalist revolution. Jose Antonio was the son of the former dictator, General Miguel Primo de Rivera. However, this was the first time that Felipe had seen the Falange in action and it seemed to him to be mindless violence intended to intimidate the ordinary working class people. His own sympathies were with the working classes.

Felipe knew of the growing reputation of the Falange for provoking street violence and had determined to stay clear of them if he possibly could. However, the unexpected nature of this attack had given him no time to think what he should do. Whilst he supposed he knew how to defend himself, up to now it had never been necessary. Should he have held his ground and fought them, he wondered? No, without a weapon it would have been a foolish activity and would have served no purpose other than to get himself more seriously injured.

At last, dusk came and he dragged himself from a pain-filled doze to get slowly to his feet, but faltered in the act and sank back to a sitting position. With some difficulty he undid his dusty tie and tied the two ends together with a one-handed knot, tightened it with one end of the tie held between his teeth, and then put it round his neck again, and finally looped it round his left wrist to take the weight of his arm. It brought him some relief and with difficulty he got to his feet again and slipped into the deepening shadows. He made his way to the lodgings of a medical student friend, Jaime, close to the University Medical Faculty. There was still shouting and noise to be heard but farther off now. He climbed the stairs to Jaime's room where there was a light burning. Knocking softly on the door, it was opened a fraction and then wider as Jaime saw who his visitor was.

"What's happened?" he said drawing Felipe in. Felipe told him.

Jaime sat Felipe down and gently examined his arm. He bathed it and sponged his face for him. Felipe felt better for this simple act of kindness.

"You already know your arm's broken," Jaime said. "It needs setting but you will need to go to the hospital. I've not long been back. The ambulances have attracted the wrong sort of attention today, I've heard of two being overturned and set on fire. When it's safe I'll take you to the hospital myself. The streets are relatively quiet now - that's why I came home. I think the Falange have had their fun for the day and are drinking themselves into oblivion somewhere. Give me five minutes, then I'll take you."

Having checked the streets outside, he hoisted Felipe to his feet, then helped him down the stairs. Outside, Jaime looked up and down the street before drawing Felipe out after him and putting a supporting arm round him. Felipe ached all over as though the cudgels had found other targets beside his arm. At each crossroad, Jaime cautiously checked the adjoining streets before proceeding. In this fashion, they eventually reached the hospital.

Jaime installed Felipe behind a curtain in a cubicle and helped him off with his shirt before fetching a doctor to him. The doctor looked exceedingly tired and asked no questions as to how he had come by his injuries. Bruises were becoming apparent all over Felipe's chest and back. He had no recollection of any blow but the one that had broken his arm, but clearly there had been others. An injection numbed the pain before his arm was set and plastered in what seemed to Felipe a long drawn out and exceedingly painful procedure. Then at last he fell into a drugged sleep in a narrow bed in a tiny room on one of the upper floors of the hospital. His last waking thought was that he had not thanked Jaime for his help and must do so tomorrow.

Next morning Jaime found Felipe sitting on his bed, looking out of the window at the rooftops of the city. He was obviously very stiff and somewhat drawn, but otherwise cheerful and ready to be discharged. His arm was plastered and in a sling and he was dressed in yesterday's tattered clothes, although someone had obviously brushed them for him. Felipe gratefully thanked Jaime.

"What now?" asked Jaime.

"I'll go and see my boss. If he'll let me, I'll go home for a week or two until this mends," he said gesturing at his arm. "I can't really afford to be off work as I won't be able to pay my rent. Or even worse he might use it as an excuse to get rid of me, and then what will I do?"

"Go home and mend that arm. By the time you're back, the troubles will be over," said Jaime with sunny optimism and a supreme lack of judgement.

9

Molly had seen Verity and Bernard picnicking by the stream that Sunday afternoon but Richard had been concentrating on his driving and had seen nothing. That was ideal as far as Molly was concerned. She knew that Verity was the object of Richard's adoration, and she wasn't going to tolerate that. As soon as she had first caught sight of Richard she had decided that he was the man for her. Already she had persuaded her father to put work Richard's way so that a partnership and financial security could not be far off. If she could get Verity off the scene then Richard was hers for the taking. Now she saw a way to this.

Richard himself was flattered by Molly's attention. She was a very pretty and fashionably dressed girl who appeared to hang on his every word. He very much enjoyed the kisses willingly exchanged in the cosy back seat of his car in secluded country lanes. Indeed Molly had indicated on more than one occasion a willingness to go further. Richard had initially ignored such signals and deliberately disengaged himself, thinking as he did so of Verity. There had shortly come a time when he was unable to resist Molly's advances any longer and they had made love in the backseat of his car, an event which they had since voraciously repeated each time he took her out. He knew that he was going to have to do the decent thing pretty soon and ask Molly to marry him; he couldn't treat a respectable girl that way and not ask for her hand, even though he regarded his heart as still belonging to Verity

Before they arrived home that evening, Molly told Richard that she had seen Verity and 'that nasty little ginger-haired office boy of hers' making love on the banks of the stream. It never occurred to Richard that Molly might not be telling the truth, after all he and Molly had spent the afternoon lovemaking. But Verity and an office boy! Richard was outraged.

Later that evening, Richard called at Verity's house and was closeted with her father for some time. Then her father called Verity to join them in his study. He was sitting in his armchair, not looking his usual self. Eventually he looked up at her, "Richard has come to see me as he was very perturbed by seeing you this afternoon in what he describes as 'intimate circumstances' with someone he says he recognised as our office boy, Bernard. He very properly drew this to my attention. What have you to say? Were you out with young Bernard this afternoon?"

Verity was astounded. "Yes, Father I was but..."
Her father gave her no chance to finish, he was clearly angry to an extent that Verity had never before seen. "Verity! I'm shocked. Shocked more than I can say that a daughter of mine should be guilty of such a thing!" He had gone very red in the face, almost purple; his face was covered in perspiration which was beginning to drip on to his shirt. Verity stared at him in alarm.

His hands went to his chest and he was unable to get out the cruel words he was trying to say to her. As he clutched his chest he slowly toppled from his chair and slipped on to the floor, a surprised look on his face.

Verity fell on her knees beside him, "What is it?" She fumbled for his pulse and found it racing. She propped him up against a chair and, seeing that he was trying to speak, she bent her head close, "Shocked, shocked," he said and then he was silent and his agitated eyes ceased to move.

Verity stared at him in horror and fumbled to loosen his collar and tie. He was terribly clammy to her touch and she wasn't sure that she could feel him breathing at all, certainly with her head close to his chest there was no sound of laboured breathing. What to do?

"I saw you!" Richard burst out. "Saw you with my own eyes! So did Molly and we were both shocked." Richard was not being truthful in this, but felt an overwhelming need to justify himself with Verity's father lying on the floor between them. "I had to tell your father."

"Shut up Richard!" Verity called over her shoulder as she ran for the hall phone and demanded that the operator contact the doctor and ask him to come at once. The operator would know where to find him on a Sunday evening.

Richard was still standing there, uselessly spluttering justifications of himself and accusations against her. Would he never stop? It occurred to her that she knew that there was one sure way of stopping him. She picked up a large vase of flowers from the hall table and hefted the vase and its contents at Richard. Whilst the vase just missed him, the water drenched him. It stopped the flow of words very effectively as he stood there sodden and dripping water over the floor.

"You're a smug, self-satisfied, pompous prig! Don't judge others by your standards and get out before I throw something else at you!" she shouted. Richard ran past her, all dignity gone, and the front door slammed after him as Verity knelt once more by her father. His face seemed to have drained of expression and his skin was cooling. She held his hand and talked to him telling how he had been completely misled by what Richard had said. She knew as she talked that it was too late, he was beyond hearing her, but she just had to tell him that he was mistaken and had misjudged her.

A knock on the door announced the arrival of the doctor, opening his Gladstone bag as he came in. He did not waste time asking her what had happened but simply tried everything possible to revive her father.

Finally he said, "It was a heart attack, I've been telling him for years to take more care with his heart but he'd never listen. I'm really sorry, Verity, but there's nothing more I can do, he died before I got here. I'll write out the death certificate first thing in the morning and you can collect it. Would you like me to call the undertakers for you?"

Verity sat on the floor with tears streaming down her face already swollen from crying. She nodded at the doctor who had known her since birth. "Please, that would be a great help, I don't really know what to do."

He used the phone to make some calls, knowing that the operator would be listening in and that the news would have spread round the small town by morning. He thought that at least it would save Verity having to tell everyone herself.

Richard had arrived at the Flemings' house without any thought but stopping this nasty little affair of Verity's. It had never once occurred to him to question Molly's account even though he had never in a lifetime seen Verity act in any way other than with due decorum. She had not explained herself and she had had the gall to call him names and had soaked him as well. It was fortunate that her aim hadn't been better, but he was extremely angry with her.

In the morning he asked his secretary to telephone and ask how Mr Fleming was. She returned, giving him a curious look, and told him that the funeral would be on Friday but she had been asked to tell him that he would not be welcome. Only then did it finally come home to him just what he had done, but he was still convinced that he had been right to tell her father about Verity's conduct, just as Molly had said he should. Whatever the consequences he knew that it was Verity's fault, not his.

10

Captain Moreno had left the Balearic Islands accompanying General Franco on army manoeuvres and was now one of the General's staff in Madrid. Franco was there as 'personal technical adviser' to the Minister for War as trouble was expected, instigated by left wing agitators and the strong coalminers unions were thought likely to support them. Moreno heard the Minister saying that the Government wanted to be ready to squash any uprising, hence General Franco's informal appointment. The reality was to ensure that the Minister, who trusted Franco's judgement and tactics implicitly, would have the General at his right hand immediately he was needed.

Moreno himself took little interest in politics; he only knew that those on the left considered those on the right to be fascists and those on the right considered those on the left to be Communists. Each was out to get the other and as far as he was concerned, as an army officer he would obey orders to quell any uprising from whatever quarter it came without any particular interest in the rights or wrongs of the situation. It was for the Generals, or their political masters, to work these things out and issue the orders.

News finally came through of the expected trouble. Franco's headquarters became a hive of activity as the Government declared martial law. The army instructions were to take over essential services and round up as many of the union leaders as they could.

The Minister of War had placed Franco in 'informal charge' of the suppression of the uprising. Whilst there was doubt at first as to what being in 'informal charge' meant, no-one was left wondering for long as a stream of harsh orders started to flow, ostensibly in the name of the Minister.

Franco called his staff and the naval officers now attached to him, to a briefing. In acknowledgement of his informal role, Franco had changed into civilian clothes, more suited to the role of adviser; he ordered his staff to do likewise. Moreno did not like the idea of dressing in civilian clothes as it lacked status. All he had ever known was the army with its hierarchy of rank and to dress as a civilian was demeaning.

The uprising in Madrid itself had only amounted to sporadic sniper fire; the Asturias region was the main problem. Moreno was not privy to Franco's thought process, and for the most part the behind-the-scenes manoeuvring was alien to him. He rejoiced when Franco issued orders, in the name of the Minister, to bring over the Spanish Legion from Africa. It was made up of mercenaries of many nationalities, had a reputation for ruthless ferocity in battle and the mere mention of the Legion struck terror into the hearts of most opponents. What an opportunity it would be if he could see action with them!

Franco continued to issue orders in the name of the Minister from the temporary headquarters he had established in the telegraph room at the Ministry in Madrid, ignoring the views of the more senior officers in Asturias.

It was Moreno who relayed Franco's instructions to the Lieutenant Colonel in charge of the Spanish legionnaires, but it seemed to Moreno that the Colonel was not in tune with Franco's thinking. Moreno had no hesitation in reporting to Franco the informal conversation he had had with the Colonel who thought his mission would be to use the natural fear engendered by the Legionnaires' reputation for atrocities to frighten the people into submission. The Colonel did not think that the Government would actually contemplate firing on Spanish civilians. Moreno reported the informal conversation to Franco in full. He was furious, which in his case was expressed by extreme iciness. Moreno hoped that it would be the

Colonel on whom Franco's fury would be vented, not him as messenger. He was not disappointed.

After a short interlude, Franco replaced the recalcitrant Colonel with Colonel Yague, who Moreno knew from his Zaragossa Academy days to be a strict disciplinarian. Yague would use any means at his command to suppress the uprising.

Franco also issued orders, using the Minister's name, to remove his own cousin from command of the regional Air Force base at Leon, suspecting that his cousin would sympathise unduly with the workers and hesitate to fire on civilians. Moreno thought that this was a reasonable response, even though he heard from others that Franco had more or less been brought up with this cousin; there was no place for sentiment in the army. These insights into command at the top were invaluable to Moreno in forming his own views. In the future, he would only have to ask himself what Franco would have done in his position to know what was the right thing to do.

Moreno was not surprised when Franco went on to order the bombing and shelling of the working class districts of towns in Asturias.

Moreno had heard that in Asturias the rebellious workers, who were mainly miners, were known to have armed themselves with arms stolen from factories and with explosives taken from the mines, so real fighting could be expected there. So Moreno was delighted when the General entrusted him with written orders to carry to Colonel Yague and told him to make haste to Asturias.

Back in uniform again, the Captain was driven to the airfield outside Madrid where a small plane was waiting for him. Moreno had never been in a plane before, he was fascinated to see the ground disappear from under them and feel the exhilarating sensation of speed and freedom as the plane surged over the rugged countryside of Spain on its way to the base at Leon. He had never much considered the role of the Air Force before, but now its role as a tactical arm in battle first struck him, an air strike against an enemy would leave them virtually powerless to defend themselves. He mused on these things all the way to Leon, where a car was waiting to take him to field headquarters.

Waiting in the ante room he could hear angry voices. Then the door opened and a general strode through, clearly furious. He slammed the door so hard the whole frame vibrated. A Lieutenant came in.

"The Colonel will see you now, Sir."

Moreno rose and followed him to where the Colonel strode impatiently up and down.

"You have orders from General Franco?"

"Yes, Sir," said Moreno, handing them over.

"Thank God for that. I must have the power to act independently of these fools." Then he sat down to break open the seal on the orders and read them. When he got to the end, he started again at the beginning and then turned to consider the map pinned on the wall, musing.

Moreno continued to stand, waiting to be noticed and dismissed.

At last, the Colonel turned to him and for the first time scrutinised Moreno's face.

"The General said that I might use you if I had need of you, rather than you go back to Madrid. Academy trained are you? What year?"

Moreno told him.

"Remember you now. I can always use a well-trained officer. Did you bring your kit?"

"No, Sir. The General didn't mention that I might be staying."

"Lieutenant, see that the Captain is kitted out appropriately" Then to Moreno, "Report here in the morning at five, ready to move."

Moreno was exhilarated as he followed the lieutenant out and along the road, all his tiredness having disappeared. He was going to see action with the Foreign Legionnaires, the best thing that could happen to him to promote his career. The lieutenant paused for a moment, "If you would like to see the bombing raids, Sir, I have my field glasses."

So saying, he led Moreno up a short track to a promontory and pointed to where they could see flashes against the night sky. The captain took the proffered glasses and focused them on the distant mountainside. As he watched, a bomb must have found a target, since flames rose hundreds of feet in the air. They were too far away to hear the explosions.

"The bombing raids started last night. I've never seen anything like it before," said the lieutenant. "They say that the devastation on the ground is just as good as from our shelling," he concluded enthusiastically. Then, remembering that this captain from Madrid was both an unknown quantity and an emissary from General Franco, he recalled himself and conducted the captain to a billet for the night without further delay.

Moreno, his shirtsleeves rolled up, sweat stained and dusty, was smoking a cigarette outside a shepherd's hut where he had been 'extracting information' from a reluctant source. Feeling that the interlude had been long enough, he ground the cigarette butt into the dust with the heel of his boot and re-entered the hut stooping under the low lintel. The dreadful sounds recommenced inside the hut but outside there was no one but a couple of sentries in the vicinity to hear them, and they were Moroccan mercenaries used to giving no quarter, so took no more notice than they did of the vultures flying overhead.

Finally Moreno emerged from the hut again, his jacket over his arm. He nodded to the two sentries who went over to assist two soldiers emerging and dragging an inert body from the hut. Shots sounded as Moreno walked jauntily down the track to report on his latest success in extracting the information required. The birds, disturbed for a moment, wheeled and cried in alarm and sped off down the valley.

"Excellent," said the Colonel surveying the list of names that Moreno had handed to him. "Arrest these men and deal with their families," he said, passing the list on to a waiting officer. "Remember, make no exceptions, we must make an example of them."
"Of course, Sir," said the officer, affronted that the Colonel would think such a thing of him. He knew that there had been trouble between the Colonel acting under General Franco's orders and the General nominally in charge of the operation who favoured moderation in dealing with the civilian insurgents. He had heard that the Colonel and the General had almost come to blows over it.
"Sir," said Moreno, "may I suggest my work might be more effective if I dealt with the next batch in their own village?"
The Colonel considered for a moment then replied, "Very well. Take a company with you and follow on an hour after the Lieutenant. That ought to give you time to smarten up," he said, looking with distaste at the dishevelled state of Moreno's attire.
"Certainly, Sir, immediately," said Moreno, smartly turning and clicking his heels to counteract the justified criticism. How did the Colonel expect a man to carry out such exacting work without getting into

an unkempt state? Oh well, he would take a wash and get his orderly to find him a clean shirt and then get something to eat before setting off.

An hour later, refreshed in every way, he got into the cab at the front of the truck as it set out to follow the Lieutenant into the recently captured town.

Incredible though it seemed to Moreno, the rebellious miners had twice repulsed the columns of attacking soldiers. They were said to be using their everyday skills with dynamite, rather than the arms that they had stolen from the armaments factories. It appeared that they didn't know how to use the rifles. Moreno had heard a rumour that certain of the union leaders were in Madrid negotiating for a peaceful settlement. The ordinary members of the unions did not know about this or they would not have fought so fiercely, often sacrificing both themselves and their families in the process. Well, it did not matter to Moreno whether they were beaten into submission or surrendered, the result would be much the same, the army would do a clear up job of all the troublemakers, or potential troublemakers, to clear the slate for the politicians.

The truck stopped and Moreno jumped out as his troops poured off the back of the lorry. The houses in some quarters were still burning; in others, the devastation caused by the bombing was apparent. He noted that the accuracy of some of the bombing was suspect, clearly the Air Force needed good intelligence relayed back to improve their hit rate. The ashes of the burnt and destroyed buildings still floated everywhere, settling like snow on the ground and covering objects with a drab grey that seemed appropriate to the time of year. Then he caught sight of some of the Lieutenant's men ahead. They had rounded up a crowd of suspects and were herding them into cattle pens in the market square. Moreno quickened his pace and went forward to carry out yet another efficient clean up job.

By the end of the short campaign, with the rebellion crushed, Moreno had grown in experience. His reputation as one of Franco's hardest and most ruthless young officers was assured and he had received his promotion to major. It had been noted that Moreno had carried out all his duties with that special attention to detail that was more usually the mark of an officer in the Spanish Legion. Moreno had not hesitated, as some had, to carry out his duties against Spanish civilians. Moreno had heard that there was a fuss going on in some quarters about the supposed unnecessary force and brutality used by the Spanish Legion. Much good may it do them to make a fuss, thought Moreno - Franco is the man to follow for sure.

11

The funeral was over, Verity's tears had dried at last. Constance had tried to find out for Verity the contents of her father's will before the funeral but had been unsuccessful, a rare outcome for her. Now they sat in the front parlour as the solicitor extracted the will from its envelope and put on his glasses.

"You may wonder why your father had a London solicitor," he said looking over the top of his glasses at Verity. "We were friends when we were articled in the same firm." Verity nodded. "You must understand that this will was made just after your mother had died when you were very young. He would have been wise to have updated his will as time went on, but he didn't. That's why his estate will be held in trust for you until you are 25. You will have money for your maintenance and this house will be maintained out of his estate by your trustees, of whom I am one. There are bequests to your cook and housekeeper contingent on their continuing to look after the house until you are 25, if you wish them to do so."

He continued, looking at Verity over the top of his glasses, "His solicitor's practice is to be sold to a neighbouring firm on terms laid out in the will. I'm afraid he makes no provision for your articles to be transferred for the remainder of the term and I have spoken to the practitioner concerned who is not willing to take on a female articled clerk, it being so out of the ordinary."

"If Verity marries before she is 25 does she get the money then?"

"Makes no difference, he was worried that someone might marry her for her money."

Verity's mind felt deadened. Since she had left school her thoughts and her time had been monopolised entirely by the necessity of learning the law, because that was what he had wanted her to do. Now in one stroke he had taken it all away again. She would have food and shelter provided for her but nothing else for another five years.

Whilst Constance worried about the house, the money, and most of all about Verity, Verity's concern was about where her life would go from here. She had no real idea about what she should do now as her thought processes had already been numbed by the shock of her father's death in such bizarre circumstances. He had not been a loving demonstrative man but he was the only parent she had known. The future was a place that now held no attraction for her, it was totally empty.

The solicitor having ascertained that they had no further questions, departed. Verity and Constance, engrossed in their own thoughts, continued to sit silently in the parlour as dusk started to fall.

Verity had felt totally unable to tell Constance about Richard's shocking accusation which had led to her father's heart attack. It was too unexpected, too unjust and she could not talk about it until she had worked it all through in her own mind. The days leading up to the funeral had been filled with all the practicalities of death. Now she had this awful feeling that she, and not Richard, had caused her father's death. She knew in her inmost self that this was untrue, but she could not help accusing herself and wondering whether if she had acted differently he might be still alive.

She did not have the same qualms about telling the whole story to Helen when she arrived for the weekend. Helen was her own age and would understand as an older person might not. Verity started telling her the whole story as they walked arm in arm from the station on Saturday morning. Bernard had been there with her at the station to collect Helen's suitcase and take it on to the house strapped to the back of his bike. He pedalled off and left them to walk home.

Verity told her all about the innocent bike ride followed by Richard's inexplicable appearance on Sunday evening with some made-up tale about her supposed intimacy with Bernard. "I asked Bernard to come this morning especially so that you could see him for yourself."

"Absolutely impossible story," declared Helen. "What is he - fifteen? Sixteen? No-one in his right mind could think that you could be having an affair with a boy of Bernard's age! I presume that Richard isn't in his right mind?"

"Molly, the limpet, is on his mind. There can't be much room for anything else, he has a very narrow mind."

"And your father believed it?"

"Apparently."

"Good heavens! How appalling! And that brought on a heart attack?"

"Yes, although our doctor said it was mostly to do with just having eaten a large meal with lots of wine and his heart being unable to cope."

"Did you tell the doctor about Richard having been there?"

"Richard ran when I threw the vase at him, so I never mentioned him having been there, no point really."

"Except for him being the one who triggered it off."

"What could that matter to the doctor?"

"Not a lot, I suppose."

"It's such a relief to talk about it, I wasn't sure that Constance would have understood, you really have to be our age to understand the vast gulf between a boy barely out of school and someone of our age which makes the whole thing quite unthinkable."

Helen squeezed her arm. "Don't ever bottle things up again." They walked on slowly through the woods as the sunlight filtered through the trees and played tricks with the shadows.

They were not far from home when they saw ahead of them a couple leaning up against a tree kissing, the man's arms entwined round his girl and her arms round his neck.

"Oh, Lord, there's Richard, let's turn back!" Verity exclaimed in alarm. Until that moment she had not realised that she had come to hate him for causing her poor gullible father's death.

"That must be Molly the limpet, running true to form," remarked Helen, as Verity swiftly branched off on to a side track before they could be spotted. It was muddier but they were unlikely to meet anyone else on it.

"She looks a frightful little harpy - what can he see in her?" Helen continued looking back over her shoulder.

"It started because her father was the new bank manager and introduced some clients to Richard - you remember I told you that he had recently qualified as a chartered accountant?"

"Well, it has certainly progressed beyond liking the extra clients, maybe he likes possessive clinging women," said Helen dismissively.

Richard had seen Verity and Helen as they approached. He dreaded to think what they had seen him doing, especially after the accusations he had made about Verity.

There was no drawing back for Richard now. He ran his hands gently and caressingly over Molly's lovely body, trying to think of ways to pleasure her. She guided him as to what she liked and responded to his hesitant touch. It occurred to him, belatedly, that he was making love with an expert in the art. Since there could be no retreat, he thought that if she might become pregnant, he might as well make a thorough job of it.

Next evening Richard did what he had to do and formally approached her father for permission to marry Molly, permission that was willingly given. All those months ago, when Molly had first set eyes on Richard and asked her father to check out his financial standing and credentials, he had done so. He had hooked Richard for her with the new clients passed his way and Molly had done the rest. "Clever girl" he thought.

The following week there were some court cases coming up in the firm's diary which Verity still needed to attend as there wasn't anyone else to do so. One was a two day divorce case in London and it gave her something to think about as she concentrated hard in court all day. Afterwards she left the court and walked through Lincoln's Inn Fields and up into High Holborn, and then on to Bloomsbury and Constance's flat near the British Museum. Constance was sitting drinking tea.

"How did it go? No, don't answer that until I've made a fresh pot of tea for you and then I want to hear all about it."

Verity went and discarded her hated grey hat, required attire for a woman in Court, and then returned to the elegant drawing room. The room had been furnished by her aunt with the best of modern decor and furniture, usually provided by the enterprising Heal's store in Tottenham Court Road. Ambrose Heal was a good friend of her aunt and often dined there along with other interesting guests.

Verity took a seat in a chrome and leather minimalist chair which in spite of its looks was remarkably comfortable. Taking the proffered cup of tea, she updated Constance with an account of the day's proceedings. After this she was silent for a while, absently stirring sugar into her tea as she thought about the case, a miserable glimpse into someone else's married life. Constance broke the silence.

"I'm glad you finished early today. I've managed to secure tickets for the new Dodie Smith play that is on at the moment at the Globe, it will do you good - Ambrose says it is very good." Dodie Smith had worked at Heal's for many years before establishing herself as a playwright and her ex-employer was a staunch supporter of all her plays.

"We'll eat out after the play, so help yourself to some of these sandwiches, otherwise you'll be hungry."

Verity ate her way through a generous quantity of sandwiches and then went off for a luxurious soak in the bath. The plumbing, like everything else in Constance's flat, was modern and efficient, unlike the bathroom at home where little in the way of hot water was ever apparent. Perhaps, Verity thought, the trustees might run to some efficient modern plumbing.

The play, "Call it a Day," was very good. Verity and Constance laughed and cried and came out feeling that the world was a better place than when they had gone in. A taxi dropped them at a crowded restaurant where they were shown to their reserved table. Verity noted that it was a table for four and looked questioningly at her aunt as the waiter brought cocktails, unasked, and placed them on the table.

"It's all right, you'll find that it is a non-alcoholic cocktail, they make them very well here."

"It wasn't that; I was wondering who the other guests are?"

"You'll see soon enough," said her aunt firmly, helping herself to a canapé.

They did not have long to wait. Verity saw that the head waiter was ushering two men through the crowd towards their table. As they approached she recognised first Roberto, last seen the night of their escape, and behind him, Don César.

"I'm very pleased to see you, Roberto," said Constance while Verity was recovering from the surprise. "I gather from César that you are over here completing your studies?"

"Yes, a one year course at the London School of Economics. Then I'll return to Spain and join my uncle in Madrid," he said, smiling at Verity rather than Constance. Verity's heart was beating so fast that for a moment she was unable to produce any speech.

"I'm pleased to see you again," he said to Verity. "I'd not realised when we met in Ibiza that you were a lawyer - we do not have women lawyers in Spain."

"Well, we're a rarity even here - it's not long since the first woman was admitted as a solicitor. But I'm not one yet, I have still got another year to go before I qualify."

"And you work here in London?"

"I'm just up for a few days for a case at the High Court," Verity explained.

"But that is very near the LSE - I come perhaps to see you in Court?" he queried.

"I don't stand up in Court to speak, I do the preparation and ensure that the barrister has all the facts at his fingertips. There's a rule that only a barrister may speak in Court, but the barrister is not allowed to speak unless he has a solicitor sitting in Court behind him."

From his look, Roberto did not understand the curious way the English legal system worked. Nor did Verity fully understand the reasoning behind it either.

"I'll come and see for myself," he said, puzzled.

From the conversation over dinner, Verity gathered that Don César was over in Britain on a trade mission on behalf of his Ministry in Madrid. He was staying at the Spanish Embassy with the rest of the mission but had naturally taken the opportunity to see his nephew, whom he seemed to hold in high regard.

The dinner conversation was animated on all sides. Verity came to life again after the deadness caused by recent events. She found that any constraints which she had previously felt in the presence of Don César had long since dispersed. Roberto had an unconstrained naturalness about him which made it seem as though she had known him for years and he now spoke colloquial English, although with a strong accent. She learned much more about Don César over this convivial dinner than she had found out on their previous meetings. He was undoubtedly an important man in the government. Given that she now knew him to be married, that presumably accounted for the fact that they had not met him in Madrid. Instead, he had appeared only when they reached Ibiza, where presumably he was not known and a close friendship with another lady would pass unnoticed.

Constance, looking at Verity's flushed face and bright eyes, thought that her plan was working well. Roberto was just the person to awaken Verity from the torpor into which she had fallen after her father's funeral. It was clear to Constance that there were things that Verity had not told her for some reason and that she found the burden difficult. Roberto was a lively, handsome and lusty young man, and she thought a fling with him was just what Verity needed, and if she did fall a bit in love with him, it would do her no harm. Roberto would be a temporary diversion for Verity before he returned to Spain. Constance thought to herself that the other part of her plan for Verity would complement this shortly. Verity deserved a lot better than to follow in her father's pedestrian footsteps.

They parted at midnight with Roberto promising to meet Verity at Court in the morning, "If I wake in time," he said.

He not only woke in time but was already in position in the front row of the public gallery when Verity took her seat behind Counsel the next morning at 10 a.m. Verity was grateful that Roberto restrained himself from waving or acknowledging her in any way other than an elegantly raised eyebrow and a barely perceptible smile. Anything more would have drawn the eagle eye of the judge who already looked as though he had breakfasted on something sour.

At long last the hearing drew to a close and Verity excused herself from the client as soon as she decently could and rushed off to find Roberto, afraid she might miss him. She need not have worried, he was waiting for her outside and greeted her by kissing her on both cheeks and drawing her arm through his. She felt his warmth against her and absorbed it, wondering how she could ever have thought that her life might be empty.

12

With Roberto in her life, Verity found that she was capable of making the decisions she needed to. It was not that she discussed her own position with him, but she had greater clarity when she was able to relax with someone of her own age who never took anything very seriously. She was damned if she was going to leave the legal profession before she was fully qualified just because of the bigotry of old men who thought it an unsuitable job for a woman.

She was clear now that she did not want to become a lifelong member of the profession; she certainly didn't intend to end up as the female equivalent of the desiccated solicitors that she had seen at the Law Society's Hall, but she had already invested over three years in studying and practising law as an articled clerk and qualify she would. She needed to find a solicitor who would take her on for the rest of her articles and was going to look for one who owed her father a favour.

Eventually the Fleet Street firm who had been their London agents agreed reluctantly to take her on as a last service to her father. This favour did not stop them from demanding a large premium from her for the privilege, and she had to apply to her trustees who grudgingly agreed to advance the money. The partners made clear that they were not really concerned about how often she attended at their offices, but said that if she did go in they would find her something to do. She decided that she would take a break first to get all her affairs in order and then she was determined to inflict her presence on them, whether they liked it or not.

Back in Ruislip, Doris had agreed to stay on as cook housekeeper for as long as Verity needed her. It would be a comfortable life, just making sure that everything ran smoothly for the weekends when Verity came home. Violet, who was looking forward to a well earned retirement with the money Verity's father had left her, agreed to come in on the occasions when Verity might need a maid, which were not likely to be frequent.

Constance was glad to be able to offer Verity a home during the week when Verity would be working in London. Constance had always hoped that this might happen and looked forward to having young and lively company to keep her young too.

Whilst Verity was in London she frequently met up with Helen, when Helen had an afternoon off, and followed avidly the advances in the distant romance between Helen and Juan. She did try gently to dissuade Helen from building up Juan into a faultless hero but knew that it was to no avail. She just hoped that if the pair did meet again neither would be disappointed in the reality of the other after their lengthy correspondence.

Whilst Helen was looking well, when she took her gloves off, Verity saw that her hands were red and raw.

"It's all the scrubbing and the disinfectant," she said, seeing Verity's eyes on her hands. "I've got chilblains too - the hospital is so cold and draughty. I really love the work especially when I'm allowed to do something more responsible than giving bedpans and making the beds. I'm moving into Women's Surgical Ward next week, that should be really interesting," she said enthusiastically.

"Is nursing what you expected it to be?"

"It's all terribly hierarchical. As a first year student nurse, I'm only allowed to associate with other first year nurses, and we're spread over all the hospital. I'm usually working on a ward with second and third year student nurses, staff nurses and, of course, the Sister. It would be more than my life is worth to do anything other than speak when I'm spoken to."

"It sounds worse than school!"

"It is, much stricter. There's someone watching over us all the time, ready to bawl us out for the slightest thing, like not washing the equipment properly, not doing the corners of bed sheets to an exact angle, keeping your own room tidy, all that sort of thing. I sometimes think that Sister deliberately goes into the sluice room to smear dirt to give her an excuse to shout at me! And then there's the cap."

"The cap?"

"Our indoor uniform includes this ghastly white linen cap, but we have to make it up each day ourselves." Seeing Verity's incomprehension, she explained, "We're issued with these white linen squares with the hospital crest on one side. The art is to make sure that they are well starched and ironed to perfection. Then you have to twist a third of it into a cap which fits your head, making certain that the crest is in the front, and manipulate the remainder into butterfly wings which stand up at the back. Secure the lot with heaps of hair grips and hope to goodness it's not windy outside. I've been late time and again through struggling with making up my cap. But now I've got friendly with a second year nurse and, if she's on the same shift as me, she helps me with my cap. Sister has stopped complaining about my cap since I've had help."

"Of course I'm not allowed to associate with nurses other than strict contemporaries, so I'm so lucky to have you here in London. Now tell me all the latest about Roberto, are you in love with him? I know I'd be if I didn't have Juan!"

Verity was very much afraid that she might be falling for Roberto, however much she had tried to stop herself. When they were apart she could rationalise all she liked, but when she was with him it was hard to not fall under his spell. There was no doubt that the world was a much more enjoyable place in his company.

May saw not only Verity's twenty first birthday, but it was also the month of the King's Jubilee, the twenty-fifth anniversary of his accession to the throne. The commemoration of this was encouraged by the Government in an attempt to bolster the morale of the country after the dreadful depression and unemployment problems of the last few years. Walking along Ruislip High Street, Verity noticed how Roberto attracted a lot of attention. London was cosmopolitan and used to people of all nationalities; Ruislip, on the contrary, was insular and a young man with the swarthy good looks of Roberto caused people to stare at him as though they had never seen the like before. Certainly, his suit was of a foreign cut and he did not wear the popular trilby hat or fedora on his head, but instead a round soft hat. Women seemed to view him as something exotic and Verity had noticed that men didn't seem to know what to make of him either. She was convinced that Roberto was the most handsome man she had ever seen, including those in the movies.

Roberto appeared to like visiting Ruislip although Verity could not at first make out what the attraction might be. He did not look at home anywhere in this provincial setting; people were awkward with him, speaking slowly and loudly to him as though he might be deaf rather than simply foreign.

They saw Richard and Molly around town sometimes, but they always pretended not to have seen Verity, which suited her just fine. It was puzzling to Roberto that this couple should go out of the way to cross roads to avoid meeting them, the very fashionably dressed girl clinging on to her partner's arm as though they could not even be prised apart. Richard, now a partner in his firm, had married Molly at Easter. Molly still clung to him relentlessly as though she were afraid of what might happen if she let go. Verity was very glad not to have to speak to Richard and tried hard to ensure that they did not go anywhere that he and the limpet might be.

Sometimes, at the weekend, Verity and Roberto took a rowing boat at Ruislip Lido and he would pull lazily round the lake, letting the boat drift into the bank. They would moor and lie in the grass looking up at the sky and the clouds drifting high overhead and the skylarks freewheeling above, whilst they talked and set the world to rights in both English and Spanish. At first, he had laughed at her attempts to speak Spanish, but when he found that she was determined to persevere, he had helped her with pronunciation and talked slowly to her so that she could keep up with a conversation.

Roberto found Bernard's Spanish even more incomprehensible, overlaid with a cockney twang as it was. But recognising the youngster's determination, he did not laugh but helped him too and referred to Bernard in his absence as 'your young admirer'.

Verity had often wondered exactly why Bernard had taken up learning Spanish shortly after she did. For a time, she had been very much afraid that he might have developed a crush on her. But his attitude on first meeting Roberto had convinced her that Bernard simply had a passion for knowledge to be obtained from whatever source was available to him. Fortunately for Verity this appeared to be his only passion. The one point that Verity was not so keen on was that, encouraged by Roberto, Bernard started to go to some political gatherings with him. Under Roberto's influence Bernard joined the Communist Party.

During the week, Roberto attended lectures at the LSE and, as far as Verity could make out, spent his evenings attending political meetings or partying far into the night with the other students. He had great difficulty adjusting both to the British hours of work and mealtimes. The later the hour, the more lively he became. On Saturdays he often came down to Ruislip in time for lunch and in the evening took the last train back to town. Occasionally, since there was no-one at all to object to any impropriety, he stayed until Sunday and Verity was able to luxuriate in two whole days of his attention.

His uncle, Don César, belonged to the Spanish Centre party which at that moment was struggling to hold on to office in Madrid. Roberto had leftist sympathies but his political allegiance seemed to be changing from week to week, according to the latest political developments that filtered out from Spain. So contradictory were his political views that sometimes Verity thought that Roberto must attend every meeting of every faction in student London.

Once Roberto had tricked Verity into attending a protest meeting with him against the British Government Arms policy. It was held one Saturday morning in a quiet London cul-de-sac and Roberto had said that they were going to look at a Saturday street market he had heard about. When they arrived at the outdoor meeting there had been a modest crowd holding up their banners to support the speaker who was haranguing the gathering through a megaphone. It seemed to Verity that many of the crowd wore the same bemused look as herself and probably had come upon this meeting by accident. She was looking around when she saw five delivery vans screeching to a halt across the end of the road, effectively blocking the exit. Out of the vans poured young men in the uniform of Mosley's Blackshirts, the British Union of Fascists.

The Blackshirts were not armed with clubs like the Blueshirts had been in Barcelona when Felipe had encountered them, instead they wore knuckle-dusters and just charged into the crowd knocking everyone down, men, women and children indiscriminately. Verity caught a blow on her back and hit the railings of one of the houses. She saw steps leading down to the 'area' of one of the houses, where the dustbins were kept, and leapt down them with alacrity and ducked down out of sight behind the bins. She could hear the Blackshirts landing blows on the crowd. There were grunts and groans and also screams from women and children. Some of the young men at the meeting, like Roberto, tried to resist the attack but were unarmed and unready to defend themselves and came off worst in the encounter. The attackers smashed the speaker's platform and tore up the banners, then retreated jeering to their vans and drove off just as a lone police car drove up.

Roberto had received a blow to the jaw which had laid him out and Verity helped him back on to his feet. His jaw looked, and was, painful. He bore the imprint of the blow for a week or two but had no serious injuries, just hurt pride.

Verity had never had a steady boyfriend before, just friends who sometimes invited her out on an impartial basis, like Richard had. She was very attracted to Roberto just because he was so very different from the other boys she had known. He made her feel special and attractive, even though her own mirror never seemed to confirm this. It was wonderful to have someone around who actually treated her like a woman rather than a child or playmate, but she was always conscious that he would be going home to Madrid again soon and that would be the end of it.

It was confusing that he had different customs and values from her own. She was apprehensive about his involvement with the Communist Party and other left-wing splinter groups. He also smoked and she hated this, but all he did in response to her protests was to blow smoke rings at her. He took as little notice of this objection as of her concerns about his left-wing political involvement, telling her that this was all part of the educational process that he had come to London for.

Roberto did not go to Ruislip every weekend, so sometimes she would stay with Constance and meet him in London. She had even gone to a political meeting with him when Harry Pollitt, the Secretary of the British Communist Party, was due to address the LSE Students' Union. Verity agreed to go with Roberto as the meeting seemed to be at the more respectable end of the range of political gatherings he attended. She had to admit that Pollitt was a wonderful orator and she could readily see how he inspired his audience. But when you stopped to examine in detail what he had said, it did not seem to her to amount to much.

Roberto had been fired by enthusiasm, as had most of the audience, and he would not listen to her criticisms of Pollitt's arguments. They had their first tiff as a result and Verity walked out on him and returned to her aunt's flat. Her aunt was out, so with no-one to talk to, Verity had first paced about the flat, still angry with Roberto. Then she felt that she might have lost him for good and wept because it had been too silly to risk losing him over such an argument. She had already gone to bed when there was a ring at the doorbell and she found a contrite Roberto on the doorstep clutching a single rose. He solemnly went down on one knee to present the flower to her, begging forgiveness as he did so.

Verity was both laughing and crying, "Where on earth did you get the flower at this time of night?"

"I cannot tell a lie," he said placing his hand on his heart in an overly dramatic gesture, "this flower was specially grown for you by the gardener in the square outside. It stood there, proud and upright, just like you, my sweet, and I had to pick it for you. It represents you perfectly and I just had to bring it to its mistress."

When Roberto kissed her she forgave him immediately. He placed the rose in an art deco vase on the hall table and departed.

In Roberto's eyes Verity had always been the epitome of cool restraint, the quintessential English lady. He both respected her intellect and was afraid that she might well be his superior in ability and acumen. That was one of the reasons why he had not attempted to develop their relationship further. Anyway, his uncle had warned him off early on and told him that the one thing he must not do was to get Verity pregnant. It turned out to be an unnecessary warning since Roberto had never got as far as romantic involvement with Verity. She helped him while away the hours in this strange and chilly country when he was bored, but romance? No.

Constance on the other hand had given Verity a little kit containing all she needed to avoid becoming pregnant, should she find Roberto irresistible. Verity had expected that he would become the great love of her life, after all he was one of the handsomest men she had ever met. She had been so grateful for his company and his attention after her father died, but it eventually became apparent to her that they had few common interests. Initially they had both tried to show an interest in things that the other was interested in but it just hadn't worked out. She was very aware of this lack of common interests, his dalliance with communism appalled her, as did his late night partying

and his lack of attention to his studies. She suspected that he found her provincial and far too serious.
All the same she wished that he had stayed just a little longer after bringing her the rose as a peace offering.

13

Meeting up at a Lyons Corner House as usual, Verity had some news for Helen. She had had another meeting with the enigmatic Mr Jones. He had typically given no hint of what it was that he wanted to see her about, just that it would be in their mutual interest to meet.

"And?"

"Well, I think he was offering me a job in the Ministry, he said he wanted to organise some training for me. I told him that I was going to finish my training as an articled clerk before considering any other kind of work and he gave me a 'Your Country needs You' sort of speech before saying that the course starts in two weeks' time, just after Roberto goes home in fact, and that if I undertook the course and passed it, a job would be waiting for me whenever I wanted to take it up."

"So it's some sort of Civil Service training course and entrance exam?"

"I think so. I'll be glad to have something to occupy me when Roberto goes home."

"You're bound to be upset. Forgive me for asking but have you and he...?"

"No, of course not! Oh I'm sorry, I really shouldn't say that to you. Truth is I've been tempted, he is very handsome, but all the same... "

"Well if you really want him I'm sure you'll think of a way," said Helen. With that they moved on to less delicate subjects.

Verity's last date with Roberto was to be a dinner at the Spanish Embassy. When he arrived to pick Verity up he was dazzled by her flame coloured evening dress, cut on the bias to show her figure off to full advantage. She was equally struck by his appearance in full evening dress which, if it was possible, made him seem more handsome than ever. Seeing their exchange of looks, Constance assured them that she wasn't going to wait up for their return but would have an early night. With a couple of sleeping pills if necessary, she thought to herself.

The dinner was a glittering affair with a good sprinkling of British politicians and their wives, with the conversation mostly in English for the benefit of the guests. The talk round the table was not only unguarded talk about what was happening in Spain, but also about the King's illness and the Prince of

Wales who would eventually succeed him on the throne. It was here that Verity learned for the first time of the Prince's reputation as a womaniser, although the company did not quite put it that way. It seemed that he had a good many mistresses from amongst the aristocracy.

"As for that Wallis Simpson!" said a lady disgustedly.

"Who?" asked Verity of the man seated on her left.

"Edward's bit on the side, don't you know?!" Verity didn't know, so he was only too pleased to enlighten her that Wallis Simpson was already married and had had several husbands and lovers. "Now she's hoping to be the next Queen," guffawed the man.

There had been not a word of this in the papers and this was Verity's first intimation that there was a lot going on which was never reported in the press. She listened avidly to all this news from far and wide. Finally their hostess, a sharp-faced woman with a vituperous tongue, indicated that the ladies would withdraw and they went to the powder room to repair their makeup.

One woman approached Verity. "I've been admiring your dress all evening; the fabric is wonderful and that halter top so flattering!"

"Thank you," said Verity smiling.

"It's no good, Alice, you could never wear a top like that, you've no boobs to hold it up!" said another woman and the talk moved on to the latest fashions, to

Verity's relief. She did not like the way Alice had come up and stroked the fabric, it made her feel very uncomfortable.

The women whiled away the time in a drawing room until the men finally joined them, reeking of port and cigars. Roberto was one of the last to emerge and came through deep in conversation with the ambassador and then disappeared from view. Verity was not alone whilst waiting for Roberto, a number of men had clustered round her and were vying for her attention. She was after all by far the youngest and prettiest woman present and they did not waste time waiting to be introduced to her. Social chitchat was not her forte but it seemed that little was required on her part other than to smile at them all and try not to drink the lethal mixture of cocktails they plied her with. There was general pressure on her to go off with them to some unknown party and she was beginning to be afraid that she would be whisked off with a crowd of people without seeing Roberto again as this was, after all, her last evening with him. Their coats arrived and hers too, and as she looked around frantically there was no sign of Roberto anywhere.

"Think I saw him go, wasn't he with Alice?" said someone. "Or was it Fiona?" said another.

The drawing room was rapidly clearing; Verity thought that she could hardly stay on if everyone else was departing, after all just where was Roberto? She plucked up her courage and approached her hostess.

"Roberto? I'm sure he has gone already. If I see him I'll say that you were asking after him," she said dismissively. She saw no reason to tell this young woman that Roberto had so annoyed her husband with his persistent left-wing talk that the ambassador had had him escorted from the building, put in a cab and sent home. Humbled by her hostess and almost in tears, Verity allowed herself to be led down the stairs by the last of the partygoers and out into the street.

Whilst the crowd of them were waiting for a taxi she slipped away unnoticed and rounding the corner, hailed a taxi to take her ignominiously home. So much for the man whom she had at first thought might be the love of her life, she reflected that night lying awake and thinking of him. She was determined that she was not going to spend her time pining for someone who did not even have the good manners to remember that he had arrived with a partner. There was no message from him in the morning and she knew he was due to catch the boat train that evening. She tried to think of an excuse for contacting her dismissive hostess one more time to ask what had happened to Roberto, but pride prevented her from doing so. She had intended to surprise him by seeing him off at Victoria station that evening, but now it no longer seemed appropriate, it would be better never to see him again.

The Civil Service course was coming up and she concentrated on that, reading avidly. The trouble was she had no idea what kind of intellectual challenges would be set for her.

She had been provided with a railway warrant for travel to Brimscombe, near Stroud, and told that her train would be met. She was to expect to be away for a month. Constance was supportive and suggested what to pack and advised her to take as little as possible with her, other than a good book.

Brimscombe proved to be a country station abounding with wild flowers, but few passengers. A car was waiting for her and she was swiftly driven away. The driver dropped her at the door of a big house and got her suitcase out of the boot without a word before driving off. Verity carried her case up the steps and into the hallway which smelled strongly of a mixture of polish and flowers, the latter coming from an enormous bowl of lilies on a centre table. A woman appeared and said that she would take her to her room, and picked up her case and went upstairs, Verity following. The woman checked her watch, "You're to be in the garden at three, by the fountain," she said and left. It seemed to Verity that she would not be troubled very much by conversation in this place. She couldn't imagine what she might be required for in the garden, unless a course in flower arranging was a requisite for civil servants, which seemed highly unlikely.

She quickly unpacked and made sure to get down to the garden early to find the fountain. There she found a number of others waiting. They were joined at three by an elderly man with wisps of hair flying in all directions. He held his cane aloft and pointed to a nearby border, "What flowers do you recognise?" he asked.

"Nicotiana," said one. "That's right. Next," he said, pointing with his cane.

"Petunia?" hazarded another.

"Angel's trumpet!"

"Potato, Sir."

"Deadly nightshade," contributed Verity.

"Henbane," suggested someone else. After they were unable to name any of the remaining plants in the border, their tutor rattled off the names as he pointed. "Woody nightshade, eggplant, capsicum and tomato," he said pointing to a plant that they could now see was a fruitless tomato plant unexpectedly nestling along with the flowers and wild plants.

"And what do they have in common?" They looked at him blankly but no-one had an answer. "Come on, you'll have to do better than this! They are all members of the Solanaceae family, some of the most poisonous plants known."

"You," he said pointing at Verity, "you identified deadly nightshade or Atropa belladonna as it is more properly called. What parts of it are poisonous?"

"I suppose the berries, Sir," she responded.

"Don't suppose, we need accuracy. If you wanted to use it as a poison, the roots are the most deadly, but every bit of the plant is poisonous. Be very careful when touching it," he admonished.

In the course of the next hour and a half they soon discovered that virtually every plant in the garden could kill in some horrible way.

"Now the Mandrake, another member of the Solanaceae family, is one of the most notorious. It used to be said that when it was uprooted it shrieked in agony. There is a great deal of folklore about it, even Shakespeare mentioned it in several of his plays," he said.

Verity was bemused, was this meant to be a lecture on botany, plants in literature, or was His Majesty's Government planning a mass poisoning of the population by introducing Mandrake into the public water system? She hoped that all would shortly become clear.

"Tea is in the conservatory before your next class," he instructed. "I hope that it is not necessary for me to stress that washing your hands is vital in case you have touched any of these plants; we don't want to lose any of you just yet." Verity thought for a moment that he was joking but looking at him she smothered her smile. Clearly he was deadly serious.

There was no talk over tea and biscuits, it was more of an anxious pause in the proceedings rather than refreshment. As they were finishing their tea, the woman Verity had met on arrival reappeared. "Report to the Kitchen Garden next," she announced.

Everyone rushed out and Verity with them, having no idea where the Kitchen Garden was as yet. She wondered whether they were now to learn of how poisonous most fruit and vegetables were, or simply pick the produce for supper. It was neither. Entering the walled garden she was lined up, handed a pistol and instructed in loading and firing it at various targets. The glasshouses at the end of the garden seemed to have already suffered as a target, there wasn't much left of them. Several instructors moved amongst them, checking their handling of the weapons, advising and rebuking them as their progress (or lack of it) deserved. When the stable clock struck seven they were told to unload their weapons and hand them in.

At supper conversation was again limited to essentials. Verity wasn't sure whether this was a rule of the establishment or just good practice in this apparently murderous company. Afterwards she went to her room with no clear idea of what she was training for and no opportunity to ask anyone, but some very uneasy thoughts about it. She made some notes in her room in case they were likely to be questioned in the morning as to what they had learned the previous day. The more she thought about her extremely curious day, the happier she became. Whilst she had no desire to become a mass poisoner, it was clear to her now that she was not heading for a staid job in the higher echelons of the Civil Service, a much more adventurous role was clearly intended and now she knew it was what she had craved all along. Action, excitement, even danger, yes!

In the morning her next session confirmed to her that she had strayed accidentally into some sort of killer's paradise. In an area of the estate known as the wilderness, her first task was to observe demonstrations of how to creep up on someone unawares and put them out of action silently, and usually permanently. This they then had to practice for several hours for themselves, although without killing or maiming fellow students or instructors, even if at times they came close to it! Certainly by lunch time Verity was covered in bruises, as well as scratches from branches and brambles, and bites from insects hiding in the long grass.

With a few minutes to spare before lunch, she went upstairs to change into slacks, Constance having insisted that she bring several pairs in an otherwise frugal wardrobe. She found that she was ravenous after the physical activity of the morning and clear that she needed to be a lot fitter than she was in order to keep up with the training. The instructors clearly thought so too as the rest of the day was spent in hard physical exercise until their unused muscles were at screaming point. That night she was too tired to make notes and she simply fell into bed and slept soundly. Whatever the future held for her it was going to be exciting and challenging, although she very much hoped that Mr Jones had not identified her as a natural killer in his selection of her.

Verity did not have much time for reflection on the course, after the first week they were liable to be called out in the middle of the night for some exercise or other that would see them creeping up on mock sentries in the dark and delivering fatal blows. She never knew what the next day or night might hold but was finding that, far from being anxious about the activities, she thoroughly enjoyed them, especially when they had the chance to devise their own strategies. Afterwards they would have a meeting in the hall, whatever time of night it was, where they were served hot food and had to report back on what they had done and why, before the instructors gave them notes on their performance with suggestions for more effective strategies.

Verity found it all exhilarating and as the days went by she spent less and less time dwelling on her loss of Roberto and that horrid last night with him, or, more correctly, without him.

The small arms training gradually expanded so that she was able to identify and use a wide variety of current weapons and also those dating back to the First World War or even before. As the instructors explained, she must be able to use any weapon to hand, so long as there was some ammunition for it. If there was no ammo available then first of all it could be used as a threat, as no-one would know whether it was loaded or not. Secondly, it could be used to knock someone out or even thrown at them. Verity remembered Richard and the vase which had missed him and thought that maybe he had a lucky escape.

Evening lectures had been introduced and they had experts giving talks on the political hotspots where trouble could break out at any time, illustrated with maps and slides of those leaders whose names they should be aware of . These lectures were interspersed with talks on basic explosives, and they would make simple devices in the basement laboratory which they would then go to a disused quarry to explode. They still had to keep up their basic fitness training every day as well as some night time exercises. Verity had found the whole course so challenging and absorbing that she was beginning to dread it coming to an end and having to go back to her normal life, whatever that was to be.

The exams, when they came, were nothing like any Civil Service exams that anyone could have thought up. Verity knew that she had been continually monitored and assessed throughout the course and the tests were wholly practical, tasks to carry out with or without a partner. She also had interviews with various strangers who plied her with questions on their particular topic.

Finally, a few days before the end of her course, she was roused in the night and told to dress for an exercise in the country, but otherwise not to take any of her belongings with her. A lorry was waiting outside and she was ordered into the back of it and handed a haversack. She recognised some of the students from the course but clearly they were not all going on this exercise. "Where are we going?" Verity asked the instructor checking off their names on his list.

"On an exercise," was the unhelpful reply and then the engine started and further conversation became impossible.

It was a bumpy, uncomfortable ride which did not prevent Verity from sleeping most of the way. They appeared to be climbing up some fairly steep hills and the ruts in the road jolted them about. It was the middle of the night and raining heavily when the lorry finally stopped and the flap over the back was raised. There was no lighting visible and the cloud cover prevented any moonlight from assisting their night vision. Verity had not a clue where they were, nor had any of her companions; not that conversation had exactly flowed.

An army officer appeared. "You two," he gestured to the two nearest the back of the truck "You get out here." The two clambered out and after a minute or two the lorry moved on. After ten minutes the lorry stopped again and another two were ordered out. The lorry moved on again and dropped another two, leaving just Verity and a man she knew as Dennis slithering about in the back. Then it stopped again and Verity was ready to get out.

The officer appeared and gave Verity a hand down for which she was grateful as she was quite stiff by now. "Good luck," he said. "You'll need it," and then he climbed back into the cab and the lorry drove off up the track, soon disappearing from sight as it rounded a bend. Verity stood in the rain staring after the tail lights of the lorry.

"Come on or we'll get drowned out here," said Dennis touching her arm. "There seems to be an overhanging rock over there, let's shelter." He led her towards the rock and they crouched underneath. Whilst it was still wet, they were at least out of the direct force of the driving rain and their eyes were becoming accustomed to the darkness.

"Any idea what on earth is this all about?" asked Verity.

"This must be the final exercise they promised us. Well, at least I was told I'd been selected for basic survival training. You too?" he said turning the white outline of his face toward her in the darkness.

"Never said a word about it. Let's see if we've got some instructions in the depths of these haversacks." He flicked his cigarette lighter and opened his haversack. It proved to contain a map of sorts, provisions including a bottle of water, a pair of binoculars, a penknife and some matches. Verity had the same in hers, minus the map but with a typewritten message saying 'Arrive by 3 a.m. Thursday. Penalties incurred if seen by any patrolling troops in the meantime.'

Dennis opened up the map. It was a curious map with all the place names erased. They could have been absolutely anywhere - they were not even wholly convinced that they were in England, it could easily be Wales with all the hills around them. All they had to go on was an 'X' which presumably marked their Thursday morning destination. What they didn't know was where they were now.

"We'd better get well away from the road and find somewhere we can rest until dawn," he said amiably.

Verity felt rain trickling down her neck as they scrambled up the hillside away from the track. If this was to be survival training, they needed to make a good start, a place of safety but with views over the surrounding countryside as soon as it got light.

Dennis was a resourceful young man who was not unfamiliar with military training. She thought he was likely to be a good partner for this exercise, someone who was unfazed by difficult conditions. He took Verity by the hand to guide her up the hillside and explained the rules of the game as he went.

"Soldiers do predictable things; we'll do the unpredictable. We've got to get from A to B, or perhaps X in this case. They won't have dropped us more than 25 miles from the target. In just over 24 hours we can be home and dry, so to speak, and enjoying some nice bacon and eggs - it's not long, is it?"

"No, let's go for it!"

They found a place to rest for the remainder of the night, high on the hillside but overlooking the path that ran along the crest of the range of hills. They cut bracken to make a roof covering for a shelter of sorts between two rocks. There was just room for them to crawl in. With the two of them crammed in, they could only move an arm or leg with the agreement of the other. Verity was to sleep first and Dennis was to wake her after two hours so that he could sleep and she could keep watch. Verity was asleep as soon as her head rested on her haversack.

Dennis whispered in her ear, "Time to wake up. Turn over slowly so that you can see out."

Immediately awake, she did as she was told. Dennis handed her the binoculars.

"Nothing so far." With that he put his head down and slept immediately.

Verity scanned the hillside. It was a little lighter now but was still raining gently. She rested her elbows on her haversack, binoculars at the ready. Dennis breathed deeply by her elbow; she hoped he did not snore.

As the light increased, Verity drew out the map and compared the features she could see. She soon had their position pinpointed and marking it in pencil, studied the possible routes open to them. She also took a look at her rations and, mentally dividing them into portions, hungrily ate her first portion. It was whilst she was doing this that she heard a slight noise not far off. She clamped a hand over Dennis's mouth in order to wake him silently. He wriggled to turn over and they watched in silence as a patrol of six soldiers came along the path below them. The patrol came slowly on, obviously searching for any sign of the fugitives but missed their hiding place. The game had begun.

14

Verity sank back in her comfortable chair and closed her eyes for a moment to enjoy the hot summer sunshine. Things had moved so fast in the past few weeks that it was quite difficult to comprehend that she was here on the terrace of the Ritz Hotel in Madrid. She would have had even more difficulty in believing that it wasn't a dream if it were not for the presence of Helen sitting opposite her, bliss shining out from her open face. As usual Helen was talking.

"Wasn't the Mezquita at Cordoba wonderful? Such a pity that we won't have time for the trip to Toledo tomorrow."

"You know it's not actually supposed to be a holiday, it's cover for us being here."

"Of course, but so far it has been so much like a holiday that it's easy to forget. It was so good of Mr Jones to arrange this trip for us."

"It's not out of the goodness of his heart - not sure he has one. Purely a business arrangement."

It was just over two weeks since Verity had arrived home at her aunt's, having successfully completed the whole of her induction course. At the end of the course Mr Jones had put in an appearance and had all the successful graduates of the course swear both the loyal oath to the Crown and an oath of secrecy. Finally they were all given appointments to meet him the following week and then at last they were able to go home.

Verity found it curious that Constance asked her very little about the course and nothing that could not be answered without infringing her oath of secrecy. Normally a woman who wanted to know everything that was going on, Constance simply asked about the food "Plentiful but not necessarily good," the journey: "A nice little country train, what I saw of the countryside looked beautiful," and similar innocuous questions. Likewise she did not ask about the Civil Service exams or whether Verity had passed them. She simply provided a comfortable home for Verity, told her of her trip to Ruislip to check that everything was in order in Verity's absence, and passed on a few messages. One of these was from the Fleet Street firm that she would shortly join for the remainder of her Articles of Clerkship saying that they would be pleased to see her at the end of the Long Vacation, the period in which the Courts were closed, which ended in early October.

"And do you have a follow-up interview?" Constance asked, referring to the recent course. Verity did, it was to be the next day at ten.

When she arrived, the enigmatic Mr Jones had handed her the brochure for Cook's Grand Tour of Spain departing 1 August. He indicated that she should read it, so she did, puzzling all the while as to what she was supposed to be looking for. Having got to the end she looked up at him.

"Think it sounds good?" he said.

"Yes, but I can't afford a twenty-eight guinea holiday - that's an awful lot of money."

"No need to worry, it's all arranged and paid for, in fact my secretary is just fixing up the final details now for you and a friend."

"What friend?"

"Let me see, Harriet? No, Helen someone, Helen Pugh," he said after rifling through the papers on his desk.

"Helen? Just what's this about?"

"I need a little job done in Madrid, matter of picking up a small package. Requires someone not known to the locals for it - you'll be ideal. Very simple and no risk attached. You're on our payroll now, of course. It won't be suspicious at all if you travel on a regular tourist package with a friend. Your friend's employer was very helpful and accommodating in ensuring she was free for this little job."

Verity had certainly never heard Helen describe the Matron of her hospital as 'helpful and accommodating' and she looked forward to hearing Helen's version. "Tell me what I'm to pick up and where and when."

"That's what I like, direct and to the point!" Mr Jones exclaimed, and went on to explain the details. "You won't need to use your own names of course, thought you might like to be Vera Foster, same initials, easy to remember. Don't want there to be any repercussions for you. Now, on your way out," he said, standing and opening the door for her, "my secretary will take you to have your passport photo taken." Verity started to retort that she already had a passport, and then halted. She did not as yet have a passport in a false name and this was clearly to be remedied immediately.

Verity thought that Mr Jones certainly only gave out minimal information. She no longer believed that, if he said that there was no risk involved, there was none. She promised herself that she would prepare for every possible eventuality so that she could act instinctively when trouble arose. Unfortunately for Verity problems sometimes arose which no-one, least of all her, had dreamt of.

When she arrived back at the flat, Constance showed no amazement at all about her sudden decision to take a holiday abroad with Helen. "An excellent idea! Do you both good," was her only comment. Verity eyed her suspiciously but soon was drawn into a discussion of what clothes she should take for the baking heat of Spain in August.

Verity rang Helen that evening and was unsurprised that Helen already had all the details; Mr Jones clearly worked quickly and efficiently. Helen had been given three weeks' leave of absence from the hospital and already had her bag packed ready to join Verity, since, as she pointed out, they had little time. They were due to depart from Victoria Station the day after next. First Verity had an appointment the following morning at Mr Jones's office to pick up their travel documents.

It was not only travel documents that were waiting for her, she was also given a fashionable hat. The clerk who handed over the hat showed her the concealed pocket in the crown of the hat, enough to take documents or a very small parcel.

She was handed a new passport, a large amount of currency, tickets and an itinerary for the Cook's Grand Tour, and Spanish and French rail timetables, "Just in case you need them," he unhelpfully explained. Her final package had been of clothes which Mr Jones thought might come in handy. They were an odd mixture of distinctly unalluring garments which she looked at in mystification.

The girls had plenty of time for lengthy discussion on the train journey. They travelled third class down to Folkestone, "Not really pushing the boat out, are they?" commented Helen. After that, they had travelled second class on the cross-channel steamer and on the French trains from Boulogne via Bordeaux to Irun on the Spanish border. Here they changed trains to the Spanish-run Madrid train as the rail gauge was different in Spain so through trains did not exist.

Helen had known that Verity was going on a training course but thought that it was a Civil Service type course. She thought it best not to enquire further, they had plenty of other things to think about. She knew that Verity had something special to do in Madrid but that was all she was permitted to know. The closer they got to day ten of their holiday when Verity would have to perform her task, the more both girls forgot everything but the importance of this mission. It was easy to avoid being nervous whilst they filled their days with sightseeing and basking in the wonderfully hot sun, but the tension was beginning to grow.

The girls were now on day nine of their "Grand Tour" having arrived in Madrid on their second day, and then had done organised sightseeing which had taken them to El Escorial and then on to Granada. After this, they had continued to Seville and Cordoba before returning to Madrid today. The next day was to be the one when Verity would pick up the package instead of their joining an optional tour to Toledo. The day after they were to continue to Barcelona where they would spend two days before starting their homeward journey. They were both looking forward to seeing Barcelona and their friends there, but had been warned not to tell their Spanish friends of their imminent arrival. Helen in particular found this irksome.

"Come on," said Verity, hoisting herself out of her chair. "The Prado closes at four so we'd better get going."

The Prado Museum hosted one of the richest collections of paintings in the world with the highlight being the collection of paintings of Velazquez. Passing through the North Rotunda, the girls headed up the stairs and into the first Velazquez Room. Then they headed right into the room devoted to Las Meninas where they, and most of the other visitors to the Prado, stood in front of the painting. It was with difficulty that Verity tore herself away to visit the principal Velazquez room, but here the luminosity of the paintings held even Helen in thrall. When they had finished viewing the Velazquez, they moved on to the El Greco paintings and then to the Goya. Finally they visited the Early Flemish Gallery and then descended to the ground floor. It had been relatively cool in the gallery, but when they emerged on to the Calle de Felipe IV the heat hit them. They could only manage to walk very slowly towards the Parque de Madrid following the street plan which they had been given.

The sight of the lakes in the park made them feel cooler and reenergised them, and they walked round one of the lakes before stopping for a cool drink at a café. The streets were incredibly dusty compared with home - something to do with how far inland they were. They sat looking at the Spanish families around them, listening to their conversations and adjusting to the local accent. Verity wondered what those same families would have thought had they had known why she was there.

Verity had been continually checking whether anyone new had sat down since they had. There did not appear to be anyone following them - no reason why they should be followed at the moment, but it was just as well to get into the habit of checking. She was glad to see from Helen's constantly shifting gaze that she too was checking, but Verity was aware of her responsibility of being the trained professional. Eventually they made their way back to the hotel, getting used to frequently crossing the road since this gave them a good excuse to look up and down the road. No-one appeared to be following them. Only when they got back to their room did they feel free to discuss the final details of their plan for the next day. Verity would go alone to the pick-up; this was ultimately her task, not Helen's.

Neither of them slept well that night. Whilst Mr Jones had reassured Verity that she would not be in any danger, he had supplied lots of back-up information that suggested to her that there was every prospect of things going spectacularly wrong. After all, why did he need an unknown like Verity to pick up a package for him? Whilst he had played down the importance of the mission, it suggested to Verity that the local agents who would normally have carried out such a task were known to the authorities and were being watched or had been arrested. The girls had carefully planned the role which Helen would play and she was ready to do her part.

Breakfast was unappealing to them both but they had to be seen to be acting normally in every way. After that they equipped themselves for the day and went once again to sit on the Ritz terrace. At quarter to eleven Verity rose and headed off for the Prado once more. There was a small queue for tickets and Verity got out her museum catalogue from the previous day to thumb through the exhibits while she was waiting. After this she loitered on the ground floor looking at some of the sculptures in the lower long gallery, keeping an eye on the time as she did so. There generally seemed to be many more people about today, but she was not sure whether more people was good or bad. Finally she made her way upstairs to the main floor and, catalogue in hand, made her way slowly to the Early Flemish paintings.

Whilst she was still in the upper Long Gallery she heard a commotion ahead of her that made her pause in her progress. The sounds receded to the ground floor, then it was quiet again. Verity, in spite of herself, was now quite afraid. Were the sounds those of the courier being arrested? No way of knowing, but she prayed that she was not walking straight into a trap. She took some deep breaths and then continued through the Rotunda and into the Early Flemish Room. Mercifully the room was empty of both visitors and attendant and she thankfully sank on to the bench to admire the two works by Albrecht Durer. She had placed her open basket on the floor by her and, as she studied the paintings her hand groped for and found the package fastened to the underside of the bench. She heard someone coming and swiftly concealed the package and was studying her catalogue again by the time a couple came in. She gave them a slight smile and then stood up and left the room to head for the stairs. She turned to exit the Rotunda and ran straight into a man heading the opposite way. In the collision her hat went flying and the man bent to pick it up for her. They were both in the act of apologising before they recognised one another; Verity was horror stricken to see that it was Captain Moreno!

It had taken a moment for Verity to recognise him in a dark suit and hat but no one could ever mistake those eyes. To her surprise, after the first flash of recognition, he beamed delightedly and greeted her in English as he handed back her hat. Ramming the hat back on her head she took her cue from him and said that she was surprised to see him in this unexpected location.

"I work in Madrid now - I'm on General Franco's staff!"

She heard herself congratulating him, and by now he had taken her arm in a proprietorial fashion and was steering her towards the staircase. She found herself having to explain that she was on a Cook's Tour of Spain with a companion and was just taking the opportunity to see some of the paintings that she had been unable to see before closing time yesterday. Whilst he murmured about the splendour of the paintings she had the impression that he knew little or nothing about them.

Downstairs he nodded to a group of men gathered at the foot of the stairs and said something to them that was unintelligible to her. Then he steered her out of the museum and into the street, gripping her arm tightly. Verity found herself almost unable to think straight in this strange situation. Was she under arrest? She was so frightened that she just went with him without resistance. She did remember however that on her last encounter with this man she had pushed him into a fountain and ended up having to escape from Ibiza; she very much doubted that he had forgotten either. His presence in the museum at a time when an informer was dropping off a package of information for a foreign power could not be a coincidence. The commotion she had heard was only too likely to have been the arrest of the informer, but if the watchers had known precisely where the package had been concealed they would have set a better trap for her. It was possible that they were searching the person arrested even now and probably continuing to search the museum, something that she gleefully thought would take them all day.

Captain Moreno, still holding her arm, took her to a café where he ordered them both coffee, without asking whether she wanted one. She thought that perhaps if she were to go to the toilet she might find another way out of the café and make her escape. She excused herself and stood up to go to the toilet reaching for her basket; he took it from her grasp.

"No need to take it with you - no-one will steal it whilst I'm here," he said smiling. Verity forced herself to smile back and left her basket with him. She knew that he would search it and that was fine because the tiny package was secured in the hidden pocket in her hat. She found there was no way out of the back of the café, so she simply used the toilet and gave him plenty of time to search her possessions before she rejoined him. She was glad that she had not been carrying the false passport or any travel documents, Helen had all of these safely with her.

Moreno studied her and, looking at her skimpy summer dress, could see that there was nowhere she could have hidden a package on her person. He found himself glad that she was innocent, as indeed he knew her to have been when he had had her listed as a spy by General Franco. It had done his career no harm, indeed it had actually done it a lot of good. He smiled at her and continued contentedly to study her admirable figure.

She smiled back. He had clearly found nothing untoward in her basket and now appeared completely relaxed. She too relaxed in the knowledge that he had not found anything incriminating.

A man came into the café and looked round until he saw Moreno, who gave him an almost imperceptible shake of the head before returning his full attention to Verity. She saw the shake and took it that she had passed the test. The question was, how to get free of him?

Since it was clear that she was stuck with him for the moment, she searched for neutral topics and had no difficulty hitting upon art. She told him how impressed she had been with the paintings she had seen yesterday at the Prado but explained that, as she only arrived from Cordoba yesterday, had not had time to see all that she wanted to see, and showed him her well marked catalogue as she talked. He smoked as he relaxed and feasted his eyes on her; it was well over a year since he had last seen her but he remembered every detail. He hadn't forgotten the humiliation of his dunking in the fountain but now had another chance to make headway with her. He felt very strongly all his previous attraction to her and deliberately brushed her hand in reaching to look at the catalogue she was holding.

She felt something like an electric shock as his hand touched hers, but resisted her impulse to move out of his range even when he moved his chair closer to hers under the pretence of looking at the catalogue with her. He was very close now, and she realised that she was powerless to move. The talk of paintings dried up and surprisingly it was he who moved first.

"I must return to work," he said simply. "But tonight I will take you to Madrid's finest restaurant," he said firmly. "Where shall I pick you up?"

"The Ritz," she replied.

"Seven o'clock," he said and departed.

"Lord, what now?" Verity murmured to herself as he left.

15

Helen was waiting for Verity at the park as they had arranged. "I saw you come out of the museum with that man holding your arm, I knew him at once! I was so afraid you'd been arrested!"

"So was I!" admitted Verity and rapidly told Helen what had happened.

"And you're going to keep this appointment?"

"I have to," Verity responded.

"Hey, you're not actually attracted to this horrible man are you?" she asked, and then seeing Verity's face she answered her own question: "You are! Oh heavens, that's all we need!"

"Look," said Verity, "if I don't show up this evening he will start searching for me and be very suspicious. We haven't got time to get away before seven. He doesn't suspect me right now so let's keep it that way - I can manage a dinner with him. Then we can go on with our tour."

"I suppose so, but we must have a plan, just in case."

"Of course, and this is what has been going through my mind," and Verity started to outline the plan that she had been forming. It was risky but so were all the alternatives. She paid a visit to the ladies' room at the Ritz Hotel to see if there was somewhere she might conceal a change of clothes in case she might have need of them. She found some panelling at the back of one of the cubicles which she was able to unscrew with her nail scissors with just enough room behind to hide her things.

She was waiting for him in the bar of the Ritz when he walked in just before seven. She was wearing the stunning red evening dress she had last worn to the embassy dinner with Roberto, brought with her on this holiday at the suggestion of Constance. The dress and the girl in it took Moreno's breath away. He was very thankful that he had worn his best uniform showing his new insignia of rank, and that he genuinely was taking her to the best restaurant in Madrid tonight, rather than some lesser place.

She stood up as he approached. "You've been promoted!"

"Yes!" he said standing tall, "I'm a major now."

"Major Moreno! Congratulations!"

"Thank you, but please call me Luis."

"Certainly, Luis."

He took her hand and they went outside to a waiting cab. Once in the darkness of the cab, he placed an arm round her shoulders and the electricity was there again between them. This time it was she who reached up to kiss him, and the kiss lasted the short distance to the restaurant and they got out hand in hand, both unwilling to break the contact between them.

Verity had decided that her best strategy for survival was to be friendly, responsive even, willing to please him and not to antagonise him in any way. This time she had the skills to overpower, or even kill him in self defence; she hoped it would not come to that. What she had not taken into account was the sheer strength of his magnetism.

The Botin was indeed one of Madrid's finest restaurants and certainly its oldest. Verity looked round in amazement as Moreno told her that Goya had worked there before becoming a painter. She could well believe it - it was so old it looked as though Goya might only just have walked out of the door. They were conducted to one of the upper floors where tables were set in a tiled and panelled room. It looked very grand and she had to admit to herself that she would not have expected him to bring her to such a luxurious place. They settled at their table and looked around the room which was only just beginning to fill. She noticed that a large table had been set up down the centre of the room for a party, but most of the tables were like theirs, tables for two, set so that each table had a modicum of privacy.

"Shall I order for you?" he enquired after they had been given menus.

"Please," she said replacing her menu on the table. At first glance she thought that she could understand most of it, but just as well not to let on that she understood any Spanish at all.

"The roast suckling pig is a speciality of the house - we'll have that." Verity agreed that it would be a good choice and let him get on with ordering whilst she relaxed for a minute or two. She had come prepared to discuss various safe topics that would give nothing important away about her, but waited for him to lead the conversation.

He explained that he had been working in Madrid for much of the past year and found it very much to his liking. "General Franco is our top general and I am privileged to be on his staff," he concluded. Encouraged by her smile he went on boastfully, "Today he entrusted me with a special assignment, to trap a man in our Ministry who was thought to be spying."

Verity felt as though her blood in her veins had turned to ice but managed somehow to go on smiling, "Did you catch him?"

"Oh yes. I never fail."

"The General must think very highly of you," she said, at a loss for anything else to say.

"He does. Look, here he comes now!" he said, rising as a party of people came bustling in. Verity also rose and, following his gaze, saw a small man entering the room wearing a uniform which was heavily encrusted with gold. She thought that Helen had been absolutely right; she should never ever have agreed to come out tonight, but too late now. General Franco looked just like the photo she had been shown of him on her course such a short time ago.

The General could hardly fail to notice his young staff officer with the stunning girl in red beside him. He greeted them and Moreno saluted smartly and, as the General turned with a quizzical eye to Verity, Moreno started to introduce them. "May I introduce an English visitor? This is Miss," and he hesitated for a second remembering, as the General undoubtedly would, that Miss Verity Fleming had been listed as a spy a year or two ago.

"Rose Watson," improvised Verity holding out her hand, which the General took and bowed over.

"Enchanted," he said in his soft high voice, "and a very pretty name."

"Thank you," said Verity, smiling her most dazzling smile at this strange cold-eyed little man whom she instinctively feared.

As they resumed their seats Moreno smiled his thanks at her, but Verity knew that she had blown it; she was not supposed to know that she had been listed as a spy and it would not be long before he realised it too. "Rose is my second name and my family call me that, I used to love roses as a child," she again improvised.

"Watson?"

"I'm not living at my father's house any more, I'm living with my aunt, so it seemed the right thing to do to adopt her name. Do please go on calling me Verity." Moreno had not in fact called her anything so far but now ran her name over his tongue and found that it had a pleasing sound. He reached for her hand across the table and put it to his lips, "Verity Rose Fleming Watson - I like every part of you and your name."

General Franco had more practical thoughts on his mind than foreign spies. When a few years ago he had been Commandant of the Zaragossa Military Academy he had insisted that all his cadets, whom he knew to be a licentious bunch, carry at least one condom with them on nights out. He had campaigned vigorously to stamp out venereal disease amongst them. If he met them out in the town he would even demand to see that they had their protective equipment with them. He had almost asked Moreno the same question but had stopped himself just in time; he trusted that the young man had not forgotten this most basic part of his training. Moreno had not. He could not work for Franco and not follow his unwritten rules.

Verity and Moreno moved on to talking about their families; he said that he had a mother and sister whom he didn't see very often but that he expected his sister would be getting married soon, and then enquired about her family. She told him about her family and the recent death of her father since the information could do her no harm, and it was much easier to tell the truth than anything she might otherwise have made up, apart that is, from calling herself 'Rose Watson'.

He offered his solemn condolences and took her hand as he did so. She wasn't sure whether he had accepted her explanation about her name but he continued to exude charm and sexual attraction. For a short time they could enjoy themselves uncluttered by the future.

Finally the meal ended and he announced that he would now like to take her dancing. She was ready for this and countered that she must first return to the hotel and tell her aunt, as he had assumed her unseen companion to be, that she was going out dancing and would not be back until late.

He accepted this and had the doorman call a cab. They reached the Ritz and he helped her out, holding her arm very firmly, and to Verity's alarm steered her straight to the main staircase and up to the second floor where he produced a room key, opened a door and steered her in before locking the door after them. They were in a bedroom, luxuriously furnished and with a balcony. It didn't look to Verity like he was intending to interrogate her, more like a classic seduction scene. There was no getting away this time unless she was prepared to leap from a second floor balcony. She wasn't going to do that, but she had come expecting him to try something of this sort and was prepared for even this, in the interests of the service, so long as she could get away afterwards. She had the skills now to disable him with her bare hands if she needed to.

After the rejection she had suffered at Roberto's hands, it hurt her to think that he was somewhere in this city now, and that he had entirely forgotten her. Verity had felt every bit of the charms of Moreno this evening and was not unwilling to be with him for just a little longer. In spite of the danger and the evil that she felt in this man, it simply added to the excitement. She could not remember when she had ever enjoyed an evening so much.

Unknown to Verity, Roberto had seen her that very evening as she left the Botin. He had been dining on the ground floor and it was the flame-coloured dress he had noticed first, a dress that was hard to miss. It was with complete astonishment that he recognised Verity, leaving hand in hand with an officer. He knew that Franco's party were dining upstairs and that Verity had come from there. It was unbelievable that Verity was here in Madrid, and had been a part of Franco's party, the man who represented everything that stood in the way of a communist take-over of the country. He knew that she was a capitalist from a capitalist country, but friendly with Franco? What the hell was she doing here? He had leapt up to follow them outside and heard Moreno tell the cab driver to take them to the Ritz. She must be staying there, perhaps he could pay her a visit tomorrow and find out what was going on and whether he could turn it to his advantage.

In the luxurious bedroom Moreno shed his heavy uniform coat on to the floor, far too hot for an August night, and pulled Verity on to the bed on top of him. Whatever her head told her, her body was giving all the wrong signals and they kissed passionately as his arms and body enveloped her.

At length Verity geared herself up for the action she knew she must take.

"Luis, darling, I'd better tell my aunt that we're going dancing, then she won't worry," she said, slipping from the bed and taking the key from his coat pocket. He reached out an arm lazily and drew her firmly back on to the bed. "I've a better idea than dancing, we could just stay here," he said, "doing this..."

It became even harder for Verity to draw away but she knew that she must get out of there fast whilst she still had a will of her own. She freed herself again and unlocked the door of their room and let herself out blowing kisses to him as she did so. "Bathroom's at the end of the corridor if you need it," he called after her from the bed. She moved silently along the corridor to where she knew the back stairs must be. She slipped down the stairs, checking at each turn that there was no one else using them and reached the ground floor where she dodged into the ladies' toilet.

Verity and Helen were not staying at the Ritz, nor ever had been - she had simply thought it might be good to establish a hotel other than their own as a temporary base. Fortunately there was no one else in the toilets and she pulled away the section of panelling where she had hidden a bag and a change of clothing earlier, just in case she might need them. She changed in a cubicle into some of the dowdy clothing that Mr Jones had provided, reluctantly placing her evening dress and shoes behind the panelling, wound a scarf over head and then slipped into the corridor and exited the hotel by a back door that she had previously located.

Bag in hand she set off to the station, trying hard not to draw attention to herself by hurrying. Helen had already left a message with their Cook's tour representative that evening to say that they had been called away by a family crisis and to arrange for their suitcases to be sent home without them. They now just had a small holdall each.

Earlier in the day, Helen had purchased from different booking office clerks third class return tickets to various destinations. Not that they would need the return half, but if they were to lay false trails they had to do it to the best of their ability.

Helen had been sitting slouched on a bench in the station for more than an hour, dressed in equally dowdy clothing with an all-enveloping hat which entirely covered her blond hair. "I may have to sleep in this blessed hat," she grumbled out of the side of her mouth as Verity sat down beside her. "Train goes in 20 minutes," she continued, "must go to the loo." She headed off towards the toilet whilst Verity studied the station exits for any sign of pursuit. She need not have worried - Moreno was dozing in his room at the Ritz and waiting for her reappearance and wondering at the interminable time that all women could take in the bathroom. It would be a while yet in his present happy state before he discovered that she was not returning to him, was not registered in the hotel, and indeed was nowhere to be found.

The girls boarded the train separately, sitting in compartments a little apart. This was especially hard because Verity was longing to tell, and Helen was equally anxious to hear, what had happened, but it was simply not safe to do so and they must not be seen to be travelling together in case of pursuit. Helen retained the vital package in her care because she was still the unknown traveller, less likely to be picked up by the police or military than Verity was.

By the early hours Moreno had discovered that Verity had escaped yet again and that neither she nor her aunt were staying at the Ritz. Verity was clearly known to the waiting staff who had served her coffee and drinks, but they said she had always paid cash for her purchases rather than put them on her room account. No one seemed to have noticed the aunt, whom Moreno had never seen so could not describe.

He had been grateful earlier when Verity had stopped him from giving her real name to the General, but it had not taken long for him to become suspicious about why she had given a different name - it simply had to be that she somehow knew she had been listed as a spy; either that or she actually was one. It seemed to him just too unlikely to contemplate that she was a spy, but the more time he had to think about it, the more possible it became. After all, he had first run into her yesterday at the Prado just after arresting the traitor and had been suspicious. But he had personally searched her basket so knew that she was not carrying anything untoward. She couldn't have taken anything to hide in the toilet at the bar, could she? He pictured her as she had been and was positive that she would not have been able to conceal any package about her without it having been apparent to him. No she couldn't be a spy, he reasoned with himself. If she was then his career would be finished.

So why had she run away from him yet again when their night together had only just begun? He was certain that she had been enjoying herself just as much as he had been and she had come to him willingly and passionately. There was absolutely no way he could admit to the General that the woman he had introduced to him earlier in the evening was a spy. Was she or wasn't she? The only way to find out was to catch up with her.

Moreno had received the report from the interviews with the man arrested earlier in the day and it was certain that the man did not know who was to pick up the information.

Moreno had already given instructions for interception of diplomatic bags where possible, but it was tricky to do without the risk of causing a diplomatic incident. He had suggested that the British diplomatic bag in particular might be worth intercepting as he thought that finding the missing package would make any risks worthwhile.

Whilst the girls slept fitfully in their third class carriages on the way back to Cordoba, Moreno sat with a bottle of brandy at the Ritz working out what to do to save his career. Above all else he had to find Verity or Rose or whatever her name was. They had unfinished business, both professional and personal.

Arriving in Cordoba at lunch time, the girls had changed wearily back into their everyday clothes in the ladies' toilet at the station and gone to a café they had been to just two days before when they were on the tourist trail. Eating as they talked, they were at last able to catch up on events. Helen found it difficult to believe that Verity, whom she had always regarded as inclined to be conventional and law-abiding, had been so attracted to the dubious charms of Major Moreno, although come to think of it, this trip itself was hardly law-abiding and conventional. Verity had changed in the time she had known her, was more outgoing and eager for adventure.

"It was really hard to stop myself," confessed Verity, both ashamed and exultant at the evening spent with Moreno. "I know exactly what he is and what he is capable of but he can be so charming and intense that it was hard to resist. Then of course I blew it at the restaurant when he introduced me to his boss. He hesitated in giving my name when he introduced me and I came in with a false name, to save him and then of course he knew that there was something wrong."

"You were very brave," Helen sighed. Now that they were no longer going to Barcelona on their Cook's tour, she wouldn't have the opportunity to spend time with Juan, free of any supervision from her parents. Verity understood this and squeezed her friend's hand and changed the subject.

"We've got to make sure we look like tourists while we are here," Verity reminded Helen whilst reaching for their guidebook.

"Blow that! The most important thing is to agree where we are going next."

The strain of the last few days was beginning to tell on Verity, the planning and execution of picking up the mysterious package had been followed by a volatile mixture of terror and attraction after running into Moreno. Then she had had to plan and carry out their escape. She had to assume that every policeman they came across, and soldiers too, were primed to look out for them, or with luck, her and her aunt. At one point on the way from Madrid the train had made an unscheduled stop, and soldiers had come through the train. She took her cue from other passengers and had simply looked at them with hostile eyes. They had walked on past - she would never know whether they were looking for her or someone else. Having reached their first goal of Cordoba, her mind was now so full that it was difficult to concentrate on the current problems, but focus she must.

"We'll stick to my plan and catch the trains we selected and finally take the night sleeper train to Algeciras and the ferry to Gibraltar."

"With all these changes of clothes, I don't think I'll know who on earth I am by the end of the day or what name to answer to!" said Helen.

Verity grinned, "Nor will I!"

In Madrid, Moreno had worked his way through all the options open to him and concluded that if he caught up with Verity it would be professional suicide for him, even if he found the package on her or that dratted aunt of hers. It would have to come out that she was Verity Fleming, the very girl whom he had persuaded General Franco to list as a spy. How then could he possibly explain his taking her out last night and introducing her to the General himself under a false name? Whatever glib explanation he could come up with he would at the least be finished as a high flyer in his career and sent ignominiously to some far away outpost to serve out his time. At the other end of the scale he could find himself implicated in the General's mind in some fiendish communist plot and summarily tried and executed.

He resolved to continue with what he now knew to be a futile search of diplomatic bags and a special watch at Spain's borders for anyone acting suspiciously. He had after all arrested the man who had planted the package and had all the credit for that operation. If possible he would foist responsibility for the border watch on to some other department so that the failure to find the package would be all theirs. He acted swiftly to implement this plan and took no steps to try and trace Verity since he was too afraid of succeeding in that task. Had the girls only known, they could have carried on with their original package tour: as it was, they wound their sinuous way out of the country, finishing as supposed Scottish tourists on their passage home from Gibraltar.

It was a strange relationship between Verity and Moreno, much stronger now for the bonds between them. Moreno now knew for sure that she was a spy, and a dangerous one at that, but he was absolutely sure that they would meet again somewhere, sometime, and that would be the real test for both of them.

Verity knew too that they were not finished with one another yet. She had enjoyed his company, his charm and even his physical attraction, but she was going to try very hard not to let any part of her mind dwell on him for the moment.

16

Mr Jones had clearly been delighted with the contents of the package which Verity had delivered to him. Verity hadn't given him a completely full account of events in Madrid, as she didn't think it necessary for him to know about her relationship with Major Moreno. Strangest of all, Constance had asked few questions about the trip to Spain, accepting what Verity told her about places visited without asking for any details other than those volunteered. However, Constance had noted the new maturity and confidence in her niece but could only guess at its source. After Spain it was back to the law and a new start in London. Bernard had left the new solicitors' firm in Ruislip telling Verity that it just wasn't the same any more. He had obtained a place as a junior clerk in a Chancery Lane firm, the centre of legal London. The rate of pay was better in London than in Ruislip and he was able to pay for his train fares and still give his mother a bit extra towards the household expenses. He had prospects with this firm. His new employers subsidised his evening classes as they were anxious that he get on well, and the key to this was education.

Now that Verity lived more or less permanently with her aunt, she worried at first about what her aunt would really think about sharing the flat, when she had always lived such an independent existence. But Connie, as she now preferred to be called, had told Verity it was something she had often dreamed of, like having a daughter of her own, and that now the dream had come true.

Verity found it a real pleasure to come home to someone with whom she could discuss everything, well almost everything.

One of the many advantages of London life had been seeing a lot more of Helen. They had become very close during their shared experiences in Spain. Sometimes Helen was able to get a pass from Matron to stay overnight with Verity at the Bloomsbury flat. They went to concerts at the Albert Hall and to films where they saw Fred Astaire and Ginger Rogers in their latest film, "Top Hat", and the Busby Berkeley "Gold Digger" films, which had them dancing all the way home. Helen in turn took Verity to some of the many dances to which nurses were invited.

As Helen put it, "Ready-made grateful partners for men who can't dance."

Above all, the girls talked, argued and encouraged one another through difficult times. Helen had found the hospital rules exceedingly irksome and at times had been near to giving up, in spite of her love of the job. Verity provided an outlet for Helen to talk it all through before going back to the hospital and she always felt better for it. Helen also found the exams worrying; in hospital life so much hung on exam results.

In due time, Helen passed each set of exams and wondered afterwards why she had worried so much. She still corresponded each week with Juan, in love with the idea of being in love with him, but after all this time, not quite sure whether she could even remember what his face looked like. But she waited avidly for each weekly letter to arrive from Spain and, if a letter was delayed in the post, imagined that the worst had happened to him.

Verity and Felipe were still exchanging letters occasionally and these provided an insight into their totally different ways of life. Perhaps because they were just pen friends, their letters flowed more freely and were passed amongst their wider friends for interest. Bernard read all Felipe's letters avidly, as did Helen. Helen for her part no longer passed Juan's letters to Verity to read, but instead read her extracts. She was afraid of being thought foolish if Verity had read the flowery compliments to Helen's beauty and person. She felt faintly embarrassed when she read them herself, let alone show them to anyone else. The girls had agreed after their trip to Spain to say nothing of it to Juan and Felipe in their letters.

It did not take long for Verity to begin to flourish in the small Fleet Street office she had joined. The firm acted as London Agents for many out-of-town solicitors and their function was to issue proceedings in the Courts and carry out all the preliminary stages of proceedings. This meant visiting all the different departments of the High Court to issue Writs and Summonses. If no defence had been filed by the defendant, it was Verity's job to enter judgement against them and then issue a Writ of Fieri Facias directed to the Sheriff to seize the defendant's goods in settlement of the claim. As their out-of-town principals inevitably sent them the wrong forms or wrong instructions altogether, Verity's task was to sort the mess out herself and progress the action to its conclusion.

As Verity was the only woman carrying out this task at the High Court on a regular basis, she found that the Court clerks were much more helpful to her than to her male counterparts. She got to know the clerks and their hopes and aspirations for themselves and their families and she always asked after their wives and sweethearts. The unmarried tended to exchange saucy banter with her and Verity soon learned to give as good as she got. Because she had willing help at Court, she attained a much higher success rate with the agency work than the firm had previously enjoyed and this was good for business.

Verity learned a tremendous amount about litigation and how to conduct it successfully. Most of this she gained by watching successful lawyers in action. She loved the Courts. A visitor entering the magnificent High Court buildings in the Strand came first to the lofty great hall off which there were stone corridors leading to the court rooms. Exploring further, there were miles of corridors containing the judges' and masters' chambers. The next building along the Strand contained the administrative hub and, to save going out into the street and in again, there was a linking corridor which was not easy to find. Because of the slope of the site on which the Courts were built, if you walked from the front to the back of the building, you were on a different level by the time you tried to exit from the back entrance. Verity thought it would be an easier building in which to escape a pursuer than the Prado, or for that matter Ibiza town. All of it was built of stone although the courtrooms were panelled with wood. The whole court building was a tribute to the Victorian vision of how justice should be dispensed, with magnificence and grandeur coming well above comfort and ease of use.

Verity's favourite place was the Bear Garden, a large wood-panelled hall with long refectory tables ranged along the walls, with well-thumbed copies of the thousand or so pages of the Rules of Court, otherwise known as "the White Book". They were there for solicitors and barristers to consult, with inkwells and scratchy pens for their use as they perched on the uncomfortable benches. This was the place where barristers met up with their instructing solicitors, and paired up with the lawyers on the other side of cases in which they were appearing before the duty Master, a species of minor judge who dealt with the hearing of summonses and made decisions on all the early stages of court proceedings.

As the Courts operated on the principle that the Judge's or Master's time was more valuable than anyone else's, summonses before the duty Master all tended to be listed for 10 o'clock. This meant that first thing in the morning the Bear Garden was a heaving mass of lawyers and Court clerks, all bellowing the name of their cases in the hope of meeting up with the other parties.

Lawyers paired off, clients not generally being involved at this stage of proceedings. Those left without a partner would keep calling out the name of their case in the hope of finding the other lawyer on their case. It was often solicitors' clerks who did the summonses so you could never be sure who you were looking for. The Court Clerk, looking for the next pair of protagonists to go before a Master, would shout the name of the case over the hubbub in the hope of finding a pair of adversaries.

Verity was very wary the first time she did a summons. Hers was before the duty Master who held court in a room packed with lawyers whose cases were all listed for 10 o'clock. The pair of the moment would go and stand before his desk and then have to argue their point before an expert audience. Verity had rehearsed to herself exactly what she had to say but was then thrown by the Master looking up from his desk and peering at her over the top of his half-rimmed spectacles saying, "Well?"

It was like being in a play where you had learned your lines but no one else had. She stumbled her way through her prepared speech and immediately the Master picked up on the flaw in her case which she had tried to gloss over. For a moment she was speechless and then she heard a voice hissing from behind her, "Tell him it's Rule 44A and he has to allow it." She repeated this like a parrot. Her opposite number came in with a counter argument and the voice behind her prompted, "He has to allow your request because of the effect of the recent judgement in Dibbins v Hobbs." Verity repeated this remembering to add "Master" at the end of her speech.

The Master looked up again, "You certainly know your White book Miss er, Miss Fleming, it's a pity some of your colleagues don't follow your example and read the

Rules before they come to see me. Order given as asked."

With that the Master moved on to the next case and Verity found herself outside the room without having identified her unseen saviour. The opposing solicitor who, before the summons, had been patronisingly offensive to Verity as a woman, now looked cross.

"You might have warned me you were going to quote Dibbins v Hobbs to the old boy and given me a chance to gem up on it – I'd never even heard of it."

"Sorry, I assumed you'd be up to date with the latest cases in the field," Verity said to him sweetly.

"Hrrmph," was the only reply she got as the man turned on his heels and swept off.

Back at the office, they were delighted at her winning on the summons, only now admitting that she had been sent on this one because it seemed so hopeless that they thought she could not make it any worse than it was. Her reputation in the office shot up accordingly.

Verity and Bernard sometimes met up for lunch in one of the cafés in the back streets around the Courts, establishments inevitably patronised mostly by lawyers' clerks. They used the time to catch up on news. Bernard now had a girlfriend, Gloria, who worked in another office in the same building as him. Sometimes Verity would catch sight of them in the lunch hour, holding hands as they walked in Lincoln's Inn Fields. She had been introduced to Gloria and was delighted for Bernard that he had found someone who clearly looked up to him and admired him. Bernard, at nearly eighteen, had shot up in height and now sported a small moustache. Verity supposed that either this was a tribute to the latest matinee idol, or was intended to make him look older, or both. It actually made him look very young.

Felipe sat gazing at his drawing board. He was working on a design for a new centrepiece for one of the larger squares in the city. All the people of Barcelona had suffered a great disappointment when a decision had been taken by the organisers of the 1936 Olympics to shift the competition from Barcelona to Munich because of Spain's internal troubles. The vast Olympic stadium had already been built and lay empty, and the disappointment amongst the public was great. They had looked forward to showing off their beautiful city to the world and now there would be no visitors, no excitement. There was a sense of anticlimax which the local Government was attempting to combat with new public projects for the residents rather than visitors. The new centrepiece for a prominent square was one of these projects.

Felipe's design was innovative and pleasing to the eye, even his Principal agreed that it was a remarkable design and, unbeknown to Felipe, was considering entering it for an important architectural competition. If Felipe's design won or received commendations from the world famous judges, his future would be assured. Things were looking good for Felipe.

But things in Barcelona were not looking good. There was a general unease that seeped down the narrow streets and passageways and into the houses infecting everything and everyone in its path. Neighbours looked over their shoulders at neighbours and stopped trusting one another. An outspoken opinion given too freely could all too easily land the speaker in jail. Young activists from the Left and the Right clashed on the streets. Disillusioned with other parties, more and more young men joined the Falange whose Terror Squads reigned on the streets.

How can you defeat mindless violence? Debate as they might, Felipe and his friends could see no end to the spiral. It seemed that the message was: join the struggle or you will be obliterated, oppose the struggle and still be obliterated. All that Felipe could do was to concentrate on his work, which gave him both pleasure and satisfaction; he was determined to leave his architectural mark on the city.

He still wrote to Verity once a month and tried to write about his life and career in an uplifting way. Much of his pleasure in his present project came over in his letters but he could not prevent the dark side of Barcelona life from creeping into his account of daily life too. One or two of his circle had joined the Falange and were revelling in it. Felipe shuddered to think of this.

He knew the pattern; they would meet up at one of the Falangist meeting places where an orator would harangue them and demand to know whether they were going to allow 'the Reds' to take over Spain. Were they going to permit their birthright to be taken away from them? Were they that lily-livered that they would stand by and do nothing? Who were the intellectuals of Spain? Was it not they who had to think for the masses, and if so, why did they not act immediately to eradicate the bourgeoisie whose aims were to destroy Spain and hand it over to the Reds? By the time the Falange poured out on to the streets they were drunk, not with liquor but with blood lust to see how many 'Reds' they could eliminate that night.

It was not only violence but the sheer pointlessness of their brutality which was the hallmark of the Falange. He understood that middle-class young men joined parties such as the Falange because they felt under threat from the workers. In some parts the workers had been burning churches and the houses of the rich landowners. But for every act of destruction, there were massive reprisals by the Falangists and other right-wingers who saw such acts as being communist motivated. Communism was seen as the great threat by anyone with money. With lawlessness growing every day it was difficult for anyone witnessing street violence to say who were the aggressors and who the victims.

In Barcelona, Felipe and Juan were startled one night to see flames shooting up into the night sky; it looked like a fire a few streets away. They had run to see what was happening and found that a church had been set on fire, flames already shooting through the roof. As they watched, the roof fell in with a great crack as the main beams gave way and the whole weight of the tiles slid into the gigantic bonfire.

A fat priest was shrieking and wringing his hands whilst the mob laughed at him and shouted insults. Things were beginning to look ugly for the priest until someone led him away to safety before he could become a victim like his church. The crowd noted that whilst they themselves were always thin and malnourished, priests were often fat and bejewelled and clearly lived off the fat of the land. Fat parasites were no longer to be tolerated.

The flames lit the Church windows which exploded in the fierce heat of the fire within. Felipe saw that nearby shops were being looted and their contents thrown on the gigantic bonfire. As they watched, beautiful antiques along with rough everyday furniture were all being used to fuel the flames. No-one in the crowd dared to intervene for fear of drawing the attention of the mob to themselves, a risk none of them dared take. Felipe felt ashamed as he turned away, ash settling on his clothes which already reeked of smoke. He was beginning to feel that in this city, which he had been proud to make his home, nowhere felt safe any more.

It was a couple of weeks later that Felipe had arranged to meet Jaime, his doctor friend, in a favourite bar one evening. Jaime arrived first. Felipe, whose lodgings were almost opposite the bar, was finishing off a design and wanted to just complete the draft before joining him. The bar was popular with many students, particularly medical students, and was generally crowded. Felipe had promised to meet Jaime at around 8.30 p.m. When Jaime entered the bar he looked round to see whether Felipe was there yet and, finding he was not, briefly thought of going across the road and hauling him away from his drawing board. Then another medical student greeted him and by the time he had exchanged greetings with him, hunger got the better of him. He ordered some tapas and wine. Felipe would be along soon enough, and clutching a glass Jaime joined some fellow students, joking with them about the days events at the hospital where, however serious the work, funny things always happened and became exaggerated in the telling of the story.

Dealing with life and death each day, they had to release the tension somehow and they enjoyed their leisure time in whatever way the could. Jaime was tired, it had been a long and exhausting day at the hospital, fighting to save the life of an elderly patient who at times had seemed determined to die but had finally been persuaded to live. Jaime had left him tucked up in bed, breathing in a regular fashion and sleeping peacefully. Tomorrow he hoped to see him sitting up in bed and taking nourishment. Work had its own rewards on such occasions.

One of the students in the group was a good mimic and soon had the others laughing as he imitated one of the more outrageous professors at the hospital. They were still laughing when the glass in the window beside them exploded as a brick hurtled through, hitting one of the students directly on the head. They automatically ducked as shards of glass from the window showered over them, but the brick was followed by a burst of machine gun fire, sprayed through the gaping window in an arc. There was no time for anyone in the bar to realise what was happening. Mirrors shattered, bottles and glasses broke in a cacophony made up of bullets, breaking glass and shouts. Then there was silence, the more ominous because there should have been groans from the injured and dying, but nothing broke the silence. The Falange had silently withdrawn, melting away down the maze of passageways.

Felipe had rushed to his window at the sound of the machine gun and seen the killers spraying bullets round the bar. There had been two bursts from the machine gun, then the killers had gone. Felipe ran down his stairs two at a time, falling down some of them in his rush. He crossed to the door of the bar and gingerly pushed it open. It was partially obstructed on the other side by a body. There were probably only twelve people inside but the place seemed filled with bodies and blood. It was the silence which was the most ominous thing as he picked his way among them, turning over bodies to see whether they were familiar faces. Many of them were.

At last he found Jaime, his eyes wide open and a row of bullet holes across his chest. He was quite dead, with those injuries it would have been impossible for him to have survived. Felipe held him and wept, for Jaime, for himself, for Spain.

17

Verity was completing the purchase of a house in the Bayswater Road area for a client. Normally, the formal completion of the purchase would take place at the office of the seller's solicitor. She, as the purchaser's solicitor, would examine the deeds against something called an Abstract of Title and then, if everything was in order, hand over a banker's draft for the sale price. In return she would receive the conveyance duly signed by the seller together with the deeds and that would complete the transaction, apart from the seller's solicitor handing over an authorisation to the estate agent to release the keys to the purchaser.

Today Verity was dealing with an extremely old-fashioned solicitor who stipulated that the purchase price must be paid in cash, so Verity had received an authority from her firm to collect £500 from their bank. The bank clerk, a polite young man, had been extremely alarmed to find that Verity was proposing to travel on the London underground with £500 in her handbag and had suggested that she ought to use a taxi and had offered to call her one. Verity let him call the taxi. Whilst she was unlikely to be reimbursed the taxi fare, if she walked back to the office from Bayswater, saving the Underground fare, she would not be too much out of pocket.

Unusually, the seller's solicitor had stipulated that completion would take place not in his office, but at the property being sold. Verity gave the address of the house to the taxi driver who sped off almost before she had closed the door. She deduced that the driver was almost at the end of his shift since he seemed in a terrible hurry, screeching round corners and just beating the traffic lights whenever he could, whilst managing to keep up a tirade against the Government's foreign policy of appeasement. Verity was grateful when he finally braked to an abrupt halt outside a terrace house.

"That's it, the one with the brown door," he said as Verity jumped out and paid him. She turned round to see which one he was indicating and the taxi sped off down the road, the driver having omitted to hand over any change at all.

All the houses in the terrace had brown doors, but Verity soon spotted a brass number plate in need of cleaning on which she could still discern the number '38'. She walked up the steps and rang the doorbell.

The door was eventually opened by a gentleman in a wing collar. Verity explained who she was and the gentleman, who finally admitted to being the seller's solicitor, looked at her disapprovingly and set off down the entrance hall and up a flight of stairs with a speed she would not have thought him capable of. Verity followed on his heels, afraid of losing him. She noted that the house seemed to be stripped of all its furniture, carpets and curtains already.

He rounded a corner and dived through a doorway and Verity, following him, was surprised and apologetic to find that she had followed him into the bathroom. But before she could withdraw in confusion, she saw that the bathroom was already occupied by a man and a woman, both in outdoor coats and perched on the edge of the bath.

"Sit down," he said waving his hand towards the bath. Verity perched on the edge alongside the man and the woman. Verity fervently hoped that she hadn't strayed into some kind of strange ritual or orgy by accident. The solicitor sat on the closed seat of the toilet and picking up his briefcase opened it and removed bundles of papers.

"As all the furniture has gone there is nowhere to sit or rest our papers, but I thought we would be most comfortable in here where the hot water tank provides some heat and there is at least somewhere to sit."

Verity supposed he had a point.

"This is my client," he said, indicating the woman whose drooping face was almost entirely hidden by a large drooping brown hat.

"How do you do," Verity said, unable to offer her hand because she was by now holding all the deeds which had been passed to her for checking.

"I expect you have already met your client," he said indicating the pinched-looking man who had withdrawn into the astrakhan collar of his overcoat.

"No, we haven't met before but I am pleased to meet you," Verity said smiling at him.

"I don't know what the firm has come to sending a secretary, a mere chit of a girl, on such an important matter as my purchase," he said, ignoring her.

"I must say I thought it irregular at the least, they could have sent their managing clerk."

"If you don't mind," said Verity calmly, "I can understand your concern but I am in fact a qualified solicitor. I'll be formally admitted to the Roll of Solicitors next week."

"Congratulations! I do apologise, my dear, a natural mistake, no discourtesy was intended," said the solicitor. "But I don't think I have ever met a lady solicitor before."

No such apology was forthcoming from her client.

Verity spread the deeds over the bathroom floor and knelt down to check them against the Abstract of Title. She felt one of her stockings ladder as she did so. It was very cold kneeling on the bathroom floor but she was not going to be hurried in this important task. She worked methodically through the deeds, marking up the Abstract as she went. At last she straightened up. The solicitor looked quite incongruous sitting on the toilet but at least he must be more comfortable than the others sitting on the edge of the bath.

Verity handed over the £500 and received the conveyance in return.

"Shall we date it with today's date?" she asked.

"What other date would you put in it for goodness sake?" responded her client. "I have never known anyone take so long over anything!" he continued.

Verity was fortunately saved from further ill-informed comment by the solicitor rising from his temporary throne and taking her arm to guide her out.

"Don't take any notice of a man like that," he said. "Very ill bred. How he found the money to purchase the house I cannot imagine and would rather not ask. I will tell your principal that you did a fine job."

Verity did not care for either the ignorant comments of her client or the patronage of the other solicitor, considering both to be equally inappropriate. Perhaps she had better anticipate more of both as she made her way in the profession and devise strategies for dealing with them. She was thinking about this as she turned into the Bayswater Road, glad to get her circulation going again after that long session kneeling on the cold floor.

A large motor showroom caught her eye. Perhaps it might be time to get a little car of her own, she mused. Then she saw it - actually she could hardly miss it as it was given pride of place in the centre of the window. A small plane in a beautiful shade of powder blue, its gossamer wings shimmering in the sunlight.

Verity stopped, entranced, it was love at first sight. It was the most perfect thing she had ever seen.

A salesman standing just inside the door opened it and came out to her.

"Why don't you come inside and have a look at 'Mirabelle', Madam, it's far too cold to stand outside."

"Mirabelle?"

"Our little plane - she's a beauty, isn't she?" he said holding the door open for her.

Verity thought that it was probably the first time she had been addressed as 'Madam' rather than 'Miss', and it made a pleasant change to be treated like an adult, especially after her experiences at the completion.

"Mirabelle is the latest model of Gipsy Moth. We are the London Agents for De Havilland, the manufacturers. You will see," he said, thrusting a brochure at her, "that the wings fold up for easy transportation. You can quite easily keep her in a garage or barn. Would you like to sit in her?"

He helped Verity up on to the wing and into the cockpit.

"It is a real plane? I never imagined that a plane could be so small. But it really does fly?"

"Oh yes, Madam. It is a fully functioning plane and Moths have been flown by Alan Cobham, Francis Chichester and Jim Mollison." He reached for a book of press cuttings and put it on a table where she could examine it.

A genuine plane it appeared to be. Even the famous Amy Johnson had apparently owned one.

The salesman had brought her a tray of tea with some biscuits. She read all the details and asked about how the wings folded for travel by road. He promptly demonstrated how to pack up the plane. Next she quizzed him about what kind of pilot's licence was needed for such a plane and he gave her all the details. It would cost £150 to buy the plane and there were a few extras which it might be worth ordering at the same time, such as an extra fuel storage tank. It could be delivered very quickly as they had just received new stocks and all that would be needed was to fit the extras.

Verity had fallen for the lovely little plane and walked back to the office in a dream. She could afford it, she decided. At the age of 21, the money which her mother had left her had become her own to do what she liked with, even though she could not access her father's legacy. She had not needed to touch it so far, but now she could dip into it without the need to ask anyone's permission. That night after dinner she showed

Connie the brochures and explained all about the plane.

"I am going to buy one and learn to fly," she announced. Connie noted the decisive tone of Verity's voice and decided that any views about the frailty of such an aircraft, and how dangerous it might be, would not be welcome. Furthermore, if anyone could fly such a thing, it was likely to be Verity. It was just the sort of thing she herself would have liked to do when she was Verity's age.

"Would you like me to go with you to the showroom on Saturday?" Connie enquired.

"Super! Thanks so much for not voicing lots of dreary objections!" said Verity flinging her arms round Connie in an affectionate hug.

On Saturday Verity bought her plane from the nice salesman who had brought her tea and biscuits earlier in the week. Connie had been looking round the showroom whilst Verity was signing the necessary paperwork. When Verity had finished she went to find Connie and found her shaking hands with an older salesman.

"It will be ready for collection next week," he said. Thanking him, Connie took Verity's arm and emerging into the street hailed a taxi.

"What will be ready next week?" Verity queried.

"They are going to telephone when the plane is ready for me. They said they could deliver it direct to Heston Airfield if that would be easier."

"That will probably be the most convenient thing as you won't want to tow it until you get used to your car."

"My car?"

"I thought it was about time you had a car of your own. I know you can drive and I particularly wanted you to have a special present to mark your being admitted as a solicitor, so I've bought you a Hillman Minx Saloon. I know you would have probably preferred a sports car but I selfishly thought a saloon car would be best, since I hope to be riding in it quite a bit. I'm getting too old for sports cars, so difficult to preserve decorum whilst getting in and out of them, never mind getting so wind-blown all the time."

Verity knocked Connie's hat to quite a rakish angle as she hugged her.

Richard and Molly now had a small daughter, Lucy. She seemed to Richard to cry an awful lot and whenever Richard went near her she seemed to be in need of having her nappy changed, a task which the nursery maid was supposed to attend to. Molly seemed to have lost interest in Lucy as soon as she was born. Molly appeared to like the act of getting pregnant, but found being pregnant boring and had absolutely no interest in the end product. She had already made Richard sell their first house and buy another larger one so that there was room for a nursery maid to live in.

In fact the whole business of being Molly's husband and earning enough money for their expensive lifestyle left him permanently exhausted. He felt that if only he could see Verity now and then he would find life less exhausting. He had not heard anything of her for nearly a year now, did not even know for sure where she was, and there seemed to be no way he could find out.

They were circling over Heston aerodrome for yet another 'touch and go' landing. "Now this time," the instructor yelled through the headphones from the rear cockpit, "think of her as a flying tricycle, but with the single wheel at the rear, so position her to land lightly on the front two wheels first, otherwise she will overbalance. Then gently allow the rear wheel to settle. Remember, continue flying her down until you think you are going to smash into the runway, then off with the power!"

Verity's landings so far had not been smooth and tended to have the plane bouncing down the runway like a mechanised kangaroo. She had tried hard to follow her instructor's directions but could not fathom what it was that she was doing wrong.

Verity concentrated on getting the two-seater trainer lined up with the runway, keeping the wings straight and level and watching her speed. The runway came up to meet her, she held her nerve and only at the last minute did she take off the throttle and gently land the 'tricycle'.

"I've got it," she shouted over the intercom.

"Great! Now on with the power and away we go again," came the voice over the headphones.

Verity did what seemed endless circuits of the airfield that afternoon and, by the time they had parked the plane, she knew she had grasped the most difficult thing in flying, how to land the plane safely: it was so exhilarating! She had sat through many hours of classroom tuition learning the rudiments of how a plane flies and the dynamics of flight. She had also had to learn about plane engines as it had been drummed into her that it was the responsibility of the pilot, not the mechanic, to make sure the plane was airworthy before each flight. It did not matter that the flying school plane had just been flown in by another pilot, she must perform all the outside checks on the plane first, looking for damage, checking the fuel and inspecting the engine to ensure that nothing had gone into the engine which might have obstructed or damaged it during the previous flight. Then it was time to start the engine and run the cockpit checks following the checklist provided for the plane, taxi to the holding point and perform the final checks before manoeuvring on to the runway when clearance had been given by the control tower.

At each stage she had to rely on her own judgement to see that everything was within the correct tolerances. She knew that if she had the slightest doubt about anything, she must abort the take-off, but, with someone watching all the time, she had a strong feeling of not wanting to look a fool in front of others.

Take-offs had been easy so long as she could keep the plane on a straight course down the runway. This meant combating both the effect of any side wind and the natural tendency of the plane to try to go in any direction other than that which the pilot wanted. It was still something of a miracle to Verity that you could point a plane down the runway, for all the world like a straight Roman road, get the plane up to a certain speed, haul back on the joystick and it took off. An automobile never took off when you did the same thing. Verity felt that by rights the plane should have reeled up and flipped over on its back, but thankfully it didn't. The sweet natured training plane simply took to the air.

It felt glorious up in the sky, flying over the English countryside, learning to use all the landmarks on the ground to navigate, just like a gigantic map spread out before her. Rivers and railways were the easiest to navigate by, and if you could find a railway line and did not know where you were, you could always fly along the line until you came to a railway station, read the station sign and pinpoint it on the map in the cockpit.

Verity loved it. It might be a miserable day on the ground but once she penetrated the layer of cloud she was free to play in the sun and the sky. She hoped that soon her instructor might allow her to go up in Mirabelle for some of the solo cross country flights which she had to undertake before she could pass her pilot's licence. Her instructor had already flown Mirabelle to check out the plane and whether it had any unusual characteristics before he would even consider letting her loose in it by herself.

As he said, "You've got to think of the poor souls living an earth-bound life beneath you. It wouldn't do to go crashing into their chimney pots, would it!"

Jimmy, her instructor, spent his weekdays teaching air cadets to fly and his weekends instructing private pupils such as Verity. He did not seem to have any home life as far as she could see. Too tall to fit comfortably into the cockpit, he was also lean, probably because of all the meals he missed while flying. Some instructors had flown in the Great War but Jimmy, now in his early thirties, was too young for this, a source of great regret to him. Verity was beginning to discover that there were many like him at airfields all over the country whose lives revolved round aeroplanes and flying and they were not all pilots.

There were those who could afford both lessons and their own planes, some of them with wonderful aircraft. Then there were those who desperately wanted to be able to fly and saved like mad to afford a lesson once a month. Not all of them were men - there were several women learning. Some people, mostly youngish men, hung about round the airfield doing voluntary jobs so as to earn a flight or a lesson without money changing hands. Some just liked to watch the planes. All these were in addition to people who actually worked at the airfield. There were mechanics who serviced the planes, fitters, ground staff who looked after the runways, both the tarmac and grass strips, instructors, control tower staff and finally the pilots who flew for a living. Heston was only a small aerodrome but it seemed to have a large shifting community centred on it.

Amy Johnson sometimes flew from Heston, as did her husband Jim Mollison. Verity had been amazed when Amy had appeared beside her in the hangar when Verity was checking Mirabelle over.

"Yours?" Amy said.

"Yes," said Verity, "but I haven't been able to fly her yet - I'm still working at my licence."

"Keep at it. You'll find the freedom wonderful and she's a dear little plane and such fun to fly."

Verity was thrilled with this seal of approval for her Mirabelle. She felt honoured that this heroine of so many long distance flights should talk to her as though she was really a fellow pilot.

She took a couple of photos of Amy and her husband standing by Amy's latest plane, Seafarer, Amy wearing a light cloche hat and not looking in the least like an aviator.

Jim Mollison was not popular with the Heston crowd, unlike his wife. He seemed to think that most of the people around the aerodrome were his inferiors and unworthy of notice; there were also rumours of his drinking.

Verity had been formally admitted to the Roll of Solicitors in a ceremony at the Law Society Hall in London. It had all been very grand and formal and she had bought a new hat and suit for the occasion. She was allowed to take two guests and Connie and Helen, like Verity herself, had been impressed with the grandeur of the Law Society's Hall. The ladies' powder room was arranged with so many complimentary bottles of scent that it was hard to resist trying them all, but Verity and Helen finally settled, like giggling school girls, for trying one scent each. It was on a high note that they emerged into Chancery Lane for Verity to begin her legal career.

Her firm said that they would be happy to offer Verity a partnership as they were pleased with her work and ready to expand the firm. She was gratified by their offer and indeed it was an honour that they were prepared to offer a woman a partnership but she was not sure whether that was what she wanted. Because of this she suggested that it might be in everyone's interest if she served six months as a qualified solicitor working in the firm before giving a response. They agreed to this, although a little reluctantly, as they wanted to start on their plans for expansion.

At last it was time for Verity to do her solo cross-country flight in Mirabelle. It was to be the qualifying cross-country flight for her pilot's licence. She had already flown solo in the trainer on a number of occasions, now she was just waiting for the right weather. For the flight, she was to fly first to Croydon airfield, report to the tower there, obtain clearance for the next leg of her flight and fly on to Eastleigh Aerodrome, then back to Heston. Verity had already warned her office that as soon as the right weather conditions came along she would need to take a day off work without being able to give them prior notice. The partners agreed but solemnly asked her to be careful as they didn't want anything to happen to her, especially now they hoped she would soon become a partner. Verity was touched by their concern and assured them that she would be as careful as it was possible to be in the circumstances. She wondered what her father would have thought of her learning to fly. Somehow she did not think he would have approved and it was probably a blessing that he would never know of the turn which her life had taken. She did miss him though.

Jimmy rang her at 6 a.m. one morning. "Today's the day. Get yourself into that car of yours and report here as soon as possible."

Verity had all her flying clothes laid out; she had been ready for this day for at least two weeks as cold fronts had come and gone but not left that all-important good spell in between. She knew that, whatever the ground temperature, it was going to be very cold up in the sky in Mirabelle. She looked in on Connie before she left. Connie had heard the telephone ring and had guessed that this was Verity's big day. Connie was very nervous about the whole venture but managed to give Verity the impression of being cool and calm.

"Good luck and happy landings!" she said smiling.

The sky was clear as Verity arrived at the aerodrome in her smart little car. She was feeling very nervous and somewhat sick. She had not been able to face the thought of breakfast before she left home and was extremely tense as she went to check the details of the flight. She refused the tea that Jimmy offered and went with him to the hangar to get the plane out. They pushed it out easily between them, and Verity performed the outside checks on the plane and then strapped herself in. 'In' was a bit of an exaggeration, Verity thought, as she could hardly be more exposed to the elements.

Verity was wearing a warm flying suit that was far too warm on the ground, sheepskin-lined boots, a leather helmet, goggles and a silk scarf round her neck ready to pull up over the exposed part of her face.

Jimmy shouted at her, "Check that your helmet is firmly fastened before you put your gloves on; you must protect yourself against the cold at all costs." She gave him the thumbs up and then shouted, "Prop!" and started the engine. It positively purred at her, she did her engine checks and then taxied to the holding point for the runway. The Control Tower gave her the signal and she taxied on to the runway, gave the engine full power and was up and away.

Jimmy had suggested flying at about 5,000 feet for most of the journey to give herself better visibility. It felt pretty strange to be up here in the sky, all by herself without anyone to talk to. She had an instant of panic when she looked down at the ground, but the feeling went as quickly as it had come and she settled to navigating across London. She had no difficulty in locating Croydon and circled over the airfield to look for the signals area indicating the active runway and clearance to land. As soon as she had clearance, she flew a tight circuit and put Mirabelle down neatly on the runway, taxied to a halt, turned the plane and taxied to the parking area. It felt good to be safely on the ground again.

She reported to the tower, paid the landing fee, checked the weather forecast again for the next leg of the flight and this time accepted a cup of tea. Then it was back down to Mirabelle to carry out the checks again and start the engine. Shortly she was airborne and on her way to Eastleigh. Once in the air she wished that she had not had the tea, but it was too late for that. She concentrated on looking for the unfamiliar landmarks which she had charted to see her through this leg of the flight.

There was some cloud, but very high, so there was no difficulty in staying in sight of the ground. There had not been many planes in the air so far. She was keeping a look-out since Jimmy had warned her that if you assumed there was no one else about, that was just the time when you bumped into the only other plane in the sky with a pilot who also assumed that there was no one else about.

She became conscious that the note of the engine had changed. She listened carefully. It seemed to be running rough. Probably dirt in the fuel, she thought, but she went on listening carefully. She also looked more carefully at the landscape below in case she had to make an emergency landing. Now what was it Jimmy had said? In choosing a field, look for signs as to which way the wind is blowing. Land into wind, otherwise it will lengthen the distance you need for landing, look for a pasture field, but search for any telegraph poles which might indicate wires across the field.

There was a lot to think about, keeping on track, maintaining height, keeping a lookout, listening to the engine note and looking for a suitable place to land if necessary. Perhaps it would be a good idea to lose some height, even though it would reduce her view of the countryside. Verity took Mirabelle down to 1,000 feet. After flying at this height for a few minutes, Verity realised that the engine beat sounded smooth again and breathed a sigh of relief. She took the plane up gradually to 3,000 feet, checked the map and adjusted her course for Eastleigh. Ten minutes later she spotted what looked like an airfield. The plane seemed to take forever to come overhead, but from the layout of the field it had to be Eastleigh Aerodrome. Verity joined the circuit and flew over the signals area to confirm the active runway and on her second circuit landed smoothly and reduced speed.

Verity found on leaving the plane that her hands were shaking and she felt sick again. She reported to the control tower and asked if there was a mechanic available to check the plane. The young man in the tower was lounging back in his chair, balancing it on two legs.

"Okey dokey!" He picked up the telephone. "Myrtle, can you find George and tell him there is a damsel in distress here. Her steed is parked on the apron and was running rough on the way here. Get him to sort it, will you?" He replaced the receiver.

"Do take a pew. I'll see this next one in and then make you a cup of refreshing tea."

"That's very kind but if you can just tell me where the WC is first, then I'd better go and meet George."

"Over there," he said with a wave of his hand, "but I can tell you from here when George puts in an appearance, so please keep me company in the meantime."

By the time Verity had returned, a steaming mug of tea awaited her. She tasted it and found that it had been liberally laced with sugar.

"Hot sweet tea is good for shock!" said the controller. "And I deduce you had a bit of a difficult run down here, so shock treatment is in order. I can see George is still finishing off a job by the hangar, so sit down and put your feet up: relaxation is in order." He placed one chair for her to sit on and insisted that she put her feet up on another, whilst he chatted on non-stop about all manner of inconsequential things.

Verity finished her tea and stood up.

"Ah! That's better, you've got more colour now," commented the Controller.

"Thank you so much," said Verity.

"All part of the service, Ma'am. Come back for an up-to-date weather forecast before you go – there's a cold front due shortly."

Verity ran down the steps from the tower feeling much better. A wizened figure in incredibly oily blue overalls had already removed the cowling from the engine and was peering into its depths. Verity heard him tut-tutting as she approached. Verity introduced herself and explained the problem.

"I thought it might be dirt in the fuel," she said.

George made no comment but continued to tut-tut, interspersed with teeth sucking noises. Then he straightened up and began fumbling in his pocket. Verity thought he was looking for a spanner, but instead he produced a battered packet of Du Maurier cigarettes and some matches, extracted a cigarette and lit it.

"How far have you come in this?" he said disparagingly. "You wouldn't get me up in one of these things. A flying coffin, that's what this is!" He seemed to be warming to his theme and was punctuating his speech with puffs on his cigarettes, which seemed preferable to the teeth sucking, although Verity worried about the wisdom of his letting hot ash fall into the engine.

"What do you think is wrong?" she asked.

"Can't say yet, can I, with you breathing down my neck!"

"I'll..." Verity said backing away. She did not finish the sentence but since George took no notice there did not appear to be much point in addressing his bent back. Verity saw that he was reaching for yet another cigarette and fervently hoped he was more competent than he seemed. She returned to join her new friend in the tower. He was busy, so she quietly resumed her former seat and studied the map again for the return journey. After that, she read all the notices on the board and was wondering what to do next when George stumped into the room, the smell of oil preceding him.

"Ain't nothing wrong with that plane, waste of time if you asks me." With that he thrust a dirty piece of paper at Verity and banged out again.

Verity saw that she was holding a bill for his services.

"Do I pay this now?" she asked the controller.

"If you've got the money on you, you pay me, otherwise you can send the money on."

Verity rose fumbling for her purse.

"Hang on," he said. "We can't send you off into the sky without finding out what was wrong. Describe to me what happened."

Verity explained it all in detail.

"So the engine was running rough and coughing and spluttering at five thousand feet?"

"Yes."

"The trouble gradually disappeared when you came down lower?"

"Yes, just when I was thinking of an emergency landing."

"Carburettor icing. It can happen even on a summer's day if you are flying high enough for the temperature to be below freezing. When you bring the plane down where it is warmer, the icing disappears - that's why George couldn't find anything. Can be fatal though if you let it develop. I don't know why George couldn't tell you that, he must have known what it was."

"I think he disapproved of both me and Mirabelle," said Verity. "Thank you so much. I'd better be on my way now."

"You can't go for at least an hour. See those dark clouds over there? They'll be with us shortly and with them rain and wind. Shouldn't last long. You can use the telephone in the pilot's room to ring through to your home field to advise them of the delay and I am sure they'll be able to rustle up a sandwich for you - pilots are always hungry."

Verity started to thank him but he brushed her thanks aside.

Verity went and phoned Jimmy who was relieved to hear from her but managed not to burden her with more advice at this stage.

The flight back was uneventful and not as cold as it had been earlier, although the wind was still chilling to Verity, if not to the engine. Well, she would watch out for carburettor icing in future and know how to deal with it. Verity landed smoothly at Heston, taxied off the runway and down to the parking space outside the hangar. It was over, the most difficult part of her pilot's licence; no other cross-country flight was ever likely to be as scary again, it was goodbye to butterflies in her stomach. She turned the engine off and prised herself out of the plane. She had hoped that Jimmy might have been there to greet her but he was probably busy with other pupils.

She had nearly pushed Mirabelle back into its place in the hangar when she looked up and saw not only Jimmy but Connie heading towards her, both beaming. Jimmy was holding a bottle of champagne and Connie some glasses.

They sat on upturned crates and toasted the successful completion of Verity's qualifying cross-country flight. With her flight test and written examinations already behind her, this was it. She had passed her licence.

"But this is only the beginning," said Jimmy. "Now you've got all the usual nerves out of the way and can find your way back to the airfield by yourself, you can start to really learn how to fly. You need to be able to fly in all sorts of weather, in as many different types of plane as you can. Then you will be able to get yourself safely anywhere within the range of your fuel limits. Anyway, duty calls. See you on Saturday morning as usual."

Connie had come on the train so they were able to drive back home together.

"I've been here for absolutely ages," she explained. "I've met some charming people. Jimmy wanted to take me up for a short flight, but I told him I wasn't really dressed for it. He insisted upon my looking at his plane and telling me all about it, but I'm afraid a lot of it went over my head."

Connie was dressed in the height of fashion in a tailored linen suit and flower-decked hat. There was no way that any sensible man could have imagined her climbing into a plane, but she still had that effect on men of all ages.

"I'm so glad you came; what a lovely surprise. I was feeling a bit deflated and then you appeared like magic and lifted me up again. I was terribly nervous this morning, you know."

"So was I, but I hope I hid it just as well as you did! I'm really proud of you," she said linking her arm through Verity's as they walked back to the car.

18

Helen and Verity were sitting in a Lyons Corner House, Helen applying butter and jam lavishly to the large plate of toast in front of her, whilst Verity watched.

"I always seem to be hungry these days. It's not that they don't feed us at the hospital, but being on my feet all day doing heavy work, I use it all up very quickly," said Helen apologetically.

Verity poured some more tea. They had been catching up on the past few weeks' events, having not met for a month. Verity had been too busy getting her pilot's licence to have time for anything other than flying and work. Helen had just taken her second set of nursing exams and would shortly be starting on the last year of her training. Living at the nurses' home, there was not much opportunity to meet people of her own age unless they were sick. So the nurses' dances and going out with Verity were the extent of her social world at the moment. Perhaps because of this, her letters from Juan were an important part of her life. They had been drawn to one another on first meeting and distance had only enhanced their romance. Neither had met anyone else to whom they had been remotely attracted in the intervening two years and each was by now certain of their love for the other.

Helen's weeks revolved round the arrival of Juan's letters, which usually ran to around six pages and Helen read and re-read each one many times over. They generally arrived at the nursing home on a Thursday, and Helen would rush through the last jobs on her shift in order to get back to the home, as quickly as possible, to collect her letter. This did not always work, because Sister seemed to have a sixth sense for when Helen was anxious to be away promptly and found lots of little tasks with which to detain her. On the occasions when the expected letter was not waiting in her pigeonhole, she would go through agonies. Had anything happened to him? Was he ill, or worse? Had he ceased to love her and did not know how to tell her so?

Helen regularly tormented herself with all of these thoughts until her fears were abated by the arrival of the delayed letter. On one occasion, his letter had arrived but the Senior Nurse in the nurses' home had forgotten to sort and distribute them. When she finally handed Helen her letter over supper the next day, she had said, "Very sorry old thing. I'm afraid I put the letters in my apron pocket and clean forgot them. Hope your letter wasn't urgent!" The other nurses at the supper table allowed themselves a titter over this, knowing how anxious Helen had been about the absence of her weekly letter.

Even worse was the teasing of some of the nurses who were jealous of this seemingly exotic romance. "Romeo, Romeo, wherefore art thou Romeo," they would chorus when she walked in, wiping imaginary tears from their eyes. Then some wag would cry out in a sepulchre voice "I'm over here!" Ruder suggestions would inevitably follow.

With Verity, Helen could let herself go and talk about everything that really mattered in her life. As they talked, Verity's eye was caught by a familiar figure across the room. It was Bernard with his young lady, Gloria. Verity waved and they came across.

Bernard was looking smart in a suit appropriate to his status as a junior clerk. Gloria looked awed by the company and held on very tightly to Bernard's arm.

"Gloria and I are just going to have a bite of supper before I go off to the Party meeting," he explained.

"Bite of supper," echoed Gloria.

"She doesn't come with me to meetings - there aren't many women members and she gets bored."

"Not many women, bored," said Gloria nodding.

Verity had never heard Gloria volunteer any direct conversation of her own. She noticed that Bernard tended to wait for Gloria to catch up.

"Does your firm know that you are a party member?"

"Party member," repeated Gloria nodding.

"Wouldn't they mind if they knew about your political activities?" Verity continued, but found herself waiting for Gloria's echo. This time it did not come - perhaps she had lost the thread already.

"Oh no. All cell members have to keep their membership secret until the time comes," Bernard replied.

Thank goodness for that, thought Verity. It would be a shame if Bernard were to lose his job because he had been misled into joining the Communist Party, just when he's beginning to make good. Bernard and Gloria moved on to a table at the back of the room to which the waitress had been impatiently gesturing them for some minutes.

Helen eyed him, "He's growing up, isn't he. He's quite the young man now and has lost that delivery boy look."

"I don't know what you mean," said Verity, ever protective of her protégé.

"Well, for a start his hair doesn't stand on end any more, he's learned to put grease on it and slick it back. And he's wearing a suit that fits him rather than someone's cast-off and he's more educated and more confident."

"I don't think he ever lacked confidence," said Verity, eyeing the table where Bernard was giving his order to the waitress.

"Anyway, what's this 'Party' business about? I take it he means the Communist Party?"

"Yes, Roberto first got him interested in workers' rights, then socialism, then communism, and he seems to have stuck with communism. I do hope he's not getting out of his depth."

"I don't think you need to worry about him, he can look after himself now. You know, I've been thinking," said Helen changing the subject.

"Yes?"

"If Civil War does break out in Spain, as Juan thinks it will, I shall offer my services as a nurse."

Verity's attention came back to Helen with jolt.

"Do you think that would be wise?"

"Wise? What has wise got to do with it? If people are being injured then I can help - that's what nurses are for. Juan says that they are very short of nurses in Barcelona."

"And if war doesn't break out?"

"Then I shall wait until I finish my training, go to Barcelona for a holiday and then, who knows? And what will you do?"

"I'll wait to see what Mr Jones has in mind for me."

"Bet he sends you back to Spain."

"I wouldn't be surprised, although I may be wearing out my welcome there. He might send me somewhere else like Abyssinia," she said, thinking about the recent conquest of Abyssinia by Mussolini's troops.

"We'll see." Helen reached for her purse, "Shall we pay half each?"

The Headlines of La Vanguardia and every other newspaper in Barcelona that morning proclaimed the rebellion of the Spanish Army stationed in Morocco against the Republican Government of Spain. Elsewhere there was an uprising of part of the army led by a number of prominent Generals. They shared a common belief that the country needed to be protected from the influx of communism which they thought was behind the massive upsurge in violence and lawlessness.

In Barcelona, the Plaza de Sant Jaime housed both the Generalitat, the seat of the Regional Government of Catalonia, and the Barcelona City Hall. The Generalitat was surrounded, as it had been ever since the news of the revolt, by assault guards whose function appeared to be to prevent the people storming the building to get at the arms which were reputed to be stored there. The plaza was packed with people, all looking to the balcony, waiting for Luis Companys, the President of the Region, to come out and address the people. If the army as a whole revolted, it was the mass of the people who would have to defend the Republican

Government against the army, and to do that the people needed arms for defence.

Juan and Felipe stood side by side in the square opposite the Generalitat with their backs to the City Hall. Felipe had been standing so long that he wondered whether he was really standing on his own two feet any longer or was simply being supported by the dense crowd around them. More and more people were trying to push their way into the square so that those who had been first to arrive were squashed so tightly there was no way they could leave until everyone else did.

The crowd were chanting for arms. They had been shouting for hours and by now were all hoarse, but still Luis Companys had not put in an appearance on the balcony.

"He's afraid," said Juan.

There were murmurs of agreement from around them.

"I'm sure he'll come out eventually. After all, if he doesn't give us weapons, how can he stand against the army?" said Felipe.

"I think the Government is more afraid of the mass of the people than it is of the army. If only we had some up to-date news! What's the point of putting up these loudspeakers everywhere and then telling us nothing?" Juan gestured to the speakers which had been erected on poles.

Juan continued, "We know the uprising has started already in some provinces. It's two days since news of the Revolt first came through and none of the army bases here has yet shown which side they are on. With all the suspense, I can't remember now when I last ate or slept." The state of his appearance confirmed this as his normally smart clothes were dusty and crumpled.

It was stiflingly hot in the square, a summer night with a clear sky, stars twinkling above them and not a whisper of a breeze coming off the sea. Being jammed in with the crowd made it that much worse, but no one was complaining. There they would all stay until they knew what was happening.

Just before 5 a.m. Luis Companys came out on to the balcony to a roar from the crowd. He did not speak but simply gestured to them to quieten down before disappearing back inside. The crowd hushed. Then the loudspeakers around the square crackled into life with the voice of Radio Barcelona.

"People of Barcelona, the troops from the Pedralbes base are advancing down the Diagonal towards us. Every man to his post!"

There was a moment's silence broken by a cacophony of ships' whistles and factory hooters, the agreed signal to tell the populace that danger was imminent. Now the whole city was alert.

The crowd in the plaza did not move. How were they to defend their city against the army without weapons?

What were the posts to which they had just been ordered? Who was to organise the defences?

The shouts for arms were renewed with vigour, the crowd surging towards the cordon of assault guards who raised their rifles to their shoulders and pointed them into the crowd. Those at the forefront of the crowd knew that they would be the first to die but did not flinch, there was nowhere for them to go. The noise grew to a crescendo as the assault guards backed up against the wall of the Generalitat, waiting for the order to fire.

But before the order could be given, one guard lowered his rifle and drew his pistol from his holster. Appearing to realise that this was a spare weapon, the guard handed it to the nearest man in the crowd. The neighbouring guards quickly followed this lead, the cordon dissolving as the guards handed out their weapons.

"To the barricades," came the cry, repeated through the square and echoing out into the surrounding streets. The crowd surged towards the Ramblas and, at last, all had something to do. They uprooted paving slabs, overturned carts and anything else to hand, to pile everything up to form two formidable barricades between which a command post was quickly established by the CNT-FAI defence committee.

Juan and Felipe found that it was the unions rather than the city or government officials who were organising the defence of the city against the army. The union leaders were detailing a group of men to go down into the sewers and another group to go down into the metro tunnels. The plan was to get a contingent of the citizenry to work their way behind the advancing troops to erect and man more barricades behind them to cut them off from their barracks. In the meantime, the opening shots of the battle could be heard.

Juan and Felipe joined the group going down into the metro tunnels, and no one challenged them. Neither of them had been lucky in obtaining a weapon, so a practical task like cutting off the advancing troops from retreat and reinforcements appealed to them. The trains had stopped running the day before along with the rest of the public transport system, a general strike having been declared. The men ran down the steps into the station, jumped on to the tracks and followed the leader into the tunnel in the direction of the Diagonal. It was not easy to run along the track because of the rough stones, the sleepers and the darkness, even when they managed not to bang into the rails. It had been past dawn when they had left the Ramblas, but it was pitch black in the tunnel. They could only make slow progress, their eyes gradually becoming accustomed to the darkness, but every time they emerged into a station, they had to re-accustom their eyes first to the light and then to the darkness of the tunnel all over again.

All around Felipe and Juan was the sound of boots echoing in the tunnel, with an occasional muffled curse as a man lost his footing and fell on to the track bed. It seemed an interminable way in the dark. Juan and Felipe were not quite sure where it was intended to emerge into the street but presumed that their leader had his instructions. Obviously they had to get well behind the advancing troops.

Now the tunnel was running close to the Diagonal and they could hear muffled gunfire and explosions. Felipe prayed that there would not be a direct hit on the tunnel while they were in it. The thought of being buried down here was not good.

Just when they thought this dark journey would never end, a hiss from the darkness ahead drew them up short. A shaft of light was released from a lantern and by it they could make out a metal ladder fastened to the wall of the tunnel.

"It's one of the emergency shafts, should come up just where we want. It will take two men to release the hatch. Hey, you two," he said indicating Juan and Felipe. "You get up there and feel for the catches that hold the cover in place and release them. Be careful, all our lives are at risk."

It was quite a climb up the shaft. The nearer they got to the top, the lighter it became. Felipe was in front, so when he reached the top he had to make room for Juan to come up beside him. In order to use both hands for the cover, Felipe took off his long leather belt and threaded it round a rung and the upright of the ladder before putting it back round his waist. Juan wound a leg round the ladder to hang on with. They hung out from the ladder as far as they could, to feel round the hatch for the catches. When they had located them, they found that they were massive but well oiled. The main difficulty was trying to reach them from the fixed ladder. Juan surmised that the maintenance gangs who normally used such shafts had special tools to enable them both to release the catches and lift the hatch cover. After a struggle, they had the cover free and they raised it a few inches, muscles straining, whilst Felipe looked out.

"I've only got a restricted view but all seems quiet. Shall we go for it?"

"Anything to get rid of this weight," Juan grunted.

"Ready? Lift!"

They lifted the cover up and to one side in one smooth move, but the cover clanged loudly as it hit the dusty street.

"Let's go, quick! Into that doorway!"

With this, Felipe popped out of the shaft and dived into a doorway. After a few seconds, Juan followed him. All was very quiet, unnaturally so. It was light and the street would normally have been coming to life by now, even though it was a Sunday, but the shutters on the houses remained firmly closed. Whether they were being watched from behind the shutters was another matter. They waited a minute which seemed like ten.

"I'll move up to the street corner to keep watch," Felipe said.

Juan nodded agreement and Felipe moved up the street in a fluid movement that placed him flat on the ground by the street corner. Felipe peered round into the next street from behind a pile of uncollected rubbish and then signalled Juan that it was clear. Juan, in the meantime, was signalling each man out of the shaft in turn. The group leader, who looked in the daylight to be a manual worker in his forties, came up beside Felipe. He was out of breath and puffing somewhat but still had a pistol in his hand and a rifle slung over his shoulder.

They took the next street at a crouching run, finally emerging onto the Diagonal.

"Set up the first barricades here," said the group leader indicating the intersection. "Concentrate on the barracks side in case they send for reinforcements. After that the opposite side, then fill in the remaining ones if there's time. We'll command all the adjoining streets from here."

Looking at the group of thirty or so men, Felipe saw that about half of them had rifles from those supplied by the assault guards. He hoped that they had some ammunition to go with them. It was clear that a troop of cavalry had already passed this way from the amount of horse dung on the roads. He was very glad to think that they had managed to get behind the advancing troops.

It was hard physical work levering up paving slabs with their bare hands. By the time the first barricade had risen to about three feet, Felipe's hands were raw and bleeding.

The group seemed to have increased in size: people who had hidden as the troops passed by, now emerged to help the resistance. Carts, packing cases, furniture and mattresses were dragged to the barricades. Nearby apartments had been broken into and anything usable brought out. Someone broke into a shop and handed out an assortment of tools to make their job easier. More men arrived armed with rifles - whether any of them knew how to use these weapons was another matter. The heat seemed worse than ever and in the distance there was the ominous rumbling of gunfire.

Juan wrinkled his nose in disgust as he saw a group of men dragging two dead horses up to fill a gap in the barricade.

Then one of the lookouts shouted, "They're coming!"

19

Scrambling for the safety of the barricades, Juan and Felipe tripped and fell in their haste to put something between themselves and the advancing troops. The union leader, Leon, had already positioned men on the rooftops and balconies on either side of the street to act as sharpshooters. Leon was a veteran of many street fights with the police during the revolutionary strikes of the last few years and was a wily tactician.

The oncoming soldiers were additional troops coming up at the double from the barracks. They came nearer and nearer to the barricades until the defenders could see the faces of the front soldiers quite clearly. The officer at the front had a large black moustache that hid most of his face; he and his men were bristling with weapons and had their bayonets fixed. Felipe, unarmed apart from a fragment of stone which he held ready to throw, found he was holding his breath waiting for the inevitable slaughter.

The first shots from the rooftop ripped through the air and took the soldiers completely by surprise as the front rank and the leading officer fell. The workers delegated as sharpshooters had decided between them to make up for their lack of expertise by holding their fire until they felt they could not miss their targets. It was not necessarily the best strategy, but on this occasion it worked because they had the element of surprise on their side.

The soldiers now faced a hail of fire from the barricade. Not only bullets, but stones and anything else that could be hurled at the troops. Much of it was wide of its mark but it gave an impressive and totally false impression of fire power. Leaderless, many of the troops took the prudent course and ran back the way they had come. Some dropped their weapons, holding up their hands in surrender as they realised they were caught in a trap from which escape would be difficult. Many were shot in the back as they turned to flee, the remainder were soon rounded up and their own guns trained on them. The weapons formed a useful addition to the resources of the growing group of defenders of the barricades.

The soldiers were herded into the cellar of a neighbouring building until Leon could find out what he was supposed to do with them. Some of the more militant workers were all for shooting them straight away but Leon maintained that, as they had surrendered, they were prisoners and should await trial by the proper authority. Felipe wondered who the proper authority was in these strange circumstances.

In the distance Juan could see that another barricade was being raised along the Diagonal, in the intersection with the Paseo de Gracia, the city centre. That might take some of the strain off their position: at least they were now unlikely to be attacked from behind. Glancing at his watch, he was amazed to see that it was still only eleven in the morning.

News was now reaching them of other battles around the city where the army had been defeated on the Plaza de Catalunya, the Calle Claris and on the quay at Plaza Palacio. It was rumoured that the longshoremen from La Barceloneta had captured some of the cannon from the Docks military base and were setting them up to fire on the army headquarters at the Capitania General. It was said that some soldiers were declaring for the Republic. The assault guards and the national republican guards were rumoured to be split about half each for the uprising and for the Republic.

A truck arrived with food and drink for the defenders and also brought news. There were cheers when they heard that General Goded, one of the generals named by the radio bulletin as leading the attempt to overthrow the Government, had been captured down at the Barcelona docks after landing from a seaplane.

The sailors on board the naval ships in harbour were said to have arrested or killed their officers who had tried to join the army uprising, and the ship's companies had now declared for the Government of the Republic.

Juan and Felipe sat with their backs against the barricade. They ate bread and sausage and thirstily drank beer. It was hot and there was no shelter from the sun at the barricades and that, lack of sleep and the strenuous activity of the morning, was making them drowsy. Every third man stood keeping lookout whilst the rest ate and dozed.

A rifle shot woke them suddenly. A man sitting nearby who had been in the act of biting a hunk of bread had fallen forward, blood gushing from his chest and soaking the bread in his hand. Another shot rang out and this second shot pinpointed the rifleman for them. Leon detailed four men to enter buildings along the side street from which the shots had come. They had insufficient ammunition to fire at the window of the building from which the rifleman had aimed as they had no clear view of him. But shots continued to ring out spasmodically from the window whenever a cautious head was raised above the barricade.

Then there was a thud and a scream and Felipe looked up in time to see the body of a man falling from the window into the street below. Felipe was not at first sure whether it was the body of the marksman or one of Leon's men, but next minute a general cheer went up, so he presumed that it was the marksman rather than a comrade who had been catapulted down into the street. More shots followed from inside the building, then another window was thrown up and three bodies were thrown down into the street by Leon's men.

"What's happening?" cried Felipe.

"They're clearing out snipers," said a man as he carefully loaded his rifle with some of their precious stock of ammunition.

"Vermin," he pronounced, spitting down the barrel of the rifle.

Sudden activity broke out in the surrounding buildings as those within decided that they had better show solidarity with the worker defenders of the city. Hastily made banners were hoisted from balconies declaring support for the Unions and the Government. There was a predominance of red material in the makeshift flags. Men sidled out of their homes to join those behind the barricades.

Leon and his men were contemptuous of those who had done nothing to defend their own neighbourhood but had watched from behind their shutters. He set them to work uprooting more paving stones to reinforce the barricades, supervised by two men with pistols.

Leon was becoming restless about what was happening elsewhere in the city. There had been the prolonged distant rumbling of gunfire but no news. He wanted to know what was going on but dared not leave his post.

"Here, you two," he said, summoning Felipe and Juan. "I want you to report to our headquarters at the barricade where you joined me. Tell them what has happened here and ask for any orders. I need to know where to send the prisoners and we need more weapons and ammunition. You have your union cards with you for identification?"

"No, Citizen Leon," said Juan.

"Comrade! Not Citizen. We are all comrades now."

Neither Juan nor Felipe had ever been a member of a union. Leon, however, assumed that any young men who had put their lives at risk in this way must be union members. He tore a couple of sheets from a notebook.

"Names?" he asked. They told him.

He scribbled out a pass for each stating that they were accredited members of the CNT and part of the defence guard at the barricade at the Diagonal and signed the passes.

"You'd better take a weapon each to make sure you get through." He gave one a rifle and the other a pistol with just a couple of cartridges for each.

"That's all I can spare. Make haste and return quickly."

They set off at a run but soon slowed down to a walking pace. It was too hot for running and they needed to move cautiously to make sure that they did not inadvertently come under fire. The streets which they knew so well had changed since they had ventured down into the Metro that morning. There was some damage from gunfire but a lot more damage had been done by the uprooting of anything that could be used for the barricades which had been thrown up at all strategic intersections.

Juan and Felipe marvelled that so much had been apparently achieved in such a short time by a mainly unarmed civilian population defending the city against its own army. The wonder of it was that, at the moment, it looked as though the resistance was being led by the CNT-FAI rather than by the Government of Catalonia. What exactly was happening? They were very anxious to find out.

Bodies were strewn in the streets through which they walked and the streets were empty. Either the dead had not yet been missed by their families or their relatives were afraid to come out and get them. Felipe noticed that some of the faces of the dead wore a surprised look, as well they might, he thought, for who could have foreseen what this sunny July day would hold. Felipe and Juan kept silent as they threaded their way through the streets. It was a new experience to have to stop at each street corner, peer cautiously into the next street and then make for a doorway before checking both behind and in front of them. They were assuming that it was only troops that they needed to avoid. If it was civilians too, they had no means of knowing friend from foe. They pressed on and made it back to the Ramblas on which crowds still thronged. They duly reported and were referred on to a nearby building which had become the temporary headquarters of the CNT-FAI defence commission.

They would never have gained entry if it had not been for their new passes. Having reported fully to a weary looking man behind a desk, who viewed them from heavily hooded eyes, they were told to wait for orders. Whilst they waited, they heard reports that a big struggle was now going on in the Plaza de Catalunya.

Then they were called forward to the desk again. "We shall take the army bases next. We need Leon to lead a party to force the Pedralbes base to surrender. Take with you the group of militiamen waiting outside."

"What about arms and ammunition?" asked Juan.

"Some of the militia have armed themselves. You will get all the arms you need when you take the base. That's all," he said, dismissing them.

It seemed to Juan and Felipe that this was the wrong way round, they would get all the arms they needed after taking the military base unarmed? The man called them back.

"The password is 'CNT' and I'd better put a stamp on those passes of yours, we may have to round up anyone who cannot produce their union or party pass. Avoid the area round the Carmelite monastery on the Diagonal; the remains of a cavalry regiment is holed up there."

Outside they found a motley crowd of men and women who were apparently now to be known as militiamen and militiawomen. Juan called out above the noise of the crowd.

"Pedralbes! Follow me!"

They did, forming into a lengthy column behind him. Felipe went along the column, detailing men and women with rifles to take on specific duties. A few had bristling ammunition belts and all were on a euphoric high with the triumphs of the day. Felipe picked up the news as he went along the column; it seemed truly remarkable when he considered what had been achieved so far in countering the military rebellion.

Borne along by the militant crowd, exhaustion was forgotten. This time they took a more direct route going by various barricades where they responded to the challenge of those defending the barricade with the password "CNT!" and passed on the news as they went. There seemed to be more people about now and the column swelled in size as they went along. By the time they got back to their own barricade and reported to Leon, there were several hundred 'militiamen and women' in the column. The militia squatted on the ground awaiting the order to proceed to the military base.

Leon, it appeared, had already been giving thought to what their next move might be and had a plan ready to implement. Leaving some of the older men to man the barricade, they advanced on the base.

Part of the plan was to make as much noise as possible in their advance. As there was no question of taking the base by surprise, they needed to sound like an unruly mob who would tear the place apart with their bare hands if necessary. Felipe thought that indeed it might be true. They would be totally unable to match the firepower of the defenders of the base. If the big guns were turned upon the crowd, they would all be massacred.

Leon had started the column chanting as they went along with much beating of makeshift drums. The chanting served to arouse the militia's level of aggression and they moved faster towards their target. As the column marched through the streets towards the base, it gathered more and more people until, finally, they surged into the plaza in front of the base and it was filled with what by then had become a bloodthirsty mob, yelling and shouting.

They were greeted by a volley of shots which had them instinctively ducking. The troops had wisely barricaded themselves in and were firing from windows and the top of the wall. The volleys became more ragged but Felipe, in the front rank, suddenly realised that the troops were deliberately firing over their heads.

"Come on," he shouted waving his pistol, and rushed for the gates. They uprooted benches from the plaza to use as battering rams. The hubbub was tremendous as they charged the gates time and time again. At last the gates gave way and the crowd burst into the barracks, trampling anyone who fell in the rush.

The sight that met them was that of officers being prodded towards them at pistol point by their men, who were waving anything white they could lay hands on. The troops were throwing down their arms into a pile in the courtyard, stripping off their caps and jackets, and merging into the crowd. The crowd fell upon the officers; Felipe knew that there was nothing he could do to save them. He grabbed at a soldier who was trying to merge into the crowd and demanded to know where the weapons and ammunition were kept. The soldier, who was terrified of the mob, was only too glad to lead Felipe away to where the keys were kept in the guardroom.

In order to get at the desk drawer where the keys were kept, Felipe had to step over the body of an officer who had clearly been shot by his own men.

"Which keys?" he demanded.

The soldier identified the various keys and Felipe scooped them up. "Where's the arsenal?"

The soldier, cringing before him, nodded and headed off down the corridors like a rabbit bolting for cover. Felipe kept up with him with difficulty and, at last, arrived at a massive locked door which would normally have been guarded.

"Open it."

The soldier took the keys which Felipe proffered, fumbling nervously as Felipe kept the pistol trained on him. At last the door swung inwards on well-oiled hinges.

"Inside," Felipe gestured with the pistol.

Now the man was even more frightened, thinking he was about to be shot.

"We were forced by our officers to fire on you. Citizen, spare me! Spare me!"

Felipe felt like kicking him but instead grabbed his arm and thrust him through the doorway. He needed to know that this was indeed the arsenal. It was.

"Get me two of the best rifles and plenty of ammunition," he said, bewildered by the racks of guns. By the time he had strapped on two ammunition belts, he felt like a brigand.

"These are repeating rifles, your honour," said his guide, "and I have placed a machine pistol and ammunition in this haversack for you."

Felipe strung the haversack over his neck. He could hardly walk for the weight of weaponry he was carrying. Whether he would ever use it he did not know but arms the people must have. The sound of the mob was coming closer. Felipe had hoped to arrange their own guard over the arsenal until Leon arrived to give orders about the distribution of arms. He realised the futility of this idea as he heard the approaching mob tearing down doors that were already unlocked in their thirst for destruction.

"We must get out of here," he said to his frightened guide.

"This way, your honour," said the man, scuttling ahead of him down another corridor, up some steps and out into the open again, to where it looked as though a fiesta was in progress.

Felipe turned to thank the man but he was already gone.

There was a big bonfire in the courtyard. Felipe wondered just what it was that the jubilant militia were burning. The stores of the base had obviously been raided as bottles of wine were being passed around. There was even a large group of militia men and women dancing the banned Catalan traditional dance, the Sardana. Two men were playing flutes to which the dancers solemnly circled.

Felipe found himself bemused. All day, they had been labouring, fighting and facing danger, they had seen much bloodshed and brutality with the Spanish Army apparently directed to fire on the Spanish people. People dying around them, ordinary people turned into militia, and then the people achieving the impossible feat of defeating a well-trained army to take the barracks. And now, a fiesta.

Felipe felt a hand on his shoulder as Juan joined him.

"It hardly seems possible, does it?" said Juan gesturing to where a large banner was being hung above the battered gates of the barracks. They moved out into the plaza and looked up at the banner. It read "Mikhail Bakunin Barracks" in large red letters painted on to white sheets which had been sewn together. Leon was obviously an anarchist as well as a resourceful man. This morning he had simply been a railwayman on the Metro. Now he was what exactly in this citizens army? A comrade colonel? He certainly deserved to be.

Felipe unloaded some of his spoils from the armoury on to his friend. Juan in turn passed his surplus rifle on to one of the other original comrades from their journey through the Metro tunnels that morning. They sat down and sorted out how to load their rifles and pistols. Neither had yet fired a shot in this whole busy day.

"We need to practise how to fire these things in case we have to use them," said Juan.

It was clear that others had the same thought from the sound of firing from one of the rear courtyards. They followed the sounds and found that some kind of spontaneous drilling with arms was in progress. A couple of men who had clearly been soldiers, but had now opted to become 'comrades', were shouting instructions to the new militia, getting them to load and fire at targets. The targets were the windows of the officers quarters which cracked and broke very satisfyingly when hit.

Juan and Felipe joined the group and fired their first rounds. They worried at first about using up precious ammunition until they noticed that the resourceful 'instructors' had boxes of spare ammunition by them and were handing out more as needed. By the time Juan and Felipe left, they were confident of how to load, aim and fire their weapons. Whether they could hit a moving target was another matter. But then neither of them had ever wanted to shoot anyone, it just seemed a necessary skill for survival on this hot July night.

They walked back first to 'their' barricade where a roster was being drawn up for mounting guard. Then, released from duty, they headed back to Felipe's rooms which were now in the building where he worked. After the bar massacre in which Jaime had died, Felipe had not wanted to stay in his previous lodgings and the architect for whom he worked had given him some rooms in the studio building he owned.

They dropped exhausted when they reached this quiet haven in a world which had gone mad. Even then, they had no desire to sleep. First, they had to make sense of what was happening. It worried them that it appeared that the Regional Government seemed to be no longer in control, although presumably it supported the National Government rather than the military uprising. When would the Government assert itself and restore law and order? Or was it already too late?

Felipe went in search of the much prized radio which his boss kept in his office. They plugged in an aerial wire and threw the wire out of the window to get the best signal. They sat close to it listening and did not have long to wait for an update from Radio Barcelona. It appeared that a central committee of anti-fascist militias was being formed as a result of a meeting called by the President with the CNT and FAI. With the regular army as the enemy, lots of private armies were forming, as they already knew. "The bourgeoisie," the Radio announced, "is also the enemy. Anyone who is not a comrade worker will be deemed to be supporting the enemy, unless they can prove otherwise."

Felipe and Juan could not follow how this strange twist of events had come about. In the morning they had set out to defend their country against the military uprising. Now it seemed as though, unbeknown to them, some kind of counter revolution was taking place. How long would the two of them be protected by the passes given to them as supposed members of the CNT when they really belonged to the now demeaned bourgeoisie? In Juan's case, he was actually a member of the land-owning aristocracy who were, according to the radio, now to lose their lands to the people, who would seize back what was rightfully theirs.

It was clear that the aristocracy were backing the military uprising but that many of the landowners and wealthy people had already fled from Barcelona. Indeed it seemed that Felipe's architect principal had already gone, a note addressed to Felipe indicated that he had left by boat for France, for what he described as 'a short holiday'.

It was true, many landowners had been too grasping and greedy for far too long. But when the people could apparently defeat the army in this way, without support from the Government which they had set out to defend, who was to stop them going on to resolve all their problems by this same force?

It was something which Juan and Felipe had not foreseen in all their endless philosophical and political discussions over the preceding years. They had always imagined themselves as standing alongside the workers, as they had today, but had never imagined that they themselves would become the enemy.

Juan started to speculate on how the situation might develop. "I know what we must do," he said.

Felipe waited to hear what solution his friend had come up with. He waited several minutes before realising that Juan had fallen asleep. He barely had time to wonder what idea Juan had thought of before he too had fallen asleep.

Outside in the street, the counter revolution of the people continued. By morning, communism in all its many guises had gripped the city, the very thing which the military uprising had sought to prevent. Communists, Anarchists, Trotskyists and Socialists, all supposedly united in the Popular Front but all fighting for their own brand of socialism. It seemed that the wealthy and the middle classes would not be safe in Barcelona for a long time to come.

20

Verity's office in Fleet Street was above a newspaper office and because of this she heard all the important news long before it appeared in the papers. The partners of Verity's firm liked to be ahead with the news and they served excellent coffee each morning to ensure that whichever of the reporters was in the newspaper office in the morning would come upstairs to the solicitors office at around eleven for a cup of coffee. They were never short of visitors from the newspaper who kept them up to date. On a quiet morning in Fleet Street the boardroom would sometimes fill to bursting point.

Mrs Pringle, the senior partner's secretary, presided over the ceremony. She had a special set of china which was kept for this ritual together with a large silver coffee pot. Mrs Pringle was a big lady with a hawk nose, silver grey hair and a large bosom. She always wore a double row of pearls which refused to hang in an orderly fashion over her ample chest, which meant she was always adjusting her pearls. For a few seconds they would rest in perfect symmetry before going awry again.

Verity had at first been somewhat terrified of Mrs Pringle's imposing presence.

"You're not afraid of Mrs P. are you?" asked the young reporters in amazement. "She's a sweetie." And Verity soon discovered that, in spite of the awesome exterior, Mrs P was indeed a sweetie.

Verity had been invited to join the morning coffee ritual once she qualified as a solicitor. They were very lively sessions of debate, occasionally on legal issues, but more often on the news of the day, which was often news that would never appear in the papers. There was, for example, an unwritten agreement amongst the newspaper proprietors not to print anything about the new King's growing involvement with the married Mrs Simpson - something to do with the proprietors' peerage prospects it was generally assumed. Verity, like everyone else, loved to hear the latest gossip and join in the speculation.

It was over Monday morning coffee in late July that Verity first heard the details of the military uprising in Spain from a young reporter, Henry. Mrs P. fussed round everyone, filling their coffee cups and handing round the home-made biscuits with which she sometimes spoiled them. Henry, his mouth full, was not easy to follow and Verity had to ask him to repeat it. He swallowed, choked a bit and, finally, was able to reply.

"The Spanish Army - they've revolted against their government. It doesn't seem to be over the whole country, but certainly in Morocco, Valencia, Seville, Zaragoza, Bilbao and, oh, lots of other army bases." He took another gulp of coffee, "These biscuits are very good Mrs P," he said, taking another.

"What about Barcelona?" asked Verity.

"What about Barcelona?" replied Henry irritatingly.

"Has the army revolted in Barcelona?"

"I don't know, old girl, can't remember," said Henry, stuffing the last of the biscuits into his mouth.

"Oh Henry! You must know."

"I think that Miss Fleming is trying to say that she particularly wants to know if her friends in Barcelona are safe," said Mrs P, refilling Henry's coffee cup.

"Oh sorry, I'm sure the wire did mention Barcelona, but I can't quite remember what it said. I'll check as soon as I get back to my desk and ring you through, shall I?" said Henry, anxious to make amends, not so much for Verity's sake as to keep in with Mrs P, who sometimes served divine shortbread to which he was particularly partial.

Verity had never mentioned to Mrs P. that she had friends in Barcelona, but she was one of those people who prided themselves on always knowing what was happening to those around her. Mrs P. also knew that there was a young solicitor's clerk from a neighbouring office who often hung around waiting for Verity. She had been much relieved to see that for these last few months the clerk often had a young lady on his arm when he called. The young lady seemed to Mrs P. to be not much more than a child, but she could see that the two youngsters were clearly attached to one another. It had put Mrs P.'s mind at rest.

From then on the reporters made sure that Verity received news of the struggle in Spain, almost as soon as they heard it themselves. The newspaper's political editor also added his contribution to the coffee debate from time to time, helping them all to make sense of events which did not even make sense to the immediate participants. The editor did not think much of idealism, communism or fascism, in fact he did not seem to have a good opinion of anyone as far as Verity could make out, least of all for the emerging leaders of the Nationalist cause in Spain.

"They've been duped," he proclaimed. "Duped into thinking that the communist threat was a lot greater than it was, the Popular Front Government was toothless but just about held the balance. Now look what's happened; Russia is backing the Spanish Communists and has gained a toehold in Spain. It's supplying them with the arms that their own Government would not let them have. The generals clearly thought they would quickly take over power but instead it will turn into a prolonged struggle and a bloody civil war. There's already news of atrocities on both sides but our esteemed proprietor has decreed that we and his other newspapers must only report barbarism on the Republican side."

"But why?" exclaimed Verity outraged.

"Dear child," he said waving his cigarette holder, "because he does not like those nasty socialists who form the elected Government of Spain. That's why."

"But he can't do that - it's censorship!"

"Censorship is what it would be if our own dear Government forbade the reporting of half the news. If a man owns a newspaper, it reports what the proprietor wants it to report. It represents only his views on life and the universe. It does not have to be 'fair', before you suggest that it ought to be," he added.

"I know," he continued, "how things really are. We have our reporters on both sides of the divide. But you will not read what I tell you in my paper or any other daily rag for that matter. It is a class struggle that can never be won," he continued as the coffee circulated and they hung on his words. "For one side to rule the country they must obliterate all the good folk who do not think the way they do - nothing else will do."

Even Mrs P. had stopped circulating with the coffee pot and was listening. Whilst it was good to know the real story behind the news, it filled them all with foreboding for the future of Spain, a country that none of them but Verity had ever visited.

Verity herself found there was no getting away from what the papers referred to as 'The Troubles in Spain.' At home, Connie was worried about the safety of Don César. She had not heard from him since the beginning of the uprising and fretted because she was powerless to do anything about it, she simply had to wait for news. Helen was frequently on the telephone to Verity asking for any news because she was worried about Juan. Bernard went to rabble-rousing meetings of his communist cell at which they were berated to take immediate but unspecified action.

Shortly Verity received one of her periodic calls from Mr Jones. He said that he had a business proposition to put to her which she took as code for another pending mission for the Department. Intrigued, she agreed to meeting him in Regent's Park at lunchtime.

Mr Jones was already sitting waiting for her by the lake when she arrived. A nanny was sitting by him encouraging a small child to throw bread for the ducks. He stood up as Verity approached, raised his hat to her but did not shake hands.

"Shall we walk?" he said, moving away from the nanny and excited little girl. "I hear that you have become a competent pilot."

Verity interrupted him, "Who told you that?"

"Jimmy, of course. He does some work for me now and then, and tells me you have great promise as a pilot. He says you have a natural instinct for it."

"Did he?" said Verity, so pleased at this unexpected praise from Jimmy that she forgot to be cross that Mr Jones had been checking up on her.

"To continue, I gather your Spanish is passable and you are acquainted with Don César de los Rios César - who could well be a key figure in the events of the next few months."

Verity was no longer surprised at his intimate knowledge of her life and friends. "What do you want?" she asked. "You mentioned some business when you rang me."

"The British Government won't take sides in this conflict in Spain. It will stay strictly neutral, but that does not mean that we have no interest in what goes on in Spain, as you already know. We've our own interests to protect and we'll protect those interests at all costs," he said grimly.

"Our Diplomatic Corps in Spain is watched all the time, it's impossible for them to go to certain places or to act freely. We're recruiting a team of resourceful people whom we may send in to Spain with specific tasks to perform, and you've already proved your worth in that respect. We may send agents in alone or with another member of the team - it's impossible to say at the moment. I want you standing by in case we need you." He stopped walking and turned to look at her. The look was both an appraisal and a question.

"What would be involved this time?"

"I can't say at present, because I don't know. I just need to ensure that you have all the necessary skills and then ask you to wait. If we do send you into Spain it would be dangerous for you, but I have no hesitation in saying that you would cope. You might be away a month or perhaps longer and it is likely to be soon. You have the Long Vacation coming up, so a little holiday ought not to cause any problems at your office, unless you had any other plans?"

Verity knew that he knew that she loved the adventure and was bound to say yes, whatever was involved, but it was nice to pretend that she had a choice in the matter. She and Connie had talked vaguely about taking a holiday but they had nothing planned, as she was sure Mr Jones knew already.

"There is no need to give any commitment now," he continued blithely. "What we would like you to do is some more flying training, instruments and night flying, that kind of thing."

"That's all very well, but there is the little matter of cost of the training," she said bluntly, "it's very expensive."

"We'd pay, of course. You might describe it as a 'Government Investment', much like the investment we make in training RAF Volunteer Reserve Pilots, just in case we might need them, or you. I'm sure you'll find it useful."

Verity gave him a sideways glance; the chance of some instrument and night flying training sounded a wonderful opportunity for her. "How soon?"

He looked at some ducks crossing the path just in front of them and sidestepped to avoid them. "If you'd arrange to have, say, the next three weeks off work, I'll fix up the flying training for you. You may discuss it with your aunt but with no one else."

With that he touched his hat to her and moved smoothly away leaving her stranded amongst a covey of mallards expecting to be fed.

He had known of course that the mention of additional flying training would hook her. Every pilot wants to go on with their training to enable them to fly further, with bigger and better planes, but the bugbear is always the cost of the training. To have it provided by the Government, without any commitment on her side, was the best lure he could offer. Verity decided to discuss it with Connie as soon as she got home that night.

Major Moreno stubbed out his cigarette as he surveyed the scene from the doorway of the villa which had become temporary headquarters to his unit in this sun-baked Andalucian town. They had had a difficult time with the uprising, having been garrisoned in one of the cities which did not support the Army's decision to take control from the Government. It had been a hard struggle, first to resist the opposition, and then to overcome it.

Many of the influential citizens throughout Spain had supported the Army, as had the Church Bishops and many of the clergy. Moreno did not have much time for the clergy himself; as far as he could see, they mostly lined their pockets at the expense of their parishioners, who could often ill afford the tithes which they dutifully paid to the Church. Not that he had much sympathy with the poor who, as far as he was concerned, got what they deserved. But the gross and careless indulgences of the clergy made him despise them. After all, when had he last seen a thin priest? Had he but known it, he was echoing the thoughts of many who supported the uprising with his views on the clergy.

Moreno's battalion had been ignominiously trapped in their fortress until relieved by the troops from a neighbouring garrison who had had a better reception. The battalion had then ruthlessly suppressed all opposition, disposing of all those prominent in the life of the town, whether they were proven opposers of the uprising or not. It was an example that was not lost on the town's population.

Citizens who had actively supported the army were appointed to govern the town, acting under the orders of a military governor. However, many citizens had taken the opportunity to 'inform' on their neighbours, alleging that they had been amongst those who had opposed the army intervention. Moreno's job was to interrogate the arrested citizens before their execution. Some he did not bother with as it was clear to him that their offence was simply to have a better house, or more land, or a better wife than those who informed on them. Whilst he did not trouble to interrogate them, they were shot in a ditch outside the town just like the others. For a ruthless man used to command, he found the willingness of ordinary men to betray their neighbours despicable. It confirmed his view that they were scum whose obliteration would be a matter of no importance. Moreno himself had his own loyalties to his Unit, his General and the Army.

Far away, he also had a mother whom he respected. He did not send home any part of his pay to support her, she had money of her own and would not have thanked him for patronising her. If he only visited her infrequently and did not even think of her very often, he knew she was proud of his achievements and always glad to see him. On a recent visit home, she had been questioning him about his marriage prospects in that irritating way that mothers have. He had found himself, much to his own surprise, telling her about a foreign girl with amazing violet eyes, whom he had met briefly in Ibiza and Madrid and whose image he could not erase from his memory.

Verity's image haunted him, with those clear, deep eyes and her independent spirit, and he often gazed at the simple drawing of her which he kept in his wallet. He had never met any other girl who was quite so elusive and alluring. He owed to her his posting to General Franco's staff for that important period in 1934, and that had led to further good postings and promotion to major for the duties he performed. Then there had been that night in Madrid last year when he had found her so bewitching. But was she or wasn't she a spy? Looking back he thought that she had brought him luck. If he ever met her again, well, who knew what might happen, it would be explosive, he knew that for sure, for one of them must triumph over the other and he was going to be the victor.

In the meantime he was looking out for a Spanish girl as a wife, with good looks and a spirited outlook. It had been made clear to him that a wife he must have if he was to rise further in his profession, it was a requirement of the job. He had looked for a suitable girl amongst the senior officers' daughters with whom he was now thrown socially, but he had not found the girl he was looking for yet. There was no hurry, there were the present troubles to deal with first.

Now he was awaiting orders from General Queipo de Llano as to his next assignment, rumoured to be a special one. There was so much waiting around in the army, the boredom of barrack room life, then waiting to see what the enemy might do, waiting for the command to attack, and endless days of waiting. He had no idea what assignment he might be given next. General Queipo de Llano was a strange man even in a mad world. He had taken to haranguing the population over the radio each evening, telling them what happened to the men who opposed the victorious army and, even more important, what happened to their families. The General spared no detail.

Did anyone listen to these tirades, Moreno wondered? He could not imagine why they would listen to the radio in order to be terrified. Moreno had found it was far more effective to move in, remove a few prominent citizens, and shoot them. The message would buzz round the town immediately. There was no understanding the complex ways of generals; as an officer all he could do was to carry out his orders implicitly, then he could not be in the wrong. In the meantime he eagerly awaited his next orders.

21

In Barcelona, in some ways normality had returned to the city. At any rate, if you read 'La Vanguardia' and other newspapers, it had. They showed pictures of families strolling where the fighting had been at its worst. The general strike was over, public transport was running again and some of the barricades had been cleared for the smoother running of the city transport system. But everywhere you looked, you saw citizens wearing the insignia of the militia, with men and women alike wearing caps and armbands to denote their allegiances and carrying all manner of weapons. Committees of this or that union had taken over the administration of much of the city. Anything you did on the orders of one committee was challenged by other committees, set up by rival unions or political parties.

So far no committee had tried to take over the architect's studio where Felipe and Juan were living.

Felipe thought that it could only be a matter of time before some union or other tried to commandeer the studio. Buildings and businesses were being requisitioned all the time and workers put in to run them.

Felipe came up with a plan to brick up the entrance to the building, which was in a dead-end passageway. They and their friends could gain access via the roof of a neighbouring building. They trundled the bricks and cement to the passageway in barrows borrowed from a building site that Felipe had been supervising, wearing workmen's overalls as a disguise. The skilled labour was provided by a workman who was indebted to Felipe for a past kindness. When the work was completed, the workman would be leaving Barcelona for his own distant village as he wanted to be able to protect his family and it was unlikely that he would return to the city for some time.

Felipe and Juan kept out of the way while the work was going on as they were known in the vicinity. Surrounded by office buildings, no one took any notice of the workmen bricking up the entrance. When they had finished, they took great care to 'age' their work so that it would be difficult for anyone unfamiliar with the area to say whether it had been done recently or a long time ago. They also stocked up on food in case they had to hide away for a while.

The temporary passes issued to them on that first day had served them well and were now covered in impressive stamps that made the original wording virtually unreadable, but they wondered how long these bits of paper would give them protection from the more violent aspects of the counter revolution. Juan and Felipe had started by giving their full support to the city defenders but as soon as the immediate threat to their own city was over, the militia had set about all the reforms of equalisation which were the backbone of communism.

Too late, the Regional President and the City Governor realised that they had lost control of both the city and Catalonia, not to the Army but to the unions who set about replacing everyone in any position of power with a union member. Many of these new appointees were good able men and women who discharged their duties well, some were not.

Arrests, incarceration and shootings were the order of the day. Had they but known it, life in the Republican and Nationalist held territories was much the same.

Felipe and Juan had witnessed the militia column led by Durruti, marching out of the city to go into battle to regain territory held by the army. It had been a splendid sight to see the column with banners waving and crowds gathered to wish them well and see them off. Both Felipe and Juan would have preferred to join the column, but having been designated as 'city defenders' they were not permitted to go.

After the column had left, they had visited one of their student friends who had been arrested, but nobody seemed to know on what charge. They took food and drink for him. The militia grudgingly produced the prisoner and they had been able to spend a quarter of an hour with him before he was taken way again. He told them he was being held in a small cell with twenty-three other men. There was no room to lie down at night and, whilst they were brought bread and water each day, there was no sanitation for the cell, just a communal bucket.

Juan promised to visit again the next day with more food and a clean shirt. But when Juan called at the prison the following evening after a day spent on his city defence duties, the guards checked their list and said there was no one of that name held prisoner there. Juan insisted that he had seen him there the day before. The guard holding the list waved it at him dismissively, "If the name's not on the list, he's probably been executed."

"What for?" asked Juan.

"How would I know? Now, out before we take you in to fill his place," said the guard and the others laughed and made a move to close in on him. Juan left; there was no sense in staying to argue things out with these louts. The offence of those arrested was mainly just being in the wrong place at the wrong time.

It was on his way back from this visit that Juan had come across another of the numerous sacked churches.

Outside the church was the most grotesque sight he had seen yet. Coffins stood propped against the wall, their lids prised off and contents open for all to see. Some of the older skeletons had crumbled and fallen forward on to the pavement where passers-by kicked them out of the way in passing. Such profanity made Juan feel sick right through. These hapless remains could just as well have been his forbears. He silently thanked God that his mother was well away from all this. Whilst his family home was in Ibiza, his widowed mother and his sister had been away for some months, on a long-planned visit to relatives in South America. Land and property he would never worry about, those who were dear to him were what mattered, that and his beloved country. Felipe's parents were in the diplomatic service and were on one of their tours of duty abroad. That meant that, for the moment, Juan and Felipe had only themselves to look after, so they could bide their time and watch and wait until the moment came, when they could achieve something worthwhile to put their adopted city back on a stable path.

Juan called into a few shops on the way home to buy provisions. He had agreed with Felipe that they would avoid the shops in the immediate vicinity of the studio where they were known. For safety's sake they wanted to give the impression that no one any longer lived at the studio, that it had been bricked up and was derelict, should anyone bother to think about it. When he finally slipped into the studio via the rooftops, he found that they had company.

"Juan, this is Professor Martinez from the University." Juan shook hands with the professor who looked in a sad way, with his clothes torn and dusty and several days' growth of beard.

Felipe continued, "The militia have orders for his arrest, they visited his home on Sunday to arrest him but, fortunately, he was out and someone tipped him off so he didn't go back. He's been in hiding since then. I saw him when I was on duty and brought him back here."

"Did anyone see you?" asked Juan anxiously.

"No, I sent the Professor on ahead up the stairs to the roof whilst I kept watch."

Juan breathed a sigh of relief. He had heard of Professor Martinez as a much respected scholar. "What about your family, Sir?" he asked.

"My wife and her sister are still at home, but I don't know how long they will be safe there," replied the professor. "I've no children."

Now was not the time to tell Felipe about what he had seen today, not with the professor already looking haggard and depressed. Instead, Juan produced the provisions and Felipe got out the wine and they sat down to eat.

Later, when the professor was sound asleep, they exchanged information and began planning. They had

no doubt that the life of the professor was in danger: there had been too many arrests and disappearance of the intelligentsia to doubt it. First, they would establish a means of communication with the professor's wife. Then they must somehow spirit the professor away out of the country.
Sitting in the darkened room they felt their spirits lift. The professor was a good man whom they were sure could be preserved to teach another generation of students. They had something worthwhile to do at last!

Verity started her advanced flying training the following week, joining a small class of RAF Volunteer Reserve pilots at Northolt aerodrome for intensive flying training. Her presence on the course appeared to cause no surprise to anyone, she was issued with a flying suit that made her indistinguishable from the other students but, whilst they slept in a dormitory, she slept in a room of her own in the officers' quarters, in a hut on the far side of the airfield.
The students laboured long hours to cover the theory and the practice of instrument or 'blind flying' as the instructors called it, because you relied entirely upon the various gauges and indicators, without looking to see what the world was doing outside the cockpit. They also practised lots of emergency landings and, worst of all, were introduced to night flying under a

series of unrelenting instructors who allowed no latitude for errors but insisted that they must do it right first time and every other time.

They covered the length and the breadth of the country, landing at airfields in Scotland, the Midlands, East Anglia and down on the South Coast. They also landed in many a farmer's field, on moors and in valleys. Once, Verity got into a field by side-slipping the plane in, and then found there was no room to take off again. Having phoned back to base from the farmhouse, she was given a splendid tea of freshly baked scones, home-made jam and clotted cream, by a friendly farmer's wife who thought Verity looked tired and anxious and could do with a square meal. A couple of engineers finally arrived with a truck, unbolted the wings of the Tiger Moth, stowed them, and then hitched the plane up behind the truck and towed it back to base. While the engineers were doing this, the Chief Instructor had come out in another plane and landed in an adjacent field to pick her up and fly back, so that she was back at base long before the engineers arrived with her Tiger Moth.

Verity was incredulous at the hours they flew. At first, the intense concentration while flying made her very tired. The instructors made it abundantly clear that they would keep them all flying until they dropped from exhaustion and, if they did drop from exhaustion, they would fail the course. This was an aspect that would have been missing in a civilian course, but at

Northolt Verity could see that it made sense. The RAF pilot must fly when he had to, whether he felt like it or not, because lives would depend on him. He must be able to fly accurately and safely at all times and so must she. Verity, like the other students, became adept at dropping asleep in a chair whenever she was able to sit down for ten minutes. When Verity looked at her logbook at the end of the first week and totalled up all her flying hours, she found to her surprise that she had now exceeded one hundred hours. She was becoming an experienced pilot able to make difficult flying decisions for herself as she rapidly acquired all the necessary skills.

The visits to other airfields were interesting. She particularly liked landing at Castle Bromwich near Birmingham, not only because she was always made welcome, but also because they did an excellent tea which braced her for the return flight. As it was the summer, the weather did not present too great a problem but there was always a risk of storms and they sometimes flew in marginal weather with an instructor to gain experience. They flew at dawn and they flew at night, which was the scariest of all.

One night she had gone to bed after the evening lecture had ended and at midnight there had been a loud knock on the door with the cry, "All students to report to the briefing room!"

Stumbling into her flying overalls, she found that they were to fly immediately. Some of the students had not even gone to bed when the call had gone round for them to get up. At least Verity had had an hour or so of sleep but her body was crying out for more. Alcohol was not actually prohibited for the students on the course, but two students who had gone out to a local pub were clearly the worse for wear. Whilst still able to stand up, there was no doubt that they were not fit to fly. The two were left behind when the others all went out to their planes that night, and they had gone by the morning having failed the course.

Verity was scared stiff when she took off into a moonless night with an instructor in the front cockpit, flares showing the direction of the runway. She watched the instruments carefully and found when she looked up that the contrast between the illuminated instrument panel and the dark sky meant that she was blinded. She turned down the panel light and tried to restore her night vision. It was not easy, but the lights of towns, whose shape she knew from the map, finally helped her to orientate and get on to the right track.

Landing at night was very difficult. The flares of the runway again tended to blind her and the instructor turned on the plane's landing lights to assist her judging where the ground was. He had insisted she keep a trickle of power on the engine instead of gliding in as normal. This made their descent much shallower and slower as she descended between the flares, took the power off and waited for the aircraft to sink, hauled back on the stick and then they were safely down.

One of the main joys in this strict regime of hard work was the planes. Verity not only flew the latest Tiger Moth variant but also the much faster Hawker Hind trainer, and the Avro 621 Tutor for acrobatics. These planes were wonderfully fast and responsive so that Verity felt she was now driving a sports car in the air. She learned not only from the instructors in the classroom and the cockpit, but also from her fellow students as they relaxed in the Mess and talked about their flying experiences, some of which were quite hair raising.

Coping with the unforeseen was what it was about. They were taught that, even if some of the systems on the plane failed whilst in flight or the plane lost a part in the air, the pilot could still get back to base safely if they used their brain and didn't panic. Sometimes, when they were up in the sky, Verity's instructor deliberately removed a fuse, or some other essential, and sat admiring the view whilst the plane started to dive towards the earth at a frightening speed, or failed to respond to the controls which Verity was handling. She learned to cope, whether the instruments and the flaps worked or not.

There was one incident on a Sunday morning which shook Verity briefly. She was walking over to her plane to do a solo cross-country flight when she saw one of the spectators behind the wire perimeter fence waving to her. The man was holding a child up and the child was waving too. Verity automatically waved back, and then recognised with a shock that it was Richard. It was not that surprising since Ruislip Manor was only a mile or two down the road, but how had he known she was there? It took a moment before Verity realised that Richard could not have recognised her, clad in flying overalls and helmet she looked just like all the other pilots, totally anonymous. He was simply there like any other father of a small child, amusing his offspring whilst the Sunday lunch was in preparation. It took Verity more than a few minutes to shake off the mixed emotions that flooded her mind when she recognised him. She hoped that he was happy. Would she ever have a normal family life like Richard, she wondered, but on the other hand did she want a life like that? Probably not.

"Are you going to start this bleeding thing or ain't you?" The voice of the mechanic waiting to swing the propeller brought her back to the present.

"Sorry, just a moment whilst I finish the cockpit checks - I won't keep you from your meal." She smiled at him, and somewhat mollified, he smiled back at her. She dismissed Richard from her mind and concentrated on the job in hand.

At the end of the second week, she took, and passed, her instrument and night flying tests. Verity went home exhausted to await orders from Mr Jones. She was as ready as she could be.

22

When Verity returned to the flat at the end of her training, what she craved most was a long soak in a hot bath, to ease all her aching muscles, followed by a long chat with Connie. It was not to be. To her surprise, Gloria was waiting for her in the sitting room, perched on the edge of a chair as though afraid to make any impression on the seat cushion.
"Gloria! How nice to see you," Verity said, hoping that she was not to have a detailed account of some squabble with Bernard. Gloria looked very distressed and, from her face, had spent some considerable time crying.
"You aunt has been so kind, so kind. She gave me some tea and said to wait here for you."
"Wait here for me?" said Verity hoping to move the conversation along. Where was Connie anyway?
"It's Bernard, you see," Gloria sobbed.

Verity sat down beside her on the sofa and held her hand which, had she but known it, was exactly what her aunt had done an hour or two ago, when Gloria had turned up at the front door in a distressed state.

"Tell me all about it. Bernard hasn't finished with you, has he?"

"No," wailed Gloria.

"Have you quarrelled or something?"

"No."

"You're not pregnant, are you?"

"No, not pregnant, not pregnant, no," sobbed the girl.

"Well, tell me all about it," said Verity, resigning herself to a long session.

"He's gone!"

"Gone?"

"Gone!"

Verity thought they were not going to progress much at this rate. "Gone where? Do stop crying, Gloria. I want to know what you mean. Take a few deep breaths, that's right, now tell me from the beginning."

The story, as it emerged, was not what Verity had expected. Bernard, inspired by the fanatics down at his Communist Party meetings, had set off to Spain to fight for the republicans as a volunteer. He had been told that, if he could make his way to Marseilles, he would be able to get a boat to Barcelona. Those encouraging him had managed to overlook the handicaps of his age and lack of military training. He had departed that morning by train and boat for France, en route to Spain.

Verity mustered what reassurance she could to calm the distraught girl whilst inwardly blaming herself for the whole thing. Bernard would never have met Roberto and been introduced to the Communist Party if it had not been for her. What had she got Bernard into? She found herself assuring Gloria that she would see what she could do, whilst knowing full well that there was nothing she could helpfully do.

It was pathetic to see how the girl was reassured by Verity's meaningless platitudes. But what else could she do, thought Verity. Bernard had gone, it was too late to put a stop to the scheme, on the grounds that he was too young. No one would be able to stop him now.

"You must write to him," she heard herself telling Gloria. "He'll be glad to get your letters." He had apparently given Gloria a forwarding address; Verity made a note of it.

Finally the girl went and Verity thankfully sank into an armchair to think things through. There was nothing she could do to help Gloria - Bernard had chosen his own course of action and would follow that through regardless. Whilst he was not officially an adult, there was no way you could call him a boy either, whatever the law might have to say about it. Verity had been affected by Gloria's wailing and sobbing into thinking of Bernard as a corpse on a battlefield. But given his lack of any military training, it was far more likely that he would be put to work in a clerical capacity than on the frontline, if the militia accepted him, that is. She told herself that the sooner she got up to date on the latest news, the better.

Verity looked at her watch. The reporters would still be in the Fleet Street office waiting for any last minute changes in stories before the presses rolled with the morning edition: she would have time to get down there and nab one of them to get the latest news from Spain. She was out of the flat and into a taxi within five minutes, tiredness forgotten.

The news was that volunteers were heading for Spain from all over Europe and even some from farther afield. Young men who identified with the Republican cause were determined to offer their services. Some headed for recruitment offices set up in London and Paris, others just started to make their way to Spain. Bernard was far from alone in his efforts to get to Spain in order to fight. The Republican cause was capturing the interest of people from all walks of life: former soldiers, university students and Communist Party members alike. Bernard would be in good company, so Verity stopped worrying about him.

Verity did not hear anything from Mr Jones during the week after her training finished. In the meantime she established that there was nothing she could do about Bernard being under age. In truth, she had not really wanted to get him recalled because it would be humiliating for him to leave as a would-be hero and then be recalled as too young for active service. But she had felt some kind of obligation to Gloria and reported back to her. If Verity expected more floods of tears, she was deceived. Gloria had received a cheerful note from Bernard to say that he had arrived safely at Marseilles and had joined a nice group of lads who were all intending to fight in Spain. Gloria had decided from this cheerful note that maybe Bernard would come back to her in the end. Verity fervently hoped that he would.

Helen was the next to bring some news at their lunch on Helen's day off. It appeared that an organisation called Spanish Medical Aid had been formed and had started sending ambulances and field hospital units to Spain to aid the Republicans. Most of the army doctors were on the Nationalist side and the Republicans were woefully short of doctors and nurses to help the injured. Helen had already signed up with Medical Aid to go out to Spain with the blessing of her own hospital. She was waiting to be told when her unit would be departing.

"We're entering Spain via Port Bou and then on to Barcelona before being directed to whatever part of the front needs our services," she said happily.

"Do your parents know yet?" asked Verity.

"Oh yes! They weren't too happy at first, but Mom and Pop have come round to it. But then they couldn't do anything else, could they?"

Verity supposed not, a bit like Gloria being unable to stop Bernard. "Will you have time to see them before you go?"

"No, but Matron said that I can do some time in the theatre before I go. She's been awfully decent about it and says she will have me back afterwards. Theatre training will be so useful for me. And the hospital staff have got together to donate money to pay for some equipment which I'm going to take out in the ambulance. Isn't that decent of them?"

"Does Juan know that you're going?" Verity said quizzically.

"I've written to him but he won't have had the letter yet."

Verity could imagine his reaction, joy mixed with apprehension for Helen's safety. But Helen herself looked so happy at the thought of seeing Juan again, and being of real use in her chosen role as a nurse, that her joy was infectious. Verity threw her arms around her and hugged her. "I'm so happy for you. You're doing what you really want to do. I'm proud of you."

Helen beamed and radiated goodwill. "What about you? I can't believe that you're going to let Bernard and me do all the work? Mr Jones is bound to have some important job for you."

"Well, I've got something in hand, but I'm waiting for instructions and not allowed to talk about it in the meantime."

"I thought so! It was so mysterious when I kept ringing you over the last few weeks, and you were never there, and your aunt avoided saying where you were or when you might be back. I did so want to talk things over with you and was beginning to think you might have eloped with some unknown mystery man and the next I'd know would be a postcard from Gretna Green!"

"I thought about it," said Verity flippantly, "but I've heard there are too many midges in Scotland at this time of year."

"Saving yourself for Roberto? Or perhaps Major Moreno?" Helen teased.

"That would be telling." In truth, Verity didn't know the answer and didn't want to think about it at the moment either.

Getting Professor Martinez out of Spain had been difficult but not impossible. They had first checked that a warrant had been issued for his arrest; indeed it had, for alleged crimes against the state. They found this quite ridiculous when he was a known supporter of the Republican cause. He was not however an anarchist, or a communist, or a member of any other party at a time when a party card was what mattered.

After discussion, Juan and Felipe decided they would have to get the professor out by either air or boat - there was no way they could risk the trains, which were overcrowded with much of the military traffic. They had no connections at the airfield so concentrated on a sea route out. Juan had been able to find out what ships were due into port by drinking at quayside bars with sailors. Next day he had gone back to the same bars and got into conversation with a Scottish skipper of a ship whose next port of call was Marseilles. Juan had done a deal with him.

Later they met up with the skipper and his two mates again at the bar by arrangement, along with the professor dressed in sailor's clothing. They loudly greeted the skipper and his mates like long lost friends, had some drinks and then all walked arm in arm through the harbour gates and back to the ship for more drinks with the skipper.

The militia at the gates did not ask for their passes to enter the quayside since they were clearly part of a party from a ship. After a suitable interval, Juan and another of their flat-mates had reeled off the ship and down the gangplank and away. Felipe left some time later, shortly before the ship was due to sail. Their plan was to confuse the militia about how many civilians had gone aboard the ship and how many had left. The skipper and his mates saw Felipe off the ship with loud farewells as they drew up the gangway and made ready to sail. The ship slipped its moorings and slid away as Felipe strolled through the harbour gates and melted away down the dark narrow streets.

The professor was safely out of Spain. His wife and sister left by train for Valencia next day to stay with friends until it was safe to return home.

Verity's problems were different, in fact the exact opposite: she was working out how to slip into Spain unnoticed. Mr Jones had been in touch, cryptic as always. She was to work out a route to fly herself and some cargo into Andalucía and there meet up with someone who was in hiding, but whom the British Government would rather like wafted from under the noses of the fascists in control of the area. Having met up with him she was to fly him out.

Mr Jones had seemed rather proud of the simplicity of the scheme. "That's all there is to it," he said.

"But why me?"

"Because, my dear, the British Government has signed a Treaty of Non-Intervention in the conflict in Spain. The Government will provide no arms or assistance to either side. But as you know, we still have our own interests to protect, and this 'Pedro' whom you will collect is very valuable cargo for us. It has to be someone unofficial who collects the cargo; if anything happens and you are captured," he said calmly, "the British Government will deny any involvement. The official line will be that you are simply a misguided

British lady with a misplaced passion for Spain. You will be quite on your own and you must understand that."

"Well, that's quite clear, I'm on my own. Are you expecting me to take my own plane too?"

"No, I have arranged for you to borrow a suitable plane from its civilian owner. It's a specially adapted Gipsy Moth, carrying extra fuel tanks and the best navigation equipment available."

"And the cargo?"

"None on the way out, other than a few supplies. You'll have to refuel on the way and we can't risk any inquisitive customs officer finding anything untoward. You will need to take some weapons of your own choosing, just in case you run into trouble. Up to you where you stow them."

They were strolling round the lake in Regent's Park whilst they talked, the water shimmering in the heat of the day. Verity was wearing a straw hat and a light cotton frock and Mr Jones was in his dark city suit with bowler and umbrella. It seemed as always an incongruous conversation to be having with him. He never asked whether she would agree to go - it was already a foregone conclusion that she would.

"Your rendezvous is timed for three days from now. The plane will be at Croydon waiting for you first thing tomorrow. Its owner will be available if you would like to do a familiarisation flight with him. He'll introduce you to a civilian pilot who can help you with your flight plan and weather forecasts and the like. A survival kit will also be in the plane for you."

"Well, I hope to goodness I don't need to catch and skin a rabbit again," said Verity wrinkling her nose at the memory of her survival training at Brimscombe.

"It is entirely up to you what you catch or kill," he said calmly. "The report I received was that you were remarkably resourceful and resilient on that exercise in the Brecon Beacons in outwitting the army patrols, otherwise I would not be sending you into the hills of Southern Spain. I will say goodbye now. There's an article in my paper which may interest you," he said, handing her his folded newspaper and touching his hat to her.

The paper felt bulky and Verity tucked it under her arm and set off for the bus stop to go back to the flat. She did not open it until she reached the privacy of her own room. There was an envelope containing paper currency, French, Portuguese and Spanish, together with a generous number of twenty-pound notes, which ought to cover most eventualities. There was also a note containing the rendezvous instructions and a hand-drawn map showing the latest information on which side controlled the surrounding area. From the map it seemed as though the Republicans held the coastal region of Andalucía and the nationalists held the territory to the North, not far above Malaga. It was not at all clear which side held the actual area where she was scheduled to land in a valley up in the hills, but one thing was crystal clear, that neither side would welcome her, so she had better be pretty invisible.

Six a.m. saw Verity at Croydon aerodrome. Connie had driven Verity's car and dropped her off, pecking her on the cheek and driving straight off without turning to wave. By six thirty, Verity was in the air in her borrowed plane with its owner, a man in a well-tailored suit, an upper class British accent and Arab looks. He had not introduced himself. The plane was registered in someone else's name, he told her.

They put the plane through its paces; it seemed to Verity to be a thoroughbred amongst planes with lots of little extras to make the job of the pilot easier. The cockpits were closed, an unexpected luxury. But the bulky wing tanks were obviously going to slow the plane down. The plane itself appeared to have been registered abroad as it bore a foreign registration number.

"Made in England, registered in Egypt, that's where my home is," said the owner.

"But don't you mind lending it to me, a total stranger?" asked Verity

"A good friend has told me that you need this plane. If the plane should be damaged in any way whilst in your care, I have others. I hope, though, that the plane will return to me - it is a favourite of mine."

Back at the aerodrome, Verity met the pilot who was to help her plan the route. He introduced himself simply as 'Bill', she did not question whether this was his real name. He proved to be a mine of information as they pored over maps and weather information. They decided that the best route would be for her to fly across France to Biarritz, and then to make a sweep round the northern coast of Spain out to sea to arrive in Portugal. From there she would go down the coast of Portugal and, either over the mountains or over the sea, around Gibraltar to head inland near Malaga. She needed to have sufficient fuel when she landed in Spain to be able to take off again and fly back to Portugal.

"Look," said Bill, "I know I shouldn't really ask this, but is there any chance you could drop me off at Lisbon? You haven't got any cargo, have you? I've got the chance of a job flying from there and I was going to have to cadge a lift from someone. If you could give me a ride I could help out on navigation and all that."

The camaraderie of pilots was very strong, they usually helped one another out in whatever way they could. "Of course! I'd be glad of your company, but I'd better make a phone call first to check. I've had plenty of experience flying over the sea but it's bit daunting when you're out there by yourself. Where's your luggage?"

Verity phoned the office of Mr Jones from a call box but was unsurprised when she was unable to get through. She decided to take Bill to Portugal anyway, he might be useful and it would look more normal to depart for an overseas flight as a couple.

Bill's total luggage was a small pilot's bag and it was soon stowed on board. They agreed that lunch in France would be preferable to having a meal in Croydon before leaving. By ten thirty, they were on their way.

23

If Bernard and his fellow travellers had expected a rapturous welcome in Spain as overseas volunteers, they were mistaken. Suspicion, mistrust and open hostility were the order of the day. The large surly official at Communist Party headquarters in a Barcelona hotel glowered at them and assured them that they were not in need of volunteers of their sort. If they had not already shown him their party membership cards, their reception might well have been worse. As it was, the official grudgingly said the British Comrades might come back in a week or so when a decision had been made as to whether foreign party members might have a role to play.

Crestfallen, they were finally shooed out of the hotel. They went to a nearby bar to consider what to do next. Bernard was the only one of the group who spoke Spanish and he chatted to Spaniards in the bar. Some of the excitement came back to him; here he was in Spain at last after dreaming of it for so long. It did not matter what that disagreeable official at Party HQ had said, he was sure he would be allowed to fight for the Communists and for the cause.

Bernard soon discovered the existence of the 'people's cafés' and eventually steered his little group to the nearest, where they were served with soup, sausage and bread. They felt much better after that. They might have received a first rebuff, but there was always tomorrow, things would be better then. They slept in an annexe to the café where others were already curled up asleep with makeshift pillows, oblivious to the chaos around them. Bernard soon fell soundly asleep too, untroubled by cares. He was in Spain, that was all that mattered for the moment.

By morning two of the group had disappeared without trace. Worse still, some of their own belongings had gone as well. Bernard had used his haversack as a pillow so he was all right, but the others had lost some of their belongings and all their money. Their righteous indignation on making this discovery caused even more problems, as the people sleeping around them felt themselves to have been unjustly accused of stealing. The crowd around them quickly became an angry mob and Bernard thought it best to get out of the place quickly, clutching his haversack to him. It was not his quarrel, and if the other fellows wanted to raise a stink about it, they must take the consequences.

He thought it most likely that the two chaps who had slipped away had taken their pick of their companions' belongings before doing a bunk.

Bernard was nothing if not streetwise. He sauntered out, his haversack over his shoulder, and decided that a first priority was to get his bearings. He bought a copy of 'La Vanguardia' and chatted to a couple of lads selling the morning newspapers. From them he got directions to another 'people's café' and set off in the direction they had indicated to get himself something to eat. Militia were on every street corner and he took note of the curious mixture of weapons and clothing which they wore. Even small boys seemed to be dressed as though they were militia, although their weapons seemed to be wooden clubs which looked as though they had started life as the legs of chairs. More alarming was when he spotted a small boy who appeared to have a pistol stuffed into the waistband of his ragged trousers. Bernard hoped that for the child's sake it was not loaded.

What did surprise him was the devastation around him. His idea of battle was based on the images of the 1914-18 war, fought from trenches ranged across the countryside. It came as a great surprise to see the evidence of conflict here in the city, the damage to buildings, trenches and barricades still barring some streets. Most of all he was shocked by the damage to the churches which he passed. Just heaps of rubble some of them, but the worst of all was when he stood where, unbeknown to him, Juan had stood just two days before. The opened coffins propped up against the remaining walls of a church, the grisly occupants exposed for all to gawp at. He had never been particularly religious himself, although his mother had made him go to church with her at Christmas and Easter. He discovered, with some surprise, that he viewed the grisly scene at the church as sacrilegious. Those who had been decently buried ought to left in peace.

Verity was tired. Her brain was tired from the concentration, her eyes from scanning the sky and the sea, and her arms from putting pressure on the joystick and making continual minor adjustments to the flight path. But most of all, she was tired of the company of Bill who, in the guise of a helpful passenger, was continually making little suggestions which undermined her confidence.
At first she had thought he was genuinely trying to be helpful to someone whom he regarded as a novice pilot - he was not to know that she had completed intensive RAF training. Eventually she had concluded that he was doing it deliberately, although for what reason she could not fathom. They were nearing the airfield at Viana do Castelo, the first place available to refuel after crossing the Portuguese frontier. The coastal lighthouse at Carreco was now visible. This airfield

was where she had decided to drop off Bill. He wanted to go to Lisbon but she saw no reason why she should give way to his convenience; after all, he had had a very long free ride this far.

"And don't forget, Verity, your best route is overland from Lisbon; it's far too dangerous for you to fly around the coast alone. I've plotted the route for you: just follow my directions and you can't go wrong."

"Thank you. It's very good of you to take such trouble for a novice like me," she said, playing along.

"Can't have you getting lost, can we?" he said patronisingly with a hearty laugh which had her squirming in her seat.

He must think her a complete idiot: there was no way the fuel would last out if she did as he suggested. She had looked at his calculations of fuel and distance on the pad. Whilst she was no Einstein, she could see that his calculations were faulty. He had not used the correct formula in the first place. When she had queried the formula, he had airily said that this was one that experienced pilots used. She let him think that she accepted his explanation and changed the subject.

The range of the plane was just over 500 miles. Verity had arranged to refuel at Faro as a last stop before flying across the bay to Cadiz, and then inland over Spain towards Ronda, and then turning south for her destination. Verity had made the arrangements at their last stop whilst Bill was busy making a phone call. She had decided that Bill was not only tedious but that there was something phoney about him. She could not put a finger on it, at least not whilst concentrating on flying a plane. She no longer believed in this new job of his in Lisbon.

Verity spotted the airfield and began losing height to join the circuit and noted the signals to indicate the active runway. As she touched down and braked firmly to slow the plane down as it sped along the runway she said, "I've decided to drop you off here, Bill. It's time for me to fly on my own. Thank you for your company and remember to take your bag with you."

"But what about Lisbon? You promised to take me there," said Bill petulantly.

"I promised no such thing, as you well know. The ride ends here, Bill. You'll have no problem in hitching a lift with all your contacts."

"But..."

"No," said Verity firmly, turning the plane on to the taxiway. "I fly solo from here."

Bill got out grim faced, clutching his bag. He did not thank her for bringing him all this way at no cost to himself. He walked off without even looking in her direction again.

Verity locked the plane and went to report to the tower. She had already decided to stay there overnight and to sleep in the plane.

Bill was nowhere in evidence, but Verity did not worry herself unduly about this. Pilots were used to finding themselves at strange airfields when they delivered planes and never had any difficulty in hitching a lift, either on another plane going in the right direction, or into the nearest town. He was presumably looking for just such a contact now.

Verity refuelled the plane. Afterwards she made ready for an early departure in the morning. The small airfield had the usual tiny bar at which pilots could get something to eat, and Verity ate and bought some bread and cheese to take with her in the morning. Later, as she settled herself on the leather seat cushions for the night, she was thankful that the owner of the plane had plenty of money when choosing the luxurious fitments of his plane so that she was assured a comfortable night.

Awaking at first light, she got out and stretched herself, then headed off for a quick wash before setting off. She would have been worried if she could have seen the figure watching her and the plane through binoculars. Seeing her heading towards the toilet block, Bill hurried towards the plane and vanished out of sight behind it.

Ten minutes later Verity returned, bright and alert and ready to start the last day of her long journey south. She was in the far north of Portugal and intended heading for Faro on the coast about 300 miles south. She would refuel again there and make a decision about what time to leave, depending on the local weather conditions. Cloud and wind could affect the timing of the flight for the last 150 miles into Spain. For preference, she wanted to arrive about an hour before sunset so that there would be enough light to select a landing place, but so that darkness would quickly hide her and the plane. If all went well, she would take off again with her passenger at first light and be back at Faro in time for breakfast.

She quickly did the outside checks on the plane and then climbed in, got the maps ready and started the engine. It was a great delight to have a plane with a starter that did not require another person on the ground to swing the propeller for her - a lot less dangerous too. She checked the instruments were reading correctly, set the pressure on the dial and increased the throttle to check for magneto drop. All was normal and she taxied on to the runway and began her take-off. Soon the plane was in the air and heading south.

Bill watched it go with an impassive face. Stuck up bitch. Well, she was going to get what was coming to her. He had realised that she was not going to take his advice about her route and so would not meet the Spanish Nationalist planes that were waiting to intercept her and force her down, to prevent the rescue of that all important figure. His contact at the Spanish

Embassy had told him to use his own initiative, so he had done just that.

Verity cruised at 3,000 feet and 100 mph - there was no need for any greater speed - she had plenty of time. It had been hot on the airfield even at dawn, but up here it was beautiful and cool and the view of the coast of Portugal was spectacular. At this height she could see the waves breaking on the shore and fishing boats dotting the sea. She told herself that she must not get too mesmerised watching the sea and the coast. It was essential to keep a lookout for other planes in the sky on this lovely morning. She only saw two planes in the sky on the whole of her flight down the coast.

Near Lisbon she had climbed to 6,000 feet in case of any planes taking off from the airfield on the outskirts of the city, but whilst she saw planes on the ground, she only saw one moving to take off, and after that she lost sight of it. After three hours she was over the lighthouse at Cabo de San Vicente, in the far south of Portugal, and she started a gentle left turn to follow the coast as it swept in a curve along to Faro.

Circling the airfield at 1,000 feet, she saw the signals and the indication of the active runway, a grass strip which ended just before the sea. The wind direction was from the sea so this meant turning inland first in order to land into wind. She circled and lined up for the runway having first checked all around for other aircraft. There was one plane only and this was out at sea and flying in another direction. Coming over the airfield boundary losing height, she aimed to land a third of the way down the runway. The wheels touched down, she cut the power, the plane bounced slightly on the rough strip and landed again, and Verity applied the brakes steadily. Nothing happened. She braked more firmly, still nothing. Now, she was virtually standing on the brakes, then, she tried pumping them. Still nothing. The plane was careering over the grass strip, eating up the distance between her and the sea. There was nothing for it but to open the throttle and go round again.

Verity closed the flaps, applied full power and prayed. The plane staggered into the air just before the airstrip abruptly ended in the sea. "Perhaps they should have given me a sea plane," she said to herself.

She flew close over the waves, building up speed before climbing to 1,000 feet and executing a long turn to take her back over the land. She automatically noted that the plane she had seen earlier must have been circling to still be close but was now heading off to sea and into the distance. As she passed to the right of the airfield, she saw that some figures had emerged from the buildings and were looking in her direction. What to do now? An emergency landing off the airfield was out of the question as the useless brakes would be just as essential there. She needed time to think and flew the plane inland for a few miles to gain time.

The only strategy she could come up with was a long slow descent that would take her over the airfield boundary at a hundred feet and at the slowest speed the plane could maintain without stalling. Then, she could land at the start of the runway, cut the power and hope the plane would run out of momentum before the end of the runway. If it slowed sufficiently, she could try turning it with the rudder pedals. She tested the rudder pedals and found them useless.

Still flying away from the airfield, she fished out the handbook and checked that she correctly remembered the stalling speed for the plane. Then she turned seawards and headed for the airfield, gently reducing speed and height as she went. She had to sideslip the plane to get lined up with the runway, visible from some miles away once you knew what you were looking for.

She was down to 200 feet; thank goodness there were no buildings between her and the airfield. She had a horrible cold feeling in her stomach as she reduced height still further so as to virtually skim the boundary hedge at 75 mph. Then it was power off, and she firmly gripped the joystick to control the plane as it bumped over the runway. She seemed, if anything, to have less control over the plane than on her last landing but the speed was coming off slowly. Too slowly - the sea was approaching.

She tried the left rudder again to start a turn but it was no use. Out of the corner of her eye, she saw that a man, who had been waiting by the side of the runway watching her, was starting to run with her and then he flung himself at the wing of the plane. He had got a grip on the wing and was being pulled along by the plane. Under his weight the plane started to turn left. It skewed off the runway but was definitely slowing now, a gentle slope of the land helping although the plane was still turning slowly under the man's weight. Finally the plane stopped, miraculously still upright.

Verity released her iron grip on the stick and turned off the fuel. She felt clammy and sick and her heart was racing, but what about her rescuer? She fumbled to open the canopy and was greatly relieved to see the man sitting on the ground by the plane.

Others came running up and helped her from the plane, and she was ashamed to find that her legs unexpectedly gave way when her feet touched the ground. Arms supported her and helped her to a place beside her rescuer. He grinned at her and showed her his boots which he had taken off. The soles were worn through from the friction of being dragged at speed across the ground. His hands too showed signs of friction burns but he was laughing and talking excitedly. She could not understand what he was saying. She tried English, which he clearly did not understand. Then Spanish, and found that he could apparently comprehend most of what she was saying, but only spoke very halting Spanish himself.

One of the others had been examining the plane and now beckoned her over. Pointing, he showed her where the brake lines had been cleanly cut through. A wire cutter had obviously been used. Her mind leapt to Bill - only he could have done this.

In careful Spanish she asked whether the plane could be repaired today. Immediately everyone began to talk at once, with much waving of hands and the universal gestures and the expressions of horror of workmen asked to do something immediately.

After much haggling over steaming cups of black coffee and slabs of bread trickled with olive oil, a deal was reached. They would repair the plane this afternoon. She understood them to say that parts must be obtained and that they could not start work until the arrival of these parts. One of the men indicated to her that he was setting off to fetch the parts needed. Verity thought it fortunate that limited mutual language prevented them from pursuing questions about why anybody should sabotage the brakes of her plane.

When the plane had been towed to a hangar out of the glare of the sun, Verity started to check the plane over. One of the mechanics had joined her and together they checked everything. There was some slight damage to the delicate wing where her rescuer had grabbed hold of it, but that was easily repairable. What she was looking for was any other evidence of sabotage. They found none. But the cutting of the brake lines left Verity with much to think about.

Clearly this had been an attempt to stop her mission. She remembered the plane she had seen as she tried to land. Was this the plane she had seen take off from Lisbon and had its pilot followed her to report back on the destruction of her plane on attempting to land? Had it waited around to see the result of her second attempt at landing? She couldn't be sure, she had been too preoccupied. She remembered seeing it heading off to sea but the pilot could easily have circled back and watched her. In that case, did whoever had employed Bill know that the she had landed safely? She had no answers, only lots of questions. She wondered, almost for the first time, who this important passenger of hers was to be.

Verity lunched with the airfield workers on fresh sardines and rough bread. She declined the red wine which they poured from pitchers, whilst wondering whether it might in fact be safer than the water she was drinking.

The day wore on interminably and Verity, sitting in the shade of the hangar, began to wonder whether they were ever going to start on repairing her plane. In the meantime she checked and re-checked her route into the mountains of Spain, memorising the landmarks on the map. She also checked the weather reports with the tower. There was a southerly breeze but nothing to worry about unduly.

Verity awoke from a troubled doze when someone tapped her on the shoulder. The mechanic beckoned and Verity rose and followed him. The plane stood outside waiting for her. Verity settled the bill for the fuel and repairs out of the Portuguese currency supplied by Mr Jones. Had he foreseen this kind of eventuality, Verity wondered? Possibly. Verity packed her bag away in the plane.

The men had gathered round smiling. She jumped down and shook hands with each one in turn and then, reaching her rescuer, she impulsively kissed him on both of his stubbly cheeks, to the cheers of his friends.

"I can never thank you enough," she said, not knowing whether he understood the words but sure he understood the sense of them. Smiling, she clambered up into the plane and they moved back to allow her to start the engine.

She taxied slowly and then turned on to the start of the runway, straightened the plane, tested the brakes against the throttle, then released them and started the take-off as the little crowd waved goodbye. She was soon in the air and, checking carefully that there was no other plane in sight, she turned the plane and set her heading to cross the Bay of Cadiz.

24

It was later than Verity would have liked. The sun was already quite low in the sky. She built up the cruise speed to make up what time she could on the 150-mile flight. Checking her heading, she made slight adjustments to keep her on course to pass to the right of Cadiz. Then at last she was over Spain and heading inland. She was not worried about any interference by Spanish planes: she had been told by Mr Jones that the Spanish Air Force was in disarray, many planes damaged by each side to prevent them falling into the hands of the other side.

It was not all that easy to see at this hour, as the sun was so strong in the west that travelling east made everything look dark ahead. There was some haze which did not help visibility either. Verity needed to head for Ubrique, and she followed the headings which she had worked out earlier to keep to her course, timing each section against her watch. This was certainly a really mountainous region, and it was one thing to look at them on a map but far more frightening to see them in reality.

Shortly, she could just make out a town which looked like the right shape for Ubrique and banked to turn away from the town. Somewhere in this inhospitable terrain lay the Sierra de Libar, her final destination, described to her as a narrow straight plateau high in the mountains somewhere above Cortes de la Frontera. The map she was working from now was hand drawn by an unknown hand, the printed maps simply showing a range of mountains with no detail other than height. The only way to find Sierra de Libar in the setting sun was to stick strictly to the instruments and the headings she had worked out. This was not a desirable course in the middle of a mountain range, but she had no alternative with visibility so poor.

She tried to quell the nagging doubt at the back of her mind as to whether it was actually possible to land in these mountains. The plan had clearly been made by someone who was not a pilot and who did not realise the myriad difficulties that mountain flying presented, not least flying into the side of a mountain that was higher than the height at which she was flying. She checked her heading again and counted off the minutes and seconds on her watch: the plateau should be coming up now.

Peering intently she made out a narrow flattish strip of ground nestling high up between the summits of two inhospitable mountains. She must be careful not to lose sight of it. She overflew the plateau and went a mile or so farther before turning in a tight circle and flying the reciprocal heading back towards it.

The watchers on the ground had seen the plane silhouetted against the sunset and then heard the engine as it flew nearer, as they watched in silence and waited.

Verity was trying to decide which direction to land in. There were no visible clues as to wind direction to help her so she intended to overfly once more and then make a decision. But heading into the sun, she saw she was perfectly lined up for a landing and decided to go for it. She lowered the flaps and dropped off the height so that she flew over the start of the plateau at a hundred feet. There were a few trees and then the ground ahead looked clear. She allowed the plane to sink down, looked to check ahead again but now could not see ahead, both because of the sun and the angle of the plane which was now nose high. All she could do was keep the plane straight with the rudder pedals.

She touched down, hoping against the odds for a clear space in which to brake to a halt. In the meantime she turned off the fuel as a precaution and the engine died out. There would be no way of taxiing the plane in the dusk once she had brought it to a halt: it would have to stay where it was until morning when she could take off at first light.

The brakes were responding this time, the wind was slight, she was going to be lucky. She was keeping the plane fairly straight as it slowed, but the last of the sun was directly in her eyes. It was never easy to see where you were going once on the ground, even on a regular airfield, and this was far removed from that. The last thing she heard was a loud bang before the plane turned over.

Helen felt that the ambulance ride all the way to Spain had become a prolonged form of purgatory. It had seemed a reasonably comfortable vehicle when they had set off in convoy with another ambulance from London. After hundreds of miles Helen had concluded that ambulances were fine if you were only taking a short ride to pick up a patient, but they were clearly not designed for the journey that they had undertaken to Spain. Helen was stiff and sore and doubtful that she would ever be able to sit down again. The roads had deteriorated the farther they went as they jolted and jerked their way across France to Toulouse, then across the Pyrenees at Puigcerda into Spain and down to Barcelona.

Much of Helen's enthusiasm had evaporated on the long, hard journey, especially during their frequent stops to repair punctured tyres, broken exhausts and overheated engine. But their final arrival in Barcelona revived her. To see the city for herself, at last, was like seeing one of the seven wonders of the world.

But it was not as Juan had described it to her. It was not the fabulous architecture of many of the buildings which caught her eye. All the buildings seemed to be draped with red and black flags and the jostling crowd in the streets, men and women alike, wore red neckerchiefs round their necks. Blue overalls were the order of the day and everywhere striking and patriotic posters decorated the walls and the windows. The signs of war were apparent, destroyed buildings in many streets, the remnants of barricades.

The hospital where they were to be based was unlike any other hospital of her experience. Flags draped that too, militia on guard with ancient rifles at the entrances to the building. Inside, patients in the corridors on makeshift beds, the wards overflowing with more patients attended by hordes of people who were not wearing nurses uniforms and whom she discovered were the families of patients. In the midst of all this chaos strode beleaguered men in white coats being pulled this way and that; somewhere in the crowds she spotted a few uniformed nurses.

The other British ambulance in their convoy of vehicles was a day or two behind them after engine trouble. George, a clerical worker who had been her volunteer driver all the way to Spain, fought his way through the throng to Helen, bearing two cups of some strong hot liquid in his large hands. Helen gulped it down thankfully without stopping to wonder just what it was. George had locked and secured their vehicle in the yard at the back of the hospital, where there were gathered a number of makeshift ambulances, identifiable as such because of the large notices in their windows declaring 'Ambulance'. George had taken the precaution of removing an essential part from the engine of their own ambulance to make sure the vehicle would still be there when they went back to it.

They finally cornered a harassed official in an office, who hurriedly entered their names on a register and then directed them to where he said they would find the 'receiving unit' for casualties, to which he supposed they would be attached. After some searching, they found it. It would not have passed muster back at home, but they immediately noticed that it had a sense of direction and purpose which had been missing in the crowded area outside the unit. Helen collared a nurse, who looked at her unknown uniform in puzzlement and then gestured to where a short hawk-nosed older woman in a starched cap stood giving directions to all and sundry. Helen approached her and got in her prepared speech quickly before she too could be despatched by this woman. The dark eyes beneath the severe cap gave her a quick onceover and then the woman summoned a girl in a makeshift uniform. The girl beckoned Helen and George to follow her, saying nothing, and set off at a run. They had a job to keep up with her but eventually all three arrived puffing and triumphant on the top floor of the building. The girl, who had a twitching nose very reminiscent of a rabbit, gave a quick wave to her right and left and then, with another twitch, vanished, just like the White Rabbit, before Helen could ask her any questions.

After a little exploration, Helen and George worked out that the nurses were quartered at the back of the building and the men at the front. They went in search of vacant beds and George, finding one, promptly fell fast asleep on it. Helen eventually found a bed in the women's quarters that appeared not to have been claimed. A nurse passing through said that she might find sheets in the cupboard at the end of the room if she was lucky. She was lucky, and had soon made up the bed and put her spare clothes in the locker beside it.

She ventured back the way they had come and, much to her own surprise, found herself back at the receiving unit. The small woman who had been directing everyone was nowhere in sight but, whatever the crisis had been, it appeared to have passed and the large room was deceptively tranquil.

A young man, clearly a houseman or its Spanish equivalent, came up and asked if he could help her. She introduced herself and explained about the ambulance parked outside and George and herself having been sent as its crew, with directions to aid and assist the wounded. She produced her letter from the Ambulances for Spain organisation and the translation which she had made of it. He scanned them and then looked down at her with a smile.

In rapid Spanish he said, "Welcome to Barcelona, Nurse Pugh! I am one of the doctors in this unit and look forward to working with you. We are grateful to you for coming to help us in these difficult times. Will others be following you?"

Helen explained that another ambulance was a little way behind them but she was not sure what other plans were afoot as they had not been completed by the time she left London. He started to reply but, in the way of all hospitals, was called away to attend a patient. Helen wandered to the door and stood outside looking around. It was early evening but still very hot. She was hungry but had no idea where to obtain any food. She stood there indecisively before noticing several nurses all hurrying off in one direction. She followed them hopefully, and found herself at the staff canteen where she joined a queue and was ladled out a portion of food. It was hot and tasty, quite delicious to Helen who had not eaten a regular meal in over a week. With a full stomach came tiredness and it was all she could do to drag herself up all those stairs to bed. Just before she drifted off her last thought was of Juan, so close but how would she find him?

Helen was awoken by the bustle of other nurses getting up in the morning. She was ashamed of having nearly slept round the clock, but it had also restored her enthusiasm and cheerfulness. Washed and dressed, she found George in the yard checking the tyres of the ambulance.

"I'm off soon; they're sending a chap with local knowledge with me today so I won't get lost first time." Helen could see he was longing to see some action. She wished him good luck and went inside to report to the receiving unit for duty. She found that it was also where they utilised all the volunteers who were beginning to appear from all over the globe. They had very little in the way of a common language. Helen was a rarity in speaking some Spanish but had difficulty in understanding the local dialect and Catalan was impenetrable to her. The girls got by with makeshift uniforms and makeshift language. Any conversation was likely to contain a smattering of English, French and Italian, as well as an attempt at Spanish. No wonder the Sister in charge went for peremptory orders backed up by hand signals.

Finding herself working alongside the White Rabbit, washing and making a patient comfortable, Helen discovered that she was from a communist country, having come to Spain with two brothers who were anxious to fight for the communists. What country she came from Helen was never quite certain, nor could she catch the girl's name. The brothers were away fighting and the girl was clearly intensely proud of them. She would continue to work at the hospital until they came to take her home, she said.

The nurses and nursing assistants were of an even more variable standard than those in an average hospital at home, since many of them had no background of nursing. What they did all share was a fierce commitment to their patients, expressed in many different ways.

Some of their patients were civilian casualties, but most were militia of some sort, many having been ferried back from the front. This was Helen's first experience of war casualties. She had not been shocked by the injuries, as some had, but found that a professional detachment enabled her to cope and observe their injuries and the effect which they had on their bodies and store away the information for future use. Much of the time she was working with the houseman and they talked as they worked, about the patient's surgical and nursing treatment, about Barcelona and about themselves.

Helen had very soon explained that she had a friend in Barcelona whom she wanted to find at the first opportunity and that this had been a main reason why she had come. She explained that her friend did not know she was coming, but at that point the doctor had been called away.

Helen fell into bed exhausted that night; the heat had been very difficult to cope with, as was the dust which was everywhere. She promised herself that next day she would take some steps towards finding Juan. At the least she could send, or perhaps deliver, a letter to the post office where he collected his mail.

25

The sound of something dripping penetrated Verity's consciousness. She lay there listening for a few moments. Then all at once she remembered the plane, the landing and hitting something: after that, nothing. The dripping could only be fuel from a fractured fuel line. She opened her eyes to total darkness and sat up, or rather she tried to as waves of sickness and pain came over her. She was no longer in the plane, that much was clear as there was no harness holding her into her seat, but where was she?

Her left arm hurt. She touched it gently with her right hand and it was sticky with what she could only presume was blood. Her head hurt and she ached all over. She peered round in the darkness, saw a lighter patch but could not make anything out. As the sickness came over her again, she instinctively leaned back and found that she was resting against something cold and damp and firm. With her good hand she explored the surface. Definitely rock. With the lack of light, not even a glimmer of sky, it had to be a cave.

She half sat, half lay against the rock surface, listening intently. She could hear nothing but the dripping sound, with possibly the sound of water passing over rock far away - she could not make out the direction. But there were no human sounds.

The rendezvous with her unknown passenger had been set for an hour after sunset with the proviso that if they did not meet up on that day, they would meet up at the same time the following day. Had the passenger been there waiting for her and pulled her from the plane? If so, where was this mysterious man now and had he abandoned her as useless once he had found her injured? She could understand his frustration at finding his pilot injured and in all probability the plane wrecked and with it his hopes of evading capture.

Verity decided that she had better take action: she needed to get back to the plane and find the medical supplies so that she could bind up her arm and do something about her head and, above all else, find some aspirin. If she could stop the thumping in her head, then she would be able to think more clearly.

With difficulty she got to her knees and started to crawl towards the lighter patch in the darkness; she did not think she could stand up just yet. She laboriously crawled some yards towards her goal, hardly noticing the rough rock surface cutting her hands and knees. Then all at once a light appeared from behind her and there was a shout of alarm. She stopped.

As the light from the lantern spread through the cave, she saw that she had been on the brink of a deep dark void open to the sky and the stars above.

Firm hands plucked her from the brink and lifted her gently as she cried out and closed her eyes in pain. When she opened them again she looked up into the familiar face of Roberto. Roberto? No wonder they had selected her for this strange rendezvous.

Roberto bent his head and kissed the dirty bloodstained face which stared up at him. Verity felt even more dizzy. She found that she was laughing and crying all at once.

"Roberto?"

He carried her from the cave and set her down gently. By the faint light of the stars, she could see the outline of the valley. He held a water bottle to her lips and she drank thirstily. There was a slight movement nearby that made her tense, the jingle of a harness as an animal moved in the darkness.

"The mules," explained Roberto. When she concentrated she could make out their outline as they moved slowly searching for grazing amongst the parched grass.

"Where's the plane?" she asked Roberto anxiously. "Did it catch fire?"

"No, no fire."

"Thank goodness for that."

"But," he continued dismally, "it is very damaged. I do not think it will fly again."

"Don't worry, I'll look at it in the morning and see what I can do," she said, trying to sound optimistic.

Roberto did not reply, and in the silence Verity was alarmed to hear a footfall behind her. Roberto, who was looking over her shoulder, seemed unperturbed.

"She's awake now," he said, looking over her head.

"That is good," said a familiar voice and then Don César was bending over her. He was holding something and Verity saw with relief that he had found her first aid kit.

"Roberto," he said "keep watch." Roberto melted away without a word.

Don César knelt down before her and opened up the box. "What's in here?" he enquired.

Verity told him and watched as he opened the lantern a crack and his slender fingers sorted through the contents by its light. He found some aspirin, extracted a couple and gave them to her with water to wash them down.

Then he produced a knife and slit the left sleeve of her blouse and slid it off her arm. All the while, Verity's mind was working overtime. Was she expected to take both of them away with her? The plane, even if it could be repaired, would only carry two not three people with the necessary fuel aboard. She had accepted Roberto's appearance here without question but it made an awful lot more sense if it was Don César himself whom she was to fly out of Spain. Didn't he have some Government job? Hadn't someone said something about him being a Government minister? Connie had never said very much about it, just given the impression that he had a high rank of some sort, and Verity had never felt the need to question her further.

As Don César's fingers gently explored her shoulder, she bit back the pain but he noticed her sharp intake of breath. He tore a strip from the sleeve he had cut off, wet it and first bathed her face, then gently wiped the blood from her arm. It started bleeding again and he held his fingers against it, applying firm pressure until the bleeding stopped, then competently applied a pad and a bandage. Verity was surprised as she had not thought that a man in his position would have such practical skills.

As though hearing her thoughts, he said, "I have gained many skills since I have been in hiding."

His fingers moved to her head and gently explored her scalp.

"No open wound to your head. You probably hit it when the plane overturned. Hopefully your headache will be better in the morning."

Verity smiled up at him, her head already feeling a bit better as the aspirin took effect.

He continued, "Your arm and shoulder are another matter. It could be a break of some kind, but I know little of these things."

"It will be fine in the morning," she said, with more optimism in her voice than she felt.

Roberto rejoined them, having obviously been rummaging through the plane because he produced her bag.

"All is quiet, but I think we should take Verity back to the cave. It is not safe to show a light out here."

They carried everything into the cave, and last of all Roberto carried Verity, placing her carefully on a rough wool blanket which smelled as though it had last adorned a mule. Roberto sat down beside her and she leaned against him thankfully. She was very tired and all she wanted to do was sleep, but there was much to talk about first.

They had shuttered the lantern and, as they sat there in the darkness, they started to tell her their story. Verity listened to an account of the uprising of the Army in Seville, where they both were in August. Don César's offices had been surrounded by rebel troops but he had been able to slip away over the rooftops in the confusion. He had gone to his home in the city, but then it became clear to him that, until the Government restored some kind of order to the city, he was not safe. The killing of innocent citizens had started: anyone who was suspected of not being entirely for the

Nationalist cause, and indeed even many who were, were seized and shot.

The favoured method was to round them up at night and shoot the captives in a ditch on the outskirts of town. Then Don César heard that a warrant had been issued for his arrest.

Roberto, a respected party member and official of a powerful union, had also heard of the warrant and had gone to warn his uncle. He had got Don César out of the city in a vehicle liberated from a diplomatic mission, using a travel warrant for official party business in the south.

Don César had wanted to go to his own home in the country to protect his estranged wife, but after a hazardous journey they had found his estate burnt and laid to waste. Worst of all, Roberto had identified the body of his aunt and her servant in the local church which had become a makeshift morgue. As a party official, he was permitted to move about but did not dare to arrange for his aunt's burial - it would be too dangerous to be identified with a victim of his own party.

Roberto had not told his uncle of his wife's death until they were hundreds of miles south in a safe house, too late for his uncle to do as Roberto knew he would want to do - claim her body and see her decently buried. Don César and his wife had not lived together for many years, but he blamed himself for not being there to protect her when she needed him. He was sad at her death even if it was difficult to be moved unduly by the death of a harsh and unloving woman when all about him was death. But he felt that he had failed her as a husband, just as she had failed him as a wife.

It was from a safe house that a message had been sent out which had resulted in this rendezvous on the plain. Don César was an important man in diplomatic circles. If he could be spirited out of Spain underneath the noses of both Republicans and Nationalists, the British thought he might be able to assist them in the shady diplomatic dealings which they covered up by an avowed policy of non-intervention in Spain's internal affairs.

Once his uncle was safely out of the country, Roberto was going to return to actively supporting the Republican cause through the Communist Party. There was no question of him leaving Spain, now or ever, he assured Verity. She believed him.

Roberto said he had seen the plane fly overhead, then return and touch down but, whilst he could clearly see the boulders in the path of the plane, it was only when the plane kept straight on that he realised that the pilot could not see them. Roberto had held his breath in horror as she rammed the rocks and the plane overturned. Expecting the plane to catch fire, he had run and hauled her out, unrecognisable in pilot's overalls, helmet and goggles.

Verity explained that she had turned the fuel and the magnetos off as a precaution as she touched down and that it was probably this that had prevented a fire. They murmured approvingly in the darkness and went on talking, first one telling the story and then the other. They told her that she was the last person in the world they had expected to fly into the Sierra Llano de Libar that evening.

Skirting round the wreckage they had gingerly carried the pilot to the comparative safety of the cave as a precaution against the explosion of the plane. Only by the light of the lantern had they finally recognised her.

They had been worried that the plane might have been seen vanishing into the mountains by those in the small town of Cortes de la Frontera, the nearest habitation. That had been at the back of Verity's mind when she decided not to over fly a second time - to circle round again might have attracted attention. The surrounding territory was held by the Nationalists, they explained. They rather thought that no one would be likely to explore this inhospitable terrain in the dark but it was best to keep watch, just in case. Don César disappeared outside to stand watch. Verity immediately fell asleep exhausted without further thought for what the morning might bring.

Richard slammed his front door so hard that the frame shook. It did not make him feel any better. The terrible scene with Molly had been all the worse for being so unexpected. He had been visiting a client in Ruislip Manor this afternoon so had thought it would be nice to surprise Molly by arriving home early and perhaps take her and the baby, Lucy, to the park. Richard liked to think that they still did things together as a family, even though this rarely happened.

He had certainly surprised her. The first thing he heard when he came through the door was the baby crying her heart out. He found Lucy in her pram in the garden, unattended and sweltering in the hot afternoon sun. Although the hood was up, the sun had obviously moved round since the pram had been positioned and she was very distressed. He picked her up and comforted her, taking her inside to find her a drink and bathe her hot little face. He remembered that it was the nursemaid's afternoon off and set off upstairs to find Molly, presuming that she was having an afternoon nap.

It was not until he reached the bedroom door that he heard low voices and, walking in found Molly in bed, doing what she did so well, with a man whose backside he did not recognise. He stood there stupefied with Lucy held in his arms.

"Darling," said Molly, and for a moment Richard was not sure which of them she was addressing, "I loved that, do it again!" The young man promptly obliged. Richard backed out unseen as the bed shook.

Richard carried Lucy to her playpen downstairs and settled her. Then he stood indecisively looking out of the drawing room window, listening to the gyrations from the bedroom above and wondering what to do about them. The gyrations seemed to last forever. Richard wondered why he had ever thought that someone with the sexual appetite of Molly could be satisfied by him alone. How long had this been going on? The two of them made love every night and she was very demanding. It had not occurred to him that she needed it in the afternoon as well.

It seemed an age before the man came down the stairs, carrying his jacket. Richard saw his face as he passed by the drawing room door but did not know him. Once the man had let himself out, Richard realised that he had been holding his breath, and let it out. He took the stairs two at a time and burst into the bedroom.

"Slut!" he shouted at her, grasping her shoulders and shaking her.

"What's the matter, darling?" she said looking up at him.

"I came home and saw you at it with your fancy man!"

"So that's why Lucy stopped her yowling," she said, wriggling out from his grasp. "I might have known the brat would stop when Daddy came home."

"You left her in the sun," he flung at her. "How could you treat our daughter like that?"

"You don't have to be with her all day. She's an inconvenience even with a nanny to look after her."
"Are you going to explain your conduct?"
"Conduct, darling? You make me sound like an officer and a gentleman! What is there to explain? You saw for yourself, or I assume you did," she said tying her silk dressing gown cord around her waist.
Molly sat down on the bed and extracted a cigarette from a case by the bed.
"How could you?" he spluttered.
"Simple, I don't get enough of it, I have needs and you are always too busy with your work. So I have a little extra on the side."
"You're my wife!" shouted Richard, wanting to hit her as she blew smoke rings to the ceiling.
"What difference does that make? I'm not an ice maiden like your dear Verity."
"What do you mean?"
"Well, I don't suppose she has ever even allowed anyone to kiss her, least of all you, her willing slave. All you ever did was hang around her like a sick dog. I made sure that she got what she deserved!"
"What do you mean, never allowed anyone to kiss her?" said Richard slowly with what felt like an ice-cold lump in his chest. "You said that she was making love to that office boy on the river bank when we saw them that Sunday."

"And you believed it: you always were so gullible," she said stroking his arm. "It has always been one of your most endearing qualities."

"You mean to say that Verity wasn't ..." Richard couldn't bring himself to say it.

"Of course she wasn't, you silly goose. But I had to get rid of her; I couldn't have you wishing you had married her rather than me. Now you're stuck with me for better or worse, remember?"

"I'll divorce you!"

"So you can go and marry little Verity instead? I don't think so. Remember that Daddy provides all your work. You wouldn't last very long if Daddy withdrew the work, would you? Daddy can be awfully vindictive when he's crossed, and so can I! I think I'll have a bath now," she finished, kissing him full on the mouth as she rose.

Richard sat with his head in his hands as the appalling implications of what she had said struck home, about their marriage, Lucy and the devastating lies about Verity.

Why hadn't he seen Molly for the slut she was? The unfairness of it all brought him to bursting point and he went out to work off his anger with a walk through the woods and to think things through.

What reason did he have all that time ago for wanting to convince Verity's father of her improper conduct, she who had never encouraged him to do more than kiss her cheek? It was, as Molly had said, pure jealousy. He had spent the time since that denouncement, smug in his self-righteousness, confident of being in the right ,and that it was Verity's conduct which had caused her father's death. He had also been mad with jealousy of that little runt of an office boy – Bernard, was it? Anyway, just what had she been doing sitting on the riverbank with Bernard? He conveniently forgot all his broken promises to Verity about Sunday outings and the ultimate betrayal of getting Molly pregnant. He burned again with jealousy, even though he now knew that there was nothing to be jealous of.

26

The first light of dawn came all too soon for Verity after a troubled sleep. The men were nowhere to be seen so she reached for her bag and extracted a fresh blouse. Somewhat crumpled but at least clean, it would cover her decently, which was more than the present one was doing. To her annoyance, it took her some time and a considerable effort to get her torn blouse off and the fresh one on, but at last she was respectable enough to emerge cautiously from the cave. Verity found the two men surveying the plane which they had clearly dragged some way from where it had landed. It was close by some large rocks which hid it slightly. It was a sorry sight and Verity's heart fell. Minor repairs she could have managed, but the cockpit and wings of the plane were badly damaged and, when she looked at the engine, she found this had taken the brunt of the impact. With no means of carrying out the complete rebuild which the plane required, it was a write-off. There was no way that any of them could escape in it. Verity confirmed what they already knew and saw their shoulders sag with despair.

"We must hide it," said César.

"Destroy it," said Roberto.

"How?" said Verity.

In the end, it proved not too difficult to both destroy and hide it, the plane being essentially a fragile craft. They broke it up and threw the pieces down the deep chasm in the caves. Verity shuddered when she remembered how close she had been to falling down into its depths. There was not even any sound of the engine hitting the bottom. Such a sad end for a beautiful plane.

As they toiled, Verity saw enormous birds gathering on the branches of one of the few trees on this parched plateau. Against the rising sun they looked sinister, and when one or two flew down from the tree, they strutted towards Verity with an ungainly waddling walk.

Seeing her looking at them, César said, "Vultures, and they're hungry. When they've had a meal, they can't fly at all."

Even shortly after sunrise, it was very hot and dry. After a couple of hours' work, all that remained of the plane was an oily patch where it had turned over. Roberto manoeuvred the rock which the plane had hit so as to hide the oil. It was time for them to move on. Their belongings had been thrust into the panniers of one of the mules, and Verity was helped on to its back. There was no saddle, she sat on sacking held in place by the panniers.

"Keep as far forward as you can," advised Roberto leading her mule. The other animal carried their supplies and other items salvaged from the plane. César had gone on ahead to act as lookout. Dressed in a dirty ragged outfit with an equally dirty shady hat, he looked very much a man of the soil. They were following a track which was invisible to Verity's eyes but which Roberto said was a shepherds' or smugglers' path.

"Smuggling what?"

"Goods from Gibraltar. Tobacco, spirits, you know, the usual sort of stuff which Governments tax heavily. Luxury goods can be bought cheaply in Gibraltar. The smugglers' paths are centuries old, they lead right over the mountains well away from where people live. Shepherds sometimes use them but know to turn a blind eye if they meet a stranger."

"So are we heading for Gibraltar?"

"For the moment. We will have to see how it goes, it's quite a way to Gibraltar, but you can see the Rock from here." They stopped and he pointed to where there appeared to be a darker patch in the cloud on the horizon. Verity squinted at it in the sunlight and then she could make out the distinctive shape of the great rock which appeared to rest against a background of clouds. Was it fifty, perhaps sixty, miles away, Verity wondered as she thought of her maps, now tucked safely into the pannier basket beside her.

The scenery was incredible now she had time to look at it. They had left the dusty high plateau and were following a rocky path winding downwards. You could see for miles; Roberto pointed out to her the Pillars of Hercules, now visible beyond the Rock of Gibraltar, away across the water in Morocco. Verity took in the colours, blues, purples and greys in the distance and the white of the rock on which they stood, and the parched faded soil on which vegetation seemed to have lost its grip. Then she snapped back to reality; this was not just a beautiful view but hostile country over which they must make their way unseen to safety.

At the moment their aim was to put as much distance as they could between the Sierra de Libar and themselves and get well away from any incriminating evidence of the landing of the plane. But they were travelling over arid rocky ground which did not offer much in the way of hiding places. Verity was startled when the first shots rang out, echoing round the mountains, but after a moment she realised what the others already knew, that it was the echo of some far away skirmish. As more rifles joined in, the noise built up and seemed to Verity to be circling them, but Roberto and César continued on their way unperturbed.

Descending the bed of a dry stream, Verity called to Roberto, "I'd rather walk than ride this mule down here."

"You're quite safe," he assured her, "well, safe as far as the mule is concerned." But glancing at her face, he came and helped her off. A low whistle to César brought him back to join them, and they sat on the baking rocks to confer and pass the water bottle round. Verity's arm and shoulder were hurting and she had become parched from the sun. Roberto took off his own hat and put it on her head, and she was grateful to be able to keep the sun out of her eyes. She felt downcast, she had come as the rescuer and was now nothing but an encumbrance. She got her maps out of the pannier and spread them out on the ground.

"We need to find somewhere to obtain more water and food," Roberto said, and went on to explain, "We usually approach an outlying farm or house. Don't worry, we're used to this. If there is nowhere to buy, then I simply help myself to whatever is available."

In spite of some hours spent bumping up and down on a mule, Verity felt that the shock of the plane crash was wearing off and she was more herself.

"What do you want us to do?" she asked.

They decided, with the help of Verity's maps, that César and Verity would keep moving with one of the mules and that Roberto would take the other and find somewhere to obtain food. They pinpointed a place where they would meet up later. Roberto memorised it and then mounted one of the mules and was away down the track. He had taken one of Verity's weapons with him. Verity and César now took one each, Verity selecting a machine pistol from the cache in the panniers. They loaded and slung the guns in belts round their waists, hidden from sight by the folds of their clothes. They both eyed one another, each wondering whether the other could fire a gun if they had to.

"Yes, I can," said Verity, "I did some training before coming on this mission."

"Good," said César. "Tell me about it."

She did, there did not seem much point in keeping it secret now that they were thrust together in this way.

At the end of her story he asked, "Does Constance know about this?"

"Yes."

He nodded in satisfaction. "We'll return to her together."

In perfect accord they moved on. With César's calm acceptance of the situation, Verity felt that maybe she did have a role to play after all. There had been all that intensive training and she could handle a gun if she had to. She decided that the time had come to become a full member of this escape team and turned her mind to planning, whilst her eyes continued to scan the mountains around them for any sign of movement.

Major Moreno had been called to the temporary Area HQ that morning and given his orders. The General had received a tipoff from a reliable contact in Portugal that an attempt was to be made to fly out an important Government figure from right under their noses. The contact did not know the exact location of the rendezvous, only that it was somewhere within the Ronda region. The General had received the call that morning but, from the General's high level of irritation, the Major deduced that, whilst the call had been expected, something had gone wrong. Clearly Moreno and his men were being called in as backup to salvage the situation.

Moreno's orders were simple. He was to find the fugitive and bring him in, alive if possible. That left Moreno with a seemingly insuperable task: it was a large region, the pickup was expected to be that night or the next day, and he had to find it and the fugitive within a few hours.

Moreno's network of informants were put on alert. Anyone seeing a plane overflying the region was to report it by telephone as quickly as possible. Moreno's men could check out the sightings with authorised plane movements in the area.

Moreno commandeered a house with a telephone in Ronda for his base and organised his men into pairs. He gave them instructions to take their vehicles round the small towns and villages of the region gleaning any information. So far, he had little to go on. Where might it be possible to land a plane in this horrible terrain? Or would it be a take-off in a plane stolen from an airfield? His enquiries as to possible landing sites had drawn a blank. No-one, least of all the pilots he had contacted at the nearest air base, would attempt to land a plane in this region - far too dangerous, they said, too many mountains. Moreno privately thought the General's informant must be unreliable, unlike his own network.

Reports came in all day as his men returned. Their reports were all the same, nothing doing. One of his men had been carefully studying the maps to search for a likely place for a plane to land. Possible landing places in valleys were all ruled out because river beds, even if there was no water in them, had far too many rocks and boulders to land a plane. Mind you, the maps of this area left a lot to be desired, thought Moreno. Locals who had lived all their lives in the mountains might know them intimately but it was dangerous to take soldiers up there when they did not know the paths and tracks which could take them safely through a rocky and inhospitable area, with deep ravines and bogs for the unwary. Moreno was not going to risk his handpicked men up there without a definite lead.

Moreno reported back to the General by phone at five in the afternoon to say that so far he had not found anything of note and had his ear blasted off by way of response. When the General paused for breath, Moreno said "Pardon me, Sir, but it might help if we knew who we are looking for."

"That's for you to discover - do I have to do your job for you?" snapped the General and slammed the phone down.

Moreno lit a cigarette and looked at the map again. The trouble was it was not a good map for military purposes. If you wanted a leisurely drive from Ronda to the coast, always assuming you could afford a car, then the map would have been fine. For anything else it was worse than useless. He had done all the groundwork for the information to come in, he would just have to await developments. There was always tomorrow, he thought, blowing a smoke ring at the ceiling as he settled his boots on the makeshift desk.

It was next morning that he heard from his informants the first report of a plane flying near to Cortes de la Frontera and then disappearing into the mountains. Maybe the bird had flown already, but he'd better check it out.

His patrols had field radios but they very rarely worked in this mountainous terrain, so he had to wait for the last of them to return before he could brief them. They were to climb to the highest points in the Cortes de la Frontera area to look for any possible landing place for a plane. If they saw any possible place, they were to examine it for any trace of a plane landing and taking off. There was bound to be some trace and they must find it, even if it was simply to confirm that the escape had probably been completed last night.

The men dispersed to their vehicles, grumbling. Mountaineering was not one of their usual activities and they did not relish the thought of any strenuous exercise in the heat since no roads would assist them in penetrating this terrain. Only one pair thought of using four-legged transport, and they set off for Cortes de la Frontera to see if they could hire a donkey or a mule to get to their nominated viewpoint.

They were lucky. The younger one, brought up in the countryside, soon found a man with a couple of working donkeys which he was prepared to hire out for the day in return for a few pesetas.

"They are valuable animals," he shouted after him, "I must have them back soon!"

"It'll save us hours of sweat," said the soldier to his companion as they jogged along at a slow pace.

"Don't they go any faster?" said the other, a lean sallow man in his thirties, who had been in the army for more years than he cared to remember.

"They go a lot faster than we would trudging up there."

"It's not right. Where is our dignity if someone sees us?"

"Shut up!" said the first, edging his beast on to the goat track which had been pointed out to them. The animals were familiar with the track and took their usual route, regardless of the intentions of the two soldiers who soon nodded off as the donkeys ambled upwards. That was how they came to reach the Sierra de Libar, rather than the lookout point for which they had been aiming.

They only jerked awake when the steady motion of the donkeys ceased.

They stood looking at the inhospitable terrain. It was mid afternoon and very hot, and even the vultures had departed to the shade.

"Let's sit under that tree by the rocks," said the younger soldier, leading his donkey towards it. The older man slid stiffly from his mount and it followed him when he let go of its rein. The animals were used to looking after their own interests, just as the soldiers were.

It was only later when one of the soldiers went behind the rocks to relieve himself that he found the entrance to the cave. His muffled voice reached his companion.

"Over here!"

They explored with interest, lighting matches to look round. It was in the flare of a match that they spotted the smear of blood on the rock wall of the cave where Verity had been propped up.

"Blood?"

"Could be, not sure how old though." He spat on his palm and rubbed it over the patch of rock. His hand came away stained.

"Looks fresh. Could be significant."

It was only when they emerged that they realised the potential of the landscape for landing a plane, although from the rocks and boulders strewn about it would not be easy. They searched for any sign of a plane having landed or any other signs left by the person who had lost blood in the cave.

"It would have been difficult to land with this great boulder blocking the way."

"But something must have happened up here for there to be fresh blood." The soldier sat down, leant his back against the boulder, lit a cigarette and puffed on it. He contemplated the sun, the rocks and the dust and finally rose throwing his cigarette stub on the ground and stubbing it out with the toe of his boot. Doing so revealed oil in the sand. He sank to his knees and stared at it.

"That plane must have landed here and hit this rock," he concluded.

"But it isn't here now so must have taken off again."

"Better report to the Major; let him work it out.

The radio refused to work so they walked back down to Cortes, letting the donkeys lead the way and simply following them. It was dark by the time they reported to Major Moreno.

The Major immediately got on the phone to the General, who cursed him and everyone else at the escape of his quarry.

When the General had run out of invective, Moreno spoke, "Just possible that the plane didn't get away. If the pilot was injured on landing, the fugitive might still be here, somewhere up in the mountains."

"And where would they have hidden the plane?"

"I haven't got an answer to that one yet, Sir, but I'm working on it."

"You've got two days, then I need you back here," and the General put the phone down.

Moreno didn't know what had made him hold out this hope to the General, other than a hunch which wasn't the sort of thing a soldier under orders was meant to have. He put his cap on and went out to find some company.

27

Helen had written a short note to Juan at his Poste Restante address, telling him of her arrival in Barcelona and her whereabouts. But several days went by without him making contact. Helen's time was taken up during the day with nursing, receiving casualties and dealing with them. Wounded from the front arrived periodically, and in between there were the injured from other more local skirmishes. Helen saw George from time to time, generally grubby and tired but with all his enthusiasm intact for a 'real' war, as he called it. He was picking up Spanish phrases as he went, although the ambulance drivers seemed to be of all nationalities, just like the nursing staff in the hospital.

George told her that the roads outside the city were difficult to drive on as they were badly potholed, and there had been some indiscriminate shelling of the roads and the traffic on them by the Nationalists, making their task even more difficult. He did not tell her about the pitiful heaps of bodies beside the road where the military had pushed all debris aside, human and otherwise, to keep the roads open. George had been told that Spanish Medical Aid might soon be sending them elsewhere and this movement of their unit could include the nurses who had gone out under the scheme too.

It had not taken Helen long to fit into such routine as the hospital had in time of war. She even ceased to notice the red flags draped everywhere and the occasional gunfire and shelling in the distance. She would be due for a day off in two days' time and had planned to go in search of Juan, borrowing a map to work out where to go. Other nurses advised against going out alone in the city, after all, she did not even know her way around. It was too dangerous, they said, and if she must go out, she ought to have someone to go with her. They fixed up that she could go out into the city the day after tomorrow with one of the junior doctors whose day off it was. Helen was getting desperate, to come all this way to be with Juan and now to run the risk of being sent to another part of Spain without seeing him didn't bear thinking about.

Juan at that moment was contemplating his future. He and Felipe had assisted six prominent citizens to exit the country via a sea route. They had taken refugees past the guard posts at the docks, disguised as crew of this vessel or that, and walked out alone some hours later. They feared that they were becoming known to the guards and had decided that they could not use that exit again. But coming up with any other way of smuggling anyone out would be difficult, and they had a steady stream of would-be clients seeking an escape route who deluged them with offers of money and jewellery for a passage out. Money was very necessary because support had to be bought. But the more people who knew about it, the more risky the enterprise became, and they decided that the time had come to at least call a temporary halt to their activities. Neither Juan nor Felipe had collected any mail for some weeks - they had done their best to disappear officially. Anyone who noted their absence from their usual haunts would think that they had gone to their homes; maybe it was really time to go home until the heat was off. They discussed booking a passage home to Ibiza. which had fallen to the Nationalists at the beginning of the uprising, then been reclaimed by a Republican force, but it was generally felt that the Nationalists would soon send a larger force to reclaim it and that would mean reprisals. There were rumours that the Nationalists carried out mass killings of anyone suspected of Republican sympathies. How much truth there was in these rumours it was difficult to guess. Juan and Felipe had their homes in Ibiza and maybe home was where they ought to be. But

Barcelona had felt like a home too for some time and it was difficult to contemplate leaving.

"It'll only be for a short time until the present troubles are over," urged Juan.

"You really think there'll be a quick solution? I wish I thought so."

"No," admitted Juan "in my heart I do not think so."

"What options do we have?" mused Felipe. "We could join the militia and fight for the Republicans, I suppose."

"If it was a unified army we might, but the militia is so divided and the 'proper' army is on the other side. I don't much want to align myself with any particular communist faction. In fact, definitely not any communist faction," said Juan firmly.

"We could head for Madrid and help to defend it against the Nationalists."

"Same problem, we'll only be allowed to fight if we join one of those 'red' outfits and I just can't go along with what they stand for."

"I hope it doesn't make me sound like a traitor," said Felipe "but what I would really like to do is to follow my boss. He's in Italy now and is sure to be working. I would like to finish off my training with him. When this war is over, much rebuilding will be needed and that is where I can be most useful. I just feel that there's no place in this conflict for those in the middle ground. We will just get mown down by one party or another because we are in their way."

Juan was silent for a bit. "I suppose, if I am honest, I very much want to go to England and see Helen again."
"Are you going to marry her?" enquired his friend.
"I'd like to, but I just don't know: we come from totally different cultures. I don't know how it would work out. I can hardly ask her to come and live here at the moment, and how could I settle in England? I don't know what it's like, so I need to go and see for myself."
They poured more wine and sat with their feet up contemplating the future.
"Ought we to see if there's any post?"
"Pointless - what post could possibly get through at the moment? Much better to make it look like we've already left."
"There are too many people who know that we're still here. We have either got to move or get out altogether."
"Look, we pick up messages at Andre's bar; few people know of our actual address, especially now everyone else has left here."
"Maybe. We must not go to Andre's again - the next escape must be our own. We need two boats out - doesn't much matter where to, so long as it is away from Spain, but we can't risk going together."
They mulled over possibilities and decided that one of them would check the harbour bars for visiting ships' crew the next day, armed with an appropriate pocketful of money to buy generous rounds of drinks.

Helen was excited and anxious about going out into Barcelona to look for Juan. She had intended to wear her own clothes but the other girls advised that it would be safest to be seen as a nurse. A young doctor met her at the entrance and took her out into the city. He was giving up his day off to accompany her, but she was a very pretty girl and he found her fair hair quite bewitching. He hurried her round some of the main sights in Barcelona like a tour guide, anxious that she should see everything in the best light. When she wanted to see where the fighting had been, he hustled her off to see the Cathedral. When she asked about the storming of the barracks, he tried to distract her by telling her about how the Sardana, a Catalan dance, was now performed outside the cathedral on Sunday mornings and that it was a symbol of their new freedom. A question about the battle for the telephone exchange saw her hauled off to admire the Palace of Music, wonderful in itself, but Helen was beginning to despair. She had longed to see all these sights, but with Juan, not this earnest young man who fancied himself as a city guide. He was doing his best and obviously wanted to avoid causing her distress about the war that was dividing Spain, but she had not come just to see the sights and all this was wasting time. When they paused for breath at a café, she tried to tackle the subject, but he had difficulty in understanding her accent and therefore what she wanted. It was when he moved his chair nearer to hers and put an arm round her shoulders that she realised just how far apart their thoughts actually were!

"No!" she said moving abruptly away from him. It was the vehemence in her voice that attracted the attention of someone else at the pavement café.

"Is he giving you trouble, Miss Pugh?" said an English voice, and Helen turned to see Bernard looking anxiously down at her. He looked somewhat scruffy and down at heel but he had never been more welcome.

"Bernard, how wonderful to see you! Do join us," she replied in Spanish and, waving him to a seat, she made the introductions.

"The doctor has very kindly been giving me a guided tour of the city, he is a most respected colleague at the hospital," she said, trying hard to avoid any hurt feelings on the part of the doctor.

"Bernard is in the legal profession," she said to Amador, who stared hard at the dishevelled young man, not believing her.

"I was hoping to join up and fight for the Republic," said Bernard "but they won't have me at the moment in spite of my party card."

The doctor, whose pride had been severely jolted by Helen's reaction to his advances, could clearly see why the authorities had refused the services of this weedy boy. However Helen had made a gracious apology and he was prepared to accept that there had been misunderstandings between them, but this did not extend to making small talk with this boy. He summoned the waiter and paid for their coffees.

"Can I escort you further or may I entrust you to your English friend to return you safely to the hospital?" he enquired.

"Bernard will see me safely back, won't you, Bernard?" she said beaming at him. He nodded, hoping that she knew where this hospital of hers was, because he didn't.

They shook hands all round with insincere expressions of mutual delight and then the doctor had gone, unaware that he was the one person with the information Helen needed most, the whereabouts of Juan, whom he had known at university.

Helen breathed a large sigh of relief and turned to Bernard. They had much to talk about. Several pots of coffee later, after they had caught up with news, she asked him where he was staying.

"Sleeping rough at the moment, Miss, nowhere in particular to go."

Helen thought for a bit. "Why don't you join Spanish Medical Aid?" she asked.

"Ain't got no training, Miss," he replied.

Helen explained about the volunteers who manned the ambulances and looked after the casualties and said that she was sure they would welcome a Spanish speaker.

"Suppose I could help," he said, scratching his head. "Just until they'll have me as a soldier." Remembering his ambitions, he straightened in his chair and tried to look like he was growing into a soldier by the minute. Helen suppressed a smile.

"Of course," she said, hoping that once he got into the Medical Aid work, he'd forget about becoming a soldier: after all, he would be fed and housed by the volunteer organisation. Verity would be pleased to know that her lost protégé was found; Helen looked forward to writing to tell her.

"Now," said Helen, "you can help me." She explained about wanting to find Juan and how he had not responded to her letters. Bernard knew all about Juan and Felipe and their friendship with Helen and Verity, but also understood that Helen had made some kind of commitment to this Juan. He wasn't sure whether they were actually engaged or not but thought that they had an understanding, just like him and Gloria. They talked it back and forth.

"So you don't have any idea where he is living now, just this post office address since he last moved?"

"That's right. I have the address of the architect that he used to work for but think he said that the architect had left the country at the outset of the uprising."

"I could check it out for you, Miss. I've made friends since I've been here," he said, gesturing at a ragged group nearby in the street who were watching them and giggling amongst themselves. "They may not be much to look at but they know Barcelona like the back of their hand. They sell newspapers, know everything that goes on almost before it happens."

"Be discreet won't you, Bernard," she said, laying a hand on his arm. This brought a chorus of catcalls from the boys. Bernard looked pleased with himself now. He was going to have a job in the thick of it and he could help Helen find her man - what could be better? He called one of the lads over and introduced him before briefing him in rapid Spanish. He gave him Juan's boss's address and asked him to find it and observe who was going in and out. He explained that he wanted a description of everyone who went in, but that the watcher must not be seen.

Turning back to Helen, he explained awkwardly that the boy would need something for his trouble, but added in English "Safest not to show him what money you're carrying, Miss."

Helen fished in her pocket and brought out a few coins. "Will this be enough?"

"Just right, Miss," and to the boy, "Same again when you report back, friend. I'll be at the Medical Aid post - do you know it?" The boy nodded and rejoined his friends.

Together Helen and Bernard made their way back to the hospital where Helen got him accepted as a volunteer and made sure he got food and a bed. Later, when George reappeared, she asked him to take

Bernard under his wing for the first few days after which she was sure the resourceful Bernard, always quick to learn, would have made himself indispensable.

28

Roberto had met up with Verity and César, having obtained some food, water, wine and even more importantly, news of Nationalist activity in the region. The locals said that army patrols were believed to be combing the mountains and soldiers had been asking whether any one had seen a plane flying over the area. It was apparent that no one in Cortes de la Frontera had seen the plane.

They had the rations which Verity had brought in the plane which they could use as a safeguard against their not being able to obtain food locally. Thankfully, the mules had been well able to carry everything they needed to take with them from the plane. It was always risky for Roberto to go into towns or villages and they needed to avoid this wherever possible. The sound of spasmodic gunfire could be heard rolling around the mountains but, because of the echoes, it was very difficult to place whether it was near or some distance away.

They continued on their way in order to put as much distance as possible between them and the Sierra de Libar. Roberto reckoned that it would be three to four days' walk to Gibraltar. Verity's arm in a makeshift sling was stiff and sore and, although it was no longer bleeding, it wasn't much use for anything either, but at least it was her left arm and she was right-handed. They had decided to make for the cork forests as they would be less likely to be spotted in a forest than out here on the mountainside. They avoided the topic of precisely where they were aiming for as none of them had an answer as yet, other than the obvious one of Gibraltar.

They rested in the hottest part of the afternoon, finding what shade they could, then moved on again as the shadows lengthened. They walked on, long after dark, until they could no longer see where to place their feet. Then they ate and afterwards talked, Verity sitting leaning comfortably against Roberto whose strength and enthusiasm were infectious. It was so good to be with him again that even in this perilous situation her confidence was restored. She had heard nothing at all from him since he left England and had assumed that whatever there was between them had finished. Now, feeling his light touch on her arm, it was as though the intervening year had disappeared. They did not talk about the past, only the future.

Roberto wanted them to head for Gibraltar. César was not so sure - he thought this would be where guards and checkpoints would be concentrated and could not see how they would get through. He had the advantage of having visited Gibraltar, as indeed had Verity, but something stopped her mentioning this. They deferred to Roberto's wishes for the moment.

Finally, they arranged a rota for staying awake on watch and, whilst the men protested about Verity taking a turn, they were also relieved as this would lengthen the hours that each could sleep. Sleeping for longer than two hours was positively luxurious after their journey across Spain.

Verity, at her insistence, took the middle watch. It was surprisingly cold in the middle of the night considering the time of year, but the cold air helped her to stay awake. Her leg muscles ached from the tough walking and she suspected that she already had some blisters on one foot, in spite of the strong boots she was wearing. Indeed she ached all over from the bruises from the impact of the crash, with the exception of her left arm, which was simply numb.

She sat listening to the sounds of the night, of insects and animals, the mules moving gently about and a faint rustling of the wind. She could not see very far as there were no lights visible anywhere and no stars. She contemplated the problem of where they should head for. It had to be the coast, but what they would do when they reached it was another matter. It would probably mean either buying or stealing a boat.

Verity wondered whether her luck had run out with the second plane crash. Then she reminded herself of her good fortune - she had survived both crashes, even though the first one had clearly been intended to write her off along with the plane. Had the second one been sabotaged too, she wondered? On balance probably not, as it had been the boulder which had been her undoing; difficult for anyone to foresee that one. Or had someone deliberately moved it, knowing that a pilot landing a plane would be unable to see it with the nose of the plane high up and blocking visibility?

But whatever the truth, she knew that she had inadvertently played into the hands of the enemy in not whisking their quarry from under their noses. She was now going to have to travel with César for some days and expose him to the risk of capture from either side. That risk encompassed her too. Far from disconcerting her, she felt very protective towards César and determined that, one way or another, she was going to deliver him safely to the British Government, and to Connie too. After all, she thought, he was free to marry now, so some good had to come out of all this.

She woke César at the end of her watch and then curled up next to Roberto, who sleepily responded by drawing her in close to him and kissing her. She fell asleep with her head cradled against his shoulder and the warmth of his body protecting her against the night chill.

They felt safe high in the mountains. By day, they might be seen from a long way off and sound also carried, a fact that they were very conscious of. Anything that could chink or clank on the mule bridles had long since been removed. If the path branched, they took the higher path, as they had a fear of anyone spying on them from above.

On the second day, Verity found the heat even more trying than the first. She needed frequent swigs of water from the wine skins to wet her parched throat. In the end she slung one of the wine skins over her good shoulder and carried it with her so that she did not have to halt their progress in order to get water from the panniers. She was feeling strangely dizzy too, waves of nausea coming over her at times.

Sometimes they talked quietly as they walked, or one of them would point out an eagle or another bird of prey to Verity and hand her the field glasses to watch the bird soaring high above. The vigilance that required them to continually scan the countryside enabled Verity to spot many more birds and animals than she would normally have done. All about her were wonderful vistas of Andalusia which she could absorb even whilst searching the landscape for signs of anyone who might be an enemy.

Around midday they heard the sound of someone hammering on rock some distance off. Roberto used the field glasses and saw a man working on the repair of one of the dry stone walls that crisscrossed the area. They decided that Roberto would go forward along the track with the mules and distract the man's attention, whilst César and Verity would climb up to the ridge and skirt round the man before rejoining the track later on.

Verity and César started to climb up the mountainside. It was not unduly steep but there were loose stones underfoot which made it difficult to keep their footing. They slowed down to minimise the risk, and each concentrated on getting safely on the other side of a low stone wall which ran just below the ridge.

Verity, as the younger and fitter, got there first and had dropped down behind the wall when she heard a small cascade of stones. Peering through a chink in the wall, she saw that César had lost his footing and had slipped a few feet down the mountain side. She was over the wall in a flash and scrambled down to him, extending her hand. He grasped it thankfully.

Roberto, hearing the cascade of stones above, acted as though he himself had slipped on the path. Whether the man up ahead was fooled he could not tell. Roberto, passing him on the track, acted liked any self-respecting smuggler using these high paths and offered the man a cigarette before laying the open packet down on the wall. They stood and smoked amiably.

"Patrols up here yesterday," offered the man.

"Looking for anything in particular?" queried Roberto.

"Reckon they were. Asking questions about a plane and whether I'd seen one land or take off. Daft it was. Only ever seen a plane once down at Malaga. They've got spies on the brain, always asking questions in the town, that's why I come up here where I don't have to talk to anybody other than my own kind." He nodded at Roberto and pocketed the pack of cigarettes.

"Salud," said the man.

"Salud," responded Roberto.

Roberto met up with the others about half a mile down the track and was surprised to see César leaning heavily on Verity and dragging one foot.

"Help me get him on a mule," said Verity. There was no time to waste getting him properly seated. They heaved him up to what would have been side-saddle, if there had been a saddle. Verity took a length of rope from a pannier and secured it round his waist and round the mule so that he could not slide off. Roberto put an arm round César's waist to support him and they set off, César's left foot sticking out uncomfortably.

It was several miles before they felt able to stop behind a cluster of boulders and gently lift him down on to a blanket. There was a lot of swelling already around his ankle. Verity probed gently with her fingers but could not tell whether it was broken or not and did not want to remove his boot in case she was unable to get it back on again. All the while César was protesting that there was nothing wrong, that he would be able to walk, that he was not going to impede their progress. Eventually Roberto in exasperation told him to be quiet; they would see to his ankle and he must ride from now on.

Verity took bandages from the first aid kit and soaked them in water before applying them to try to reduce any further swelling. What he really needed was some kind of stick to help him move about, but there was nothing they could utilise on the mountainside. César took the painkillers offered and swallowed them down with wine. Verity hoped the alcohol would also help dull the pain.

Verity observed that César's colour was not good. There was a greenish tinge to his complexion which she did not like the look of - shock perhaps. They really ought to get a doctor to see him but doctors meant towns. They had intended to keep well away from the town of Alqueria de la Frontera after crossing the river, but Roberto now steered them towards it.

They had hoisted César back on to the unresisting mule and could see by his face how painful it was. The mule ambled gently along and César clung on to it, beads of sweat on his face. Neither Verity nor Roberto had any medical training, but clearly César needed proper medical attention as soon as possible. Whether such help might be available at Alqueria de la Frontera was anybody's guess but they were going to have to seek help, whatever the cost.

In murmured conversation, Roberto and Verity agreed that they would look for a sheltered place just outside the town and then Roberto would go in to find a bar where he could obtain information.

They could already see the town ahead: it had been visible for some time, perched on the top of a hill with a ruined castle commanding the landscape. Nearing the town, they took refuge in a copse of cork trees on the outskirts. Roberto cut César a stick to use as a walking aid. They agreed that, whilst Roberto was gone, César should stay on the mule in case he and Verity had to vanish further out of sight. They checked weapons and ammunition and then Roberto took the road into town.

As he entered the hilly town, he was passed by an army car with flag flying from the bonnet, clearly a Nationalist officer's car. Roberto noted that there were three soldiers in it as well as the officer. Fortunately they took no notice of Roberto who shortly found a bar where he sat down and ordered a drink. Locals had learned not to converse with strangers - it was too dangerous - much better not to know. They might be regular visitors from Gibraltar visiting Alqueria, as people had done for well over a century, or they might be smugglers or even customs men on the trail of the illicit trade in tobacco and spirits. Local custom was to make no enquiries of anyone: if you knew nothing you could not let anything slip to the wrong people, whoever they might be.

Refilling Roberto's glass the barkeeper said, "Don't know what you're here for but the best place to find it is at the Hotel Inglés," he said, jerking his thumb to indicate the direction. Roberto nodded, drank up and left.

He found the stable for the inn where he could see several horses' heads peering out of the stalls. A stable boy came up and raised an eyebrow at him. Roberto offered a cigarette and lit it for him; the boy dragged gratefully on it.

"Any doctor in town? Bad foot," Roberto said casually, indicating his dusty boots.

"No doctor in this town, not now."

"Where will I find one?" Roberto asked passing over a few coins.

The boy looked at the coins in his hand, much more than the usual tips from guests at the inn and decided to be helpful. "Think we've got one staying at the moment, foreigner booked in for the night. Want me to call him?"

Roberto nodded and handed over some more coins. The boy counted and pocketed them before disappearing up the stairs into the inn. Roberto kept a watchful eye on the street, particularly for that staff car. He smoked another cigarette sitting on an upturned stable bucket.

A man came out "You wanted me?" he enquired in heavily accented Spanish.
"You're the doctor?"
"Yes."
Nothing for it but to trust this man.
"I've got an injured man with me, slipped down the mountainside earlier today and hurt his ankle, might be broken. There's also a girl who has injured her shoulder."
"Did she slip too?"
"No."
The doctor looked him over wondering whether this travel stained man was one of the bands of guerrillas he had heard about. He didn't want to be lured out to some mountain hideaway but, on the other hand, he felt bound by his professional ethics to aid anyone who was sick or injured. He made up his mind.
"I'll look at them but it had better be somewhere on the outskirts of the town, not here." The doctor thought for a moment. "There's a chapel, a shrine to some saint or other just below the castle, it should be deserted at this hour. Look, I'll show you." He picked up a stick and did a sketch map in the dust. "Got it?"
Roberto nodded and erased the sketch with the toe of his boot.
"In one hour, inside the chapel and keep out of sight. Shouldn't be disturbed there," and he turned and went back inside. Roberto slipped away.

After some arguing, he and Verity agreed that she and César would go to the rendezvous taking just one mule. Roberto would remain in the copse with the other mule, with all the supplies. They unloaded the panniers of the mule which César was riding, so that they had nothing suspicious with them. Verity was carrying a gun hidden in her clothing from the cache in the plane, a very handy machine pistol which she had been trained to use, but thought it best to say nothing about this to Roberto as he had no idea she could even shoot. He kissed her briefly and disappeared deeper into the copse with the laden mule.

Verity, leading the other mule carrying César, took the overgrown path Roberto had indicated on the outskirts of the town. It wound round the base of the castle walls towards the shrine. She felt for the security of the gun and ammunition and, reassured, hoped fervently that she was not walking into a trap.

29

Bernard waved to Helen as she entered the hospital canteen for breakfast. "Hey, Miss! Over here."
Helen went over to where he was sitting with several of the other volunteer ambulance crew. She had not seen him for a couple of days and found that Bernard's appearance was transformed. Dressed in his office suit with nice white shirt and tie and an armband signifying his status, he looked what he was, smart, savvy and good at his new job. He also looked infectiously happy and had the knack of making others cheerful too, whatever the language barrier.
"I've heard from my friends," he said, switching to English and digging out a notebook. "Two chaps, youngish, early twenties seem to be living there, as they stay overnight." He went on to read a description of two men that sounded very much like Juan and Felipe. "They act very cautious, entering the building next door to the address, and my friends thought they

probably gained access over the roof as there didn't seem to be an entrance to the architect's building - where there should have been a door it's bricked up. Offices next door have a workers' committee on the first floor, no one living on the premises. These two don't put on any lights in the building they enter, but a faint light sometimes shows in the architect's office next door. Do you think that's them, Miss?"

"Bernard, I'm sure it's them," Helen was ecstatic and felt very much inclined to burst into tears and hug Bernard. Juan was there; she would be with him soon. Taking a deep breath to calm herself, she went on, "Do you think your, er, friends could take me there? How long would it take?"

Consulting his notes he said, "Sounds as though the best time to be sure of them being there is to arrive about seven in the morning. I would need to be there too, Miss, not safe to let you go on your own with my friends."

Helen nodded - she would feel much better if she had Bernard with her for this tricky meeting.

"Tomorrow morning?" she asked.

"Meet you at the hospital entrance at six, just so long as I'm not out with the ambulance. I'll keep the lads watching in the meantime, just to be sure."

Helen felt confident that he had things in hand.

"Oh, Miss," he went on. Helen turned back to face him. "I've written to Gloria now I've got a proper job like.

Told her to tell Miss Fleming I'm okay." Helen beamed at him and went to get her breakfast.

Felipe was worried. "I'm sure this place is being watched," he said, looking out of the window and indicating.

"Do you mean the newspaper boy," said Juan, "why would he be watching us?"

"They've never sold La Vanguardia on this street before. They've been doing it for three days now. The boy selling the papers changes during the day but they never leave the pitch and they always seem to be watching when we go in or out."

"Don't be paranoid, they're just lads trying to make an honest living in difficult times."

"I think we ought to get out as soon as we can."

"As soon as we can find two willing skippers, we're off. I'll be down at the quayside bars today as usual. May be we should simply take any boats we can and not be fussy about the destination."

"You're right. Whilst you're out, I'll begin to remove all traces of our living here."

"Good."

It was much later in the day that the phone in the architect's office began to ring. Juan was shocked to hear it as he had not even realised it was still working. He stood stock still until it finally stopped. Who could be calling? Were there really people out there who were trying to track them down, as Felipe had suggested? He crept to the window and saw that a paperboy was still down there behind his stand, sitting on a step with his hat tipped over his eyes. Was this unusual? Wouldn't they normally disappear in the heat of the day to await the distribution of later editions of the paper? He really didn't know, it was just that ringing of the telephone in the empty office which had rattled him.

It had not been until the afternoon that Helen remembered that Verity had given her the telephone number of Felipe's office in case she should need it. She tried once from the Hospital Administrator's office and then tried at intervals whenever she was free. No-one answered.

Felipe returned in the evening and burst in through the door very excited, "I've done it! I've got a skipper whose boat is calling at Italy to agree to take me tonight and he sails in the early hours. And I think I've got you a berth on a boat leaving for Africa tomorrow evening as a crew member! What do you think about that?"

Felipe outlined the details; they would pull the party trick just once more. He had already been to round up friends to make up a rowdy party to accompany the skipper and his mates on board but he stipulated that Juan should not be there: it would be too dangerous for him to be seen on the docks two nights running. Juan said that he would watch from another bar as he must know that Felipe had got away safely.

"So long as you make no move if anything goes wrong," stipulated Felipe.

Juan nodded.

"I've been busy," went on Felipe producing some dirty clothes from his bag. "They're a seaman's clothes."

"They smell like it," retorted Juan.

"They are the clothes you will wear when you sign on tomorrow to serve on the coal ship that is coming in, and these," he said, waving some papers triumphantly, "are your identity documents showing that you are a registered seaman, your permit to enter the docks and discharge papers from your last ship."

Juan gaped, "Just how did you get those?"

"Poor soul got too drunk and was arrested, then assaulted a guard and the rest is history. One of my contacts whipped his spare clothing and identity papers before the guards could seize his effects. The coal ship never has enough crew, always short-handed and looking for additional men. The skipper always frequents a particular bar and if you approach him there, he will sign you up without any questions asked, particularly if he has a jug or two first."

"My dear friend," said Juan "how can I ever thank you enough?"

Felipe clasped his hand, "Just make sure you get away safely, that'll be my thanks."

At ten that night, Juan embraced Felipe at a quayside bar and then hurried off to a bar further down the street where he could observe the proceedings. As the hours passed, he watched as a rowdy party developed, apparently centred on a tall fat man, who could be distinguished as the captain of a merchant boat, and some drunken crew members. Juan knew that the captain had already been well paid for his services with final payment to be made when the ship was safely at sea and the fellow played up well, finally standing up and with open arms clearly inviting the drinkers to accompany him to his ship.

The motley group swayed and lurched their way along the street past where Juan was sitting, Felipe with one arm round the captain. Juan watched as they approached the dock gates and the guard post. The captain waved his hand expansively as he rolled past, shouting that these were his friends and they were going to have a party on board, the best party ever and everyone was welcome.

To Juan's horror, the guards stepped forward, barring the way with their rifles. The message was clear, only the crew would be allowed past. An argument seemed to be going on, and then they were turned back, only the sailors being let through. Juan saw Felipe detach himself from the group and then, to Juan's horror, he saw Felipe jump into the water. The guards ran forward, rifles at the ready. Juan started to rise from his chair, Felipe was going to try and swim for the ship and it wouldn't work, they would shoot him in the water. A rifle cracked, once, twice.

Somehow Juan managed to stay in his chair, remembering his promise to Felipe. Then as he watched, the rest of the group, after a brief hesitation, teetered towards the dock in a rowdy singing laughing group and promptly fell or jumped off the dock after Felipe. Those who didn't jump were thrown off by the guards with choice epithets following them. There was complete chaos.

At last an order was shouted, and some of the sentries were dispatched to guard the gangplanks of individual ships including the one whose captain and mates had now retreated on board. The crew were clearly rattled as they appeared to be getting under way immediately.

Some of the party were still larking in the water, others were heading for the nearest steps to get out of the filthy oily water. Fortunately the guards took no further interest in the sodden group. There was no sign of Felipe; had he made it to the far side of the boat and managed to clamber on board? The boat was edging out slowly from its berth and making its way to the dock entrance.

Juan lingered until all the swimmers had come out of the water. Then he waited at the bar where the customers were discussing 'those idle wasters who've nothing better to do than swim in the docks'. It was three in the morning before Juan gave up his watch and made his way back to the architect's office in low spirits, not knowing whether his friend was alive or dead.

Once home, he sat looking glumly at the seaman's clothes and papers until his head finally sank on to his chest. He hardly seemed to have slept at all when he was awakened by someone knocking on the door. Starting up and looking wildly round for escape, he at last realised that a male voice was calling out in English, "Visitor for you!"

Juan threw open the door, and there was Helen, who fell into his arms laughing and crying, watched with a wide grin by a young man wearing an ambulance section armband.

"Juan, this is Bernard, I'm sure I've mentioned him in my letters."

Juan firmly grasped Bernard's hand and took an immediate liking to this young man with the infectious grin.

"If you'll excuse me, Miss, I'd better be off to work now."

"I can't thank you enough, Bernard," Helen said, kissing his cheek so that he blushed. "It was Bernard who tracked you down when you didn't reply to my letters," she explained to Juan.

Bernard tactfully disappeared. Juan closed the door and took Helen into his arms. It was a long while before they surfaced enough to talk. There was so much to catch up on and so much to say to one another to declare their love, that for a long while nothing made much sense to either of them.

They had to confine themselves to the bare essentials. Helen grasped that Juan and Felipe had been running an escape route for people in danger of being arrested and shot. Now they thought the authorities might be on to them and it was time for them to disappear and Felipe had made his bid to get out of the country only a few hours ago.

Helen suggested that it was highly unlikely that a few random shots fired into the water in the dark could have killed him. It was much more likely that he had boarded either the ship leaving for Italy or another boat. Juan thought about this and became a little more optimistic. Helen worked on this.

"But how can I leave now you have come to me here?" he said, stroking her hair.

"Darling, it's vital you leave tonight. You must sign up on that coal ship."

"You want me to be a sailor? You like sailors?"

"I'll like this one, just so long as you don't have a girl in every port," she said, kissing him again.

"I can't desert you," he said resolutely.

"You won't be deserting me, silly! I must know that you are safe if I'm to be able to do my work here."

It was only then that Juan glimpsed how hard it had been for Helen to come all this way to attend to the injured and sick in this war, far from home, and how difficult the work itself must be. He pressed her hand to his lips, then knelt in front of her.

"Miss Pugh," he said formally, "will you be my novia, my betrothed, my wife?"

His eyes held hers as they widened, and then she smiled and held out her hands to him.

"You may have to ask my father's consent - he's a bit old-fashioned that way - but my answer is definitely yes!"

Juan walked her back to the hospital in the early evening. She was going to be in trouble for having been absent all day without leave, but these brief snatched hours with Juan were worth it. Helen had Juan's real identity papers in her bag and his bank books for safekeeping. She also had some other keepsakes from him. He just had his seaman's clothes in a bag with him. On her advice, he had not shaved nor washed himself or his hair as it was essential that he looked the part of a just sobered up seaman.

They stopped for a coffee in a café near the hospital and sat looking at one another.

"I'll go to the cloakroom to change and leave my old clothes there. I think there's a back way out, and I'll use that and set off for the dock and a life of hard labour," he said. "But you must leave first, I want to see you reach the hospital safely before I go."

They stood up and Helen turned and left quickly, only looking back when she had reached the entrance to the hospital. She waved at the dark figure silhouetted against the lights of the café, then ran up the steps.

As she neared the casualty ward, she became aware of the pandemonium surrounding the ward. A fleet of battered ambulances stood outside, blanket covered stretchers everywhere, the cries and screams of the wounded mingling with agitated cries from those trying to attend to them. She flung her cloak and bag into a locker and plunged into the chaos.

"Which ones shall I deal with?" she said, grabbing the arm of a passing colleague. He paused wiping his brow with a bloody hand.

"Over there, start over there," he said pointing.

Helen joined a little nurse who was flapping around ineffectively over a group of four stretchers. Helen started with the end one and checked his wrist pulse - none was apparent - felt his neck and flashed a light in the staring eyes. This one was beyond need of help, which was not surprising as it looked as though half his chest had been blown away. She pulled the blanket gently over his face and moved on to the next one.

The little nurse had joined her now, relieved to find that someone knew what to do.

"Are these casualties from the front?" Helen asked her.

"No, they say the Nationalists are bombing the roads leading to the front; most of them aren't even soldiers," she said, tears brimming up again in her eyes.

"Help me with this one; no time to cry," said Helen attending to another stretcher case.

Caked in mud and blood with a dirty bandage round his head, it was difficult to see the man's features other than that he was slightly built. He was murmuring, she bent her head to catch what he was saying as she started to gently peel back the blankets to look at his injuries and check for bleeding. It took a moment to realise that it was mixture of Spanish and English as he kept repeating, "Don't let them take me leg. Not me leg."

Helen removed the blankets and saw that the man's left leg had been blown away. A tourniquet had been applied at some point to stop the bleeding and she called to a young passing doctor, "Shall I ease this off and redo it?"

He nodded, "Get him prepared for theatre and into the queue, he may stand a chance."

Helen worked swiftly changing the bandages whilst the little nurse cleaned him up. It was only when she glanced up momentarily from her work that she saw the man's ashen face properly. It was Bernard.

Helen stayed with him until he went into the theatre, then she worked like an avenging angel doing more work than she would have thought humanly possible. There were women and children amongst the casualties too. How could the Nationalists do such a thing? But outrage was no use. No, the best nursing was what was needed and these innocents should have it. Helen rallied those who were flagging, urging them on and on.

It seemed many hours later that Bernard was carried back into the ward, and Helen went to his side and helped settle him in the bed. She started to fall asleep as she sat holding Bernard's hand. There was still a mixture of night nurses and day nurses on the ward, as some of the day girls had just snatched a few hours' sleep before coming back to the ward. They were all exhausted. A Sister approached Helen.

"This man is your compatriot, the young ambulance man?"

Helen nodded.

"Go and rest. You have looked after our compatriots, we will do the same for yours. It will be many hours before he comes round. I'll send for you at once if there are any developments."

Helen was suddenly more weary than she had ever thought possible.

"Thank you," she said simply, and began to move her leaden feet in the direction of the dormitory and bed.

Hours later someone gently shook her shoulder. "Your friend is awake now and asking for you. We think he is going to pull through."

Helen fell out of bed in her rush to go to Bernard's side, tears of relief making it difficult to see. He managed a weak smile when she sat down by him.

"They've taken my leg then?"

Helen nodded, unable to speak.

"Expect they needed it for the war effort!" he said.

"Oh Bernard, I'm so sorry!"

"I'm thankful to be alive, Miss. Think they got some of our people. One minute we were driving along trying to avoid all those craters in the road, next minute we were one of those craters!"

"I'll make sure you get the best nursing possible," said Helen determinedly.

Bernard was quiet for a bit, and Helen sat holding his hand. She thought he had slipped off to sleep but then he opened his eyes and looked at her. "I'm going to be well in time to dance at your wedding, Miss." Helen leaned forward and kissed him on the cheek.

"I'll make sure you keep that promise!"

Juan too thought of Helen as he stumbled around in the bowels of the vile smelling dirty coal ship as it clanged and creaked its way to sea. Shouted orders followed him wherever he went. Mostly he did not even understand what it was he was supposed to be doing until a crewman pushed him into the right place and handed him a shovel. But he was grinning in the dark: he was on his way to freedom and a new life, and he shovelled away at the coals as though his life really did depend on it.

30

Major Moreno was leaning against the bar at the Hotel Inglés. He had sent his men out to check the town but in the meantime was interested in any visitors at the hotel and exactly why they were there.

It appeared that there were several middle-aged foreign ladies travelling in Spain who had taken refuge at the hotel on their way to Gibraltar. With them the Major was at his most charming and gallant: after all, they posed no risk to anyone. He was a bit suspicious of two men who had arrived that day, one British and the other apparently French. The British man claimed to be on the staff of the Governor of Gibraltar and to have come out to hunt wild boar, a favourite sport of gentlemen quartered in Gibraltar. The Frenchman was apparently being entertained by the idiot British man. Moreno was mistrustful of anyone who could be stupid enough to hunt wild boar in the middle of a war zone. But he could understand foreign visitors such as the ladies getting trapped and had promised them an escort through the Nationalist held territory down to Gibraltar.

He would keep a watch on the hunters' activities for the short period they were here, just to make sure that they were what they said. In the meantime he signalled for another glass of liquor.

Verity had left César and the mule out of sight and was reconnoitring the area around the shrine, which turned out to be a chapel. With whitewashed walls and big wooden double doors, it sat on the hillside just below the ruins of the castle. Verity was watching for any sign of activity or any indication that anyone was already there; it was not yet quite the appointed hour. Having checked the outside, she slipped through the open doors at the front with her gun in her hand and the trigger cocked ready to fire. She flitted round the inside like a wraith making no sound. Then, satisfied, she went outside again and gave a low whistle. An answering one came from César. He rode down the track from behind the castle.

He came in using his makeshift walking stick and Verity settled him in a pew behind a pillar to wait and then looked outside to check the track down to the town again. The shrine looked as though it had already received the attentions of the military of one faction or another, for there were only shards of glass left in the windows and the main door was damaged and incapable of being closed.

Verity had already noted that there was another entrance to the shrine at the rear, presumably for the clergy. She found the entrance to the sacristy and at the far side was the door to the outside. Some keys hung on the wall and one of them fitted the door lock and she opened it. All was quiet, and she went back into the shrine and took up a position where she could see along the town track through one of the shattered windows, having pocketed her pistol.

A man fitting the description of the doctor appeared on horseback, slipping down easily from the saddle and throwing the reins of his mount loosely over a railing as he briskly approached calling out, "Doctor Suchet."

Entering the shrine, he said in halting Spanish, "I don't know who you are, nor do I want to know, but I thought it best if I appeared to be going out for a ride."

Verity said nothing but took him to where César lay out of sight. Then she resumed her lookout through the window. She could see the track and keep watch, but with the lengthening rays of the evening sun, it was difficult to tell whether there might be any movement in the shadows or whether it was the effect of the dying sun. The doctor's horse had easily slipped its reins from the railing and, unsecured, had wandered off out of her line of vision up towards the castle track;

clearly either the grazing was better there, or it had sensed the presence of the mule.

The doctor worked quickly and efficiently on his patient. He could not feel a break in the patient's ankle or leg and decided that it must be a torn ligament in the ankle, hence the fierce pain. It needed strapping up tightly and, with rest, the swelling would go down in a couple of days. The doctor dunked his bandages in the stoop of holy water by the entrance for want of any other source of water and then began strapping the ankle. The patient said little, answering questions tersely with what the doctor recognised was an educated Spanish accent. The clothes were rough though, peasant type clothes. The doctor knew better than to ask any personal questions. He gave an injection of a strong painkiller and finished tying the support bandages. He wished that girl would help him instead of spending her time staring out of the window. He helped the patient sit up, already more comfortable as the injection took effect.

It was then that Verity hissed urgently, "Get out!"

The doctor looked up in surprise, doubting what he had heard.

"Army patrol approaching up the track. Use the sacristy door over there. You'll find a path leading away round the castle, take that. And thank you."

The doctor grabbed his bag and fled through the sacristy door. Verity had already decided that in the event of an attack it was best to leave the main door ajar and cover it with her pistol, rather than cut off a line of possible escape for them. It was better that external appearances were normal. There was just a possibility that this was a routine patrol rather than that someone had followed the doctor.

"Start making your way to the sacristy," she called to César in a low voice. "I'll meet you back in the copse." She heard him make his way out as fast as he could and was glad that he had not chosen to debate her order. Then she rested her machine pistol on the ledge of the window and held it steady, spare ammunition at the ready.

The first words from outside dashed her hopes of it being a routine patrol.

"You're surrounded, come out with your hands above your heads!"

Unlikely that they have us surrounded, thought Verity. Roberto had seen an officer and three men in a staff car. If they had followed the doctor here, there wouldn't have been time to send for reinforcements; it was only an hour and a half since Roberto had arranged the meeting with the doctor. She made no response: they might as well think that their quarry had flown. Her task was to delay them here for long enough to allow César to get back to the copse, where Roberto would hide him. It was César's safety that mattered above all else.

The soldiers crept forward taking advantage of every bit of shelter available, rifles at the ready. The officer had a pistol in his hand.

Verity was reluctant to fire the first shot, she could probably get one of them first time and possibly wing a second one, but that would leave the others to return her fire.

All of a sudden, they came forward in a rush, yelling with the bloodcurdling cries that had already brought fear to many in the campaign. These were not just foot soldiers but Moors, the most feared soldiers of all. For a second, Verity was paralysed and then she fired, spraying the courtyard with bullets. But still they were coming on. She had definitely hit one because he had dropped his rifle and then fell forward on to the rough stones where he lay unmoving. The officer scooped up the rifle as he ran past and in an instant was pouring bullets through and around the open door.

Verity used the moment to jump down and run for the shelter of another pillar, away from where they would expect her to be. One of them tried to rush the door but Verity fired at the floor of the open door so that bullets ricocheted up to meet them. They were uncertain where the fire was coming from and ducked back behind the door frame. She resisted the temptation to put some bullets through the door frame as this might pinpoint her position. Their lack of knowledge of where she was, and indeed how many people there were inside, were her main cards to play at the moment. She had to hold them here for long enough to allow César to get away. She tried another ricochet shot but this time they had her pinpointed and fired in her direction. Then a shot came from the other side of the chapel. Verity thought for a moment that she was indeed surrounded but then realised that the shot had been aimed at the soldiers who were spraying fire through the door opening.

Another shot came from somewhere over the other side of the chapel but still she could not see who was firing.

Then bullets started to pour in through one of the windows, a soldier having climbed up the outer wall. Verity ducked out from her pillar and fired rapidly at the figure in the window who fell with a cry. But this had diverted her from the doorway and they were in, taking shelter by the font as they potted shots at her. She dived from behind the pillar and sheltered crouching behind a pew. She raised her head and fired again then, crouching, ran the length of the pew before diving across the aisle. There seemed to be scuffling movements coming from various parts of the chapel, there was a pause in the shooting as no one quite knew who was where. Verity cautiously peered this way and that but could not see where the two remaining soldiers were, nor where the other unknown gunman was. She hardly dared breathe and, as the pause continued, wondered whether she could make a dive for the main door, but she was on the wrong side to get through in one movement; she would have to go round it and that meant offering herself as a target for too many precious seconds.

Then a familiar voice spoke calmly and clearly into the silence.

"We have your companion. We'll shoot him through the head in 30 seconds unless you come out with your hands up." This was followed by a noise that sounded like someone being throttled.

Verity thought César had come back to fight and they had caught him. It was his safety which mattered most.

"Throw your weapon on to the floor," instructed the voice. Verity threw it on to the floor.

"Kick it to where I can see it," said the voice smoothly as though asking her to pass the salt. "Now come out from behind that pillar."

Verity stepped out.

For a moment she stood facing Moreno six feet away. Another soldier stood behind him but no César. Moreno and Verity recognised one another at the same second. Then a movement at the side of the chapel caught her eye and turning her head slightly she saw a man standing aiming his rifle directly at her. He started to squeeze the trigger as she stood mesmerised. Then everything happened at once.

"No!" The cry was cut off by the rifle firing as someone launched himself at her carrying her down to the floor. Two more almost simultaneous shots and screams, and then the echoes of the sounds died away and there was silence as the dust resettled in the sun's dying rays.

The man on top of her was a dead weight. There was blood over both of them. She did not know whether it was his or hers or both. It was only as she tried to shift the man who had thrown himself in front of her to protect her, that she saw it was Moreno. He was bleeding heavily from a wound in his chest. She struggled to get out from under him and, freeing herself, laid him gently on the floor.

His handsome face was ashen and his breathing barely perceptible. His eyes flickered open and he tried to smile. "Have I redeemed myself?" he whispered.

"Yes," she said and bent over and kissed him. He responded and then gave a sighing breath and was still. Verity fumbled for his wrist but could feel no pulse. She tried the one in his neck and that too was still. There was blood everywhere but it had stopped gushing out from his chest. She automatically checked his jacket pockets with one hand whilst reaching to pick up her pistol. She stuffed his wallet and papers in her pocket and, still kneeling on the chapel floor, reloaded. All was quiet.

Then she pulled herself up by grasping the back of a pew. She could not see anyone. Cautiously she moved towards to where the other soldier had stood. He lay on the stone floor with part of his head blown away.

Verity averted her gaze and started to slowly and cautiously search the chapel.

It was on the floor behind a pew that she found the man who had aimed the point blank shot intended to kill her. She found him lying on his back with sightless eyes gazing at the chapel roof. It was Roberto, the once ardent suitor, who should have been safely waiting in the copse to receive his uncle. She closed his eyelids and made the sign of the cross over him. No time for long farewells - this was war and she was a participant. They were dead and she, by some miracle, was alive. She sprinted for the sacristy door and out into the cooling air and freedom.

31

Verity found César on the ground not far along the track, rubbing his head and looking extremely groggy. "He knocked me out," César explained as she helped him up; at least, thought Verity, Roberto had baulked at killing his uncle. César saw that she was covered in blood but now was not the time for questions. She heaved him unresisting on to the mule and then she started off at a run along the track leading the animal. It responded gallantly and they gained the sanctuary of the copse as dusk was falling. It was the mule who found its companion, tied to a tree well away from where they had expected to find it. Verity climbed on to the second animal and urged it towards the track into the cork forest where she allowed the mules to find their own way deep into the woods, sure-footed as ever in their own environment. Verity and César were ducking under the branches that loomed up at them in the gloom. Verity clung to the neck of her mule and trusted that the animals were not trotting in circles but taking them to safety. They came to a gate in a stone wall and Verity reached down and unfastened it; they went through and she refastened it behind them.

She began to think she was hallucinating when she saw that another animal was now following. When it came alongside her she saw that it was a pony. It passed them and trotted confidently ahead, the mules following. Verity was now having difficulty in stopping herself from shaking uncontrollably, reacting to violent events, the shock of betrayal and so many deaths. They had warned her about this kind of reaction at Brimscombe but she had no idea she would feel quite so bad. Her head felt as though it was almost exploding as her mind fought to make sense of so many lines of thought. All her cherished ideals and principles seemed to have been blown away with the gunfire. Who was friend, enemy, lover in this maelstrom? It simply made no sense that the man she had once thought she loved had tried to kill her, whilst the one whom she had known to be her enemy, a man reputed to be dissolute and feared, had given his life to save her. Had she idealised the one and condemned the other and got it all wrong?

Verity remembered how her attraction to Moreno had nearly overwhelmed her in Madrid. She knew the attraction had been mutual: had she mistaken his for lust? Could events have been different if she had not been so conventional and inhibited? Might both

Roberto and Moreno now be alive if it had not been for her? Verity became aware at last of the pain in her arm, and felt thoroughly weary and longed for sleep. She thought that this must be how soldiers feel after a battle, numb with exhaustion as they try to make sense of what has happened.

The mules crossed a wide drying riverbed and afterwards what looked like another tributary. There was very little water in either but the animals were able to find something to drink before continuing. The terrain was densely wooded and they seemed to be passing through a steep-sided valley well up in the mountains when the hooves of the animals clattered on stone. Looking up, Verity saw that they were passing under a stone archway into a paved yard, then the mules stopped.

Verity slid stiffly from her mount and helped César off his. He seemed to be in better shape than her now, thanks to the painkilling injection from the doctor. They could make out the outline of a building in front of them, quite a grand building by the shape of it, but in total darkness.

"Must be a hunting lodge," whispered César. "This a prime hunting area for wild boar. I'll light the lantern."

Having retrieved one of their lanterns from the panniers, he lit it and held it up. It showed an imposing ivy-clad doorway with the name 'San Juan de la Pena' over the door. He grasped the knocker and knocked. There was no response. He tried the handle and to his surprise it turned. He limped over the threshold into the hall and placed the lantern on a chest.

Verity was struggling with the fastenings of the mules' panniers and heaved them on to the ground. The mules, freed of their burden, trotted off after the pony, presumably towards the stables and food - at least the mules had a host for the night.

Verity dragged their belongings inside and closed the front door, drawing the bolts across it. César in the meantime had found a kitchen and a kitchen pump and had drawn some water. There was a fire laid in the grate and he decided to risk lighting it. Tonight they needed warmth and hot water; in the depth of a valley in the forest it was unlikely that any smoke would be seen. Feeling much better, he placed a large heavy kettle on to heat.

Verity had sunk on to a kitchen settle, exhausted now that the immediate danger was over. César looked at her.

"Before we talk, you must wash off all that blood. Any of it yours?" he asked matter-of-factly.

"Not really sure, maybe some of it," she replied.

César had found another lamp and hobbled off with his stick to explore. She undressed and poured some of the water from the kettle into the sink and started to wash herself. César came back with towels and soap for her and then sat discreetly looking the other way into the fire. At last Verity was satisfied that she was reasonably clean. Now she could at least examine her wounds. The one from the plane crash seemed to have reopened and bled copiously. It looked as though she had simply bruised herself when she was pushed to the chapel floor. She thought she might have hit something on the way down, which might account for the extent of the new bruising that was beginning to appear, that or the impact of Moreno's body; otherwise she was okay. Her arm hurt like mad, but that was all and it was probably an improvement on the previous numbness.

She wrapped the towels around her and went and sat by the fire. César had already delved into the first aid box from the plane and had a dressing ready to put on her arm. First he poured some antiseptic over - it stung horribly. Then he placed the dressing over the wound and bandaged it firmly in place and wrapped a coat round her, one of a selection hanging by the back door. She saw that he had been burning her bloodstained clothes. The contents of her pockets were laid out on the floor.

Seeing her surprised look he said, "Don't worry about clothes, there are plenty in the wardrobes here. There is bound to be something that fits you. Are you warm enough for the moment?"

Verity nodded.

"I take it Roberto is dead?" he asked.

"Yes," she whispered.

"Did you kill him?"

"No."

"You should've done - he was a traitor. He tried to catch us both in that trap. I've had time to think on the way here and can make sense of a lot of things I couldn't understand before. That boulder your plane hit for one; we had cleared the area of rocks ready for a plane to land. Then he had me hide in the cave out of sight. Next thing I knew he told me that your plane had hit an obstacle on landing. It should not have been there, Verity, he must have rolled it there once I was out of sight. But how could I suspect my own nephew?" He paused before going on.

"Tonight, as I made my way along the path from the shrine, I met him, he hailed me, put his arm round my shoulders as though to explain why he was there, but instead knocked me out." César paused. "Tell me what happened at the shrine after I left."

Verity told him about how the soldiers had rushed the chapel, and then went on, "I could not understand what was happening when someone else was firing from the back of the shrine. I thought at first you had come back with a gun."

"I should've done," he responded, "but you remember that Roberto insisted on our leaving all the weapons behind in case we were searched. Clearly you thought for yourself and took a weapon anyway - a pity I didn't have the sense to do the same."

Verity went on, "The unknown gunman wasn't shooting effectively, I couldn't understand what was going on. Then the soldiers pulled a trick, making out they had someone captured. I assumed it was you, they made it sound as though they were throttling you. I followed instructions to drop my gun and came out from behind the pillar. That was when the officer and I recognised one another, standing there face to face. We knew one another immediately - it was Major Moreno. He had extraordinary hypnotic eyes. For a moment I thought he was planning a horrible revenge on me and then I realised that there was something different between us; I didn't have time to put a name to it. We just stood looking at one another for a second."

"Then I caught a movement out of the corner of my eye and turned. Roberto was standing there with a rifle pointing straight at me. It took me completely by surprise. I thought he loved me and instead there he was with this triumphant look on his face as he started to squeeze the trigger. No warning, no farewells, he just squeezed the trigger. I just stood there mesmerised, but the major anticipated it and hurled himself at me, knocking me to the floor. There were other shots and I stayed where I was until the shooting stopped. Then when I picked myself up, I found that

Major Moreno had taken the full impact of the bullet which Roberto had intended for me. The major was still alive but the blood was pumping out of him," she said, reliving the scene. "He died a few moments later."

"A brave man, an enemy, but in the end a gallant man," commented César.

"Yes, a brave man. Did I misjudge him all along?"

"I don't think so. In Ibiza, he had a reputation as a man who took advantage of women and then treated them cruelly, especially if they were pregnant. Don't forget that he was the one who issued an arrest warrant for you."

"Did you know I was listed as a spy after that? All the same, he saved me from Roberto. I may have badly misjudged them both," she said thoughtfully. "I think that what happened after Roberto fired at me was that the remaining soldier fired at Roberto, just as Roberto turned and fired his next shot at him; at any rate they were both dead when I went to look for them. I was glad Roberto was dead because otherwise I might have had to finish him off myself," she said shuddering. "I was thinking it all through on the way here and what I could not make out was just who Roberto was working for and why he wanted to kill me."

"I may have the answer, but it's guesswork," said César. "I think he was a Republican supporter. He'd become a Communist - did you know? But whatever his politics he wanted me dead, particularly after he found my wife had died. I have much wealth in Spain and elsewhere and he was my only heir. His task, self-appointed or otherwise, was to make sure that I never left Spain alive. Maybe there never was an arrest warrant out for me. Later on he'd not expected that arrangements could be made for me to be whisked out of Spain, he didn't know about all my diplomatic contacts. I think that in the end he didn't care which side killed me, so he set up that trap for us to walk into. But he needed to ensure that you were dead because you might talk. He wanted the Nationalists to shoot you and was obviously confident they would kill you immediately, but when they failed to do so, he had to make sure of your silence."

They gazed into the flames which were greedily consuming Verity's clothing.

Verity said slowly, "All of the army patrol were killed, so we stand a chance of getting away. No one will know who they encountered at the shrine; they will think it was Republican activists or guerrillas. We stand a much better chance of escape now than when Roberto was alive."

"You're right," he said sitting up straighter. Although there's the doctor, he'll know."

"The doctor is unlikely to have told anyone where he was going. You heard him say that he had come on horseback to make it look like he was simply out riding."

Verity gathered Moreno's papers up and examined them. No orders or anything useful amongst them but the one thing that did surprise her was discovering in his wallet a carefully preserved drawing of a girl. It was the drawing that Helen had sketched of her so long ago in Ibiza. It came as a shock that he had both found it and kept it with him in the intervening years. What was she to make of that?

Verity was feeling stronger now. They had found some brandy and helped themselves. For a habitual non-drinker, Verity found herself surprisingly grateful for the fortifying effect it had on her.

"Let's find some new clothes," César said, leading her to a bedroom where there was a wardrobe stuffed with men's and women's clothing, footwear, hunting rifles and ammunition, but then this was a hunting lodge. César decided to help himself to some fresh clothing as after weeks in the same clothes, it would be a luxury to wear a clean shirt. Whilst Verity dressed herself in this year's ladies' hunting gear, he washed himself in the kitchen sink and then put on his new clothes.

Verity raided the adjoining larder and found some cured hams and spicy sausages hanging there. A further search revealed whole cheeses waiting in their muslin for consumption. Verity carried her booty into the kitchen and laid them out on the kitchen table with some plates and knives. They found that they were ravenous and felt altogether better after eating.

"What do you think about keeping watch tonight?" asked Verity.

"I think we need a decent night's sleep in proper beds," he said firmly. "We're a long way off the beaten track and ought to be safe at least for tonight."

They were awake before dawn. Verity, to her surprise, had slept soundly and without dreams. She got up and went cautiously outside. It was going to be another lovely sunny day. She walked down to the stables and found the mules and their friend, the pony, contentedly munching some hay. There were also some horses in an adjacent field, although the gate to the field was open. All this suggested that there must be someone living here to look after the estate. There was a small stone house behind the stables but no sign of life there. Verity looked through the windows, everything looked neat and tidy and well cared for. Maybe whoever lived here, perhaps housekeeper and stableman, had gone away for some reason but, if so, they might be back at any time.

Returning, Verity found César sitting on a bench in the courtyard contemplating a lemon tree. It had a gorgeous scent. Verity sat down beside him.

"You look very much the aristocrat at his hunting lodge this morning," she said, greeting him with a kiss on his freshly shaven cheek.

"I am an aristocrat, it just happens not to be my hunting lodge. And you look very much the female of the species: those high leather hunting boots look extremely fetching on you," he said giving her an appraising look.

César noticed that Verity even walked differently wearing these expensive clothes, there was a touch of hauteur and grandiloquence that were not a normal part of the Verity he knew. She saw him eyeing her and smiled at him.

"Let's eat and go," she said firmly, "it's too comfortable here."

"Certainly, Senora," he said reaching for her hand and raising it to his lips to kiss it.

Verity fled to the kitchen and had spread out some food on the table by the time he hobbled in. He had now added a rather nice jacket to his outfit.

Over breakfast they discussed their next move.

"Did you take all the packs and everything off the mules last night?" he enquired.

"Yes, the mules are simply loose at the moment but not showing any inclination to wander. There are horses in the paddock too; we'd do best to take them and leave the mules."

Verity had already explored the lodge. It was single-storey but rambling and she realised that the owners must entertain extensively with hunting parties as there were no less than three drawing rooms. Wild boar heads were mounted on plinths on the walls of one of the drawing rooms - looking at the ferocious tusks she hoped not to meet a live one in the forest. On the wall in the hallway was a map of the estate so she'd sketched a copy from this. She'd also found in a desk documents indicating who owned the lodge. She showed them to César now.

"Are you thinking what I'm thinking?"

"That we should take on the identity of these people?"

"Yes. They probably only visit occasionally. Even then they'll only entertain their own kind on the estate so may not be well known in the area."

"We'll take the horses and one of the mules to carry things. The hunting rifles as well, but we'll have to leave everything else behind that might indicate our true identity. Shall I be your daughter?"

"Certainly not! You'll be my wife," he said firmly, "I'm not having any soldiers making eyes at you."

"Aren't I a little young for your wife?"

"Not at all - a man with a young and pretty wife is always much envied! Have you the maps from your plane?" he continued.

Verity fetched them and spread them out over the table.

"I think we'll have to avoid heading straight for Gibraltar," he said. "We'd never get across the border. We'll head for the coast and then try to find a boat to take us either to Gibraltar or, even better, to Portugal."

They pondered over the maps.

"I think I've an idea," César said at last. "There is a famous nature area here," he said, pointing to an area to the north of Cadiz. "It is close to Sanlúcar de Barrameda and covers a wide area. It's ringed by swamps, the Guadalquivir river and the sea, so no one lives there, which is why the wildlife flourishes. I went there once with my parents when I was young," he said musingly. Then continued, "If we're lucky we might find a boat, otherwise we can make our way along the coast on horseback, although we'll have to cross the estuary at Huelva at low tide, and the coast is a bit tricky from there on. But until we get to Sanlúcar, we can travel openly with our new identities."

Verity drew a route map in her notebook and incorporated the map into a drawing of a butterfly to disguise it should they be stopped and searched. For good measure, she also drew a quick sketch of one of the wild boar heads, adding what she hoped was a reasonable representation of the boar's body. César was already feeding all their maps and papers into a small fire in the grate. He destroyed Roberto's things without stopping to look at them. Then he packed a leather satchel he had found with a spare shirt for each of them. Verity put some cheese and ham into another satchel with apples for the horses, filled the water containers, and cleared away all signs of their stay. She also ensured they had plenty of ammunition for the hunting rifles, whilst César disposed of the ashes from their fire and re-laid the fire in the grate so everything looked as before.

They had neither heard nor seen anyone since leaving the shrine. They set off on horseback, leaving Roberto behind them for ever.

32

Verity and César rode out through the forest, tall and erect on the best horses that the hunting lodge had to offer. One of the mules followed them on a rein, laden with their supplies.

It was just as well that Verity had made a map of the estate because otherwise they might have spent the rest of the day wandering round in circles without ever leaving the estate. Even with the map, it took them forty minutes to reach the boundary. As they left the dense forest behind them and headed up out of the valley, they could again hear the distant boom of guns and the reality of war was with them once more.

The noises of battle pursued them all day, sometimes distant and sometimes alarmingly near, as the sounds echoed back and forth between the mountains and the valleys. Sometimes they would see black smoke rising up as a shell found its target. At other times, it would be the rattle of rifle fire that accompanied their journey. They paused at midday to rest the horses in the shade of some olive trees and gave them apples to eat and a leather bucket of water to drink from. Verity used their one pair of binoculars to scan the hills for any signs of activity, but there were none. They rode openly, rather than travelling furtively as they had done in the days since the plane crash. Even so, they saw no-one and as far as they knew, no-one saw them.

It was getting to be dusk as they rode boldly into Arcos de la Frontera, a hilltop town named by the old frontier between Christian and Moslem Spain. César stopped at the first inn that they came to, guessing correctly that the premier establishment of the town had been taken over by the military of whatever side was in power here. The innkeeper assured him that he had a good room to offer them and César went and inspected it before accepting the room and having the horses and mule led round to the stable and their supplies locked away in the tack room. The innkeeper stopped César when he started to give their assumed names. "Senor, in these troubled times it is best that I do not know who my guests are. To me, you will be simply the gentleman and his lady in Room 5."

César's ankle was barely troubling him this evening. He had the pain killers supplied by the doctor yesterday and managed to walk with only a slight trace of a limp. Verity was sharing the painkillers and whilst she held herself a little stiffly, anyone observing her would put it down to a day spent in the saddle.

Their meal was served in a room that also held other travellers. There were two ladies sitting together and Verity was amazed when she heard their English voices, loudly discussing the other guests whilst blissfully unaware that anyone might understand them. At one moment, Verity was about to laugh at some funny remark they had made when César caught her eye and frowned at her. She responded to him in Spanish and they carried on a desultory conversation whilst continuing to listen in to their neighbours' chatter.

They soon gathered from the ladies' talk that they were in Nationalist held territory and Verity was all ears when she heard them talk of the shocking killing of "that nice Major Moreno" and his men. The Major had apparently been gallant towards them and promised them safe conduct back to Gibraltar. The surrounding area had apparently been searched for guerrillas but none had been found other than one unknown body at the shrine. The ladies had been delayed whilst the army searches had been carried out, but when they finally departed they had not headed straight for safety but decided instead to fit in a bit more sightseeing.

Verity and César took their time over their meal in order that they could glean as much useful information as possible from the talk around them. Finally, they went up to their room and discussed their route for the next day, modifying it to take account of the army movements that they had heard talk of during dinner.

César announced that he was going to sleep in a chair by the window. Verity was not certain whether he meant to keep watch from the window or what his intention was, so she said nothing and went to bed and to sleep.

In the morning, they waited until residents of the town were up and about before leaving the inn since they wanted to appear as normal as possible. They could hear the sound of the stomping of army boots and shouted commands not far off, it was not a reassuring sound.

They passed various army patrols bristling with guns before turning off on to a track which Verity was sure would shortly take them into the forest once more. Fortunately they had not been challenged, their haughty demeanour had halted the one patrol which had seemed likely to challenge them. Verity was glad that the wide leather hat she was wearing hid most of her features.

They rode deep into the forest for several hours before they stopped to rest the horses. They sat quietly, listening to the sounds of the forest whilst the horses and mule munched away. Verity's sensitivity to sound had become heightened. She thought she could hear a different sound above the ordinary forest sound. She signalled to César to stay where he was and crept quietly away.

Some distance off she found the source of the sound, a charcoal burner going about his work. She skirted round to make sure there was only one man and no apparent weapons to hand. Then circled back to the track and approached openly along it. She greeted him and in response to his nod, asked if she could rest there for a few minutes.

"Bring your horses up if you like, won't be no interference here," said the man, one of those countrymen who could be anywhere between forty and seventy.

Verity felt ashamed that she had thought she could fool a man whose natural habitat was the forest. She nodded and shortly returned with the horses and a reluctant César.

The charcoal burner looked at him intently but there was no recognition on his face. Satisfied he turned away and brought out some cold sausage which he proceeded to slice with a fierce looking knife before holding out slices to them. They accepted and sat down to eat.

"Soldiers up this way yesterday," he offered. "Looking for somebody I guess, didn't find nothing." They nodded. He looked at them speculatively.

"If you're heading for some particular place, your Honour, I might be able to help. I know all the smugglers' paths over this country from here to the coast, if you're wanting the coast."

Verity looked at César. Should they trust this man? But what other help were they likely to get? She made up her mind.

"Thank you, we were thinking about Sanlúcar."

The man nodded thoughtfully. "I can take you along routes that them soldiers will never find. There'll be a price of course, couldn't take the risk without something for my troubles."

"Of course," said Verity ignoring César's warning frown.

"You'll not be wanting that mule once you reach the coast."

"True," said Verity.

"That's a good looking animal, I'll take it on and if you should ever come back, I'll have it safe for you."

Verity held out her hand and he shook it. The charcoal burner looked at César and then back at Verity.

"Don't say much your father, does he" he commented.

Verity stifled a laugh; César frowned even more.

They were underway shortly, their guide sometimes leading them on foot and sometimes riding the mule ahead of them. They did not seem to be following any discernible path and César whispered his doubts to Verity as they ducked under the branches of trees.

"What choice do we have?" Verity threw back at him.

When the forest finally gave way, they were high on a mountain path with what looked like the world at their feet. The views were wonderful and they paused, forgetting for a moment that they were running for their lives. Then, the peace was broken by the sound of heavy gunfire which seemed to roll all around them. They moved instantly, before Verity realised that it was actually thunder. The storm broke over them shortly, the first rains of autumn after a long dry summer, throwing the water down in blinding sheets on both the travellers and the parched earth.

Verity had never seen anything quite like this. The water ran everywhere, streams forming where there should have been none, the earth turning into an instant quagmire. Thunder continued to roll overhead and lightning forks came in rapid succession. Verity had never liked thunderstorms and for a while worried that the lighting would get them, if the Nationalist troops did not. They were leading their mounts now as the horses were slipping and slithering, as indeed they were too.

As they plodded on, hardly daring to take their eyes from the ground, the rain turned to hail and stung their faces and arms. The ground was covered in the stuff now, almost like snow, the animals too were covered in it. Verity shook her head and a cascade of hail fell off the brim of her hat and down her front. César laughed, then he roared with laughter, standing shaking helplessly, and Verity caught it from him and laughed too. He looked liked a walking snowman.

Their guide turned back to find the cause of their laughter and saw them pointing to one another doubled up with laughter. He was going to hush them but shrugged instead, who would be likely to hear them in the middle of this storm?

The weather did not let up that day and they did not make as much progress as they had hoped. Verity was not sure what distance they had covered. The view was blotted out by the storm clouds. As it grew dark, Verity felt that they had turned from the direction of the coast and then found the reason as their guide led them up to a shack. Another man, clearly a charcoal burner, came out hearing their horses. His worried face lit up at the sight of their guide and he greeted him volubly. The accent was so thick that Verity could not follow what was being said. She hoped that César could and looked at his dark profile as he strained to follow the conversation.

Their guide came up, "You are welcome to stay the night with my friend," he said expansively, indicating the door of the hut. Verity was prepared to trust them and thankfully slid down from her horse and started fumbling with the saddle fastenings with hands that were numb from the cold. César took the saddle from her and strode to the hut and disappeared from sight.

Their guide had unloaded the mule and Verity followed him leading the horses. A barn loomed up in front of them and he led the way inside. It looked to Verity more spacious than the charcoal burner's hut, but then it was well stocked with wood and cork, precious commodities in this land. Their guide companionably talked to her as they made the animals comfortable and fed and watered them. They would be best to sleep in the barn he said, the hut was small and she and her father would want their privacy. It was too late now to disabuse him of César being her father, so much for his plan of being thought of as her husband.

When Verity entered the shack, their host was settling a large pot on to a rough hewn table. It smelled very good. He explained that he had just taken it out of the kiln where it had been cooking slowly all day. They sat down on a bench and cut hunks of bread from a couple of loaves and dipped these into the pot. The stew was delicious, although from the quantities it appeared that they were probably consuming their hosts' food for a week. They tried to eat sparingly but were urged and encouraged to eat more; it was clearly a matter of hospitality and Verity gave up protesting and enjoyed the food. When she asked what it was, the charcoal burners looked at one another and then said, "Wild boar". Clearly they were not allowed to kill wild boar themselves, so Verity made no further enquiries and managed to bite back the comment that she had never tasted wild boar before.

The wine skin went round and the men grew more talkative, apart from César. He spoke little, just enough to preserve the decencies. One of the charcoal burners lit their way to the barn and said that they would rouse them in the morning.

Verity made herself comfortable on some straw up under the leaky roof, but César prowled about restlessly as they listened to the rain hitting the roof.

"What is the matter?" she asked finally.

"I don't trust them. These men are from gipsy stock, thieves and vagabonds, you just can't trust them".

"I don't know how you can say that when they have been so kind and helpful."

"But why?" he retorted. "Just why should they help a couple of apparently aristocratic strangers? We are their natural enemies over hundreds of years. It doesn't make sense."

"Because they are good decent people who help others in times of trouble," she responded.

"They're after something, mark my words. They're probably going to fetch the soldiers from the nearest town, wherever that might be and reap any reward going."

"It's impossible to talk to you when you are in this mood, I'm going to sleep."

Although Verity lay down it was some time before she slept. Was she too trusting she wondered? Just because she had been taken in by Roberto, did not mean that two helpful and humble men were going to betray them too. She fell asleep without resolving the debate in her own mind.

When she woke it was because daylight was entering the barn; she sat up and stretched, then rubbed her stiff limbs. She could see César asleep a little distance from her. She clambered down as quietly as she could and then stopped short. The mule was gone, so were its panniers. Had their guide indeed betrayed them and sneaked away in the night to inform on them?

She looked cautiously out of the doorway but there was no sign of anyone and it was impossible to see any specific tracks on the muddy path already churned up by their entry into the barn last night.

Verity slipped out of the barn and headed towards the charcoal burner's hut. She could see no sign of anyone. She knocked tentatively on the half open door of the hut. There was no answer. She poked her head round the door but there was no-one there.

She raced back to the barn and shook César awake.

"Get up! You were right, they've gone and so has the mule and the panniers. We must get away!"

César leapt up and then stumbled as, forgetting, he put his weight on to his bad ankle. Cursing, he hopped round whilst Verity quickly saddled first her horse and then his. She seized their remaining belongings and tied them to the saddles.

César, mounting his horse, seemed to be trying to stop himself from repeating, "I told you so!" too many times. He was about to go off in a direction away from the barn and hut when she stopped him.

"I think we have to go back down the track we came up on, I think we diverged from the real path in order to come to this refuge."

"Some refuge!" he grumbled, but followed her down the track.

It had stopped raining at some point in the night but was still very muddy underfoot. The parched earth had been incapable of absorbing the rain that had fallen with the result that the top few inches of earth had become extremely wet and slippery.

Verity rode in front, all her senses heightened as she looked for danger. It was not easy to concentrate on the way ahead but she decided that her horse could best pick its own way through this muddy expanse. She kept her eyes looking ahead and soon found the place where they had diverged from the path; they turned on to the track to head towards the coast again.

Once they were clear of the forest, she could see the sea not too far off. She wished that she had a better idea of precisely where they were aiming for. She stopped and let César come up alongside her.

"Can you make out where we are from the landscape?" she asked him.

He studied the terrain for a minute.

"I think that is Jerez over there to our left," he indicated.

"So if we head straight for the sea, Sanlúcar would be on our right?"

"Yes, but it might be better to aim even more to the right, so as to reach the vicinity of Sanlúcar a little way up the estuary."

Verity had drawn out the field glasses to survey the landscape. The one place that she could not see was into the forest behind them.

"We had better put as much distance between us and the forest as we can, we don't know whether there is anyone out after us." César nodded and they set off again.

Out in the open the ground was firmer and they could ride faster. Now Verity could see that there was a road down below, obviously the road from Jerez to Sanlúcar, which they could avoid by heading toward the estuary. They were covering the ground fast. If they had been betrayed, and Verity still felt it was an 'if' although César was certain, they would have gained time by leaving the barn long before they would have been expected to. But what if their pursuers were even now travelling along the road to Sanlúcar by car? It did not bear thinking about.

There were still no figures in the landscape indicating pursuit. They rode on.

They were taken by surprise when they saw a solitary figure riding towards them from a track at an angle to theirs. Verity soon recognised their guide of yesterday riding the mule. He hailed them.

Verity greeted him with a smile while César lurked in the background scowling.

"I had not expected you to rise so early," he said in surprise. "You thought that I had deserted you or perhaps betrayed you?!"

Verity reassured him as best she could, she could do it easily since she had believed in him, but César from his looks clearly still thought the worst. The man could see this and turned back to Verity.

"Thank you for having faith in me. Not everyone trusts our kind, they say we are gypsies and worthless. I have been busy this morning, I thought if I were to go ahead, I could find somewhere for you to wait out of sight in Sanlúcar. Then I could concentrate on finding a means for you to leave without suspicion. It would be as well," he continued looking at Verity, "for you to change your clothes before we go on."

Verity looked at her arm and saw that the blood had seeped through the dressing again and on to her blouse.

"Thank you, Senor, for all your kindness," she said and slipped down from her horse.

Taking a clean blouse from her pack and a fresh bandage, she walked a few paces away from the men whilst they studiously looked the other way. She was struggling with the bandage when hands came to her assistance.

"Look, I'm sorry but I'm still not sure about him, we must stay on guard," César whispered whilst bandaging her arm neatly. Dressed in a fresh blouse, Verity wiped a damp cloth over her face and then replaced her leather hat and remounted. Whilst she was doing this, César packed their hunting rifles away in the smart leather cases and stowed them on the mule.

They rode into the outskirts of Sanlúcar later that morning and followed at a distance behind their guide until he stopped under a tree. He indicated the entrance to a courtyard across the way and Verity rode in and then waived to César to join her. It was an inn, a somewhat shabby one, but it had stables and food and drink and clearly no questions were asked of its guests. César paid for a night's board and lodging in advance. Whilst he was doing this, Verity went out to the stables to confer with their guide.

"I will wait on the quay for the fishing boats to come in, buy fish and listen to what is being said. Then I'll come back and tell you."

Verity pulled some coins out of her bag, "You will need money to buy fish," and she slipped a generous amount of coins into his hand, it was more than a month's money to him but in small denominations so that he would not look suddenly wealthy. He thanked her and shook hands with her again.

César insisted on taking a seat outside the inn where he could see up and down the road. Verity left him to it and wandered about a little. There were boats moored along the quay a little way away. This inn was at the furthest end of the town from the quay, really the place was just a fishing village. Positioned here they could slip away tonight, always assuming that there was some means of slipping away.

At the worst they would have to wait for low tide and ride across to the reserve which Verity could tantalising see across the water. But they would need a local guide for that, it would not be worth risking drowning because of ignorance, having come so far and survived so much.

She returned to join César and dozed gently in her chair, reviving when the landlord set a table in front of them and placed before them a jug of wine, some bread and plates of fresh sardines. Their spirits revived.

"We've got this far, against the odds," said Verity.

"Sorry if I've been too doubting, but after Roberto..." he trailed off.

Verity wished he had not brought up the subject of Roberto. "Roberto is dead, we are alive" she said resolutely.

"I know, for us there is always tomorrow," he responded.

"Don't you have a word for it - Mañana?"

"We often use that when we are trying to put off what we do not want to do," he said "but for both of us, yes, there will be a tomorrow."

This was the most positive thing he had said for a while, so Verity left it at that. He had to grieve for those he had lost, it was unreasonable of her to expect him to share her growing optimism.

Looking down the road towards the quay, she saw the figure of the charcoal burner walking up the road towards them. She slipped out of her chair and went round to the stables, ostensibly to check the horses. The man joined her there, carrying some fish wrapped in a cloth. He placed his parcel down reverently, he did not usually eat so well.

"Not possible to cross the estuary on horses," he said, "channel's too treacherous. But my fishing friends say that they are already doing a trip tonight and they could make space for you."

"Fishing friends?"

"Good men who know how to keep secrets."

Smugglers thought Verity, that explained a lot.

"When, where, how much?"

"I will come for you shortly after dark. I need to get you down to the quay without being seen, they will depart as soon as you are on board. You can negotiate your own price with them according to where they take you."

"The horses," began Verity, stroking one of their heads.

"Where would you like me to take them?"

"They belong on the Alqueria de la Frontera Estate."

"I'll lead them back and let them loose on the estate."

Verity reached for her purse again but the man stopped her, "I have been paid enough."
Verity felt slightly embarrassed, she did not want to offend him again.
"We will always be in your debt," she said seriously.
He shook his head and she left it at that.
She went back to César and told him what was happening.
Shortly after dark, having ostensibly retired for the night, the rattle of a pebble against their window told them that it was time to go. They slipped out, wearing dark clothes and carrying the few belongings they had left. They followed their guide as quietly as they could, taking shelter when a vehicle swung on to the road, so as to avoid being caught in its lights.
The town was very quiet. There was no official curfew here but everyone knew that being out at night was dangerous. At last they reached the quay and their guide indicated a gangplank on to a boat that by its smell was a fishing boat. Hands reached out to help them on and they were hustled down out of sight. There was no time to even thank their guide, ropes had been cast off and the boat's engine had started up. As though this was a signal, other engines started up nearby and there was a general clanking and noises that indicated a fishing fleet setting off for a night's fishing.

Verity and César sat in the dark in a cabin for half an hour or so before a crewman came down and lit a light.
"Safe to go on deck now if you wish."
They went up and felt the breeze, which was increasing in strength every minute. They could see nothing but it was good to be out in the air. Two other figures joined them, both coughing and spluttering. One of them was promptly sick over the side. Verity offered a handkerchief and it was when a voice thanked her in English that she realised that these were the two lady travellers whom they had last seen at the inn in Arcos de la Frontera.
Verity put her good arm round the one who had just been sick and repeated the advice that her Aunt had given her on her first fishing boat trip.
"Relax, breathe slowly, don't try to fight the motion and it will get better."
"But my dear, you're English!" said the lady whose eyes were only just becoming adjusted to the dark. "How come you're here? And with your husband too?"
"Mary, don't ask tomfool questions. It's not our business, we all want to reach Portugal, that's all we need to know," said her companion.
Later, when the sickness had abated, they sat companionably huddled together against the wind. The ladies were regaling them with details of their trip through Andalucía. Their stories were notable for their not mentioning the civil war at all. If it were not

for the fact that they were clearly getting out of Spain illicitly, you would have thought they had not known there was a war going on.

Their boat turned away from the fishing fleet once they had reached the fishing grounds and they chugged on, with the riding lights extinguished.

It was only when the dark bulk of the Portuguese coast was looming large that the older woman, who had not introduced herself, bent towards them and addressed them by name, their real names!

She whispered, "Trust me! We're nearly there, please do what I say."

There was no time to ask questions, the boat had stopped offshore and a dinghy was bumping up against it. Barrels and other cargo were handed up on deck and then the four of them were helped down into the dinghy and their belongings handed down after them. Money exchanged hands. Very shortly, the dinghy was scraping the shingle of the beach. The rowers jumped out and steadied the boat for them and handled them ashore.

Following the ladies, who suddenly seemed to have become younger and more active in their movements, they walked quickly across the sand and shingle and up a winding path. They reached a road where a vehicle was parked without lights. There did not appear to be any driver with the vehicle. The unnamed lady opened the driver's door, got in and started the engine, whilst the other efficiently stowed all the luggage in the boot.

Verity and César climbed in the back of the car. They moved off smoothly and almost silently without lights. They travelled for some time, enough at any rate for Verity to dose off in the back of the car. Her instincts told her to trust these two elderly ladies. César sat alert and suspicious, but asked no questions. Verity awoke as they bumped down a rutted track to a farm where dogs barked at their arrival. As soon as the ladies emerged from the car, the barking turned to yelps of delight as the dogs jumped up trying to lick them. Lights had come on in the farmhouse and a smiling couple greeted them in voluble Portuguese.

Ushered in to a warm farmhouse kitchen, their bags were taken from them and they were shown to bedrooms. Separate rooms, Verity noted. Verity washed herself with a jug of warm water and then returned to the kitchen where food had been laid on the table.

Coming into the kitchen after her, Mary said, "Emmeline will be along in a minute, do help yourself to some food."

César joined Verity and then the older woman came in from outside and bolted the door.

Sitting down in the warmth of the kitchen, Verity and César gratefully accepted food and drink and asked no questions. Eventually, the older woman leaned back in her chair and spoke to them.

"Time for explanations, I think. My name is Emmeline and this is my sister Mary. We live here on this farm on a more or less permanent basis, have to go back to Blighty every now and then of course, but we've made our home here. You're quite safe now. I'll have you out of Portugal by tomorrow and on your way back to Mr. Jones. He was getting quite anxious about you, you know," she confided, "Constance too."

Verity looked at her stunned, César did too.

Mary joined in, "So he contacted us. Emmeline thought we could combine a bit of sightseeing, well, more gathering information as to which side was where of course, with finding out what had happened to you."

"We found out that your plane had been seen over flying Alqueria de la Frontera and the army were trying to track you down," continued Emmeline. "I got the impression they were expecting you. They found traces of a plane having crashed up in the mountains, but nothing more; sabotage I expect? Major Moreno was so informative talking to his sergeant when he thought that there were only a couple of old English biddies present in the hotel, who couldn't possibly understand Spanish. Then he received a tip off and went haring off with his men in the hope of surprising you at the shrine."

You were there in the town?" asked Verity.

"Oh yes! It seemed an obvious base. After all, we knew where you had intended to land and it wasn't far away. We took in a lot of other historical places so that we looked typical oblivious tourists. Quite enjoyed ourselves, no-one takes any notice of elderly ladies. I presume you had to kill the Major and his men? I gather it was quite a bloodbath."

"It was, but no, as it happened I didn't kill the major, quite the contrary, he saved me from a bullet."

"I told you he was really rather a gallant," said Mary nodding at her sister.

"Nonsense!" said Emmeline "Let Verity explain."

Verity told them all that had happened, with César filling in some of the detail.

"Quite remarkable," said Emmeline. "Mr. Jones certainly knows how to pick his agents!"

"Are we really safe here?" asked César, looking from one to the other in mystification.

"Absolutely," said Emmeline. "The only people who know you are here are the local smugglers and they're not likely to tell anyone."

"And Aunt Constance?" Asked Verity.

"An old friend, we've done quite a bit of work together in the past," explained Emmeline.

Verity looked at them in amazement as her brain whirred and fitted unexplained things into place. César simply didn't know what they were talking about any more.

"We thought you might prefer a sea voyage back," Mary said. "There's a boat we can get you on tomorrow evening."

"It's not another fishing boat is it?" asked Verity anxiously.

"No dear, Lisbon is a scheduled port of call for a number of ocean liners, so we're booking you on to one," explained Mary. "With a nice cruise back, you'll be as right as nine pence by the time you dock at Southampton. You both look as though you could do with a bit of a rest," she concluded, looking at them over the top of her glasses.

Days later, Verity sat on her steamer chair on the deck of the ship, sipping a cup of broth brought by an attentive steward. César was playing deck quoits as though he had not a care in the world, and Verity was enjoying the sunshine as she watched him. Relaxed and at peace she was also working out at long last that her entrance into the service of Mr Jones' department had to have been the work of Connie. Why she hadn't seen it long ago she could not imagine. The encouragement, where any normal aunt would have advised caution; the failure to ask natural questions to which the answers might have been compromising; she had to be the source of Mr Jones' knowledge of everything about Verity. Indeed the intensive travelling Connie had undertaken in the last decade for no apparent purpose probably had had a purpose, one known to only a few people; clearly Connie was an experienced hand at this game. What a woman she was! Verity was so glad that she had been instrumental in bringing home what Connie longed for most, César.

She could barely wait to get home to ask lots and lots of questions, whether she would receive any answers was another matter.

Verity had mourned for Moreno but not for Roberto. It was clear to her now that at some stage in their relationship, she had become a bloated capitalist in Roberto's eyes and any love he might have had for her had turned to hate. She would never know that Roberto had seen her in Madrid with Moreno and drawn his own conclusions. Verity could not go on loving the memory of someone who had hated her so much that he had tried to kill her.

A young man in uniform appeared at her side.

"Madam, we've received a telegraph message for you. Would you care to follow me?"

Verity followed the young man to the telegraph office where the operator handed her a message.

It read, "WELL DONE STOP REPORT BACK WITH CONSIGNMENT SOON AS DOCK STOP NEXT ASSIGNMENT AWAITING YOUR ARRIVAL STOP JONES".

He doesn't waste time thought Verity, well neither would she. She made her way back to her chair in the sun, determined to make the most of this and every opportunity which came her way.

COMING SOON

The Tears of the Crocodile

Another Verity adventure

Arriving in Egypt Verity finds herself with a fiancée she has never met, a prospective mother-in-law who resembles a gorgon, a mysterious death to resolve and an espionage mission to complete.